Another Summer

Another Summer

A NOVEL

KARA KENTLEY

Linden
Lake

LINDEN
LAKE

Copyright © 2025 by Kara Kentley

All rights reserved.

This book is a work of fiction. Names, characters, places, and incidents are the product of the author's imagination and are used fictitiously. Any similarities to actual event, locales, or real persons, living or dead, are coincidental and not intended by the author.

Cover design by Nicolette S. Ruggiero
Cover artwork © Shutterstock
Interior design by Zoe Norvell
Developmental edits by Savannah Gilbo
Line edits by Michele Chiappetta at Two Birds Author Services
Proofread by Andrea C. Neil at Two Birds Author Services

No portion of this book may be reproduced, stored in a retrieval system, or transmitted in any form or by any means without the express written consent of the publisher or author, except as permitted by U.S. copyright law. Thank you for supporting the author's rights.

Paperback ISBN-13: 979-8-9928054-0-6

E-book ISBN-13: 979-8-9928054-1-3

For Jim, Ryan, and Caroline
*This never would have happened without your love,
encouragement, and support
I am forever grateful*

xo

CONTENT GUIDANCE

Please be advised that this book contains on page, detailed descriptions of panic attacks, drawn from my own personal experiences. I hope I have handled the subject with compassion and sensitivity.

For those who experience panic attacks, help and resources are available through the National Mental Health Hotline at 866-903-3787

For a more detailed list of other sensitive content, please visit karakentley.com/contentguidance

CHAPTER ONE

Avery

SATURDAY, MAY 13

After a decade away, Avery Easton wanted this place to feel different. Something akin to jamais vu, that sensation where a familiar place feels foreign. But the second she opened her car door, the scent of fresh pine filled her lungs, and she remembered everything about Linden Lake.

While most people associated the woodsy aroma with Christmas, pine reminded Avery of Maine and the evergreen summer she'd spent here a decade ago. Diving off the old dock; sneaking into vacant cabins for stolen kisses; stargazing in favorite sweatshirts, with flashlights to point out the constellations. The coming weeks would be a playlist of memories on shuffle, each one taking her back to *that summer*.

Love tells a lot of lies. Especially first love.

Some of those lies she'd told herself. After so much time and distance, trusting she'd put her first heartbreak in her rearview mirror might have been the biggest one. Long before she'd turned down the gravel driveway, every sight since she'd crossed the state line brought back memories of Miles. Napolitano's Pizza, Roger's Grocery, and the bank sign with the time and temperature, where she'd asked him his favorite time of day. He'd later amended his favorite time to 3:59 p.m., the exact moment of their first kiss.

Avery studied the lodge, not yet open for guests, and sighed. The original plan had been to leave her furniture in storage and travel all summer before starting her MBA in the fall. Her best friend, Lily, had called Thursday, with a tearful voice so desperate, Avery packed her things and drove up from Virginia. Sam Cooper had suffered a heart attack. The Cooper family needed help running the administrative side of the resort. Avery had done the job for only one season, ten years ago, but Lily claimed nothing had changed.

Avery walked around the side of the pine-shingled lodge, past the century-old log pillars of the front porch, and out onto the granite ledge from which the lodge commanded a magnificent view of Linden Lake sparkling in the sun. She bounded down the small footpath to the shore and out onto the old dock, the cool lake air heightening her senses. Closing her eyes, she lifted her face to the warm sun. Tiny waves lapped at the dock pylons. Ah, tranquility. People came here to replace the pings and dings of the modern world with birdsong and leaves rustling in the soft breeze. Once warmer weather arrived, the lonely call of a loon would join this meditative soundtrack.

Every summer began as a new ripple on the lake. A blank slate, waiting to be filled with fresh memories. Montressa Lodge might not have changed in the last decade, but she had. She wasn't nineteen and naive anymore. Age brought wisdom. This summer, she'd create a new playlist of memories. *That summer* didn't need to factor in. After all, one could never step in the same body of water twice.

"Pepper." A husky voice called out from somewhere behind her, instantly goose-bumping her skin.

Only one person called her Pepper.

Miles gave her that nickname after learning her parents had picked her name off the label on a bottle of Tabasco Sauce. Avery's stomach flipped. The tiny hairs on her neck stretched toward the rhythm of his footsteps. She forced a smile and turned around.

He broke out in a jog along the lakeside trail, past the cabin where she'd trapped the squirrel, past the marina where she'd waited for his shift to end so they could sunbathe and swim. Past the outdoor kitchen where every Montressa employee learned to flip a blueberry pancake onto a plate. At least a hundred had hit the ground before Avery eventually plated one. Thankfully, the Coopers' puppy licked the failed attempts from her shoes.

She tore her eyes away from Miles and focused on the boathouse-turned-cabin at the far end of the property. Time hadn't lessened its charm. She'd treated the night they'd spent there as a pledge. He'd turned it into a tryst. Avery shook off the thought, glanced at Miles jogging up the path, and summoned the strength to protect her heart.

She wasn't supposed to see him again until Lily married Nate Cooper in the fall. There'd be bridesmaid duties and friends to buffer the shock. As the only bridesmaid, Avery had picked her own dress, one cut low enough to show off the tiny freckle near her heart. The one he used to kiss. She'd dreamed of exuding a hotness that simultaneously said, *take me* and *you'll never have me*. Hundreds of times, she'd imagined coyly saying hello as his jaw dropped.

She raised a hand to her messy topknot and cringed.

This was not that.

No makeup, her comfiest leggings, and a favorite sweatshirt had made sense for the long drive on short notice. She'd planned on showering once she settled in.

Miles stopped running a few feet shy of the dock.

"Avery." Her name came out breathy and deep, smoother than the lake and still capable of making her just as wet. That had not changed.

Still tall, still handsome, with two days of dark stubble and hair a little windswept, as if he had just stepped off the ski boat. Gone was the Yale Track sweatshirt. In its place, a trim navy Henley hinted at every muscle beneath. Lightweight gray athletic joggers skimmed his toned legs. Miles had an almost post-workout glow, as if he'd just completed a marathon without sweating. He looked perfect.

Where Miles was all sinew and sin, Avery's aesthetic screamed *abandon all hope, ye who enter*. She regretted sticking the gnawed paintbrush she'd found rolling around the floor of her car through her messy topknot.

She waited for her stomach to sour. Instead, it filled with fireflies. Miles was smart, charming, and sweeter than maple syrup. But not perfect. A decade ago, he'd held her like a treasure before discarding her like trash. He would always be Sharpie on white shorts. Unerasable, ruinous, a stain the lake couldn't wash away.

"Hey," she said, trying to sound calm and casual, as if they'd known each other once, but it hadn't been meaningful. Except *that summer* had been significant and life-changing. For her, anyway.

"Hey you." He smiled, the wood planks squeaking under his feet as he walked toward her. "I always hoped I'd find you right here, on this dock."

If she'd known she was standing in the place he'd always imagined seeing her again, Avery would've moved to the new, larger ski dock the second he called her Pepper. This had been their spot. The old dock had twin pylons on opposite sides at the end. They used to lean back on them, facing one another, her painting and him reading, bathed in the golden glow of a setting sun. She used to stretch out her legs so her foot could lean against his thigh. He'd finished *War and Peace* that summer. They'd been so happy. Until they weren't.

Miles opened his arms wide, fingers twitching in search of an embrace. A dazzling smile spread across his tanned face. After a decade of silence, Miles Magrum wanted a hug. Avery's jaw dropped at the audacity.

As he stepped closer, she stayed planted in her spot. Almost automatically, she placed a hand in the middle of his chest to stop him and his aura from destroying her composure. Too late. That long-lost, intoxicating, woodsy scent wafted ahead of him. Miles still smelled clean and cedary, like warm pine after an August rain. He had his own signature pheromone. She'd never let it weaken her resolve again.

Under her hand, his chest felt solid. She'd loved the boy he'd once been, but all indications were that Miles was much different as a man. Lily said his life had become a red-carpet step and repeat of gorgeous women. If he'd wanted to contact her, he would've. And he hadn't.

Miles lowered his hands and gave up on the hug. She backed up a step to make sure he knew she'd drawn a line on the dock. One he shouldn't cross.

"It's great to see you." He rubbed that dark stubble on his jaw, as if things weren't going the way he expected. "The Coopers appreciate you coming. I'm not sure if you've heard the latest, but Sam's stable and in New York, at one of the best hospitals in America. He's scheduled for a quintuple bypass Monday morning."

"Sounds like he's in excellent hands," she said. "It's been a whirlwind few days. How're you holding up?"

"Good, thanks for asking. I'm worried, but he'll be fine. No more drawn *buttah* with his *lobstah*, but fine."

Like her southern accent, Avery wondered if uncomfortable situations brought out Miles's New England accent. Or maybe it had been an attempt at humor. It had been so long since they'd joked about anything, she didn't know.

"It's scary," he said. "We're all…"

Miles shook his head and cleared his throat.

Avery regretted refusing the hug. As the only child of only children, Miles had little support. Sam's son, Nate, had been Miles' best friend since preschool. Which made Sam Cooper almost like an uncle to Miles. Miles probably needed the comfort of an embrace.

"You were nice to send your jet to take the Coopers to New York," she said.

It came as no surprise Miles owned a jet. He'd created CashCache, an app that taught a world of spenders how to get themselves out of debt and start saving. News of its sale to a large financial institution for an undisclosed sum had been hard to avoid. Undisclosed sums typically had a lot of zeros and commas.

"Oh, I don't own a jet." He waved off the idea. "Flying commercial creates less of a carbon footprint. I chartered one to get Sam to the best cardiologists."

Deep down, Avery knew he hadn't hired a jet to show off. If Miles loved someone, he'd go to great lengths for them. If he didn't, he wouldn't so much as call or text. How he'd treated her was proof of that.

"Miles," she said. "I'm looking for Lily. Have y'all talked today?"

The second she said "y'all," he cocked his head to the side and smiled—a sign he'd caught her accent too.

"No, I'm not sure she knows I came up last night. But you know Lily, she's always late." He laughed a little too loud. "I came over to check the waterfront and saw you standing here. Like a vision."

Funny he called her a vision when he'd done the ghosting. Nothing good could come from broaching that topic today. Avery frowned and resolved to keep everything on the surface.

"I'm sorry you drove all this way to work at the front desk." Miles rubbed his stubble again. "I hoped you'd return for something happier, like a vacation."

Avery shook her head, surprised he couldn't see why she hadn't come back here until now. Vacations were for making new memories, not reliving painful ones. She'd taken trips with Lily almost every summer, but never to Maine.

"I'm not here on vacation," she said. "I'm here to open the resort."

"So am I."

For a split second, the world fell so quiet she could've heard a pebble drop clear across the lake. Lily hadn't mentioned Miles being here. Seeing him at a wedding was one thing. Working with him sounded like hell on earth. One of them needed to go, and she had the summer off. Given his active social life, she'd let him off the hook.

"I'm sure you're busy." Avery straightened her shoulders. "I've got this. Go back to New York and your red carpets."

She waved him away like he'd vanish and become a ghost again. Instead, he widened his stance and crossed his arms. Miles wasn't going anywhere. She felt a tingle of attraction at his big dock energy.

"Nate and his mother are staying at my apartment in the City, and he asked me to get the waterfront ready," he said.

They stood there in silence, and Avery stared down into the crystal-clear water. She could see every rock on the bottom.

"I'd already planned to be here most of the summer. At my new house," he said. "I'm working on a project."

Miles hooked his thumb over his shoulder, across the cove. He must have bought a house on the other side of the point.

"If you need anything, I'm a paddle away." He pushed up the sleeves of his shirt.

"Paddle?" Avery stole a peek at his forearms, more rippled than the lake and just as inviting. When she lifted her head, he smiled. He'd caught her ogling. Heat rose in her neck.

Miles ran his teeth over his lower lip, as if gathering the courage to say something. He'd done that right before he asked her out the first time, before he'd kissed her, and again right after she'd told him she loved him.

"I bought the Red House."

The air left her body. At nineteen, that had been her dream house. He'd heard her ideas for it as they'd sunbathed on the floating dock, planning a future that never came. He could have given her a second to absorb this news. Instead, he waited for a reaction.

"The A-frame?"

He nodded and she gulped down the bitter taste of acceptance. Since she'd never returned to the lake, she'd given up claim. But she never thought Miles would take it for himself.

Out on the point, the Red House's triangular roof glistened in the sun. The spruce green pines behind it complemented the fresh crimson paint. Large boxes sat on a pallet by the front door, partly covered by a blue tarp, its edge flapping in the breeze. Solar panels covered half of the roof. She put her hand to her heart to steady the betrayal moving through her chest.

"You should see it." He smiled like he'd won a prize at a carnival. "Come for dinner. Tomorrow. Six."

It was a dreamy Maine lakeside cabin, an A-frame straight out of a hot cocoa ad, nestled among the tall pines, with a big porch and a long dock made for getting a running start before jumping off the end. She'd always wondered if it was equally as quaint on the inside, but she couldn't hand him a reprieve for their very public breakup. Or the ten years of silence.

As if reading her thoughts, Miles cleared his throat. "Our best friends are engaged, and it'd be nice if we could be in the same room and not be…"

He didn't finish his sentence.

Not be what? Mad at the guy who left her crestfallen and crying in a parking lot?

"We should talk," he said. "About us."

He stared out over the water.

"About us?" She waited for him to make eye contact. "There's no us, Miles. You made sure of that."

He shifted on his feet and dug his hands into his pockets.

"That summer," he said.

A sour taste rose in Avery's throat. A decade ago, he'd walked away with his dignity intact, leaving her crumpled on the pavement. When she'd finally stood, long after he drove off, there were tiny pebbles embedded in her knees. Hearing him call it *that summer* was an emotional gut punch.

"I'd like to move past it," he said.

Of course he would. He'd ruined it.

Avery recited the words she'd practiced hundreds of times in the mirror, still unsure she believed them. "Listen, I granted your wish and gave you space. Ten years of space. And I do not need to see your house."

"But you want to." He smiled in slow motion, one side of his mouth lagging behind the other.

Teasing her about the house he'd stolen from her was both infuriating and seductive. Those chestnut eyes widened as if he knew exactly what she wanted. Hoping to silence the traitorous thrum radiating down her middle, Avery reminded herself they'd never been friends.

"You can leave." Again, she shooed him away. "Go back to New York. I've got this."

Miles straightened and made himself taller, which only made him more alluring. She didn't remember his chest being so broad, or his arms being so muscular. He'd changed in the last decade.

"Well, if you think you can open this hundred-acre resort in a month with your lists and that sweet southern accent, I won't stand in your way," he said. "Especially if I get you so up into your feelings that you can't handle having me around."

Avery bristled at his massive ego. Her accomplishments were more than lists and southern charm.

"Don't you dare insinuate I can't do a job I once did or run a business," she said, pointing at the lodge. "I founded and sold a successful stationery company. For a lot of money. I got into a top ten business school, and I'm starting my MBA at Dartmouth in the fall."

Miles's playful demeanor grew sullen. His gaze fell to the dock planks.

"It's been a decade, Miles." She pointed at the lodge. "You can't waltz up like some kind of athleisure local hero, expose your forearms, and invite me to dinner expecting forgiveness."

When he didn't respond, she kept going.

"I appreciate you saying hello," she said. "But your ten years of silence still stings, and dammit, Miles. No one told me you'd be here."

"I can leave," he said. "But if my presence bothers you this much, we should talk. Our best friends are getting married in October, and I don't think we want this"—he swirled his hand between them—"at their wedding."

Avery crossed her arms over her chest. She didn't see the point in talking. They were different people now, and this felt like all she could muster.

"I didn't come here for you," she said. "I came to help the Coopers. I'm okay with you being here. But please don't make me pass through the second circle of Hell every time we meet."

"Lust?" Miles grinned. Like a devil.

Avery rolled her eyes. This new Miles and his big dock energy had grown tiresome.

"The second circle of Hell," he said with an infuriating, intoxicating smirk, "is lust."

She should have known this. A decade ago, they'd both discovered their schools offered a class on Dante's *Inferno*. He'd signed up at Yale and she'd done the same at Vanderbilt, agreeing they'd study together via Skype. She grimaced at the memory of taking the course and reading the book on her own, hoping he'd call and apologize so they could finish the semester as planned. It never happened.

His eye twinkled. Sarcasm and sunlight suited Miles. That had not changed. Neither had the dent in his chin. She resisted the urge to press her thumb into it, feel his stubble, watch his lips part softly in anticipation of a kiss. If he had been anyone else, she'd jump into his arms and wrap herself around him.

"We can discuss the *Inferno* when you come for dinner," he said. "I'll let you pick another circle."

"The ninth circle is for betrayers of special relationships. They're frozen in a lake of ice."

"Perfect. I can tell you've imagined me there already." He winked. "And we happen to have a lake."

Avery bit back a laugh. Miles couldn't know he'd acclimated her to future betrayal. It had made it easier for her to break the engagement off with her fiancé, Trent, when he'd cheated. After being fooled twice, she'd given up on finding someone who committed to her the way she committed to them.

Miles reached across the dock and rested a heavy hand on her shoulder.

"Come on, Avery." His melty chestnut eyes begged for forgiveness. "This first time may be the toughest part of seeing each other again."

She hoped so. She couldn't open this big resort by herself, but she'd never admit that. At least not to him.

She looked up at the lodge. Lily stood at the top of the path, rubbing her brow, as if warding off a headache.

"You two okay down there?" Lily shouted down.

"Yep, just discussing Dante." Avery glared at Miles. "I should get off this dock before he moves on to *War and Peace*."

"'Nothing is so necessary for a young man as the company of intelligent women,'" Miles said.

Lily laughed. Avery scowled, annoyed he could pull quotes out of thin air so quickly.

Miles raised his hands in surrender, his shirt lifting to reveal a trail of hair below his navel. She couldn't see the rest of his abdomen, but she remembered those peaks and valleys. A luscious playground which should come with a warning: *Abandon all hope, ye who enter. He will break your heart.*

Miles motioned for Avery to leave the dock first. As she passed by, she recalled how he used to rest his hand in the small of her back. A tingle pulsed through her, and she reminded herself yet again that allowing his hand to brush her there, or anywhere, would let in a lie.

He headed down the lakeside path toward the marina and, beyond that, out to the Red House. His house. Avery's gaze shot darts at his back.

She bounded up the path to hug her best friend.

"What was that?" Lily asked, as they walked into the vacant lodge.

"Nothing. Just setting boundaries before your wedding."

Lily huffed out an exhale, and Avery shivered under a blanket of guilt. Lily didn't need to add another burden to her busy month. May was crazy for teachers, with a zillion end-of-year picnics, graduations, and whatnot. Her future father-in-law's heart attack happened three days ago, sending her fiancé to New York for who knew how long. Lily and Nate did not need a war breaking out between their best man and maid of honor.

Avery rested a hand on Lily's shoulder. "Everything'll be okay. Miles and I are adults now. We can handle this."

CHAPTER TWO

Miles

SUNDAY, MAY 14 - MOTHER'S DAY
For the last decade, Miles had hoped the next time he saw Avery, they'd be alone so he could apologize. After which, they'd spend hours catching up. As entrepreneurs, they had a lot in common. But thinking time had lessened her pain had been foolish, assuming she'd accept a general apology was arrogant, and calling her Pepper hadn't been the flex he'd imagined.

She'd seemed annoyed to see him, but there had been flirty moments when a familiar buzz arced between them. She'd blushed when he'd caught her checking out his forearms. At the mention of Dante's *Inferno*, a warm tingle had rippled through his chest. The promise of feeling that way again was the silver lining urging him to keep trying.

His ten-mile run earlier in the day had only heightened his confusion. Right now, he wanted to talk through the confusion with someone.

It had been a couple months since he'd seen his therapist, and contacting her on a Sunday was out. Searching for a friend who understood his past, he scrolled through his texts.

💬 **B&E Production Assistant:** Remote fine. Please confirm for Tuesday

After selling CashCache, the app he'd written to help people get out of debt and start saving, Miles had taken a part-time gig as a financial correspondent on *Bright and Early*, a national morning television show hosted by another former Montressa employee, Victoria Evans. This Tuesday, he'd been assigned a segment on the effects of rising interest rates on student loans. He could film remotely from the lodge, which had better internet and less construction noise than the Red House.

💬 **Wes:** Welcome back. I will text you every day until you pick countertops. Seriously, pick something!!!

The past winter, Miles had hired Montressa's head of maintenance, Wes DuCharme, as his contractor. Miles flew up from New York as needed to follow the progress of the renovation and answer Wes's questions. For weeks, a box of granite samples had sat gathering dust in the Red House's unfinished kitchen. Wes wanted to wrap up before Montressa opened, but Miles hadn't realized choosing finishes would be so hard. He could've hired a decorator, but he'd used one for the Manhattan apartment he'd purchased after the sale of CashCache and hadn't liked the results. Despite its feature in *Architectural Digest*, the space felt cold and impersonal, as if he lived in a museum.

💬 **Nate:** Dad doing well, ready for surgery tomorrow.

💬 **Nate:** Thank you for the jet and use of your tricked-out apartment.

💬 **Nate:** Your couch. WTF! Is it supposed to be a nest?

Miles chuckled. No one knew Miles like Nate Cooper did. They had been best friends since preschool and had grown up on the lake together. But Nate had fielded enough questions about Avery over the years. Now

Nate was engaged to Lily, Avery's best friend, and no engaged couple should have to deal with unresolved, simmering tension between their best man and maid of honor. Besides, bothering Nate while his father waited for coronary bypass surgery was selfish.

The obvious choice was his Manhattan friends—former child actors Hayes Preston and Anna Catherine Page. He and Hayes had been playing phone tag all week. They needed to discuss plans for their project: a bereavement camp for grieving families, with counselors and various professionals to help navigate the loss of a loved one. Like Miles, Hayes also lost his mother at a young age and had become a trusted sounding board. Miles had his eye on the perfect spot: an abandoned corporate retreat.

Linden Lake's loose heart shape mimicked the leaf of a linden tree, from which it got its name. The north shore resembled the top of the heart, with the Red House in the point between two half-moon coves. Montressa occupied the entire western cove, Bramble Beach sat on the eastern side. Past the end of the beach sat the retreat. It wasn't for sale, but his goal for the summer was to purchase it.

The wood floors squeaked as he walked through his empty house. His mother had always said creaking floors were how Maine lakeside cabins said hello. The sound made him feel at home. He opened FaceTime and called Hayes. Anna Catherine answered before it rang. Perfect. He could wish her a happy first Mother's Day and get some advice.

"Anna, that was a faster pickup than a Kardashian at an NBA game."

"The Kardashians have moved on to rappers, Miles. Catch up." She sat bathed in the sunlight of their den, propped up with pillows all around.

"Happy first Mother's Day."

"Thank you. I love being a mama, even if meals take forever because Lennox insists on nursing after I spoon-feed her solid foods." Anna smiled and dropped her gaze to her nursing baby. "Mother's Day must be a hard day for you. I never met your mom, but she raised you, so I'm honoring her today too."

His throat tightened. Maisie Magrum had been amazing. Eleven years later, he still missed her hugs, her laugh, and her worn-out Birkenstocks by the back door. For the rest of his life, not a day would go by without reminders of her.

Good actors knew how to let a moment sit, and Anna Catherine quietly waited out his sadness. The compassion and safety of their friendship meant the world to Miles.

"Thank you, Anna." He smiled as he wiped away a tear.

"How's Sam?" she asked.

"Stable. I came back to Maine to help at Montressa, and you won't believe this. Avery's here."

"Wait! What? Tell me everything." She looked off screen. "Hayes, get in here. Miles ... Avery ... oh my God!"

Hayes appeared on screen, leaning his head close to Anna Catherine's.

"When I got here yesterday, I went over to check on Montressa and survey the waterfront. And there she was, standing at the end of the old dock."

"And did she look like all your dreams?" Anna Catherine asked. "Please tell me you said hello."

"She looked great. Like she did that summer. She has gorgeous reddish-blond hair that glimmers in sunlight. Her eyes are this deep gray. They change color depending on what she wears. She's mesmerizing." Miles rubbed his stubbled jaw and shook his head. "I couldn't keep my head straight and I called her 'Pepper,' which made her uncomfortable. It got worse from there. She used to be fun to joke with, but I may have been obnoxious."

He'd had ten years to plan that moment. Tell her he had missed her so much he often searched for her in crowds. Thank her for suggesting he get therapy to help him deal with his grief. He should've called her after she'd left Maine a decade ago, but he'd waited too long. So long, it felt like time had run out. Each passing month of doing nothing made the fear he didn't deserve her come true. Despite having accidentally become a popular plus-one in Manhattan's social scene, there had been no one else.

He stopped at the sheet of loose plywood currently serving as his kitchen counter and opened the box of granite countertop samples to distract himself. He placed a green tile next to the red cabinet, immediately thought of Christmas. Wrong season. Like most lake houses, the Red House was a summer house. He set the green tile in the rejection pile.

"She hates being surprised." He held up another sample and thought of Avery's warm hand splaying across his chest, stopping his hug on the dock. "Things got contentious quickly."

"No." Anna Catherine lifted a hand to her mouth.

"I get her reaction," he said. "I don't remember much about our breakup except that it happened right after I saved Max Perry's life. I froze up inside and got so panicked, I said things I didn't mean. Whatever I said was terrible enough she left without saying goodbye."

"Miles." Anna sighed. "Saving a child from drowning is a trauma. I can't imagine how she felt seeing you again, but deep down, she must know you weren't thinking clearly when you broke up with her."

"Well, yesterday she told me to go back to the City after she brought up the second circle of Hell and I pointed out that circle is lust."

"No!" Hayes covered his eyes and shook his head.

"I couldn't help it. I needed to ease the tension, and she used to love light teasing." Miles rubbed the back of his neck. "Maybe I should come back to the City until she's gone. But they need my help at Montressa."

Before Sam's heart attack, Miles had planned to spend the summer at the Red House. Now, he wanted to help the Coopers, who had been there for him countless times during his mother's illness and later, after she passed away. Leaving Maine also delayed plans for the bereavement camp. He looked out his back window, across the lake to the corporate retreat. Two people in yellow neon vests stood on the shoreline. Maybe a survey crew. His realtor might know.

"Miles, you've wanted another chance for a long time." Anna Catherine brought him back to Avery.

"I know, but I ruined my chances a decade ago."

"You were young," said Hayes. "And understandably lost."

True. But now, their best friends were engaged, and they needed to get along. The last thing he wanted was to cause a scene at Lily and Nate's wedding. The Avery he knew wouldn't want that either.

"It's one sighting," Anna said. "Make a plan for next time. First, no bringing up lust."

Miles chuckled and told them every detail of the dock encounter. When he got to the end, Hayes and Anna Catherine stared at him. What felt like minutes of silence passed.

"I should leave, right? I don't want to upset her. It's foolish to think of getting back together." He dropped a granite sample onto the plywood counter in frustration.

"Dude." Hayes rubbed his forehead. "After ten years, you can't just walk up and expect her to say yes to a dinner invite. You gotta work up to that."

"But I have to say I am sorry before we can—" Miles shook his head. "Say it works out. She starts her MBA in the fall. No direct flights from La Guardia to Hanover, and it's a five-hour drive to Dartmouth from the City. I checked last night. Distance'll challenge a relationship, so maybe I shouldn't try."

"Miles, oh boy. I have never seen you like this. Let's see if we can help." Anna paused and lifted Lennox to burp her. "What's your favorite film where the guy wants his girl back?"

He should've known she'd ask that. As former child actors, Hayes and Anna Catherine had come of age on set and viewed everything through the prism of film. Miles always picked the same movie to irritate her.

"*Die Hard.*"

"Yes!" Hayes pumped his fist. He loved *Die Hard* too.

Anna rolled her eyes.

"Don't fight me, Anna Catherine. *Die Hard* is a romance." Miles laughed, and the tension in his shoulders loosened. "John McClane goes to Nakatomi Plaza to win Holly back."

Hayes nodded. "When Hans Gruber falls to his death, John and Holly get their happily ever after. Genius analysis, Miles. I'm going to add this to your Wikipedia page."

Hayes loved editing Miles's page. The whole thing was an inside joke.

"Last December, you two claimed *Die Hard* is a Christmas movie." Anna frowned. "And now it's second-chance romance? No. How about *Crazy, Stupid, Love?*"

Miles vaguely remembered that movie.

"Is that the one where Ryan Gosling fights Kevin Bacon?" he asked.

"Mm-hmm." Hayes gave Miles a thumbs-up. "Ryan whips off his ring, ready to avenge his friend, even though they aren't getting along at the moment. That movie is a bromance, not a romance."

Lennox burped and Anna elbowed Hayes. "Hang on, Miles. The baby needs to switch sides. Hayes, take the phone."

Miles placed a black granite countertop sample next to his brick red cabinet. It reminded him of Tiger Woods on Sunday. Winning.

He picked up his phone. The brownstone's ceiling filled the screen, and all he could hear were voices as Hayes made sure Anna was comfortable. Miles waited, his screen aglow from the light of the brownstone's den. Hayes asked if she needed anything and went to get Anna a glass of water. Miles loved the way they cared for one another. This. Miles wanted this. Getting up in the morning. Figuring out the day together. And every time he dreamed it, he saw Avery. After that summer, he'd thought about calling her or showing up at Vanderbilt, but at twenty-two, he didn't know what to say, how to sound sincere, or how to fix his mistakes. The little voice telling him he'd never deserved her didn't make things any easier. At some point, he'd waited too long and ever since then, he'd told himself it wasn't meant to be.

He replaced the black sample with a white marble veined with strands of gold. Hmm. His mind floated back to *Crazy, Stupid, Love* and the other thing Ryan Gosling did in that movie.

"Anna, did you pick this movie to trick me into doing the *Dirty Dancing* lift?" he asked the ceiling on his screen.

Anna picked up the phone. "No, but if you do, please film it for me."

Hayes returned, and she took a sip of water. "Steve Carell tries to win back his wife with small gestures. Before the fight, he's built a mini-golf course in their backyard to recreate their first date. You need to remind Avery of why she fell for you. I know you're different today, but the guy she loved ten summers ago is still in there."

Hayes kissed her temple.

"Anna Catherine is the smartest person I know," he said. "Miles, give us some memories of that summer. What happened the first time you talked to her?"

"I was on a run, and on my way up Montressa's driveway, she drove by, accidentally hit a puddle, and covered me in mud." He laughed. "She stopped and apologized in this sweet Southern accent. A couple days later, I saw her at Napolitano's Pizza. I was with friends, and she didn't notice me. I sat there watching her, and it felt like no one else was in the pizza parlor. She forgot to take her cookie when she picked up her order. I figured she worked at Montressa, so I stopped by on my way home. I found her on the dock, painting. I walked up and said, 'You forgot your cookie.'"

Miles's mind drifted back in a daze. She'd invited him to sit with her. That had been the first night they'd seen the loon as he called for his mate. Avery had shimmered in the rosy, golden glow of the setting sun. The blood in his head had taken the superhighway to his pants. He had grabbed a life jacket and placed it in his lap as if that were perfectly normal. Thankfully, the loon distracted her.

"Bring a dozen of those cookies to the lodge," Hayes suggested. "She won't feel singled out, but she'll know you brought them for her. What else? What did you wear that summer?"

"I drove the ski boat, so mostly board shorts, tees, and sweatshirts. She always stole my sweatshirts."

"Smells imprint themselves on our memory. Did you wear cologne?" asked Anna.

Anna was right. The day before, Miles noticed Avery didn't smell like coconut sunscreen anymore. She smelled grown-up, beautiful, and a little Southern. Something floral, but not a flower he recognized. He couldn't remember what he'd smelled like in college.

"Possibly Axe body spray. I lived at home, and the residual scent never left my room after middle school. Sometimes I open a box of stuff from home, and I can still smell it."

"Oh Miles, I didn't know how far you've come." Hayes laughed.

"We all have, Hayes," Miles said. "That summer, after running in the morning and driving the ski boat all day, I probably smelled like sweat and sunscreen, with undertones of motor oil. And I had my baseball cap on backward all the time."

"Okay, women go nuts over the backward baseball cap. That'll take her back," said Anna Catherine. "What was she wearing yesterday?"

"She was a mess."

"You said she was gorgeous."

"She was. A gorgeous mess. Like if you dropped a bottle of rainbow sprinkles. It's a big mess, but so pretty. Like that. Ratty sweatshirt, leggings. Like a college student who had been in the library all night, cramming for exams."

He'd resisted the temptation to pull that paintbrush from her topknot, allowing that strawberry blond hair to cascade over her shoulders.

"Ooh," Hayes said. "She is still into sweatshirts. You should 'accidentally' leave one at the lodge. She will keep it because it smells like you, like Taylor Swift's scarf in *All Too Well*."

Anna took the phone.

"She wanted to look hot when she saw you again and got nervous when she didn't measure up to your recent plus-ones. After getting up who knows how early and driving halfway up the East Coast?" Anna clicked her tongue and shook her head. "I feel for her."

"But I told her she looked great."

"From her perspective, you had to say that. Next time, try not to surprise her so she can prepare and feel more comfortable. And keep the conversation light. No Dante, like some condescending professor."

Part of him hated how much sense they made. At least getting her back seemed possible.

"Got it," he said. "And thank you."

"Remember," Hayes said. "She's in *your* neck of the woods. Expect her to feel uncomfortable. What did you used to do there, for dates?"

"Canoe to an island for a picnic. Stargaze. Swim. Napolitano's Pizza has a video game arcade. There's a drive-in theater fifteen miles up the road."

Anna and Hayes both had the same blank expression, mouths half open, like they were witnessing something they'd never encountered.

"It's rural Maine, not the West Village. But thank you. I've got this." At that, Miles changed the subject. "Speaking of the Village, where are we with NYU?"

"They want to discuss how many therapists we need. After my film opens Memorial Day weekend, I'll have more time to meet with them."

Miles let out a sigh of relief. Their bereavement camp might work. Anna leaned in again. "I know you grew up in the land of maple syrup, but Avery needs molasses. Take it slow."

"Ayuh." Miles nodded. Over time, he'd taught Hayes and Anna that "ayuh" was how Mainers said *yes*. "I got it. I'll see her on Tuesday. Nate called a staff meeting. I'll let you know how it all goes."

After they hung up, Miles opened his post-run bottle of chocolate milk and flicked the cap into the basket on top of his fridge. Linden Dairy still sold serving-sized glass bottles of chocolate milk, and although they'd replaced the metal caps with plastic, the little bottles were his favorite part of coming home. That, and fresh blueberries. He spent eleven months of the year waiting for blueberry season and looked forward to its return. Frozen blueberries simply weren't the same.

He threw on a jacket and headed outside. The lake sparkled on cool, crisp days like this. He scanned the water as he zipped up his jacket. No sign of the survey crew at the corporate retreat, so he texted his realtor. He watched two ducks swim along the shoreline as he walked to his garage. If he got lucky, the birds would nest nearby. Avery loved baby ducks. She loved baby loons more, and the loons should be here soon. They returned every spring and nested in the cove between his house and Montressa.

Dust billowed out into the sunlight as Miles swung open the old wooden garage doors. He carefully uncovered the Mail Jeep, a 1985 Dispatcher he'd bought in high school from a retired postal carrier. He'd refurbished it a couple of years ago and kept it as an "around the lake" car. The passenger door no longer unlatched and slid back while driving. It was safer now, but he'd always loved how Avery had screamed and then laughed hysterically every time it had flown open. He smiled, put his key in the ignition. The Mail Jeep revved to life on the first try.

As Miles pulled the car out of the garage and into the gravel driveway, he felt a flutter of excitement. Avery had always loved this car.

He'd park right in front of the lodge, where she couldn't miss it.

CHAPTER THREE

Avery

MONDAY, MAY 15

Avery's grandmother, Mimi, used to say lost things had a way of resurfacing exactly where she'd left them. Forty-some hours had passed since the incident on the dock. She'd moved into the loft apartment above the lodge, done three Peloton rides, and reoriented herself with Montressa's sprawling campus of guest cabins. The entire time, her mind kept replaying the conversation with Miles, arriving at the same conclusion again and again. Dredging up a past they couldn't change was pointless.

Once she'd finished her morning shower, Avery headed down the loft's outside staircase on her way to the front desk inside the lodge's lobby. Her breath hitched when she saw Miles's Mail Jeep parked in Montressa's circular drive. The refurbished 1985 Jeep Dispatcher hadn't lost its novelty. She jiggled the passenger-side door handle to see if it still didn't latch properly. He'd fixed it. As she peeked inside, her breath fogged the window in the chilly spring air.

He'd let her drive it once, but she enjoyed being his passenger more. Because it had been used to deliver mail, the steering wheel was on the right, enabling the postal carrier to reach mailboxes. Originally, there hadn't been a passenger seat, but Miles added one in high school. The passenger sat on the left, normally the driver's side. That change in perspective had felt the way he made her feel: off kilter, in a good way. Every time he shifted into reverse, he looped his hand behind her headrest as he looked out the back window. That simple, protective gesture never failed to send a flutter through her. When he turned to face forward and shift out of reverse, they often locked eyes and leaned in for a kiss. *That summer*, she'd craved any excuse to go in reverse.

There would be no going backward this summer.

She shook her head, walked into the lodge, and distracted herself with work. Everyone was concerned about Sam. Concentrating on lodge business could ease their worries a little and might push Miles out of her every thought.

Montressa had passed down from Cooper to Cooper ever since it opened in 1926. Over time, the Cooper family bought the surrounding land and Montressa now sat on ninety-nine acres, with twenty-two cabins sprinkled through the property. The centerpiece was the lodge, which housed the front desk, office, lobby, dining room, and six hotel-style lodge rooms. Avery was staying in the loft, a small apartment above the office with its own set of outside steps.

At the end of last summer, Sam retired, and his son Nate took over running the resort. Each Cooper updated the resort to fit their generation and Avery expected Nate to do the same. He'd planned a staff meeting tomorrow via Zoom, and she didn't want to join in without having made herself useful, especially since Miles was working so hard on the waterfront. Early this morning, from the loft window, she'd noticed a neat row of freshly washed kayaks down at the marina beach.

She spent the morning getting familiar with the front desk and office. The L-shaped front desk sat in one corner of Montressa's spacious rectangular lobby. There were two doors: the driveway door which opened to the back of the property, and the lakeside door. The front desk faced a sitting area with couches, a coffee and tea station, and the puzzle table, a guest favorite that saw heavy use all summer. A large stone fireplace climbed up one wall.

A hallway behind the front desk led back to two offices. Nate's office, which had *General Manager* painted on the door, looked out over the glimmering lake. The other office belonged to Nate's mother, Laurie, who still managed reservations. Lily would join Montressa's staff as activities manager once school ended. She was waiting a couple of years to decide whether she wanted to keep teaching or join Nate in the office year-round.

Avery knew of nothing more aggravating than someone rearranging your office and vowed not to meddle with Laurie's system unless necessary. She decided to work from the front desk, which had a counter for serving guests and a lower, more functional seated workspace. It was more fun to work from the lobby anyway, given its view of the waterfront and proximity to the fireplace. Someone, probably Miles, had left a maple-blueberry donut by the phone. He'd always bought two. One for his post-run breakfast, the other for her. She set it aside. Time to work.

No thinking about Miles.

As Lily promised, everything was pretty much the same except for a new laptop. A sticky note pasted to the top cover said, "no password." That wasn't very secure. On the wall, the giant chalkboard still held Montressa's famous handmade reservation chart. Dates ran across the top and the names of each cabin down the left side, leaving a square for each day of the summer. At some point, someone had switched from chalk to Post-its to block off each reservation.

On the board, sticky notes contained the names of some of the longtime families who came every year: the Schwartzes, the Longneckers, the Lipscombs. The Michaelsons still reserved half the resort for their family reunion week, which staff used referred to as "Hell Week". Avery laughed at the memory.

Handwritten reservations led to double-booking. It had happened the summer she had worked at the front desk, thankfully on a slower week when someone's reservation could be upgraded.

"Tell me they are not still using that old board," she muttered to herself as she opened the laptop. Montressa should've modernized once Nate took the helm, but scanning the computer revealed they used it for emailing guests and internet browsing. She wondered if Nate ever considered purchasing scheduling software to keep track of reservations.

It was easiest to focus on the issues she could fix, such as answering general inquiry emails and clearing Nate's calendar. No appointments today, but Tuesday, *fix steps* showed up on his schedule, shared with *Wes DuCharme, Maintenance Director, Montressa Lodge*. Wes had been a cabin steward ten years ago. He must have stayed on. She dialed his cell, and after they'd caught up on the last ten years and she'd congratulated him on his new job title, Wes confirmed he'd rebuild the rotted steps to the lake tomorrow.

The next item on the calendar was *Paulson Carter*, no information listed. A Google search revealed Paulson Carter's job title as Chief of Emerging Markets at Carter Hotels in New York. He had graduated Phi Beta Kappa from Yale the same year as Miles. She could ask Miles about Paulson, but tracking down an email address and sending a message took less time and avoided another lecture on Dante's *Inferno*.

Late afternoon, with nothing left to resolve on the calendar, Avery finally got up from the desk and walked to the window. Her gaze traveled to the waterfront, where Miles and the maintenance crew were attaching the floating ski dock to the fixed dock. Avery put her hand to her necklace and ran the charm back and forth along the chain. Miles had on a baseball cap, jeans, and despite the chill, a faded Yale Track T-shirt. Every arm muscle tightened as he pulled the rope to bring the floating dock into place. He lifted the cement anchors as if they were foam and carefully dropped them in the water, avoiding any splash.

One thing hadn't changed. He still took her breath away.

She wondered what his life was like now. For ten years, she had avoided all things Miles, never searching for his name or asking Lily about him. Once Lily and Nate had started seeing each other a couple of years ago, Lily had dropped hints and small bits of news, but Avery never took the bait. Until he'd called her *Pepper*. Her curiosity had soared ever since. There was no sign of it stopping until she answered her questions and moved on.

Ignoring the ping of an incoming message on her phone, she walked back to the desk and typed *Miles Magrum* in the search bar of the open browser tab. Two and a half million results. Gulp. The top of his Wikipedia page mentioned him being the founder of CashCache, America's most downloaded personal debt reduction app. He'd sold it three years ago to a financial institution for "an undisclosed sum." The page also had sections for his cameos in Hayes Preston films and mentioned his upcoming thesis, "*Die Hard* as a Contemporary Romance." The only thing the page lacked was a *personal life* section.

Back at the search screen, the images tab presented a Miles Magrum multiverse. On red carpets, at sporting events, and reading on the subway. Miles at the Met Gala, in a navy tuxedo so tailored, someone must've had to peel it off him later that night. In the VIP tent at a Hazel Matheson concert. Avery felt a sour pang of jealousy creep into her throat and promptly swallowed it.

She landed on a photo of him throwing a football in the surf on Montauk. Fading sunlight bathed every ripple of his abdomen in a golden shimmer. And what was at the top of his hipbone? She zoomed in and gasped. A blurry tattoo that resembled a bug in the exact spot where a firefly had landed the day he'd asked her out. They'd been sunbathing on the floating dock, their pinkies so close, it felt like they were touching. The sensation had set her insides abuzz. She'd told him a firefly in daylight was good luck, so he'd tried his luck with her. He'd asked for her favorite date activities because *that* Miles only wanted to make her happy.

Until he didn't.

She zoomed back out, reminding herself that her Miles disappeared that day in the parking lot. They didn't know each other anymore. In fact, the more she thought about it, Miles doing anything sweet for her now was irritating. Nothing could make up for his callous behavior. The less she talked to him, the better.

Avery found herself unable to stop staring at the photo of Miles—all sinew and sin. She tried to convince herself it was anger blooming in her stomach, but anger didn't tingle in her thighs. Her cheeks flushed at how quickly her search had spiraled. She knew better than to explore this rabbit hole.

Beside the front desk, the lakeside door opened. Miles stepped inside and rotated his baseball cap backward. Feeling caught, she quickly closed the laptop and spun the office chair to another part of the desk, hoping to appear like she'd been doing something else. After he left, she'd exit the page and clear the search history.

"Hey," he said.

"Hi." She smiled at him, doing her best not to appear guilty.

"Lily here yet? I got a text she wants to meet with us."

Avery lifted her phone and saw the text as a second message popped up.

◯ **Lily:** Running late. Be there soon.

"She's late." Avery rolled her eyes, annoyed Lily might be giving them more time together on purpose. Lily had sent a text earlier asking Avery to "be nice" next time she saw Miles. Avery hadn't replied. She wondered if Miles got the same text. He damn well should have.

Miles drummed his fingers on the desk and surveyed the open lobby.

"This place never changes, does it?" His scan of the room landed on the reservation board. He pointed at it. "Please tell me that's here for nostalgia."

Avery swiveled her chair toward the board.

"Nope. They appear to be using it." She kept her gaze on the board to avoid the inevitable swoon of seeing Miles in a backward baseball cap.

"There's no online reservation platform on their computer."

He reached across the desk and picked up the laptop.

"No," she yelped. "I already checked."

"I trust you." He leveled her with a soft stare. "But maybe it's in a hidden folder. The Coopers aren't exactly tech savvy. I am."

"I am too, and I already checked." She reached for the laptop a second too late. He had opened it.

She didn't have to see the screen to know he'd discovered a very alluring photo of himself in the surf. Miles lifted his head slowly, a self-important grin lighting up his face.

Avery's body temperature rose to near fever level with embarrassment. Even her fingers blushed red. She shielded her eyes and shook her head. This was a nightmare. She wished she could make him go away. Forever.

He hit what had to be the back button.

"Avery Easton," he said slowly. "Were you googling me?"

An obnoxious question, given the answer was staring at him.

"Yes," she said. "I, um... It was the first time. I've never done it."

"The first time, right." He let out a self-satisfied snort.

She sat up straighter, determined not to let him get the better of her.

"Don't pretend you're innocent," she said. "You're remarkably up-to-date on me. I've avoided you all this time. Sure, I caught little updates here and there, but I didn't have the big picture and... Can we not do this now? I mean, seeing each other again is hard enough."

Embarrassment got the better of her. She swiveled the chair away from him. Her situation gave new meaning to *wanting to crawl out of your own skin*.

"If you want to see me shirtless, ask," he said. "I'm a nice guy. I'd do that for you."

Avery covered her eyes again, hoping he'd disappear. She felt certain he'd flashed his *Inferno* smirk again.

"Please don't make this worse," she half-begged, half-groaned. "Can you leave? Please?"

Silence, footsteps, and the once-familiar scent of warm pine after an August rain. Miles smelled so good, she imagined him after a shower, a white towel wrapped around his waist. The abs from that football photo. Warm skin, a little damp. He used to jump in bed with her after his post-run shower and snuggle into her. What a wonderful way to wake up.

Her chair spun a quarter turn. She peered through her fingers, took a deep breath, and dropped her hands. There was Miles, on one knee, concern filling his chestnut eyes. Avery's breath hitched. That backward baseball cap. He no longer resembled his red carpet Google search results. He looked like he had *that summer*.

"Hey," he whispered. "Don't be upset. It's funny."

Avery rolled her eyes. She wasn't a cafeteria. He couldn't pick whatever emotion he wanted.

"Do you know how many times I've googled you?" he whispered, as if he understood. "I've never—"

Montressa's back door blew open, and in walked Lily. Miles stood and his arms fell straight down his sides, as if he'd done something he'd been warned about.

Avery sighed through gritted teeth before standing to greet Lily. He'd never what? Maybe he'd never googled her, or maybe he had. She wanted to know.

"Great news." Lily opened her arms. "Sam's out of surgery and doing well. He's going to be okay."

Miles hugged Lily, their shoulders dropping with the release of their collective worry. Lily hugged Avery next. As the two friends separated, Lily assessed Avery with a furrowed brow.

"Your face is red. Did he upset you?" She pointed at Miles.

Avery hoped Miles would save her from further embarrassment by not mentioning the googling to Lily.

"It was nothing." Avery rubbed Lily's arm. "Silly things."

Over Lily's shoulder, Avery noticed the breeze had nudged the door to the circular drive open a crack and snagged the opportunity for a break from her friend's inquiry. As she walked over to shut it, a wet, black nose peeked around the edge of the doorframe and Sam Cooper's snow-white golden retriever came into view. Upon seeing Avery, his tail beat against the door. His eyes had aged in the last ten years, but his puppy enthusiasm remained.

"Aw, Casper." She leaned down, welcoming the wet kisses on her face. "You remember me."

Casper placed a paw on her arm and whined. He pranced over to the front desk to sniff where Avery had been sitting. Lily was still assessing her with a furrowed brow and set jaw.

"Miles," Lily said.

He'd returned to the front desk, his attention buried in the computer. The quick movement of his fingers on the trackpad, clicking and scrolling, probably searching for a reservation system. His brow furrowed deeper with each failed folder.

"Miles Magrum."

His head jerked up at the sound of Lily's terse teacher's voice.

"What? I didn't do anything."

Lily stepped halfway between them and pointed, Spiderman-meme style, as if they were about to be put in detention.

"Listen, both of you." Her voice boomed. "Try to get along. For Nate's sake. And mine. Like it or not, you're an important part of our wedding. Right now, the Coopers are in crisis. Nate doesn't need your angsty bickering added to his list of worries. Miles, don't antagonize her. You like to push buttons, and Avery's are easy to push."

That seemed unfair, but Avery kept quiet. Teacher Lily made her want to recite her times tables to redeem herself.

"And Avery, I was there for you when you left Trent." Lily's voice softened. "Being there for me means acknowledging Nate's best man. He's a nice guy and as loyal as they come. Try being friends."

Avery and Miles both spoke at the same time.

"We are friends," he said.

"I'll try," she groused. They had never been friends. They'd only been more. Until they weren't.

Miles tilted his head in question. He almost seemed hurt. Avery knew better than to make a promise regarding Miles. Seeing him in those clothes reminded her of how he used to turn his baseball cap backward and pull her into an empty cabin for a kiss. Those stolen kisses often led to exploring every inch of one another before returning to work.

"Let us know if we can do anything to help you and the Coopers," Miles said to Lily.

Typical of him to charm the teacher.

"I'm glad you offered," Lily said. "Could one of you take care of the dog until school lets out in June? It's hard for me to feed and walk him before I leave in the morning."

"Not me," Miles said, holding up both hands.

"Nice." Avery scowled. "Volunteer to help and refuse the ask."

"That's not getting along." Lily shook a finger at Avery. "To be fair, Miles and Casper Cooper share a history of mutual jealousy-fueled hatred."

"I don't hate him," Miles protested. "But I'll be traveling, and I have my morning TV gig. When I'm here, I'll be down at the water, which holds all kinds of temptations for him. And the nights? My house is a construction zone."

Casper emerged from around the desk, holding the maple-blueberry donut in his mouth. He titled his head back and ate it in one gulp.

"That donut was for Avery." Miles stepped toward the lakeside door and turned the doorknob. "Avery, my friend, good luck with that menace of a dog. I'm here anytime you want to see the gods. I mean goods."

He rotated the brim of his cap to the front and winked. Avery needed to avoid these daily doses of his annoying, yet attractive confidence before his backwards baseball cap and the scent of warm pine after an August rain weakened her resolve. She'd find a solid reason to send him back to the City.

Once Miles closed the door, Lily sized her up.

"Avery, are you okay?" she asked. "When I walked in, things seemed awfully tense. I thought you'd moved on. You never ask about him."

"It's fine. We're just getting used to one another." Avery shrugged. Casper pushed his wet nose under her hand, asking for a head rub. Dogs always made you feel wanted and loved.

"I'll take care of this sweet boy"—Avery scratched behind his ears—"if you tell me what you want to do for your bachelorette party. Also, I have your wedding invitations ready to proof."

"Now that Sam's going to be okay, seeing what you painted for us and catching up sounds nice," Lily said. "So does food. Want to grab a pizza at Napolitano's?"

Avery nodded. She had missed Napolitano's molasses cookies more than those maple-blueberry donuts anyway.

CHAPTER FOUR

Miles

TUESDAY, MAY 16

For a Tuesday morning with Monday morning energy, Miles was crushing it. Most people hadn't begun their workday, but he'd already completed his remote segment on student debt for *Bright and Early*, ordered a pallet of replacement planks for the dock, reached out to an art therapist asking for information about art therapy for bereavement camps, lined up site visits to observe camps in Georgia, Minnesota and Wyoming, and signed up for fall classes at NYU on grant writing and non-profit administration. Next spring, he'd need two more classes to graduate with a master's in public administration, specializing in non-profit management.

The *Bright and Early* shoot had been a breeze. No subway commute, no studio crew, and no idle time during commercial breaks. Just him, founder of everyone's favorite personal finance app, sitting in the lodge's conference room, talking to an America he couldn't see about rising interest rates and student loans. Miles was more efficient on his own. If only he could work remotely all the time.

The wood-paneled walls of Montressa's conference room made a fantastic, rustic television backdrop. The pine boughs swaying outside the picture window almost resembled a digitally generated background.

"Did anyone hear what Miles said?" co-anchor Victoria Evans asked. "I was busy waiting for a moose to pass by."

Every question from the *Bright and Early* hosts had been about Maine, not debt. He hoped Avery watched and promised himself to do as Lily asked and be nice today. Getting along meant not repeating the emotional nails on a chalkboard of the dock and avoiding another Google incident, though he'd been flattered she'd peeked into his life.

In anticipation of Nate's virtual staff meeting, Miles traded his sport coat for a gray tee and navy cotton fisherman sweater. He expected Nate to put him in charge, and the local staff wouldn't want a Manhattan suit running the resort. Avery had always loved running her hands over his soft clothing. With any luck, she wouldn't be able to resist this silky-smooth cotton sweater. A day ago, she hadn't reacted to "classic Miles" the way Anna Catherine had promised.

He had a couple minutes to turn this remote television studio back into the lodge conference room. He put his ring light back in its shipping box and placed it in the corner for next time, logged into the Zoom meeting, and connected to the wall-mounted speaker bar and camera so Nate could see everyone. The housekeeping and maintenance staffs rarely used computers, and coming to the conference room was easier than logging on. They'd arrive any minute.

Miles placed the molasses cookies he'd brought from Napolitano's on a plate borrowed from Montressa's kitchen and set them at the end of the long table. He put the box of counter samples on the table as a reminder to give them to Wes, who was replacing Montressa's waterfront steps today.

Wes had texted last night saying if Miles didn't make a choice today, he'd have to wait until September to install the counters. The current front-runner was a sleek black granite, but before his decision was literally set in stone, Miles wanted to be sure. He sat down, opened a bottle of chocolate milk, and went through the samples while he waited.

Avery arrived first, Casper hot on her heels. She placed her tea, a black Sakura Pigma Micron pen, a couple of blank pieces of paper, and a tube of mint lip balm on the table in a neat line. Anna was right. Minor details conjured up major memories. That brand of lip balm, with its distinctive green tube, always made him think of Avery. Which happened a lot because a box of it sat at nearly every CVS checkout counter.

"Ooh, samples. What are these for?" Avery dug through the box of granite tiles as Casper slumped to the floor.

"My kitchen. These are my cabinets and the floors are walnut." He plunked the red cabinet paint swatch on the table, hoping the samples would entice her to come see the Red House or at least help him pick the right granite. "Wes is on my case. I have to pick countertops today. What do you think? Black soapstone?"

"Mimi says red and black looks like the Devil's lair," she said, rearranging the tiles.

He took a sip of his chocolate milk. Dante's *Inferno* was not the vibe he wanted in his kitchen.

"How is Mimi?" He smiled at the memory of Avery's grandmother's visit to Montressa ten summers ago. She'd charmed everyone at cocktail hour, holding court on the front porch, wearing a colorful caftan while sipping on dirty martinis. Mimi had found Miles so charming she'd bought Avery a box of condoms and attempted to give her *the talk*.

"She passed away last year," Avery said. "I miss her."

"I'm sorry." Miles knew that pain and wished he could take hers away. "She's with your Grandpa Banks now. What'd she call him? Her 'kismet mate?'"

"She mashed both words together. They were kis-mates." Avery let out a contented sigh. "I can't believe you remember."

"I remember a lot of things."

For a quiet moment, neither one looked away. Miles recalled Mimi explaining this phenomenon. A kis-mate eclipsed a soulmate. It was your one true kindred spirit. An elevated love pulling you both toward a shared destiny warmer than the sun and just as bright. Kis-mates were rarer than rare. Miles wasn't sure he'd ever know a love like that. The closest he'd come had been with Avery, but who knew what love was at twenty-two? He wasn't sure he knew now. Avery twisted her lips, as if pondering something too. And wow, her irises were the same emerald green as her sweater. He used to tell her what color her eyes were and wondered if her jilted fiancé had noticed the tiny, beautiful things that no one else mentioned.

She might have read his thoughts, because Avery broke the stare. She turned her attention to the box on the table.

"Ooh, look at this." She pulled out the white granite with gold veining. Miles sat up straighter. If his dreams ever came true, they'd share a kitchen one day, and he wanted her to love every inch of the Red House.

She traced a finger along the veining of the granite. "I love the gold flecks in this one. Contrasted with the red cabinets and walnut floors, it'll brighten the space. If you want stunning, this is it."

Miles returned the samples to the box and laid the white one on top because once an Avery-approved option existed, nothing else would do.

"Thank you," he said. "I can't wait to cook you dinner in my new kitchen."

When her face fell flat, he wished he could take it back.

"Because we're friends." He gave her what he hoped was an encouraging smile.

"We were never friends, Miles. Friends call or text each other," she said. "I helped because my conscience can't allow that precious A-frame to be possessed by the literal kitchen from Hell, regardless of its occupant. The Red House deserves better."

Ouch. He placed the sample box on an empty chair and leaned across the table, resting on his elbows.

"I like to think we could be friends," he said. "Friends who forgive one another."

She picked up her pen and let out a frustrated groan.

Miles echoed her groan. Everything became about something else with her. The countertops now bore the burden of their combined history.

"Nate is taking forever to join this Zoom," she groused. "And where's the staff for this staff meeting?"

"I don't know." Miles slumped back in his chair.

The room fell silent, except for the scratches of her pen sketching. Given how things were going, she'd probably draw him as a demon.

Casper moved under the table and plopped to the floor again.

"I brought molasses cookies ... for my friends," he said into the tense silence. Like every other workplace in America, Montressa's staff turned to vultures when they saw free food.

She looked up from her drawing, eyed the cookies, and then him. She remembered those cookies. He was certain of it.

"Good morning from the penthouse." Nate's face loomed large on the conference room's wall-mounted television screen. Behind him, Miles's apartment sprawled over his shoulder. There was his Boa sofa, woven to resemble a bird's nest. Beyond it, a stunning view of lower Manhattan.

Avery must've missed the Architectural Digest spread on her Google search because her mouth fell open at the glimpse into his city life. He wondered whether she liked it or if she noticed the crisp design didn't match his casual personality.

"Miles." Nate hooked a thumb over his shoulder. "What is up with this sofa? My sister said Kendall Jenner has the same couch and it cost—"

"Hey Nate, let's not say that aloud." He pulled at his collar to release the heat rising on his neck.

Avery straightened up in her chair and clapped her hands together.

"Nate, good morning. How's your dad?" She smiled brightly, her voice confident, not a trace of the earlier aggravation. Perhaps Nate's current situation had given her a little perspective.

"It's a good day." Nate smiled. "Mom and I took shifts and got some sleep. Dad walked a little. We all watched Miles on *Bright and Early*, and now everyone's on cloud nine because the lodge shined on national television."

Miles smiled to himself.

"Mom wants to know if Victoria is coming in a couple of weeks when the show films live from Montressa."

At the mention of *Bright and Early* coming to the lake, Avery's head lifted from her doodling. Victoria Evans had worked at Montressa with them that summer. His expertise on personal finance had led Victoria to campaign for him to be a regular on the show. For reasons unknown to him, Avery hadn't liked Victoria. Sometimes people rubbed you the wrong way. He'd had a few of them in his life.

"Yes, Victoria and I will broadcast live on June 30th." Miles tried to keep his voice as neutral as possible, but Avery bristled. It might not be the best idea to bring Victoria here when he was trying to reconcile with Avery, but it was too late. Maybe they'd get along after all these years. Then again, Avery held on to grudges.

"Avery," Nate said. "Stick around. They'd probably love some footage of you water-skiing."

"We'll see." Avery frowned, confirming Miles's fear she'd leave once she'd done what she came to do—or as soon as Victoria arrived, whichever came first. And that would be a shame because Avery was a great water-skier.

"Let's talk Montressa." With so little free time, multi-tasking was necessary for Nate, and he typed as he spoke. Miles knew the feeling. His phone buzzed on the table.

"Wait, isn't this a staff meeting? We're the only two here." Avery pointed her pen back and forth across the table.

"Ayuh. The dream team," Nate said. "Together at last."

Avery winced and concentrated on her paper.

"Updates," Nate said. "Opening Day is June 16th. Housekeeping promises to have all the cabins deep cleaned and ready by then. My sister and I are taking turns in New York so I can be back in Maine when the summer staff arrives May 30th."

Avery wrote *May 30th—staff, June 16th—opening day,* and *June 30th—B&E* on a fresh sheet of paper. Over on her doodle paper, she was either drawing devil horns or branches. Time would tell.

"Maintenance," Nate continued. "Miles, Wes says you've been a tremendous help with the docks. After he finishes the steps, he'll paint the boathouse interior. We haven't used it in a few years, but Lily says it could be our cutest cabin. Back when my parents converted Montressa's original boathouse into a rental, people loved that we'd found a new use for an old building. People still love repurposed spaces, but the interior is outdated. Avery, you've got an eye for things like bedding and paint colors. Any chance you'd redecorate it?"

Avery frowned and forced a smile. "Um, sure. Whatever you need."

"Since it's not used as a boathouse anymore, I'm thinking of renaming it." Nate winked. "What do two you think of 'Rendezvous?'"

Avery shielded her eyes with her hand. Reminding her of the place she and Miles had spent their first night together would not help them get along. Nate was trying to keep the conversation light, but he hadn't been on the dock, caught her googling, or witnessed them picking countertops. The cringeworthy moments needed to stop.

Miles glared at Nate and shook his head. "Nope. Stick with the Boathouse."

Nate cleared his throat.

"I keep a list of things people need us to pick up at Marden's and go get everything at the end of the week," Nate said in a business voice. "Can one of you handle that?"

"I got it." She wrote *shopping at Marden's* under *Boathouse*. Evidently, Avery still lived by to-do lists.

"Do y'all have a computerized reservation system or is it all on the board?" she asked.

"Just the board," Nate said. "Guests love that thing, but it has limitations. I know I need to..."

As Nate prattled on, Miles watched Avery roll her pen back and forth across her lower lip in thought. Miles couldn't take his gaze off her pink, pouty mouth. She bit the cap. Lucky pen. He'd missed her playful nibbles and those mint-lip-balm kisses. Maybe she tasted more sophisticated now. Something like tea. Sweet tea. With mint. What he wouldn't give to find out just how delicious her kiss had become.

Blood pulsed through him as a heat centered between his legs. He wanted her the second this Zoom ended. Here. On the conference room table.

His phone buzzed, and he paid it no mind. For a brief second, he closed his eyes and inhaled. Under the table, a weight landed in his lap. The weight moved. Was that her foot massaging him? His eyes flew open to find Avery adding another item to her list. A snort followed by a quick, dog double-sneeze brought him back to reality. Miles looked down to discover Casper's white muzzle rooting around in his crotch. He hadn't heard the dog get up.

"Dammit, Casper!" he yelped, and pushed away from the table.

His chair rolled into the wall and Casper emerged, tail wagging. Miles caught the dog's mocking sideways glance.

"You're a menace, Casper." Miles pointed at him.

Nate burst out laughing. "Man, the look on your face before you left the frame. Priceless."

"Miles!" Avery chided him as she clapped for Casper to come over to her. "Don't yell at him. Dogs feel shame."

"He's untrained," Miles growled as his phone buzzed again. The phone could wait. Right now, his sweater glistened with dog slobber. "He used me as his own personal Kleenex."

"It's not your fault, Casper." Avery kissed the dog's head. "Miles's clothes can easily be mistaken for tissues."

Avery remembering his soft clothes would feel like a victory if she weren't kissing the dog whose drool covered his abdomen.

"Well, it's not my fault." Miles glared at her. "And I can't wear this dog snotfest."

Avery raised an eyebrow. He took the accompanying stifled laugh as a challenge, stood, and lifted the hem of his sweater.

"Lighten up." Avery rolled her eyes. "Dog saliva is cleaner than human saliva. You basically got sprayed with hand sanitizer. It'll dry."

She'd chosen the dog. Over him. Forget being the nice guy Lily wanted him to be; he'd gleefully push every one of Avery's damn buttons.

Holding her stare until the last possible second, he slowly removed his sweater. Cool air greeted his stomach as his T-shirt rose with it. He couldn't see her reaction, but he had worked hard for this body, so he flexed his abs in case she compared this view to the one from her Google search.

When the sweater finally came off, Avery's gaze was fixed on his hip, her pout now agape. Miles tensed. The firefly tattoo. He'd wanted to show it to her when he could explain. He reached down to lift the waistband of his jeans but accidentally pulled the elastic of his boxer briefs. If she'd missed the tattoo, she didn't miss the Tom Ford logo.

She met his eyes, slowly closed her mouth and swallowed hard. Whatever she'd seen, she'd liked. He leveled his stare, raised an eyebrow, and slowly freed the hem of his tee from around his chest. Avery's head fell to her drawing. His phone buzzed twice.

"Someone really needs to get in touch with you." Avery didn't look up. At least she'd drawn pine trees and not a demon.

Nate sighed. "Yeah Miles, maybe you should check your phone."

Miles felt bad. Nate didn't need this right now. He and Avery needed to stop making a fuss over trivial things like dog slobber and granite samples. The phone buzzed again. Despite his curiosity, he didn't pick it up.

"Miles." Avery tapped her pen on the table. "You're swamped. Go back to New York. We have enough staff, and things haven't changed much around here. I can run the front desk blindfolded."

Blindfolded. What he wouldn't give for a night with her and a blindfold. Oh, the things they could try. The pulsing heat returned, extinguishing any chance of him going back to New York.

"One person cannot replace Sam, Laurie, and Nate. I'm not sure two of us can, especially if we're"—he took a chance and winked at her—"blindfolded."

Avery tucked a tendril of loose hair behind her ear, touching the spot he used to kiss, her coy smile a sign her mind had gone to the same place.

He leaned across the table. If she wanted him to leave, he'd stay.

"I worked here for eight years and ran the waterfront for three." He flexed every arm muscle for her viewing pleasure. "How about you take land, and I take water?"

"But, you're too"—his phone buzzed again, and she tapped it with her pen—"busy."

"I'll get whatever that is later." He pointed at his phone. "I can handle it."

On the Zoom call, Nate nodded. "That's a good plan. You both know how to run the resort. Let me know if you have any ideas to improve Montressa. We need more stars on those ratings. I want to add a website and maybe social media, but that'll have to wait until winter, when I have the time."

Casper stood and meandered to the end of the table. In one swift motion, he grabbed a molasses cookie off the plate.

"First thing on the list," Miles tapped her list. "Train that dog." Avery scowled.

"And Nate," he said. "There's room for twelve for your bachelor party canoe trip. We've got the bros from high school, three from your college brew crew, Wes, and me. Let me know who should fill that sixth canoe."

"How about Hayes? He's cool, and Lily suggested asking him to do a reading at the wedding," Nate said, checking his smartwatch. "Listen, I gotta go. I'll think of another person. Thank you. I appreciate your help more than you know."

After wishing him well, Avery stood, shook her head, and left. Her drawing remained on the table. Silhouettes. Five pine trees, the moon above, a moose below.

His phone buzzed again. He checked his texts. Every single one was from Nate.

○ **Nate:** Dude, put her on tv so she has to stay longer
○ **Nate:** OMG. Stop watching her play with her pen. You look ready to pounce
○ **Nate:** Noooo. Do not come between her and Casper
○ **Nate:** Damn! She is checking out your six-pack
○ **Nate:** I think she saw the tatt
○ **Nate:** She's not over you
○ **Nate:** WTF! You've been waiting for this. Get it together.

Getting it together was harder than he'd expected. Going out with women one time required little emotional investment. Trying to win back someone you hurt required perseverance, humility, and vulnerability. If he couldn't find them, Avery would leave.

"Have you seen my lip balm?" Avery reappeared, patting her pockets as she'd done so many times ten summers ago. "I swear I brought it in here."

"You did, but I haven't seen it." He looked under the table. Nothing. He walked around to her side of the table and checked each chair as she peered into the box of samples. Nothing. He shrugged and gave her his best smirk. "Maybe Casper ate it."

"You blame him for everything." She rolled her eyes and started to leave.

"Avery," he said, lightly circling her wrist with his thumb and forefinger. "I'll be in New York part of next week on business. The rest of the time, I'll try to stay out of your way."

She glanced from her wrist to him. He wasn't the only one feeling the buzz jumping between them. A tiny gasp evaporated off her lips as their gazes met. Aware he'd touched her without asking, he let go. She brushed something off his shoulder.

"So soft," she said in an almost whisper.

"Snuggle," he said.

Her eyes grew wide.

"Oh, no. Miles, I wasn't trying to, we're not, um—" She stepped back.

"No," he said, grinning. "My fabric softener. It's Snuggle."

"With the bear?"

"Ayuh."

Avery's cheeks flushed. "I'm not sure if this is more or less embarrassing than you catching me googling you."

"I'm not qualified to answer that. After all, a dog sneezed on me and I acted like a petulant child."

She let out a nervous, stilted laugh and he said a silent wish for her to find the humor in all of this and let it loose. Miles wanted to hear her contagious, genuine laugh again. He'd recognize it anywhere. His favorite time to hear it had been when they talked nonsense in bed after sex. If it went too far, she used to cry happy tears. Sometimes she'd even snort, which only made them laugh harder.

This laugh lacked that kind of sparkle, but it was a start.

"Pepper," he said, with what he hoped was a comforting smile. "We'll get past the awkward part."

She frowned at the use of her nickname and nodded. "That's not why we're here, Miles."

Maybe not, but with any luck, he'd earn her forgiveness. A monumental task, but he had time. The Lodge was empty until the summer staff arrived at the end of the month.

CHAPTER FIVE

Avery

FRIDAY, MAY 19

Casper had been lethargic and constipated for the last two days. He'd stopped eating and lost interest in walks to the mailbox or along the lake, which he usually loved. Avery had fed him a little of the canned pumpkin Lily dropped off to soothe his tummy, but he'd slept under the desk all morning.

Avery took the warm dog draped across her feet as a sign to put off investigating the Boathouse today. This left time for researching other resorts' websites and reservation systems. A new reservation system should be at the top of Nate's list.

Over the last couple of days, Miles had made good on his promise not to bother her, quietly slipping in and out of the conference room for his remote shoots and Zoom meetings. Every time she passed the conference-room door, the meeting with Nate replayed in her head, her thoughts alternating between irritation and desire. His firefly tattoo resembled a sketch she remembered drawing that summer. She'd carefully hidden their initials in the lacy lines of the firefly's wings. There'd been no way for her to closely inspect his ink, but it made no sense for him to ghost her yet permanently alter his body with a memento of their time together.

One thing was certain. Her college boy had become all man. The abs flexing as his shirt lifted confirmed this broader, sturdier Miles knew how to use his body. Given his dating history, he probably knew exactly what to do with hers. His deliberate delivery of the word "blindfolded" still echoed in Avery's head. She covered her eyes in embarrassment, despite being alone in the lobby. She hadn't pined for a man this hard in a long time. The Pine Tree State was living up to its name.

"Enough," she said to herself as she opened Montressa's laptop. "No thinking about Miles."

Casper's head jolted up at her voice. He cocked his ears, tilted his head. Finding nothing concerning, he dropped back to the floor.

Recruiters interviewed MBA candidates in the fall. And while redecorating the Boathouse sounded fun, she needed something impressive on her résumé to fill the gaping hole of unemployment since the sale of the Peppered Page last year. Nate had mentioned he needed a website and social media accounts. She could spin that as a marketing plan and impress hiring managers. She planned to research other small resorts before lunch. First, she needed to answer Montressa's emails.

The elusive Paulson Carter remained on the calendar. Avery's second internet search yielded an email address, which sent back an automated reply. A message through LinkedIn went unanswered. She'd done everything except talk to Nate and Miles. But Nate had enough going on, and Avery wasn't willing to risk another embarrassing conversation with Miles.

If Paulson showed up, she'd send him on his way, do some research, and figure out which Nancy Meyers movie to watch with Lily later.

Picking Miles's countertop had made her crave a pretty kitchen. Maybe *It's Complicated* and some croque monsieur for dinner.

Casper let out an unenthusiastic woof at the sound of gravel crunching outside as a black car rounded the circular drive in the wrong direction. Avery walked to the door and peered out the window. The door of a shiny black Rivian SUV swung open and vintage Air Jordans, white as snow, hit the gravel.

"Oof, those won't stay white long," she muttered as opened the lodge door. "Can I help you?"

Mr. Air Jordan's blond hair was gelled back, the sides cut with precision and enough length on top to look sleek and stylish. A dress shirt with the top button undone gave a glimpse of a chiseled collarbone. He tugged a shirt cuff out from under his blue blazer, revealing a massive Breitling watch and silver fish cufflinks. Although roughly her age, he oozed the superiority and sophistication of a much older man. He was out of place in the Maine woods. This had to be Paulson Carter of Carter Hotel Group. Clearly, he didn't get any of her seven messages.

He pulled off his wire sunglasses, fighter-pilot style, in one deliberate sideways swoop. Piercing blue eyes met hers. She palmed her hair in an attempt to appear presentable and thanked whatever possessed her to wear her most flattering jeans today. He mounted three stairs in one step and tucked his sunglasses into his shirt pocket.

"Hi, I'm Avery." She smiled and stuck out her hand.

"Avery, Paulson Carter. Carter Hotel Group. It's a pleasure." He shook her hand firmly, covering it with his other hand. His hands were warm, probably from the heated steering wheel. This close, he smelled expensive. "I'm glad I ignored your messages."

She disregarded his flirtation. "The Coopers aren't here and we're not open for another month."

"Well, I was in the area and wanted to see the place." He cleared his throat. "How's Mr. Cooper feeling?"

"Better," Avery said. "But maybe you should come back later. Nate should be home by the end of the month."

"My father had a heart attack too. It's tough to see someone strong laid low," he said. "I met Nate and his father at the Northeastern Hospitality Conference. Sam seemed like a fighter to me. He'll get through it."

Paulson might be more handsome than his profile picture, but chit-chat wasn't on her agenda today.

"So, can I help you with anything, Mr. Carter? Maybe directions back to Portland?"

"You can call me Paulson. Mr. Carter is my father." He corrected her with a drop-dead gorgeous smile. "If you have time, I'd love a tour. But if you're busy, I can explore it myself."

With a smile like that, Paulson was hard to turn down. It seemed he knew Sam. He must be on the calendar for a reason. Maybe Nate wanted his advice on how to modernize. The walk would be a good way to get ideas from a hotel professional. Besides, it was a pleasant morning, and Casper loved new people. Anything to help him perk up sounded like a good idea.

As if he heard her thoughts, Casper plodded outside and sniffed their visitor. Paulson kneeled and rubbed Casper's chest. At last, a guy with a soft spot for dogs.

"I hope it's okay if Casper tags along. Word of warning, he's not very well trained." Avery hoped Miles wasn't within earshot to hear her vindicate his feelings.

"Of course," Paulson said, scratching the dog's ears. "Who says you're not trained? Casper's a good boy."

Paulson had a special voice for dogs. Even better.

Avery and Casper led Paulson down the path that ran between two cabins to the lake. Every few steps, he lifted his phone and snapped a photo.

"Do they host weddings here?" he asked.

"Um, not that I know of, but I bet they could if you're interested."

"Well, I'd need to find the bride first." He let out an uncomfortable chuckle and blushed a little.

She nervously lifted her hand, tucking a loose hair behind her ear. Paulson seemed like someone who'd marry a travel influencer. They could share their love of hotels on blogs, vlogs, and socials. Fiancée or not, he'd given her an idea. Montressa was the perfect venue for destination weddings.

"A lot of our families come back every year," she said.

Paulson stopped and stared at the sun-dappled lake. His jaw went slack. Like a siren from a Greek epic tale, Linden Lake had a way of transfixing anyone who passed by and he was no exception. The spring birdsong from the neighboring trees only enhanced the experience.

"Gorgeous." He smiled. "I see why people love it here."

Ah, so he understood what made this lake special.

"I'm curious." He narrowed his eyes as if interested in her opinion. "Montressa has almost no online presence. Is that to keep it exclusive? If it works, it's genius. I love the feeling of having something everybody wants but can't find."

Exclusivity may not have been the Coopers' intent, but Paulson had a point. Purposeful or not, being hard to find wasn't helping reservations. Nate needed to expand his opportunities, not limit them. Avery wished she'd brought something to make notes of all of these great ideas.

"They rely on repeat bookings and word of mouth," she answered. "Everyone has a story of how they found Montressa. Their kids go to camp nearby, their grandparents honeymooned here, a friend recommended it."

"I first heard about it from a Yale friend. Well, classmate."

She wondered if Miles had ever mentioned her once he returned to school after the breakup. Telling Paulson she dated Miles back in college felt a little too familiar, so she kept quiet. Oblivious to her thoughts,

Paulson stared at the lodge, deep in thought.

"I like the rustic feel, but if it were mine, I'd tear it down and start fresh."

Avery gasped and lifted her hand to her heart. She searched his face for a sarcastic smirk or teasing wink, but his eyes narrowed and his mouth twisted in thought. Maybe he didn't understand the allure after all.

"What? Why?"

"It reminds me of the camp from *The Parent Trap* with all these log cabins. People want modern amenities. Being suitable only for summer isn't maximizing the location's full potential." He raised a hand and skimmed it across his view. "Imagine a glass-front, modern hotel and matching glass-front villas, all with views of this spectacular lake. Cross-country ski trails, a skating pond, a row of lakeside cabanas with hot tubs over the water, a Jet Ski marina. All less than an hour from the Portland Jetport. Being open year-round brings steadier jobs to the people who live here."

Avery envisioned overcrowded beaches, noisy Jet Skis. No more cookouts and bonfires. The loons would lose their home. A sting rose in her throat. That would ruin this place. She loved the historic lodge and log cabins. Guests used to say Montressa reminded them of a summer camp for adults. You couldn't manufacture that kind of nostalgia. She tucked the loose piece of hair back again and stood straighter.

"I love it the way it is."

Paulson silently continued down the path. And she wondered if he'd been trying out his ideas to get her thoughts. And why was he *in the area*? No one came to the lake a month before opening day without a reason.

"So, Paulson," she said. "What brought you up here?"

"I was checking out the lake," he said, "and I'd always heard about Montressa. Nate suggested I stop by."

They passed Miles's blue canoe, beached in the sand, and walked around the bend. Montressa's small marina consisted of three docks, one with boat slips. Miles looked up from fixing a motor. He stood, wiped his hands on his pants, and strode down the dock toward them. Upon recognizing Paulson, he seemed to grow larger with each step; his chest expanded, his jaw tightened, and his pecs flexed under the waffle Henley shirt.

Paulson's left hand came to rest in the small of Avery's back. She tensed.

"Miles Magrum. I was just talking about you." Paulson offered a fist bump with his free hand.

Miles bumped back unenthusiastically, a frown accompanying his annoyed stare. "Paulson. What brings you here?"

"I was in the area and had to see the lake you used to talk about," Paulson said.

Miles's eyes flicked to Avery's, and something in his glance told her this was news to him.

"Miles, you like to fish?" Paulson mimed casting a fishing rod. "Seems like a good place for a fishing—"

"The resort's not open until mid-June." Miles cut him off. "If you want to fish, make a reservation. Otherwise, leave." He pointed to the driveway.

Avery's jaw dropped. More big dock energy. Maybe Miles hadn't expected to see Paulson today, but it wasn't like Paulson was being a jerk. And Miles loved to fish. She'd never seen Miles act so rude.

Paulson checked his Breitling and pulled his cuff-linked sleeve back over it.

"I need to get back, anyway." He sounded defeated. Maybe he'd seen this side of Miles before. "Thanks for the tour, Avery. I enjoyed meeting you."

As he walked off, Miles whispered, "Did we know Paulson was coming?"

"I did and I tried to contact him, but he didn't respond." Avery matched his whisper. "I thought he wanted to book a vacation or something. Or help the Coopers. Why were you so rude to him?"

"Because Paulson doesn't help people. He buys them, wins them over, or competes with them. I'd never accept his help."

"You're making him sound evil. He seemed nice."

Except for wanting to tear the place down. Granted, that was a big deal, but it would only add fuel to Miles's rage fire.

Miles released his dart-shooting glare from Paulson's back, fixed his gaze over the water, and ran a hand down his stubbled jaw. She wasn't sure whether to stay on this dock, go after Paulson and apologize for Miles's behavior, or take the long way back to the lodge and avoid them both.

"The way he touched you." Miles gritted his teeth. "He's trying to charm you. Whatever you do, don't go out with him."

He could not be serious. Her dating life wasn't Burger King. He couldn't have it his way.

"Excuse me." Avery put her hand on her hip and glared at Miles, channeling her own big dock energy. "You don't get to tell me who to date."

"I'm not. I'm telling you who *not* to date."

He walked back to the boats. Avery followed, hot on his heels. Casper trotted beside her, clearly taking her side in this ridiculousness.

"Same thing. And you are the very last person who gets a say in who I date." Well, maybe not very last. He was right in front of Trent.

"He's not a good guy, Avery." Miles's stare grew cold. "Paulson treats people like business transactions. He'll divest himself of you when he decides you're no longer needed."

"And who are you to gatekeep everyone else? You sleep with a new woman every night and act like it's admirable. But if he did the same, it's transactional? If I did it, I'd be slut-shamed. How come you get your own set of rules? Entitled people like you are the worst."

She crossed her arms over her chest.

"That's unfair. I'm honest about commitment. Women who date me know what they're getting."

Avery stared across the cove, chewing her lower lip. Her history with him told a different story.

"I didn't know what I was getting. I still don't. Explain to me what I got." She shifted her gaze and narrowed her eyes at him. The only way off this dock was past her, and this time, she wasn't letting him walk away.

Miles took a minute to gather his thoughts. His chiseled jaw relaxed, softening his expression. His chestnut eyes turned the color of maple syrup.

"You knew from the start I was broken. I was too young to understand that you're never done grieving the loss of a parent, especially if you bottle it up inside. Which doesn't justify how I ended things." He let out a tired sigh. "After the trauma of saving Max, I said things I can't take back. I made mistakes. I should have called you afterward. At least to say I was sorry."

His face filled with an astounding sadness that made her stomach clench. He stepped toward her, and his warm hands cupped her shoulders. "The one good thing that happened the year after my mom passed was you. You're the only woman who's ever had all of me, and I couldn't have picked a better person."

Avery's heart tightened into a ball. Like her, he'd hurt all this time too.

"Since then, I haven't wanted to give my heart to anyone." His voice cracked and he rubbed his jawline. "That's what I've been trying to tell you. But you haven't given me the chance."

With one hard swallow, all her words vanished. Had Miles never had another girlfriend? Maybe he had but had held part of himself back. Avery could relate. She'd loved Trent—but their love had never come close to what she'd felt for Miles. For the last decade, she'd thought Miles hadn't felt the same way when all the while, their breakup had broken him too. He'd closed his heart and never opened it again. Assuming he was happy had been easier than learning Miles had given up on love. She'd never wish that on anyone, especially him.

They stood side by side, watching a pair of ducks out on the water. Casper paced the dock, sniffing and panting. A gentle wind rustled through the trees. If they hadn't been discussing their relationship's aftermath, she might've suggested they eat lunch on the dock, like they did that summer.

How had they wound up here, staring out at the lake, him finally admitting the depth of what he'd felt a decade ago? It was all so profoundly sad, she wanted to reach across the inches between them, wrap an arm around him, and pull him to her. Bury herself in his chest and smell her Miles. The one who smelled like an evergreen forest after a light rain, with notes of lake air, sweat, and chocolate milk.

A little bit like earth, a little bit like water, a lot like heaven.

She stole a glance at his hand as it flexed and relaxed. They couldn't go back to what they'd had, and she wasn't sure that was what he wanted. He kept saying they were friends.

Neither one moved, and a small part of her knew that was for the best. The comfort of his embrace wouldn't heal the last decade. She couldn't process this new information standing so close to him. Especially when his deep, broody stare channeled the hot model in a glossy cologne ad.

Casper stopped pacing and crouched beside Miles, eyes wide, face straining. And there on the dock, he finally found relief. Out came a tube of lip balm. Avery gasped as her hand flew to her mouth. It took everything inside of her not to giggle.

"Well, look at that." Miles's smug grin was beautiful. They laughed, the tension releasing into the light breeze.

She pulled a poop bag out of her pocket. "Um, I'll clean that up."

Miles took the bag from her hand.

"Nah, I'll get it." He nodded up the lakefront path, where Casper was plodding back to the lodge. "Go take care of Casper. Poor guy needs a little TLC."

The dock creaked as she walked off. Avery thought about turning back and admitting to Miles how often she had thought of him in the intervening years. She'd tried not to, but she often mistook runners in the park for him. Milk bottle caps sent a ripple through her heart. Eclipses, meteor showers, strawberry moons. She'd watched every astronomical event because knowing both of them might be looking at the same thing felt like a warm hug.

Avery made a deal with herself to peek back at the dock once she reached the bend. If their eyes met, she'd worry about Casper later, run back, and wrap her arms around Miles. They would figure out the rest. If not, she'd leave him be.

By the time she turned around, he'd turned his focus to a boat engine, his ratchet wrench clicking as he loosened a spark plug.

CHAPTER SIX

Miles

THURSDAY, MAY 25

After six busy days and five restless nights in New York capped off with a delayed flight and a bumpy landing in Portland, Miles wanted to apologize. He hoped the small gift he'd brought Avery adequately conveyed his regret for telling her who not to date. At the very least, she would use it.

He'd spent a good few days in New York, sleeping in Hayes and Anna Catherine's guest room so as not to bother the Coopers, who were staying Miles's apartment. Hayes had set up a meeting with the grief therapy team at NYU, and they'd walked out excited about their camp. The visit coincided with the premiere of Hayes's new action movie, *Counterblow*, which Miles attended solo. He only wanted one person on his arm these days, and how best to apologize to her had been on his mind the whole evening, even when the audience had cheered at his cameo.

Inside the lodge's front door, Casper sniffed every inch of Miles's pants, his tail wagging wildly.

"Hey boy, you okay?" Miles asked after Casper whimpered. And then Miles realized he'd been wearing these pants when he had visited Sam the day before. The poor dog missed his best friend. At least Casper had Avery loving on him. Lucky dog.

Once Casper calmed down, Miles searched for Avery. As he placed the gift bag at the empty front desk, he heard rustling from the back office. Miles started through the door at the same time Avery walked out. They collided, and she let out a yelp.

"Miles, you scared me!" Her hand clutched her chest in shock.

"I didn't mean to startle you." He held up his hands in surrender. "You okay?"

"Yeah." Avery took a couple of deep breaths and leaned back against the doorframe. "I thought you were in New York."

"Just got back." He settled against the opposite side of the door frame. "I saw Sam yesterday. He felt good enough to beat me at chess and backgammon. But Nate's emotionally fried, so I burned some frequent flyer points and got Lily a ticket to New York tomorrow for Memorial Day weekend. He needs her."

"Thank you. I talked to her last night and she misses him. She hasn't seen Nate since she dropped the Coopers off at the jet you chartered. They've been so scared and stressed. How are you doing?" Avery asked, reaching across the doorway to squeeze his arm.

A buzz jolted through him, and he could have sworn she felt it too, because her eyes jumped to her hand on his sweater. They were standing so close, he could smell that mysterious flower perfume of hers.

"I'm worried about them all, but especially Nate," he sighed. "He's shouldering too much. He'll be okay, but it's hard to see your friends struggle. And I'm realizing how much he worried about me while my mom was sick. I want to fix everything for him and I can't."

"He knows you're there for him and I'm sure that's a great comfort." Avery tilted her head and smiled. "I'll drive Lily to the airport. I can stop at Marden's on the way back and tackle everyone's list."

He thought for a second about offering to come with her. Maybe she had softened after hearing how much she had meant to him. But they weren't ready to spend a day running errands together yet.

"Listen, I want to apologize," he said. "I had no right to tell you who to date. Paulson gets under my skin. He's everything I hated about my time at Yale and in New York, wrapped up in one human."

Miles ran his hand down his face. "It's not my place to make demands on you. I'm sorry."

"Thank you." Avery nodded.

He cocked his head toward the front desk. "I brought an apology gift from the Big Apple."

She walked to the desk, examined the white bag with red letters, and smirked. "You brought me an apology gift ... from CVS?"

"Yeah." He rested a shoulder against the doorframe. "I've got a three-foot-long receipt to prove it."

"CVS has this thing called an app." She winked. "You load it on your phone and it magically sends you digital receipts."

Seeing Avery's playful side felt like a big shift. Maybe spilling his guts the other day hadn't been such a bad thing. Miles struggled to keep from grinning. Her eyes sparkled when she flirted. It took everything in him to stay firmly planted in the doorframe and act naturally.

"I'll have to look into this, what did you call it? An app?"

"It saves paper, Mr. Carbon Footprint."

"An ironic sentiment, coming from the girl who made a fortune selling paper."

Avery giggled and Miles knew he was on the brink hearing that laugh he loved.

"When I play rock-paper-scissors, I always choose paper," she said.

"Then we will end in a tie. I choose paper to honor the industry of my home state," he said. He couldn't help but marvel at the silly things they had in common. "Down East, we play rock-paper-chainsaw, because ... lumberjacks."

"Ooh, an added level of danger."

He thought about replying he liked a little danger, but she reached into the bag and pulled out the case of lip balm. Her deep, honest, belly laugh filled the room. Miles's heart jumped at the realization that all he wanted for the rest of their lives was to be the person who made her eyes sparkle like they were now.

"I think of you every time I'm at a CVS checkout," he said. "There's always a case of them by the register."

He lifted his arm above his head and leaned a forearm against the side of the door frame, resting his hand on the top edge. Anna Catherine had made him practice this pose earlier in the week, calling it *swoon worthy* because it conveyed his interest while lengthening his body. She'd proclaimed *the door jamb lean* a rom-com hero signature pose. Miles found it unnatural, and wildly uncomfortable, but he wasn't about to throw away its potential for magic.

"After Casper, I figured you needed backups," he said. "You used to lose lip balms all the time. And hair ties."

"Thank you." Avery pulled out a tube, opened it, ran the balm over her lips, and broke into a satisfied smile. "I don't care if it's from CVS. This is the most thoughtful gift you could've brought me."

"I'm glad you like it," he said. As he held her stare, a warmth filled him. Finally, a relaxed moment. It felt welcome, almost perfect. He would've asked anyone else to go get coffee in hopes it turned into a date, but he needed to take this slowly, even though it seemed like Avery might say yes. Maybe the door jamb lean worked.

He shifted in the doorframe, and cool air hit his abdomen. Seriously, his arm might fall asleep up there.

She leaned against the desk and playfully pointed a finger at him. "I can't believe you, with all of your model girlfriends, were jealous."

"Um, well, I wouldn't refer to them as girlfriends. It's more like I went on some dates. None of them reached girlfriend status." Miles scratched the back of his neck with his free hand. "Wait, how did you know who I've dated?"

Avery's blushing, guilty face had to be one of the best things he'd seen all week.

"Oh, that's right, I caught you googling me." He opened his mouth wide to feign shock.

"That's not the point, Miles!" Her newly dewy lips twisted. "Are you saying you didn't sleep with *any* of them? Not one?"

"Well, I wouldn't say that." He raised an eyebrow. "Definitely more than one."

She crossed her arms over her chest, flattened her mouth, and stared out the window at the lake. Her pout was cute, but he didn't want to sound like the player everyone labeled him as. Especially to her.

"Look, I know my life appears glamorous," he said. "I don't go to many parties, but I get photographed when I do. Friends have premieres or charities have galas. It sounds fun, but being in a big room with a lot of beautiful people can feel far lonelier than being by yourself. When seven people are sitting at a table set for eight, that empty chair speaks volumes. If I bring a date, people don't try to set me up with their coworker, sister, or friend, or worse, offer me an invitation to join some exclusive celebrity dating app."

"Oh, Miles," she moaned and wiped away a fake tear, "you win the pity party."

"I'm not asking for pity. My life feels, I don't know, empty?" He readjusted himself in the doorframe. As an only child of only children, Miles should be used to being by himself. But sometimes it felt awkward, and not just at parties in the City. He loved this lake, but it could be isolating out there on the point, in his red A-frame.

"Montressa is kind of lonely with no staff around," she said, as if she had read his mind. "Lily's busy with the end of the school year. I'm trying to make myself useful whenever I can, but at night, there's nothing to do here. I've binged so many shows I may finish Netflix."

She scanned the series of Post-its on the wall. Miles stepped out of the doorway and planted himself next to her. Avery's warm shoulder brushed his upper arm.

"A couple nights ago, I fell asleep watching *Bride Wars* and had nightmare about the reservation board," she said.

Miles had never seen *Bride Wars*. It sounded like a reality show, but if it caused nightmares, it must be a horror film.

"In my dream, instead of double-booking the Plaza at the same time as my best friend Kate Hudson, I double-booked Montressa's entire summer." Avery let out a laugh. "I kept saying we needed a new system, but Nate wouldn't listen to me."

Miles surveyed the board, chewing the inside of his cheek. "It's a wonder they don't double-book more often."

"I don't think there have been many opportunities lately. I've taken one reservation since I arrived two weeks ago." She frowned. "People don't know about Montressa. Here I am complaining about having nothing to do at night, but it's peaceful and beautiful."

"Yeah, I've run the numbers in my head," he said. "In my estimation, at about fifty percent capacity, Montressa operates at a loss. If that happens for too long, they'll have to sell or declare bankruptcy."

Her head popped up, a spark of determination in her eyes.

"After Nate asked for our ideas, I've been thinking about how to fix this." Avery rifled through some papers on the desk. She pulled out a pad with a handwritten list.

"This place could be full." She pointed at the reservation board. "People want escapes, nature, serenity, rustic charm. That's Montressa.

Except they can't find us because the Coopers haven't modernized. People used to go on the same vacation every year, but not anymore. They get information from a device, not a mailed brochure." She pushed the pad into his chest, almost as a challenge. "I'm making a plan."

Avery stood in quiet confidence as Miles skimmed a list of what seemed to be random thoughts: quaint, rustic, water, *The Parent Trap*, log cabins, camp for adults/families, fishing, swimming, water sports, weddings, family reunions, social media, website, reservation system. Her plan was clearly in the preliminary phase.

Avery rocked on her feet, clasping her hands and letting them go. She wiped them on her jeans and finally rested them on her hips.

"This is a good start," he said. "Let me help you."

She rolled her eyes.

"I don't need you condescendingly telling me it's a good start. I'm building an actionable framework," she said. "You're not the only one who knows how to run a business."

She tried to snatch the pad from his hand. Yet again, the tiniest misstep had undone his goodwill. Flirting time was over. He held onto the edge of the pad in frustration.

"I said I'd help." He gritted his teeth as he pulled. "I didn't mean to insinuate I'm the only one who can do this."

"Okay." She pulled the pad away with a forceful tug. "So, what else should be on there?"

So as not to rattle the rattlesnake, Miles focused on her ideas. Countless people had thought about promoting the resort, but none attempted to fix it. Miles had checked out the Peppered Page website a few years ago, when he'd heard she'd made it big. It had been more than a standard storefront site. Customers could personalize their stationery, add their own photos, and see a preview of the finished product. He wasn't sure whether she'd written the code for something that complicated or hired someone.

He could design Montressa's website himself, blindfolded. But working together meant late nights, leaning over a screen, their faces close together. A chance to get close to Avery with no outside interference. Perfect, if she'd go along with it.

"I can help with the website." He steadied his voice. "That's the most important item on here."

"Of course your task has to be the most important." Her shoulders dropped like a deflating air mattress.

She seemed to think they were competitors. Rivalry was the last thing he wanted.

"It's the one thing I can do to make your plan go faster," he said. "I want to help."

She chewed her lip. He waited for her to think it through and realize collaborating saved time.

"Fine. You take the website, I'll work on social media," she said.

Miles's shoulders dropped. She'd separated the tasks. She had to know a seamless product would be better.

"We should do it together," he said, testing the waters. "For continuity across platforms."

"But you're busy getting the waterfront ready, appearing on *Bright and Early*, and then there's your work, which is…What are you doing now?"

"I'm starting a non-profit," he said. "A bereavement camp."

Everything about Avery softened. Her jaw let go and her shoulders relaxed.

He licked his lower lip, unsure what to expect.

"For kids who've lost a parent?" Her green eyes turned dewy.

"Not just kids. It's for families going through a loss," he said. "But I have time to do this too, and I want to help Nate. You said you have nothing to do at night. Me too. We should combine forces."

Avery toyed with her necklace, running the pendant back and forth across the chain.

"I know you want to help Nate, but I wanted to do this myself. It's selfish, but I'll be interviewing for jobs again soon. I sold my business fourteen months ago, and this last year is a gaping hole on my resume. I can't put *planned a wedding that didn't happen* above *founded and sold the Peppered Page*. Designing and implementing a marketing plan shows employers I've done something."

This pad full of ideas was more than a brainstorm. It was a plan for proving her worth. Selling her business should've made her feel invincible, but that success shared the same space with what she saw as a failure. Miles understood dueling emotions. He'd had them that summer. So much grief and so much love occupying one space. The good parts never got the celebration they deserved because the painful parts overshadowed them.

"Avery, you founded and ran a successful business which you sold for a lot of money. That's no small feat. If I interviewed you, I'd ask why you're pursuing an MBA when you should be teaching the class."

She dropped the pendant and ran her lower lip along her teeth.

"These are great ideas." Miles pointed at the pad. "But for a project of this scope, you can sit at the head of the table, but you can't sit there alone. All I'm asking is to be on the team. Or at least in the room. So I can learn a thing or two from you."

She grimaced and shook her head.

"I don't think it's a good idea for us to work closely, Miles," she said. "When we're together, it doesn't go well. Look at today. You gave me a sweet gift and next thing, we're bickering. Trying to be friends is hard enough. And I'll be leaving soon, and you'll go back to your life as a scabrous rake."

Scabrous rake sounded awful. Sometimes it felt like she ignored his good traits in order to stuff him into a box labeled "model-dating, money-hungry villain." He needed to show her who he wanted to be.

"What if I don't want to be a scabrous rake?"

"Ha." She snorted. "You have an amazing apartment. Famous friends. All those fabulous premieres and parties and galas. VIP tickets to Hazel Matheson concerts. You're going to give that up?"

"I just told you how lonely that life is. Maybe I don't want that anymore."

Their discussion felt like part of a bigger conversation, one he'd envisioned happening in one sitting. But maybe it needed to come out in pieces, over time. She could build trust in him if they collaborated on a shared project.

Every job interview he'd conducted had a turning point. A moment when he knew whether the applicant was right or wrong for the job. Miles put one last effort into selling her on what he could contribute.

"Perhaps you can put my scabrous nature aside to help our best friends." He tilted his head toward the reservation board. "Working together ensures a seamless integration across all mediums. I don't have your artistry or eye for detail, but I can be the data science behind it. Using the reservation cards from years past, I'll create a database with an algorithm that prioritizes who has been coming here the longest and how much they spend once they are onsite. Every fall, the program will automatically favor families who come every year before opening reservations to the public. It'll reward loyalty and make next year's reservations smoother. New guests will find Montressa through your marketing talents, and they'll want to come. Prior guests will follow social media and remember why they love it here."

It was one hell of a pitch. She had no other way to get this level of help so quickly.

"Miles..." She hesitated. "You think we can do all of that?"

He nodded. "I can't. You can't. But *we* can. And I don't care who's in charge because we're working for our friends."

Avery ran her teeth over that full lower lip again as she studied the reservation board, considering his offer. She nodded, maybe to herself.

A moment later, Avery looked him straight in the eye and lifted her chin. Her hair fell back, exposing her neck. Avery with a mission was all sultry determination, and so damn attractive. He wanted to kiss that spot below her ear, but pushed her allure aside and met her stare with equal tenacity.

"Let's do it." She extended an open hand. "For the Coopers."

He grasped her warm hand and shook it. "For the Coopers."

A pact. He'd fought harder for this job than any other because he wanted it more. One opened a bottle of champagne in moments like this, but champagne was still too intimate. So he did the other thing people do in this situation.

"Thank you," he said. "You know you're amazing, right?"

She blushed and he caught a sliver of hope in her wistful smile, as if she were thinking about something she liked, or maybe loved once.

7

Avery

SATURDAY, MAY 27 - MEMORIAL DAY WEEKEND

Avery parked her car and popped open the trunk. After dropping Lily at the airport earlier in the morning, she'd spent a couple of hours at Marden's Surplus and Salvage tackling the list of requested supplies for various departments at Montressa. The store had everything: clothing, flooring, cosmetics, hardware, and home goods at dirt cheap prices. Maintenance needed driveway markers. Housekeeping needed sponges, travel-sized toothpaste, and shower caps. She'd bought her entire list and more. Avery left items for the lodge in her trunk and loaded all the bags containing items for the Boathouse on one arm.

With Lily's school year ending soon, and now that things were tolerable with Miles, Avery looked forward to spending her summer at the lake. She'd bought inflatable floats in anticipation of long afternoons chatting with Lily in the cool water. Her giant loon float was pretty accurate, but Lily's "moose" was more of a mythological hybrid with the rounded head of moose and the pointy antlers of a deer. A *doose*. Lily would love that.

On the way to the airport, she and Lily had discussed the bachelorette party. Lily decided on an early August visit to puffin-cruise-renowned Boothbay Harbor. Between Sam's heart attack, Nate's prolonged absence, and her duties as junior class sponsor, it had been a stressful spring. A couple of days relaxing and poking through a seaside town with Avery and a few friends from high school and college sounded perfect to Lily.

After the bachelorette party, Avery had a week to settle into an apartment in Hanover before starting her MBA at Tuck, Dartmouth's business school. She needed to find a place to live, yet kept putting it off. Spending a summer with Lily was more fun to think about, but Avery needed to start her apartment search. She'd vowed to forego her usual Netflix binge and spend her evening making reservations for the bachelorette trip and scoping out apartments online.

Avery squinted in the late afternoon sun as she lumbered along the path to the Boathouse. The shopping bag handles looped around her wrists cut off the circulation in her arms. Maybe she shouldn't have taken all the bags for this project in one trip, but she hated to be inefficient. If memory served, she'd purchased the perfect linens for the Boathouse.

Finding the door locked, she put the bags down and massaged her sore forearms. She hadn't grabbed the key earlier because she hadn't expected to come here first. Since the Boathouse sat at the edge of Montressa's property, it would be a long walk up to the lodge to retrieve it. She texted Wes, hoping he was nearby.

💬 **Avery:** I'm locked out of the Boathouse. You close by?

While she waited for his response, Avery walked to the end of the

Boathouse's private dock, shielded her eyes, and studied the Red House. Ladders were everywhere as a crew removed the manufacturer's stickers from the new windows and cleaned the glass. If she couldn't own the Red House, she was content seeing the quaint A-frame getting the love it needed.

A jingle of keys pulled her out of her thoughts.

"You should see the countertops they installed yesterday." She'd expected Wes and his raspy grumble, not Miles and his deep, syrupy voice.

Avery scrambled for a plausible reason for gawking at his house.

"Oh, I was just checking to see if the loons were nesting yet."

"Funny you didn't see me, since I was in the cove looking for them. I waved at you. They haven't come yet." He pulled out his keys and unlocked the Boathouse door. "It looked like you needed the master key."

Avery busied herself picking up her bags to hide her embarrassment. Miles leaned down to help, and she could have sworn his hair tickled her temple. This close, he smelled like chocolate milk. The scent of warm pine after an August rain hit her a second later.

"Whoa. Was all this on the list?" Miles peered into a bag.

"Sometimes I deviate from the list." She laughed. "And there may be returns. I haven't been in here yet, and I bought things for the Boathouse I remember."

He stepped inside and flicked the light switch. "Well, let's test your memory."

Avery hesitated, unable to will her feet to move forward. Going in *there* with *Miles* might bring old feelings to the surface. She could still picture them ten years ago. Tearing off each other's clothes. Tumbling onto the scratchy lace bedspread. And Miles so close she could count the golden stars in his beautiful chestnut eyes. He'd asked if she was sure. She had never been so sure of anything in her life.

But now...

She shook her head. They were adults, and that night would always be a part of her. She needed to stop avoiding their past and learn to live with it.

Avery stared straight ahead and crossed the threshold.

Like their relationship, the Boathouse had deteriorated. No wonder the Coopers hadn't been renting it. Sunbeams gleamed through the dirty windows of the quaint cabin, dust floating aimlessly through the light. They placed the bags on the desk beside the door.

Once Montressa no longer needed a working boathouse, Sam and Laurie had transformed it into a small cabin. That had happened about twenty years ago and to be fair, most of the work remained in good shape, but it could use an update. Avery took inventory. To the right of the desk, the same couch sat in front of the stone fireplace. A tiny bathroom and wet bar divided the back wall, and to the left stood the bed, its frame worn and chipped. Part of the Boathouse's charm was that one could lie in bed and watch the lake. The entire wall facing the water had French doors that opened onto a small deck, and below it, the dock. It needed some paint and a thorough cleaning to clear out the musty smell.

"It looks exactly the same," she gasped, trying not to reveal how self-conscious she'd become.

"I asked the Coopers to preserve it, given its historical significance," Miles said.

"You what?" She finally looked at him. He shrugged with a half-smile. The gleam in his eye confirmed he meant it as a joke.

"Oh, Miles." Her voice croaked. Sweat beaded on her forehead and upper lip.

Miles paused and searched her face. When she studied him in return, he shoved his hands in his pockets and looked at his feet, perhaps a delayed realization at the unlocking of a time capsule. Avery's stomach clenched.

"Do you need help, or should I go?" he asked.

Avery wanted to prove being here with him wasn't a big deal. Plus, at six-two, his height might be helpful.

"I have a couple of things to check. Could you hold up a curtain for me?"

She peered inside the nearest bag. She could do this. He could help with one minor project, and they could both go on their way. No harm, no foul.

"Look, a gift from Mimi." Miles pulled a giant box of condoms from one of the other bags. Of course, the universe pointed him to that bag.

The heat of embarrassment burned in her cheeks. Lily had desecrated Avery's tidy list on the way to the airport, writing CONDOMS - MEGA BOX with a Sharpie, in huge letters. She'd said Miles came up with the idea to make Montressa a sex positive resort, and Avery had fallen for it, resulting in another heated blush. And to be fair, it had been wonderful to hear Lily's laugh.

"Lily put them on my list. I pinkie swear!" Avery lifted her pinkie finger and wriggled it.

Miles studied the gold box with a roaring black tiger on the label and quietly placed it on the dusty desk between them.

"No matter how we try, there seems to be no escaping this." He fiddled with the sleeves of his Henley. "Should we talk about what happened in here?"

"I, um... Miles, I—"

She couldn't understand why she could plan this whole discussion when she was by herself, but couldn't articulate any of it whenever they were together. Maybe his deep woods aroma wiped her brain clean. She let out a ragged breath.

He touched her shoulder, and she flinched.

"I want you to know I don't regret that night or any of our other ones," he said. Miles's eyes searched her face. He wanted an answer she couldn't find the words for. On a topic she wasn't sure she'd ever be ready to talk about.

"I don't want you to regret it," he said, taking another step closer.

She picked a loose thread off the folded duvet cover in her hand. He'd taken gentle care of her every time they'd slept together, but that first night he'd been especially respectful. She'd felt loved. Knowing how it ended, she'd go back and do it again. But she would never tell him that. At least not now.

"I just don't understand what happened after that." She shook her head.

"Truth is," he said in a weakening voice. She straightened up and faced him. If he was finally going to apologize or give her a reason for his abrupt departure, she wanted to watch him say it, despite being on the verge of tears.

He didn't finish. Miles Adam's apple bobbed as he swallowed his words in one gulp. His eyes flicked to the door.

"Oh, you got in."

Avery spun to find Wes by the door, toolbox in hand, taking inventory of the tiny cabin. His eyes landed on the box of condoms. He walked over and picked them up with his free hand.

"Two hundred and fifty Golden Tiger condoms," he said, setting down his tools. "Rawr."

Wes waved the box at Miles.

"How long does one of these last you, Miles? A month?"

Miles grabbed it mid-air, as if it were a pesky fly.

"It's not mine," he grunted, shoving the box into the desk drawer. "And finishing that box in a month would take eight a day. That'd be really hard."

"That's what she said." Wes laughed at his own joke.

Avery felt her cheeks, neck, and hands burning. She needed to get Wes out of here before her whole face morphed into a tomato.

"Thank you, Wes," Avery said over his laughter. "Sorry to make you come all this way."

"Again, that's what she said." Wes wiped a laughing tear from his eye. Crimson-cheeked Miles patted Wes on the back. "See you later, Wes."

Wes stopped laughing and opened his toolbox. "While I'm here, I figured I'd turn on the water. Prime the pump after the long winter. You know, make sure the pipes are flowing." He was the only one laughing at his own innuendo. Wes wiped his eyes again, pulled a wrench out of his toolbox, and headed to the bathroom.

"You two are no fun."

Avery had an overwhelming desire to melt into the floor. Of all their interactions since her return, Wes's off-color ribbing might have been the most cringeworthy. Miles put both hands over his eyes and slid them down his cheeks, assuming the exact pose of Edvard Munch's famous painting, *The Scream*.

Wes returned a minute later, leaving the tub running. "Just need a couple minutes to flush the line."

The three of them froze, eyes anywhere but on one another.

Avery needed to move past the embarrassment, so she focused on her reason for being in the Boathouse. She walked to the bed, unfolded the new duvet, and tossed it open. It settled on the plastic-covered mattress, setting free a wave of dust. Wes sneezed. At each corner, she pulled the duvet into place. The bed was a queen. She'd bought a king size. A bigger bed would fit in this room.

"I have an idea." She snapped her fingers. "I can create a month's worth of social media posts using different vignettes of one beautiful cabin. The exterior of the Boathouse screams getaway. To make people imagine themselves in here, it needs to be dreamy. But, we're gonna need more than new curtains and bedding."

Miles and Wes scanned the room as if trying to imagine her vision. Avery ran a thumb along the post of the worn bed frame, her nail making a new chip in the crusty, old varnish. When she rocked the frame, it creaked.

"This bed needs to go," she said. "It should be a king, and not squeaky."

At that, Wes nudged a stone-faced Miles.

"Help me out here, Wes." Avery snapped her fingers again to divert his attention from Miles, who stood frozen in place. "Do you have a king bed frame in storage?"

"Not anything 'spectacular' or 'dreamy.'" Wes shook the bedpost, which rocked the entire frame back and forth toward the wall. "Ayuh, this one's a wall-banger. Whatcha thinking besides sturdy?"

"Woodsy and relaxing. Like Montressa. Maybe made of tree trunks or branches."

Wes stopped shaking the bed, took the tape measure off his belt, and measured from the ceiling to the floor. He gave Avery a crisp nod.

"We had to cut a couple of birches last spring," he said. "They're in the room behind the laundry. Wood cures well back there. We save them 'cause you never know when they'll be useful. Sometimes I make mirrors or cut them for table legs. Never tried a bed, but I think I could do it."

Avery's entire face lit up, excited Wes was on board.

"OMG!" Avery bounced on her toes. "I've seen plans for tree beds on Pinterest."

"No Pinterest." Wes put up a hand to stop her. "My girlfriend Jeanette loves Pinterest. Those damn DIY instructions might as well've been written by a raccoon under the light of a new moon. Tell me your idea, and I'll figure it out."

"Understood." Avery smiled. She appreciated his hesitation. Pinterest fails were the worst.

Miles remained glued to the floor, deep in thought. Avery wondered if he was still ruminating on whatever he'd tried to say before Wes arrived.

"I'm giving Home Depot half my paycheck," Wes said, "and I never get reimbursed. You know what she gives me for Christmas and my birthday? Home Depot gift cards. It's like she's buying me gifts for herself. You ever heard of toilet paper math? I call this girlfriend math."

Avery laughed, but part of her attention remained on Miles. They made eye contact, and her smile seemed to bring him out of his trance.

"Oh Wes, you'd do anything for Jeanette," Miles said, rubbing his hands through his hair, mussing it enough to look like he had just climbed out of bed. *That bed.* Rumpled morning Miles used to paste gentle kisses across her bare shoulders and show up late for his early morning running workouts. These days, she awoke to kisses from Casper. And there was no lazing around. The dog needed to go out.

"Ayuh. And there's benefits to dating the girl who owns the Lakeside Diner." Wes patted his stomach as he walked to the bathroom to turn off the tub.

"She's lucky to have you," Avery said as he left the bathroom.

Wes grabbed his tools and stopped on his way out the door.

"New countertops in the bathroom would help." He pointed at her. "Just don't ask Miles to pick them. He takes forever."

Miles grimaced, picked up a curtain, and unfolded it.

"You pick paint colors. I'll do a rough drawing of the new bed and check Uncle Henry's for leftover countertops," Wes said. "Miles, I can't wait for the canoe trip for Nate's bachelor party. Jeanette'll be out of town at her cousin's wedding, and I'm so happy to miss that. Her family's a piece of work."

Lily had mentioned the guys still needed one more to fill out all six canoes for Nate's trip. Hayes had texted he could come a couple days ago. Ned needed to find a twelfth man who liked being on the river.

"Jeanette says you haven't stopped by the diner for breakfast in a while." Wes elbowed Miles and gave him an exaggerated wink. "You're everyone's favorite customer."

"I've had a lot going on." Miles shrugged. "Tell her I'll stop by soon."

"What day? I want to make sure I'm there," Wes said.

"Why?" Miles leveled him with a dark stare.

"I just thought we could grab a bite to eat together," he said. "I'll even buy *your* breakfast for once."

"Aw, Wes, that's so sweet," Avery said. "Isn't it, Miles?"

Miles nodded with a grunt.

"Carry on, you two." Wes stepped outside and closed the door.

Avery handed Miles the curtain to hold up in front of the French doors facing the lake. As she considered it, he smiled at her as if remembering something. She felt her heart skip, half wanting him to finish what he had tried to say earlier.

"I forgot how a project energizes you." He wiggled the curtain. "What do you think?"

"I love them, and with that birch tree bed"—she blew a chef's kiss into the air—"I'm envisioning perfection."

He swung the bottom of the curtain in her direction, and together they folded it. He made sure to keep the original creases, and she wondered if he remembered that mattered to her.

"Everything okay?" she asked as she set the folded curtain on the desk. "You got a little quiet earlier."

"I was wondering if you still paint watercolors. Or did you get tired of it after creating design after design for the Peppered Page? Some people stop enjoying something once it becomes work."

"I got lucky. The painting part of my job never felt like work. I still love it, but I've had a lot going on lately." She gathered her car keys and the empty bags. "I brought my paints."

"Your work has a breeziness to it that fits with the dreamy vibe you described. Your stationery had that."

Sometime in the last few years, Miles must've wondered about her enough to search out her stationery.

"For the website, what about watercolors mixed in with actual photos?" he asked.

Painting Montressa had been one of her favorite activities that summer. The lake had moods, and she loved capturing them. She couldn't wait to dig out her brushes and tubes of watercolors.

"That's a great idea." The doorknob spun in Avery's hand. She spun it again and pulled. Twice. "Hmm. It won't open."

Miles reached in and twisted it one way and then back the other. It opened.

"I hate you did it in one try." She smirked as she switched off the light and stepped outside.

"I got lucky," he said.

When their eyes met, she could have sworn he was referring to something else. The amber glow of the setting sun had turned his eyes the color of maple syrup. A tingle let loose somewhere deep inside her.

"I'll put the doorknob on Wes's fix-it list." She swept a stray hair behind her ear.

Miles placed a hand on Avery's shoulder and circled his thumb under her clavicle. *Fireflies.* They had never called this buzzing sensation in her stomach butterflies. After the day a lightning bug landed on him, they'd felt fireflies. It had been a long time since she'd felt them.

"We're making progress now that we're in cahoots," he said, lifting his hand.

"Cahoots? We are not in cahoots."

"Oh, we are in cahoots. We're opening a resort, remodeling dusty cabins, and collaborating on a website." He counted on his fingers. "That's cahoots."

Avery giggled. "No one, except maybe Lorelai Gilmore, says cahoots anymore."

"I'm bringing it back," he said as he followed her up the path.

They might not be in cahoots, but if they got the website and social media accounts up before *Bright and Early* filmed, the resort might fill for the summer.

"Us being in cahoots only happened because I want to finish what

I started. For our friends."

"Ayuh, so do I." He pivoted toward the path that led off Montressa's property, past Loon Cove, and out to the point. To the Red House. His broad shoulders, those jeans that hung just right over his hips. Avery was glad she'd be around until mid-August. Maybe he would finally tell her whatever he'd started to say back there in the Boathouse. Wondering about it sent a firefly thrum through her middle as heat rose in her chest. She needed to tamp those thoughts down. This guy ghosted her for ten years.

The more time Avery spent with Miles, the more it felt like he held a lit match, the flame flickering while he decided which of two firecrackers to light. One would make her glow, the other would burn her whole world down. Again.

8

Miles

MONDAY, MAY 29

Miles had been grating cheese when his father called to say he and Lily's mother, Dorothea, had reached the Appalachian Trail's halfway point in Pennsylvania. In keeping with trail tradition, they'd each eaten half a gallon of ice cream. Miles hoped his father had chosen the lactose-free version.

Dorothea had never tried to replace Miles's mother. If anything, she'd done everything she could to honor her, including accompanying Mark Magrum on this hike. Thirty-two years ago, Mark had met Maisie out on the trail. Halfway through their trek and halfway through their half gallon of ice cream, Mark Magrum had proposed to Maisie with a paper ring he'd fashioned from a trail map. They'd married atop Mount Katahdin, at the journey's end. A year later, they'd named their son after the miles they'd walked in the woods. Today's stop made Mark miss

Maisie and Dorothea had encouraged Mark to call the other person who missed her just as much—his son.

Miles relayed the promising news about Sam, who had moved to a rehab facility a day ago. If his healing continued, Sam could come home to the lake in a couple weeks.

Miles had also been thinking of his mother when his dad called. Before she left this world, Maisie Magrum taught her son how to make his favorite dish, macaroni and cheese. It was also his father's favorite.

Upon hanging up, Miles whisked the roux. Milk and the heap of shredded Maine cheddar sat nearby, on the counter Wes had installed three days ago. As Avery had promised, the white granite with gold specks brightened the space. She had a gift for finishing a room, and Miles had enjoyed seeing the sparkle in her eye as she'd reimagined the Boathouse the day before. He'd been thankful she'd diffused the tension Wes created with his not-so-subtle innuendos.

Wes could be bothersome in more ways than one. As soon as the counters were installed, Wes started sending reminders to pick a backsplash. Ten texts in the last day. Samples sat propped against the wall, but every time Miles considered them, he became more confused. The one he'd picked in the morning grew too dark in the evening light. If only he could convince Avery to come to dinner, he could get her input. But she remained insistent on keeping some distance between them.

A heat rose in his cheeks at the memory of Wes noticing the condoms and embarrassing Avery and Miles. And it wasn't just Wes. Nate had hinted at them getting back together in the staff meeting. If it struck Miles as invasive, Avery must be feeling it too. Everyone should respect her privacy, especially if she didn't want to get back together. The next time he saw Wes, he'd ask him to tone it down.

In that awkward moment, Avery's diversion tactics had worked. The tension evaporated when she'd enlisted Wes's help with the magical tree bed. Miles couldn't figure out if she wanted to erase the memories they'd made in that bed or lovingly care for their special place. Either way, a wave of guilt and regret over how he'd ruined their euphoric summer washed through him, and he'd shut down. When she asked if everything was okay, he'd awkwardly brought up her painting to hide his anxiety. He should talk to his therapist about why he'd frozen and disengaged, but it had been a while. Maybe when he returned to the City.

His phone vibrated on the counter, breaking his spiraling thoughts. His realtor had promised to get back to him today. Maybe she finally knew whether the corporate retreat was for sale. On his morning paddle, he'd sat offshore in his blue canoe and envisioned the healing that could happen there. He and Hayes wanted to call it Camp Luciole.

Hayes was FaceTiming him. They'd been phone-tagging all week. Miles answered, propping his phone against the backsplash samples so he could keep his hands free.

"Miles! What up? What up?" Hayes's million-dollar grin filled the screen. "Our late-night idea over grilled cheese sandwiches is gathering enthusiasm. Every day we get closer and closer to opening our camp. NYU has four grief counselors willing to come to Maine next summer. They suggested rounding out the staff with graduate students."

Hayes lifted his arms in victory.

"Excellent." Miles pumped his fist. "I think I found the ideal spot. There's an abandoned corporate retreat—"

"Ooh, an abandoned retreat." Hayes wiggled his fingers in front of his face. "Like in *Scooby Doo*."

"I hope not. I'm no match for those meddling kids." Miles laughed. "Seriously though, it's got log cabins for the families, a couple of common buildings, and a sandy waterfront. I have my heart set on it. If only it was for sale."

"No way! That sounds perfect. We need to get the word out. Anna and I were thinking a gala in August would be a fun way to raise awareness and bring in some capital. Something big, with a camp theme.

What do you think?"

"Great idea," Miles said as the timer beeped on his digital watch. It had been his running watch in college, and he'd kept it because it reminded him of the day he'd run a sub-four mile. He shut off the burner and strained the pasta. "The seed money you and I put up can carry us some of the way, but we'll need money to purchase a property and renovate it. I've signed up for fundraising and grant writing classes this fall."

"Wow, Camp Luciole is happening, and it feels good. Right?"

Hayes was right. Their camp would provide grieving families with a comforting and nurturing space to heal, share stories, and remember loved ones. They'd experience moments of sadness, but the goal was for everyone to leave with hope, support, and coping strategies for the real world, including referrals to services in their hometowns. Miles and Hayes just needed a place.

"I can't believe it." Hayes wiped away a tear.

"Same. Imagine when it opens."

Miles felt a pang of excitement and a tingle of nervousness. After his mother died, he and his father hadn't shared their pain. In the rare moments they'd caught each other crying, they hadn't talked. His father had patted him on the back and mumbled to *carry on*. It wasn't until Miles first met Avery over a year later that he slowly began to share his pain. But he'd been reticent to truly open up and reveal how much sorrow he held back in order to keep his composure.

Holding it in came with a price.

Ten years ago, in the days leading up to his breakup with Avery, Miles had come to dread summer's end. Avery had been a break from his cycle of perpetual grief and in a matter of days, there would be eight states between them. Money and distance would keep them apart, not to mention his busy cross country and track schedules.

Rescuing young Max Perry unleashed an emotional logjam in Miles. Parts of that day were a blur, and others were a vivid photo montage that still swept through his mind at random times. Miles remembered spotting Max out in the lake and hurdling a picnic table on his way to the water. His reaction was so quick and so instinctual, that he'd heard his own heartbeat and nothing else. Supposedly, Nate was beside him, checking the child's pulse, but Miles didn't remember that. He recalled the Max's first breaths, and the moment he opened his hazel eyes. Through tears, Mr. and Mrs. Perry had called Miles a hero. Everyone declared it a miracle, except for Miles. That moment confirmed his worst fear. Forever didn't exist. Anything could be taken away at any moment. It hurt worse when it was someone you loved. Maybe not loving someone could protect him from that pain.

He'd callously discarded Avery, who was headed elsewhere anyway, pushing away the one person who kept him afloat. The nagging sense he had transformed her sunshine into rain kept him up at night for months, his chest pounding beneath what felt like a granite boulder. Racked with guilt and a swirling vortex of emptions he didn't understand, Miles started running late at night and taking extra showers so no one would see him cry. The following spring, halfway through his last semester, he walked into Yale's student health center at his lowest low and found therapy. Seven years later, he met Hayes at the Met Gala. Finally, a friend who had also lost his mother. Camaraderie was its own therapy. He hoped their camp provided that for others.

The roux was ready.

"I've never said this, but every day, you help me heal." Miles added the milk into the pan. "And Anna Catherine too. Thank you."

"I feel the same way about you." Hayes wiped away another tear. Tears were okay in their friendship, not something they hid. "Anna says we should celebrate when we visit. She wants you to bring Avery."

Miles whisked the milk and turned down the burner to let the sauce thicken. Avery coming felt possible, but not certain.

"It'd be nice if Avery came," he said. "There's been a tiny bit of progress, but we aren't at 'let's celebrate with my best friends' yet."

"I'll take a little progress." Hayes pumped his fist.

"Avery was the first girl who understood me."

"I know, man. I—hold on." Hayes's voice got farther away.

Miles stopped stirring. On his phone's screen, Anna Catherine battled with Hayes for the phone. As always, she eventually won.

"Ooh! Ooh! Ooh! I heard my name. And did someone say Avery?" She did a double-take and leaned closer to the screen. "Miles, are you cooking?"

"Hello, Anna." He blew her a kiss. "This morning I caught a big trout right off my dock. It rained all afternoon, and being stuck inside made me want to cook. I'm pan searing the trout and making haricot vert and Mom's macaroni and cheese as sides. I may dry off a chair and enjoy this alfresco. It's a gorgeous night. The lake is a mirror. I can't wait for your visit."

"Only a few weeks until we spend the Fourth of July at Montressa." Anna Catherine wriggled her shoulders in excitement. "Just so you know, I'm not coming for the fireworks. I want to meet Avery."

Miles added the cheddar and stirred, smiling to himself. He liked the idea and hoped Avery wouldn't leave when *Bright & Early* came to film the week before the Fourth.

"So..." Anna Catherine rested her head on Hayes's shoulder and gave Miles a dreamy smile. "What were you saying about Avery?"

"I don't know. When I'm alone with her, it's great. But when other people are there, it becomes a mess. They mean well, but pressure is the last thing we need." Miles exhaled, his lips flapping in frustration. "The inevitable jokes about my dating life make it hard to convince her I'm not the player she thinks I am. And then there's the ribbing about our past."

He hadn't planned to get into this now, but Anna Catherine and Hayes were his ride-or-dies for advice.

"She must be special if she gets you flustered," Hayes said.

"She is," he said. "Mom had been gone a little over a year when I met Avery." She'd only been at Montressa for a couple of days when Sam had sent the two of them to Portland to pick up some new kayaks. When they'd finished lunch, the boats weren't ready and after being away at school for several months, Miles had the overwhelming urge to visit the beach where he and his father had scattered his mother's ashes. Not acknowledging his mom's memory would keep him up all night. Feeling self-conscious about being sad in front of a girl he had just met, he'd driven to the beach without explanation. He sat alone on the jetty for at least an hour and Avery had let him sit, quietly wading along the shoreline, picking up sea glass. When he finished and tried to explain, he'd choked up.

"That was such a hard time for me, and she understood how to reach me. You know how the other person cries and you end up comforting them?"

"Yep," said Hayes. "You become their support when you're the one who needs it most."

Anna Catherine nodded.

"Exactly. She didn't do that." Miles said. "She gave me a hug and gently wiped my tears away with the cuff of her sweatshirt. It was actually my sweatshirt. I lent it to her after she refused to wear the plastic bib and got lobster juice all over herself at lunch."

He let out a sad laugh. That day, Avery had explained how her grandmother Mimi described grief as a balloon trapped in a room with a button on the wall. In the beginning, the balloon is so full, it's constantly pushing the button. But as time goes on, the balloon deflates a little and bounces around the room, pressing it less and less. That image had given him hope.

"I will never forget her saying she could hold space in our friendship for me and my grief. She hugged me and I can't explain why, but I let myself be comforted. Later, she picked up a piece of heart-shaped sea glass, put it in my hand, and told me it was a sign my mother hadn't left me. I still have it."

Anna Catherine and Hayes were both speechless.

"What?" he asked.

"And you let her go?" Hayes asked.

"Did it ever occur to you the heart-shaped glass was your mom's way of telling you Avery was the one?" Anna Catherine believed the universe sent signals.

Miles felt a weight drop into his stomach. "No, but that sounds like Mom."

Maisie Magrum would have appreciated the care Avery took of other people's hearts. That would've been all she needed to know.

Miles carefully transferred the macaroni and cheese to his mother's vintage CorningWare baking dish. The recipe didn't taste the same when made in any other dish. He dotted the top with tomatoes and sprinkled crushed, buttered saltines over the top.

"Miles," Anna Catherine said. "I feel like I'm watching Food Network."

Miles licked a dollop of cheese and cracker off his finger.

"Secret topping reveal. Mom said these saltines are the only ones to use." He held up a box of Premium crackers.

"Yum." Hayes smiled. "How come you never cook fancy dinners for us?"

"Because we're always at parties or Hayes's movie premieres." Miles laughed. "And I do cook for you. How many times have we ended the night at your kitchen table, confessing our deepest secrets to one another over my grilled cheese sandwiches?"

"I adore a midnight grilled-cheese confessional." Anna's jazz hands shimmied over her eyes. "We need another one soon."

He put the dish in the oven, set the timer, and wiped his hands on a towel.

"What's Avery's vibe now?" Anna Catherine asked.

"When we're alone, there are moments where she softens. But when people interrupt and embarrass us with cringe comments, one or both of us shuts down." He got the trout out of the fridge and seasoned it with herbs and pepper.

"But you said there was progress," Hayes said.

"There is. I convinced her to collaborate on a website and reservation system for Montressa. But yesterday we were in the cabin where she and I first slept together. Ten years ago, we thought no one knew. Turns out everyone did. Anyway, the head of maintenance came in and did his best Michael Scott impersonation. I think we were both already contemplating our history there, and his *that's what she said*s upped the awkwardness, and oh"—he placed his hands over his eyes—"I was rattled."

"You two are like Hugh Grant and Julia Roberts in *Notting Hill*." Anna put a finger to her mouth in thought.

"Because I own an oddly specific travel bookshop, and she owns my favorite Chagall painting of goats?" Miles smirked at Anna.

"No, because their relationship is perfect when they are by themselves. Other people, the media, and her stardom complicate everything."

"You need to find yourselves a quiet park bench," said Hayes.

Anna smacked Hayes's bicep. "Hayes, you watched that movie? Without me?"

"Ace, I watched it because you love that movie. And there was a set delay." Hayes shrugged on camera.

Anna grabbed his face from the side and planted a huge kiss on his cheek. Miles felt a swell in his chest. He wanted that with Avery.

"Dude." Hayes laughed as Anna Catherine kept kissing his face. "Take her on a nighttime stroll and break into a locked park. She will get all swoony over a bench and presto. That's your lover's bench."

"Ugh, Hayes. This is rural Maine, not Gramercy Park," Miles said. "Plus, I have to get her alone first. She's at the front desk and I'm at the waterfront most days, and there are other people around."

"Don't do it at work. I didn't get Anna Catherine to fall for me on set. I found her in the evening, after we'd wrapped for the day."

Hayes was on to something. Avery had mentioned feeling lonely at night. Miles glanced out his front window. Across the cove, he could see her sitting on the old dock, leaning against a dock pylon while she painted under a golden-pink sky. A popular staff hangout in the afternoon, the dock had been empty most evenings that summer. So many sunsets, he'd sat opposite her while she painted, their legs stretched out and touching, sometimes overlapping. His and hers pylons. They didn't need to break into a park. That old dock was their bench.

"I never know where your movie references are going, but you two are geniuses," Miles said. "Avery's in the exact spot where we used to sit. And I think I should be just a boy, paddling up to a girl, asking her if she wants to share this dinner I made."

"Oh Miles, that's so romantic." Anna Catherine's hand clutched her heart. "But one thing. She needs to feel safe around you, like she made you feel on the beach. Listen to her and don't try to fix the situation. She won't confront the past until she trusts you. Allow her the space to do that, or it will doom your future together. Until then, keep reminding her of what you had that summer."

He wanted to earn back the trust he'd lost when he had broken up with her. The shrinking image in his rearview mirror of her sobbing on the ground as he drove off still haunted him. For so long he'd told himself love belonged to other people. But there had been glimmers of promise since Avery's return to Maine. If he tried, his dreams might become reality.

The only way to get there was to end this call and go after what he wanted.

"Got it. Thanks."

After a minute of goodbyes, they finally hung up. As Miles seared the fish, his only thought was how to help Avery relax around him. Trust grew in small steps.

A moment had presented itself to make this quiet night theirs.

Miles wrapped two plates of dinner in foil, picked out a bottle of wine, and set out for the shores of Montressa in his blue canoe.

9

Avery

MONDAY, MAY 29

Dipping a brush into her palette again had been such a rush. Portraits of the lodge sat drying on the dock, their edges held down by stones. The lodge was both part of the waterfront and part of the forest beyond, and Avery couldn't fathom why Paulson suggested destroying such a marvel. Montressa's massive columns had been hand built in the 1920s out of tree trunks with the knots and branch knobs still visible, as if the lodge had sprouted out of the granite ledge upon which it commanded an impressive view over Linden Lake. She'd never seen columns like them, and houses in the South had columns galore.

 Today's rain had given her time to catch up on a few things and Avery finally inquired about a couple of apartments in Hanover. Sometimes she wondered why she waited so long to check something so simple off her list. Pressing "send" on a few emails made her feel productive. Late in the afternoon, the rain cleared. Now Montressa glowed in a golden-pink light, one she hoped was a precursor to a colorful, prolonged sunset. Leaning against the dock pylon, her back to the water, she decided the website needed a view of the lodge with this serene sky in the background.

In a couple weeks, chatter and laughter would drift down from the porch as guests shared early evening cocktails. Kids would play freeze tag on the grassy lawn above the beach. For now, she had the entire waterfront to herself. The calm, peaceful sunset cast Montressa in a lustrous golden glow, all of it mirrored in the still water. A tinge of breeze kept the bugs away. Her belly grumbled, but this ethereal vista wouldn't last all night. She could eat later. For now, she'd rather paint.

Adding art to the website was a great idea. In her research, Avery had noticed beach resorts used watercolors on their websites to evoke a carefree "sun and sand" brightness. She dabbed her brush into the lemon yellow, added a tinge of raw sienna, and mixed them next to the pool of opera rose shades dominating her palette tray. The pink and yellow edges blended beautifully. Sunsets cycled through a panoply of color, so she added a small pool of crimson. The last time she'd seen a red this deep was on Miles's cheeks in the Boathouse. The hue of her face must've mirrored his.

Embarrassment returned to her cheeks at how hard it had been seeing Miles in their favorite cabin, the one they used to sneak into when it was vacant. Avery's stomach tightened at the memory of Wes making an uncomfortable situation mortifying.

"Pretty night, eh?" Miles's voice floated over the water.

She hadn't noticed him gliding up to the beach in his blue canoe. For a second, she lingered on the vision of him bathed in a luscious, golden pink. He beached the canoe, got out, pulled the boat farther onto the sand, and lifted a cooler out of the bow.

"Mind if I join you?" he asked as he walked down the dock. "I brought food."

"You did?" Her heart softened at the kind gesture and her stomach grumbled its approval. "I skipped dinner so I could capture this perfect light before it fades."

Avery abandoned her work and motioned for him to sit at the opposite pylon, his pylon. He kicked off his Crocs next to her Birkenstocks and sat down. Relaxing barefoot on the dock had been their thing. She wondered if he remembered sitting here as clearly as she did. He handed her a warm plate. While he poured the wine, she removed the foil and savored the perfection of the first forkful of macaroni and cheese.

"Oh my God, Miles," she said, mouth still full. "This is heavenly."

"I can't take credit. It's Mom's recipe, and she said the lake air makes everything taste better." His contented smile held the warmth of treasured memories.

Miles seemed to talk about his mother more easily now. That summer, anything related to her had cast him into melancholy, anger, or sadness. Now his mother's memory seemed to provide comfort. There was something so sweet about a busy man taking time to make his mother's recipes.

As they ate, he told her about his plans with Hayes and the bereavement camp. Miles using his personal experience to help others wasn't a surprise. But she worried about him revisiting his pain repeatedly.

"Miles, you're so kind," she said. "But can I ask something? Do you ever worry about reliving your own grief every summer?"

He paused and thought about it, the sun still bathing him in an amber glow. He picked up his book and settled it in his lap. Miles held onto books like a toddler held onto a security blanket. They were his barrier for uncomfortable situations, and she'd asked a probing question.

Her heart grew heavy for him. Maybe she shouldn't have said anything. From now on, Avery promised herself to be more empathetic. She'd been hard on him when she'd first arrived.

"I appreciate you bringing that up," he said, his finger tracing the corner of the cover. "But I want to give people what Dad and I didn't have. It took me too long to find therapy and even longer to find Hayes, who also lost his mom. I think I can handle it."

Relief washed through Avery at the news he had found support. When they'd broken up, she had suggested he get therapy. He had vehemently refused. She'd always wanted him to find peace. A warmth bloomed in her chest.

"The lake is good for healing. It can rain and rain until at some random moment, the sun comes out and gives you this." Avery set her plate aside and waved an open palm out over the lake. "And it feels like everything will be okay. I always feel more centered here. There's a peace that comes from being so close to nature."

He took a sip of wine and fanned the pages of his book. Seeing him do it again was so terribly cute her heart melted a little.

"That's grief in a nutshell," he said. "The rain and rain and random sun."

Avery swallowed the lump in her chest. The boy who couldn't talk about his pain had come so far since they'd first met. Miles was using the lessons of his own journey to craft a sanctuary of peace for others.

"Do you have a name for your camp?" she asked.

"Camp Luciole." Miles thumbed his book.

"Luciole. French, for firefly." She gasped. "A light in the darkness. Perfect."

A relaxed smile crossed his face.

"Ayuh. I've got a lot to learn. I'm working on a master's degree in non-profit management at NYU. I just picked my fall classes. This summer, I'm going to Georgia, Minnesota, and Wyoming to observe bereavement camps. The Minnesota one doesn't allow cell phones. I want to see how that works so we can make an informed decision for our camp. And then there's finding a property," he said. "Remember that corporate retreat, over past Bramble Beach? It closed a few years ago. It may be for sale."

She didn't remember it. Next time she walked Casper over there, she'd check it out.

"I hope you get it. You seem to enjoy a canoe commute." She took a sip of wine. Her foot fell against his warm thigh. He didn't seem to notice, so she left it there. "And thank you for dinner. I'd forgotten you could cook."

She picked up a clean sheet of paper and he opened his book. The end of the dock felt familiar again. The two of them facing one another and doing what they had done so many evenings that summer. She painted. He read, the Red House over his shoulder. It would be so easy to fall back into this. To open her heart to him again and forget about everything that had happened the day they broke up, and afterward.

Avery moved her foot away from his thigh. Going back was risky.

"Whatcha reading?" She washed her brush in a cup of water.

"*War and Peace.*" He didn't raise his eyes, which made for a pleasant view of his thick eyelashes.

She wondered how many times he'd read it. He'd finished it a decade ago and was holding it in @lovetrainnyc's viral post of him reading on the subway. Counting now made three times, unless he opened to favorite scenes to pass the time. Or for comfort.

Miles uncrossed his feet, which repositioned his leg. His ankle now rested against her thigh. His choosing to touch her made a familiar energy buzz through her. She'd never sat with anyone else like this. She'd missed it.

"Funny," she murmured.

"What?" Miles placed his finger on the page where he'd stopped reading.

"We are both doing the same things we used to do. You're reading Tolstoy and I'm painting the Red House." She smiled.

He pointed and flexed his foot, his pinkie toe grazing her thigh. Avery's stomach did a little flip.

"You still like the Red House?" he asked.

"It's my favorite house on the lake." She made a private wish for him to brush her with his foot again.

He glanced over his shoulder. "Yeah, me too. You should come see it."

And for the first time, Avery thought visiting his house sounded nice.

"Maybe," she said.

"Progress." He smiled and rubbed her again with his foot. Like a compass finding true north, every hair on Avery's legs vibrated and leaned toward him. That tingle felt so good, she felt the urge to flirt. It could've been the wine, but she'd barely had any. She took another sip.

"Imagine how many likes Montressa's socials could get for a photo of you reading in the wild." She summoned her best playful smirk.

"Anything for Montressa." He looked at the sky, clearly embarrassed. "Just let me know you're taking it. The subway one took me by surprise."

Avery had wondered about that photo. People saw an undeniably handsome man reading on the subway, but she knew the boy inside, who took a book everywhere as a portable barrier, useful for avoiding interaction. That photo must've felt like an intrusion.

She watched as he placed his bookmark, closed his book, and checked the top edge to assess how far he had read. After all this time, his signature move hadn't changed.

He cleared his throat. "So, how's it feel to be painting again?"

"Like I never stopped," she said. "Thank you for suggesting my work for the website."

"I hope it's not a burden. I feel bad I gave you more work."

Miles acknowledging her work and respecting her time made Avery want his perspective on losing her livelihood.

"The Peppered Page's buyout required me to submit new designs for a year. I sent them my last watercolors in January." A blackfly landed on her leg and she whisked it away. "It's different when you have to give it over to a company. It stops being yours. I'm glad that year is over."

"Is that why you're getting an MBA?" he asked. "Because word of warning, there's more handing stuff in where you're headed. It's school."

She had never considered that. Going back to school made sense to everyone else but felt murky to her.

"It's hard to explain."

"Try me." He set the book aside, keeping his eyes on her. The fading light softened him into an irresistible mess of dark hair and ever-darkening eyes. Dusk suited Miles. And his foot resting against her thigh suited her. To stop the fluttering inside her chest, Avery dipped her brush in the lemon yellow. Soon it would be too dark to paint, but painting was her security blanket for talks on this dock.

"Getting engaged to the wrong person made me doubt myself." She puffed her cheeks and blew out a long breath as she swirled the yellow with the crimson, creating a vibrant scarlet. "I was never sure if Trent loved me or loved having me. He encouraged me to sell the Peppered Page, so I could stay home and not ask where he had been when he came home late. I let my life become about him, and the dreamer in me faded away. Thankfully, he left before he could claim half my company as his."

"I thought you left him." Miles's eyes darkened with concern.

She expected the words to sting or to draw up old hurts, especially coming from Miles.

"People say that to make me sound strong, but I wasn't. I woke up one morning to a friend's texts and photos of him with another woman. He admitted there'd been others but left me to do the breaking up. One day, everything aligned perfectly. The next, everything was uncertain. After Mimi's funeral, I moved into her house in Charlottesville, stuck and afraid to be myself again. I like that an MBA will make me hirable and keep me safe."

Miles brow furrowed, his eyes still focused on her. Having someone listen and not tell her what to do helped.

"Leaving your fiancée takes courage," he said with a small nod. "Lots of it."

He leaned forward and laid a hand on her knee. She'd admitted things she had never said aloud, and her revelations and the excitement of his comforting touch swirled together on her internal palette. She had unexpectedly blended a deep shade of vulnerability and entrusted it to him.

"I have great news." He winked. "I saw the dreamer yesterday. She redecorated a cabin in her head and talked a man into crafting some kind of bizarre tree bed."

Avery shook her head and smiled. That had been instinct, same as when she'd picked his counters. It had been fun. She set aside her painting and stared out at the darkening lake. There was more to the puzzle, and maybe he needed to hear it all.

"I think I picked the MBA because a top tier program admitted me despite the zero on my transcript," she said. "I failed my first semester of sophomore year."

That was the semester after they had broken up. She felt like she should say something else, but it shouldn't be up to her to make the wrong feel right. She watched her words sink in. Her pain began the day he left. She'd waited two days for him to come around and when he didn't, she knew he'd abandoned her emotionally. There'd been no choice but to distance herself physically. She'd cried the whole way back to Vanderbilt.

He scrubbed a hand down his face, releasing a sigh that sounded like defeat, or maybe regret.

"Avery, I, um." He swallowed and closed his eyes.

Avery didn't want remorse; she needed him to understand she had struggled. Her transcript proved there was no forgetting what happened. So did the firefly tattoo on his hip.

"I worked my way out of the hole," she said before he could respond.

"Dartmouth has a prestigious program. Someone there thinks I have potential, and it seems foolish to waste that."

Truth was, a business degree had never been one of her goals. She'd always envisioned herself in the arts. She might not trust Miles with everything, but he was listening and he might share how he had navigated life after selling CashCache.

"This feels good." She held up her brush. "But I don't know if lightning can strike twice. An MBA could mean never designing something again. And designing things is my thing."

Her voice cracked at the realization getting an MBA was playing it safe. Pursuing another artistic endeavor risked defeat. The little voice in her head telling her she'd crash and burn was so much louder than the one telling her she'd succeed. This was a lot to admit to a man whose ideas never failed.

Miles's stare intensified into something which could easily have been mistaken for seduction in another context. He gave her ankle a gentle squeeze. A long, lonely cry echoed through the quiet. Over his shoulder, two small black shadows glided out from the cove between Montressa and the Red House.

The loons were back.

Miles nudged her leg and lifted a finger to his lips. She widened her eyes in excitement. His foot stayed touching her thigh. They waited quietly as the black and white birds swam closer and glided by.

Loons were dramatic, with their black-and-white striped collars, spotted backs and lingering, eerie calls. She loved how the babies rode on the mother loon's back and hoped to see that again this summer.

After the loons left, Miles let out a deep sigh.

Avery studied him. He shouldn't look this enticing. It could've been the light or the way he encouraged her to find her own way.

"Hey," he whispered, lightly kicking his foot against her thigh, his gaze seeping into her like a solemn promise. "The only opportunity that's foolish to waste is the one you want. You don't need someone else to validate your potential. Your success speaks for itself. The trick is to believe in yourself. I'm guessing you have two lists. You show everyone the first one. It has the MBA on it. The other, you keep hidden because you're afraid if you write it down, it won't come true. That's the one that matters. You know you're amazing, right?"

His words echoed through her, and for the first time in a long time, Avery felt understood. He still knew her better than she knew herself. With his warm thigh resting against her foot and his smile lit by the pink haze, it became easy to forget how long it had taken to heal after Miles broke her heart.

He fixed his hair and picked up his book, fanning the pages.

A rogue paintbrush rhythmically rolling down the plank beside her broke the silence. Miles reached across her and picked it up before it fell into the gap between the planks. His hand whisked over her jeans, sending a gush through her middle.

"You've got a runaway," he said, handing her the brush.

"Don't want that," she said, reaching out. Her fingers landed on his and stayed there. Touching Miles's warm hand after he'd called her amazing lit up all the right places. That overwhelming urge to place her thumb in the dent in his chin bubbled to the surface.

Avery glanced away, thinking about how much she'd revealed. At how close they were to *something*. It felt nice to lean into Miles, but she knew better. This was nostalgia, not reality. It made no sense to cross a line she couldn't come back from. If her career confusion proved anything, she needed his friendship.

She felt the urge to process this somewhere else, by herself. She stood, stretched, slipped on her shoes, and tried to sound casual.

"I should go. The blackflies are out, and I don't want to get eaten. Plus, I need to let Casper out." She collected her things and headed up the dock. "Thanks for the dinner."

"You're welcome, and thank you for letting me join you," he called after her.

Avery didn't exhale until she unlocked the door to the loft. She shook her head, attempting to clear her confusion. Miles had cooked her dinner. There had been touching, understanding, listening. She'd revealed so much, ignoring the truth she'd learned the hard way ten years ago. Basking in Miles's warmth led to shivering in his shade.

CHAPTER TEN

Miles

MONDAY, JUNE 5

It was a good thing Avery had a list going because Miles would never remember all of her changes for the website he'd constructed in the evenings while visiting the bereavement camp in Georgia the previous week. She'd spent the week helping Nate train the summer staff, and Nate said this was the first summer he could remember everyone completing their paperwork before opening day, much less with ten days to spare.

This evening's weekly staff bonding activity was a showing of *Wet Hot American Summer* at the drive-in theater in the next town. With the whole staff gone for a couple hours, Miles suggested they discuss the website before things got busy preparing for Montressa's opening weekend.

Avery bubbled with ideas for the website's fonts, text layouts, menus, headers, widgets, and sidebars. Because dealing with money called for clarity, Miles had designed CashCache's site to be simple and easy to navigate. Vacations were different. People needed to imagine themselves at Montressa, so visuals mattered. He listened because Avery had studied a lot of resort websites in the last week.

He'd have to start over in some areas, but Montressa's would be the most beautiful website he had ever designed, thanks to her visual acuity. He'd never enjoyed a project more. Whenever she leaned closer to the screen for a better look, his head filled with her floral scent and his heart filled with hope.

Still, he was wary. A week ago, hopefulness had deteriorated into regret after she had admitted failing out of school the fall after he broke things off. Her confession made her uncomfortable, and she'd made up an excuse about the one blackfly she'd seen and left quickly. He'd do everything he could to avoid another abrupt departure.

Having her lists in his life again was a symbol of their shared purpose. She also made one for herself that included finalizing brand colors and fonts, neither of which Miles paid attention to when he'd founded CashCache. He'd chosen green, the color of money. According to Avery's quick lesson in color theory, he had chosen wisely. Green evoked security and hope—perfect for getting out of debt. For Montressa's brand colors, she took inspiration from around the lake.

They had been in the office a while, and his eyes ached from screen glare. They'd reached a good stopping point, but he wasn't ready to leave. He wanted to end the evening on a fun note. There wasn't a bar nearby where he could take her for a casual, celebratory drink, but he had a better idea. One that might remind her of their past.

He checked his watch. Earlier in the day, his StarSky app had notified him the International Space Station would fly over Linden Lake tonight. It was due to arrive in about fifteen minutes.

Avery put down her pen and stretched her arms overhead.

"I'm gassed," she said through a yawn. "Let's make these changes and meet later this week."

"Ayuh. I've got brain fry," he said. "I am going to the dock to watch the International Space Station flyover. Come along if you'd like. There's enough breeze tonight to chase away the blackflies."

It was a nerdy ask, but she used to enjoy stargazing with him. Her lips twisted in thought.

"That sounds cool," she said. "And Casper needs to go out."

She grabbed his leash and the three of them walked to the dock. They didn't need flashlights given the full moon. The heavens reflected on the still water, filling the lake with stars. Avery sat at the end of the dock and Casper plunked down next to her.

"He must be tired." Miles laughed as he sat on the other side of her. No way was he letting the dog get between them.

"Yeah." She reached out and ran her hand over Casper's head. "I made Casper run to the mailbox with me today."

"Good for you. My mom always said a tired dog is a good dog." Miles gazed at the sky and his mouth fell open as his head fell back. Stars relaxed him. "We got a clear night, maybe a bit too much moonlight, but we'll be able to see it. There's Venus."

"I like that you still stargaze."

Hearing Avery remembered things about him made his heart skip a beat. During their dinner on the dock, she'd remembered how much he loved *War and Peace*. They'd left before the stars came out that night. This could be the night he finally got what he had wished for on countless dark skies for the last ten summers.

"After all this time, you still view the heavens with wonder," she said, tipping her head back.

"Because you can never know it all." He glanced at her. "The universe is ever-changing."

The trace amount of light from the lodge illuminated her soft hair. Avery in profile was beautiful. He wanted to stay next to her on this dock all night so he could keep feeling this tingling in his chest.

"Where do I look?" She nudged his thigh with hers.

"It'll come from over there." He pointed across the lake. "It takes about two minutes to traverse the entire sky."

Miles traced its path with his hand, swooping it over her head until his hand rested behind her on the dock. When Avery didn't seem to mind, he silently congratulated himself. "I love a clear night. You can't see stars in the City."

"You see other kinds of stars," she said, rubbing Casper's belly. "That reminds me, I set up social media and flooded it with images. We need likes and shares. I hate to ask this, but is there any chance Hayes and Anna Catherine would post about us? They could come stay in the Boathouse once the bed goes in."

He liked that, but he had someone better in mind.

"I'll ask," he said. "My neighbor in New York, Symona Beauvais, has the most followers of all of us. I'm sure she'd help."

Symona had a busy modeling schedule, and he often watered her plants while she traveled or helped her hang artwork. Some nights, they sat on his nest couch and talked about how, as children growing up in rural communities, they had never imagined the lives they had now.

"Wow. Symona would do that?" Avery asked.

"Yeah. The night I moved in, she knocked on my door, asking to borrow sugar."

"That sounds like code for something else." Avery giggled. He took it as an invitation to tell her about his life in New York. Anything she'd read came from an unchecked source. He wanted her to know the truth.

"Honestly," he said, glancing at her to gauge her interest, "it seemed like a prank. Fashion Week had just ended, and she and her friends were drinking and baking cookies. I went because I was starving and curious. They'd made a pitcher of some cocktail they had invented and named 'the runway.' It was pink but tasted like a margarita. They asked me to take photos, so I did."

Miles shrugged. He'd been tipsy and shouted comedic directions in an Australian accent. They'd loved it. His photos set off a social media inundation of girlfriend groups, holding trays of baked cookies and fancy pink drinks. It still didn't seem real to him.

"You took the Pink Posse photos?" Avery's mouth dropped open in awe, her eyes wide. "That hashtag trended for an entire summer."

"I know. I still tease Symona for not crediting the photographer," he said, raising an eyebrow. "So she kinda owes me."

"Is that how you ended up dating her?" Avery asked, rubbing Casper's ear.

"Oh, we never dated," he said, happy to clear up the misconception. "She'd gone through a nasty breakup, and didn't want to show up solo to the Met Gala. I agreed to be her last-minute plus one."

"So you went as friends." Avery's mouth opened in surprise. He bit back the urge to kiss her and searched the horizon for the space station. Anything to keep him from making a move he'd regret.

"Yes, friends. I was a fish out of water. Her stylist picked out my clothes and gave me lessons on walking the carpet and posing for photos. Talk about surreal. Everyone hugs everyone, regardless of whether they know them." He laughed at how naïve he'd been back then. "The Met Gala red carpet is super stressful. As a former college athlete, I can confirm I have never sweated like I did that night."

"Symona's best friend is Hazel Matheson," Avery said. "She used to play small bars in Nashville. I'm a HazMat; that's what they call her fans. I feel like we went to college together."

"I remember that. You, with your sundresses and cowboy boots." He grew hard at the memory of her straddling him in the Mail Jeep a decade ago. He'd lowered those shoulder straps and kissed her shiny shoulders. It was the only time he'd ever had car sex. He wondered if she'd done it that way with anyone else.

"I tried to get tickets for her tour this summer," Avery said, scanning the horizon. "But they sold out in seconds flat."

"I'll text her and get us tickets."

Avery's shoulders fell, and Miles realized the two of them going to a concert sounded like a date. He'd gone too far.

She reached out on her other side and ran her hand down Casper's back.

"Miles," she said, a croak in her voice. "I'm glad everything worked out for you. What an amazing life you have."

Miles wanted to tell her everything wasn't as rose-colored as it seemed. How every summer, he'd hoped she'd come back to Linden Lake. That he found himself searching for her in every crowd. But whenever he revealed too much, she found an excuse to escape. He was pushing that boundary now and needed to back off.

"I guess," he sighed. "But celebrities are just people with a heightened sense of image. It's hard to tell who some of them really are and whether you have anything in common. I met Hayes at the Met Gala. His struggles grounded him, and I respect that when he's not on set, he's a New Yorker on the subway, just like everyone else. He calls me his normal friend, but sometimes I'm more like a third wheel."

"Have you had a girlfriend?"

"Yeah." He let out a laugh, leaned over, and lightly bumped her with his shoulder. "You."

"No, after us," she said. "Has anyone been more than a date?"

It was only natural for her to be curious. He should admit the truth. After all, she had shared so much the last time they sat here. He drummed his fingers on the dock behind him and resolved to give her the real him, not the glossy image.

"No," he said, allowing the weight of it to sit there for a moment.

"But you meet so many beautiful people."

"Trust me," he said. "It's like the first night on *The Bachelor*. Anyone who asks to steal you for a second has an ulterior motive. The people who seem perfect are the least put together."

This could easily apply to him. On paper and in public, he came across as confident, always sure of his next venture. The one viral photo that captured the real him was the one of him reading on the subway. The lost boy in a man's body, reading so no one discovered the inner Miles, who wanted things he couldn't have. Things far more elusive than red-soled shoes and nice cars.

"I know what you mean," Avery said, patting his knee. At some point, she must have stopped petting Casper and moved closer. "I thought I knew Trent, but he hid a lot from me. Talk about ulterior motives. I think I always knew the truth, and maybe part of me believed I could fix him. I just had to be the perfect girlfriend, fiancée, wife. A recipe for happiness. Except it meant he never got the real me either."

"I feel that," he said. "I never pursue beyond the first date because I have the sense we're both hiding ourselves."

Subsequent dates meant opening himself up, and he hadn't met someone worth doing that for since Avery. But maybe that wasn't true. He'd always thought she understood him from the moment they met, but he'd kept so much hidden from her back then. Stuffed his pain into a box after his mother's death. He thought he'd put enough nails in the lid to hold it down. The pressure had built until an emotional cyclone blew it open. Avery couldn't have known everything swirling inside him. Not without him sharing it.

Maybe he'd been too self-centered to consider her side of their story. The way he'd ended it lacked empathy. She must've felt blindsided. All this time, while he'd been dreaming of a future for them, she'd awoken to the certainty it was over. He'd made her think that.

"Mimi was onto something," she said. "Kis-mates, or even simple kindred spirits, are rare. Understanding each other on a visceral level ...

that's nearly impossible. I'm not sure how you know it when you see it."

Miles wanted to say he believed Avery was his kis-mate, but a lump blocked his throat. What Avery described sounded wonderful and frightening. Two warring emotions he'd become acquainted with that summer.

Avery crisscrossed her legs, sat up straight, and pulled the pencil out of her topknot. All that gorgeous hair cascaded past her shoulders. His fingers prickled with an urge to run his fingers through it, pull her in, and ask for another chance.

But years of no contact had made them ghosts. They recognized but were no longer intimate with the figure beside them. She probably thought if he'd missed her, he would have done something about it. And when he didn't, she had taken his silence as final. She didn't know that by the time he'd gotten up the courage to call her, as his finger hovered over her number, which he'd kept all that time, Nate had called to say Avery was engaged. Miles had waited too long.

His gaze shifted to the horizon just as the space station arrived. Her gaze followed. Miles let her call it because he remembered Avery's joy in finding what she searched for. She pointed to the light moving over the horizon.

"There it is!" She wiggled with excitement.

Together they watched the bright light rise into the sky, their necks gradually falling back until they had no choice but to lie on the dock.

As they settled back, he dropped his hand next to hers. The simple brush of their pinkies set his insides buzzing. His head reeled with a thousand thoughts of how to convey how much he had missed her.

"Miles," she said.

"Mmm," he answered.

"As your friend, I feel like I need to tell you to go on more second dates. And some third and fourth dates. Until you go on so many, you lose count."

An acrid taste rose in his throat at the suggestion of dating anyone but her. It was dark enough she might not have seen him nod anyway, as if considering her advice.

"It's not like I should give relationship advice, but I think the secret must be getting past the mirage," she said, staring at the sky. "It takes time to grow something."

"Right," he said. "Thank you."

And then, as if making a promise, he extended his pinkie finger and wrapped it around hers. She squeezed back and kept it there. A tear stung in his eye at the realization she still wanted to be friends. That was more than she'd wanted a month ago. But still not enough.

"How fast are they going?" she asked, breaking the silence.

"Five miles per second."

"I wonder if it feels that fast on the inside."

Five miles per second felt like the speed at which his heart had fallen to earth at the word "friend."

Resting on the dock, they gazed at the only moving star in the sky, which wasn't a star at all. It was a series of heartbeats inside of a flimsy shell, hurtling through an endless abyss at five miles per second, constantly circling the only life it had ever known. Its occupants would return transformed.

He was different now too. Maybe he could be a better man for her.

He studied her silhouette, her full lips parted in wonder. He wanted to roll on his side and pull her to his chest and capture the way they felt before he'd saved Max Perry's life and ruined his own.

But he had also ruined hers. And she had put up a wall to protect her heart. Miles knew two ways to take it down. She clearly wasn't up for a leap of faith. He'd have to disassemble it, brick by brick and slowly, which ran counter to Avery's love of getting things done.

Just as quickly as it had appeared, the Space Station disappeared over the tops of the tall pines behind them. Avery sat up, their pinkies no longer touching.

Time. They needed time together. And maybe more stars.

She crossed her arms, rubbing up and down her shoulders.

"You cold?" he asked.

"I'm good, it's fine."

If everything was fine, she wouldn't be shivering. Miles took off his flannel and wrapped it around her shoulders. When she moved her arms into the sleeves, he felt a piece of her barrier crumble as she accepted his warmth. The voice in his head told him to take it slowly. So he rose and helped her up.

They walked Casper back to the loft, talking about the space station and how the night sky was so spectacular at the resort. She brought up watching the Perseid meteor shower with him on the floating dock that summer and said she watched it every August. He'd forgotten how much Avery liked simple things. Although he knew she could handle them with grace, red carpets and bright lights would never win her over. She was all about sunsets and stars.

He told her about his fall classes, and she mentioned she had a Zoom with her MBA advisor later in the week to pick her curriculum. Miles felt honored she'd started sharing little bits of her life with him. However she opened up, he'd take it. If he could create more of these moments—the two of them together, no pressure, no outside influence—maybe they had a chance.

Miles didn't ask for his flannel back. He wanted her to hold on to it. She used to love stealing his clothes. After he'd ended things, she'd left all his clothes in a brown-paper bag in the Mail Jeep. The only thing missing was the sweatshirt he'd given her that first day in Portland. She'd either kept it, lost it, or burned it. He preferred to think she still had it a drawer somewhere and thought of him when she came across it.

At her door, he mentioned three planets—Venus, Mercury and Mars—would align with the moon in the night sky Friday night. And she said she'd set a reminder so she wouldn't miss it.

CHAPTER ELEVEN

Avery

TUESDAY, JUNE 6

Cool mornings called for hot tea and Avery couldn't get the kettle in the lobby to boil fast enough. She dropped a tea bag in her favorite mug, the one with a moose on it, and yawned. Someone needed to tell Casper it was too early to be this bouncy. He'd stolen the newspaper she used as a fire starter and torn it to shreds. Avery groaned as he proudly paraded a log he'd snatched off the firewood pile around the room. At ten, he had the energy of a puppy. She needed caffeine for this.

While the water heated, she checked her emails. Her Zoom with her MBA advisor, Emily Prescott, started in twenty minutes. Perfect. She had plenty of time to drink the first cup, brew a second one, and set up the conference room for her meeting.

Avery hadn't slept well. Sometimes she ignored all her hard work and convinced herself the Peppered Page getting snapped up by a larger company for a hefty price amounted to dumb luck. Her designs had cultivated a loyal celebrity following, but she'd spent hours last night second-guessing her talent, worrying Professor Prescott might question whether a boutique stationery founder belonged in a seedbed of future Fortune 500 executives.

For good luck, Avery had worn Miles's soft flannel shirt as a bathrobe while she dried her hair and put on makeup. Mornings at the lake were brisk, and the flannel felt as if it had never let go of Miles's body heat. Under the hair dryer, his woodsy smell had lifted off the fabric like steam. If some of his business sense mixed in the vapor, all the better.

To silence her own thoughts, she switched on the lobby television to *Bright and Early*. Victoria Evans sat center screen, bantering with the other anchors. Avery wondered if they found Victoria's lack of a filter annoying.

Victoria had made nineteen-year-old Avery self-conscious. She'd called it "being helpful" when she'd said Avery's jeans were unflattering or suggested Avery reconsider her freshly cut bangs. Her prediction Avery and Miles would never last stung the most. Avery still hated that time proved Victoria right.

Normally, Avery turned off *Bright and Early*, but she wanted to see the local weather after the news, so she muted it. Victoria had always loved the spotlight, and she'd perfected the perky morning host vibe. She had too much energy for someone who started work before the sun rose. Without sound, she was almost tolerable.

The kettle beeped just as Casper ran to the door. Unlike other times, when he seemed to get riled up over nothing, this time he barked ferociously at the crunching gravel. A few seconds later, brakes squeaked in the circle. Two freight trucks cut their engines as she opened the door.

The drivers had fifty new mattresses for Montressa. Avery was here alone. Everyone was off-property running errands or attending water rescue and CPR training in Portland. With everything else going on,

Nate must've forgotten about the mattresses. He didn't answer his phone, and a series of frantic texts to the staff confirmed no one knew anything about them. She'd have to cancel the Zoom. A frazzled search of Nate's desk yielded an invoice and a list of the number of beds assigned to each cabin. She slid it into a clipboard, started the delivery crew on Lupine Cabin, and breathed a sigh of relief when Miles's Mail Jeep pulled into the driveway.

"Miles," she said as he slid open his door. "I have my Zoom with my MBA advisor in ten minutes. Can you—"

"Go, I've got this." He took the invoice. "And good luck."

Something between them had changed in the past couple of days. Miles seemed more relaxed and helpful. Avery felt less apprehensive and more confident they could be friends. She couldn't wait to tell Lily. As junior class sponsor, Lily was knee-deep in putting on prom planning. Avery hadn't talked to her in a week. They had a lot of catching up to do.

"I'll check in later." He glanced at the clipboard and led the crew carrying two mattresses toward Lupine.

She watched him walk away. The confident stride, the clipboard, those jeans, and his Henley with the sleeves pushed up to reveal his sinewy forearms. Miles in charge was worth appreciating.

Oh, who was she kidding? Miles was hot. Period. She could admit that as a friend, right?

Eyes still on Miles, Avery walked to the lodge and almost ran into a large birch tree trunk that did not belong in the middle of the path to the office door.

"Whoa, cowgirl. Get your mind off that boy for a second." Wes laughed. He held the birch upright, as if it were a bed post.

A heat rose in Avery's cheeks. Wes didn't comment on her beet red complexion.

"Sorry, I was pulling these out of storage and missed your texts," he said as he shook the tree. "I have four of these, almost exactly alike.

What do you think of using them for the bed?"

Avery composed herself and evaluated the branch. The gorgeous silver birch bark was prettier than she'd imagined. If the finished bed equaled her vision, the Boathouse would resemble an indoor woodland sanctuary.

"Perfect! Can the branches spread across the ceiling?" she asked, fanning her fingers overhead. "It'll be like sleeping under a tree."

"I'll cut one, and you can give me your thoughts before I proceed. If Miles doesn't need my help, I can work on it now. I'll check in with him and have him send a king mattress over."

Wes hoisted the branch onto his shoulder and set off toward the Boathouse. "I'll text you and let you know."

"Okay, but I'll have my phone on silent for an hour," she yelled after him. "I'll be in a meeting."

By the time she returned to the lobby, there was no time for tea. At the conference room table, she took three deep breaths and logged on to Zoom.

Emily Prescott popped up on camera, bright-faced and glowing. Avery quickly checked her own camera. She looked less frazzled than she felt, but her makeup could've used a touch-up. Victoria would've had opinions on this. Avery hoped Professor Prescott didn't.

After introductions and small talk, Professor Prescott asked Avery to call her Emily and mentioned she had ordered her wedding invitations, baby announcements, and Christmas cards from the Peppered Page. Ah, a connection. Avery relaxed.

The first year of the MBA program included classes in analytics, accounting, and management; three things Avery hadn't enjoyed as an entrepreneur. There were no electives until second year. Emily suggested Avery get her résumé ready and offered advice on navigating the on-campus recruiting process, which sounded competitive and very corporate. After the meeting ended, Avery needed a moment to process what she'd signed up for.

Less than thirty seconds after restarting to the kettle, a black Rivian SUV pulled into the driveway behind the trucks.

"Ugh!" Avery groaned to herself. After the mattress fiasco and the information overload of her Zoom, the last thing she wanted was more drama.

Paulson got out, circled the SUV, opened the passenger side door, and Casper tumbled out. Avery laughed and pulled open the lodge door.

"Casper, what is going on?" she asked as the white blur sped across the lobby, pulled a stick from the kindling pile beside the stone fireplace, and returned to Paulson.

"No playing inside, boy." Paulson calmly took the stick.

"I was driving by, and found him sniffing around the mailbox," he said, nodding at Casper as he returned the stick to the pile. "I figured he wasn't supposed to be there."

Casper must have taken a little walk during the mattress confusion.

"Paulson, I am so sorry." She absentmindedly bundled her hair into a topknot. "It's been a crazy morning. These trucks showed up and we weren't expecting a delivery and ... thank you."

"It's okay," Paulson said. "Anything I can do to help?"

The lodge phone rang. It could be Miles, who might call the desk as opposed to texting, in case she was still in her meeting.

"Hang on." She held up a finger. "Don't leave. Let me take this."

Paulson nodded and attempted to make Casper sit. The dog was still hyper. Avery opened the bottom desk drawer, pulled out a chew toy she'd bought at Marden's for this type of situation, and handed it to Paulson. It worked like a charm.

The caller wanted to rent a cabin and as she answered their questions, Paulson wandered over to the electric kettle, lifted the moose mug with her tea bag still inside, and pointed at it. She nodded. Finally, tea. He filled her cup and brewed one for himself, silently asking about sugar and lemon. He dropped her tea off and carried his as he explored the lobby, porch, and dining room while Avery answered the caller's questions. Paulson stood in front of the muted television and watched Victoria unveil this month's book club pick.

Why did Miles find Paulson annoying? Paulson brought Casper back home, and brewed her tea, taking care to get it exactly the way she liked it. That was caring.

When she hung up, Paulson turned from the television with a sheepish grin.

"I read the books Victoria picks every month," he said. "I'm a fan."

"She used to work here," Avery said, trying to hide her smile.

"So she knew Miles before they landed on TV." His eyes widened. "I keep asking him to introduce us."

"I would, but I haven't spoken to her in ten years." Avery shrugged. Paulson was too sweet for Victoria. When *Bright and Early* came to the resort to film, Avery planned to avoid her at all costs.

A mattress passed by the window next to Paulson, as he examined a photograph of the Cooper family welcoming guests to Montressa on the wall. Paulson's clothing today was half city, half local. An unlikely merger of L.L. Bean and a steam iron. No wrinkles sullied his plaid flannel and the crisp crease in his khaki pants legs could only be from a dry cleaners, yet he looked content. His eyes were soft and his shoulders slack. Paulson pointed at Nate in the photo.

"What if Nate chose not to work for his father?" he asked, walking to the front desk.

"I don't know, Paulson. I think it's more like he works with his father, not for him."

Paulson nodded once, in slow motion. Avery could have sworn working *with* and not *for* someone was a new concept for the son of America's most famous hotel magnate.

"My father"—he shook his head—"is a lot. Imagine me after five espressos. I have trouble making friends because I'm too much. I enjoy being right, and I like everything top-shelf, but I don't know if I want to be like Dad. He doesn't have friends because he treats everyone as if they're expendable. He lives for a frenzy. I like peace. Give me a fishing rod, a babbling brook, and birdsong. That's my happy place."

Avery always assumed her peers were all adults now and she was the only one who hadn't figured out what she wanted. Maybe part of the adult experience was being adrift.

Paulson lowered his head and pulled a loose thread off his flannel. "Mom left us when I was ten; just vanished. So, Dad's all I have. I don't want to let him down, but I'm not sure I want to be the next him."

Avery took a sip of her tea. She could relate to heading down a path with a nagging sense you'd taken a wrong turn somewhere along the way. Paulson had access to everything anyone could want. Yet he'd hinted at having no relationship with his mother. Given that he and his father shared the same name, his father had come up the first time Avery googled Paulson Carter, without the "IV" suffix. Paulson's father ruled the boardroom with brash tactics and head games. Maybe he had been like that with Paulson's mother and was still that way with Paulson.

Avery's stomach tensed. It felt like a deep conversation to have with someone she barely knew. He must be lonely if he chose to discuss it with her.

"I think we all question our choices at some point," she said.

Paulson nodded slowly. As if shooing something away, he waved a hand between them.

"Sorry, I'm babbling. I should discuss this with my therapist or my best friend since middle school," he said. "No matter how much time passes, he understands me in that inexplicable way only people from your past do. Do you have friends like that? I like to think we all do."

Avery nodded. Years had passed, and Miles still sensed she kept a list of aspirations in her head because writing them down meant making them real. He understood her fear of failure, but didn't judge her for it. Lily was like that too.

Paulson's brow furrowed, and he pierced her with a deep stare.

"I know I said I'd tear it down," he said, "but I like it here. It's peaceful. Truth is, my father wants me to find—"

The front circle door swung open, and Miles walked in, his head buried in the clipboard holding the mattress invoice. "Success. We can put this mattress mayhem to bed."

He stopped laughing at his pun when he saw Paulson.

"Hey, Miles." Paulson smiled and waved.

Again, like an inflatable holiday lawn decoration, Miles magically grew in size. He stood taller, squared his jaw, and broadened his shoulders until he was all muscle, height, and chisel. She couldn't decide if this defense mechanism was protective or competitive, but this strong, confident Miles hadn't existed ten years ago. Avery fiddled with her necklace, running the pendant back and forth along the chain.

"The Coopers aren't here," Miles growled.

"Oh, I returned a runaway Casper and took the opportunity to say hello to Avery." Paulson smiled and faced Avery, his back to Miles. "So, does this place have a bar?"

She caught Miles rolling his eyes, but Avery refused to assume there was an ulterior motive behind every question Paulson asked.

"For cocktails?" she asked as she took the clipboard from Miles. "We mix drinks in a room off the kitchen. People take them out on the porch or by the lake."

"The hotel bar is my favorite place in a resort," he said. "It's where parents grab a child-free moment, couples reconnect, siblings reunite. It's jovial because everyone is on vacation. And each hotel bar has its own personality. You can tell a lot about someone based on their favorite one. Miles, what's your favorite hotel bar in the City?"

"The Marlton," Miles grumbled as he leaned against the tea counter.

A snarl brewed beneath his scowl.

"I knew he'd pick something in the Village." Paulson snapped his fingers. "The Marlton is intellectual and broody. Ideas percolate in front of cozy fires. You want the next great American novel? Someone at the Marlton's bar is writing it. Or reading it."

Well, Paulson had kind of nailed Miles. She wondered what bar Paulson liked.

"What's yours, Paulson?" she asked, taking a sip of tea.

"We refashioned a former Post Office building into a hotel. The rooftop bar is called Postcards. The team transformed the ceiling into a giant postcard. Every table has postcards and pens. I enjoy sitting at the bar, sipping a top-shelf Manhattan, and watching people come in the door. The first time they always gasp. I love a good gasp."

Avery could almost see a coupe glass in his muscular hand, peeking out from a French cuff. If Paulson was right and a person's favorite bar painted a picture of their personality, his was a modern take on a classic.

"What's your favorite drink?" he asked.

"Depends. Either champagne or a Lemon Drop." She smiled and rested her elbows on the front desk.

"Sweet but also tart, and elegant." Paulson raised a finger to his mouth in thought and then pointed at her. "I'd say Bemelmans at the Carlyle. There's always a pianist or a jazz trio. On any given night, you can find a movie star, a mogul, and a socialite. Bemelmans has murals by the guy who wrote *Madeline*."

"Oh." Avery grabbed her heart. "I loved those books. The little girls all in a row."

"Let's go." He slapped the counter. "Our jet can fly us to New York on Friday."

Across the lobby, Miles's head popped up from his phone.

Paulson raised his eyebrows expectantly, those piercing blue eyes hopeful. Avery had to admit she'd walked herself right into his offer.

"We can shop and maybe see a show," he said. "You can stay at The Carter on Park, in your own suite."

He turned to Miles. "Miles, come with us. And bring Victoria Evans. We'll do a hotel bar crawl."

The irony of the suggestion made Avery half laugh, half cringe. Sitting at a bar with Victoria was her worst nightmare. And Miles's was sitting at a bar with Paulson. If she and Miles could get to the right place, they'd find humor in this, but they weren't there yet.

She glanced at Miles, slowly rubbing his stubble, an act which conveniently hid his expression.

"Oh wow, Paulson. That's kind of you, but I have plans this weekend." She unclipped the mattress paperwork from the clipboard and stapled it together. "Maybe in the fall, when I'm in New York for interviews."

Miles stopped rubbing his jaw and pierced her with a questioning stare that melted into something else. He glanced away. She could have sworn he'd smiled at the prospect of her coming to New York.

"Here's my number," Paulson said, handing her a triple-thick business card. "Next time you're in the City—bar crawl. And you're welcome to stay at any of our hotels. I'll comp you."

"Thank you." She took his card and glanced at it. She walked him to the door and thanked him for bringing Casper home. Miles walked to the front desk when he heard the door shut.

"He seems nice." She shrugged and ran her thumb over Paulson's card. It had been a while since she'd handled triple-thick card stock. This was premium paper.

"Nah, Paulson always wants something," Miles said.

"I think you're a little hard on him. He's more self-aware than you think. He knows he's exuberant. It's hard working for his dad."

"Oh, come on." Miles groaned. "Like all nepo babies, Paulson had the easiest road to success."

"I don't know. I get the impression Paulson's father has expectations, and Paulson didn't get a choice." She picked up the mail Paulson had left on the front desk and flipped through it. Paulson had not only saved Casper, but he'd kindly brought in the mail.

"Agree to disagree." Miles stuffed his phone in his back pocket and smiled at her. "I'd love to stay and psychoanalyze Paulson Carter, but I'm heading out to visit a property."

"The corporate retreat?"

"Ayuh." He smiled. "I'm trying not to get my hopes up."

"Ooh! I hope you get it." She knocked on the wood counter for good luck and held up crossed fingers.

He crossed his fingers and pointed them at her.

"And I hope you get a quiet, warm, sunny afternoon," he said as he headed out the door to the circular driveway. "No more surprises."

CHAPTER TWELVE

Miles

FRIDAY, JUNE 9 – ONE WEEK UNTIL OPENING DAY

It was dark out. *Darker than the inside of my pocket* as Sam liked to say.

"Dammit, Casper." Miles scanned the road as the Mail Jeep crawled ahead at fifteen miles per hour, its bright headlights illuminating the pine-lined roadway. A white dog should stand out in his high beams.

"Have you seen *13 Going on 30*?" Anna asked through his AirPods, ignoring everything related to the missing dog.

Miles rolled his eyes. Another rom-com. Perhaps he should reconsider seeking advice from two former child actors who had left normal lives in their rearview mirrors during middle school. Their rom-com tips hadn't worked so far. Avery still referred to Miles as a friend. For a guy who kept people firmly in the friend zone, Miles should know how to wriggle his way out of it without a rom-com's help.

"Yes, I've seen it." He stopped and pointed a flashlight into the woods. "But I don't see the correlation. I don't dance and haven't held onto her beloved childhood dollhouse all these years. I met Avery when she was nineteen, not thirteen. I don't know if she had a dollhouse."

Anna Catherine let out an exaggerated stage groan.

"First, didn't you learn about symbolism in that fancy college? The dollhouse signifies Matty never forgot Jenna. Show Avery you never gave up on her." Anna said. "And second, we need to fix this whole 'I don't dance' thing. You gotta let loose a little."

He admitted Anna had a point and before ending the call, promised to give it some thought. Convincing Avery he had never forgotten her would be so much easier with a tangible item like a dollhouse. Words were more challenging, and his only option.

He paused just inside Montressa's driveway, removed his AirPods, cut his engine in case the dog barked, and shined his flashlight where Paulson had found Casper before filling Avery's head with ideas about dreamy top-shelf hotel bars. In Miles opinion, he'd picked the wrong one for Avery.

"Casper! Casper!" Avery's voice echoed from farther up Montressa's driveway.

Miles started the Mail Jeep and drove on, gravel crunching under his tires. A few seconds later, he pulled up beside Avery, leaned over, and slid open the passenger door.

"Get in," he said.

Avery slumped into her seat, the scent of her shampoo filling the Jeep. What flower was that? Something southern and delicate.

"Sorry to text you so late and thank you for coming. I couldn't find anyone in the staff dorm. I guess they're all asleep. And Nate is at Lily's. I left Casper in the lodge after dinner while I watched a movie and grabbed a shower," she moaned. "We do it every night. When I went to let him out at bedtime, the front door was open, and he was gone. I've been searching for a while. I even brought hotdogs. His favorite."

The last thing that dog deserved was a hotdog, but Miles kept his opinions to himself.

They drove up the driveway, calling for Casper. Nothing.

"Let's take the other fork where the driveway splits and check the Cooper compound," he suggested.

Past where the Montressa property ended, the Coopers owned three winterized houses that reminded Miles of *Goldilocks and the Three Bears*. Sam and Laurie lived in the big house. Beyond it was a little guest cabin. Nate had recently purchased the medium-sized house from his parents. It sat directly across the cove from the Red House but needed some updating to become *just right*. For now, Nate and Lily lived in Lily's apartment, close to the high school.

Miles parked the car outside Sam's house and pulled a flashlight out of a milk crate behind the seats.

"Come on, let's check every door," he said as they got out.

She called for Casper a few times. Nothing.

"Dammit, Casper," Avery muttered.

"He'll be back," Miles said. "I'm sure he has a plan."

Miles wasn't sure Casper would be back, but Avery needed reassurance. If Casper had a plan, it was to ruin quiet moments, like the ones everyone had been enjoying earlier in the night.

"I thought I had a plan," she said. "Get an MBA. Be ready for any career. But my first semester classes will be everything I hated doing at the Peppered Page. I knew this going in, but now that it's real, I'm second-guessing myself. If I'm honest, an MBA was the simplest answer to the question, 'what's next?' after I sold my business—"

"For a lot of money," Miles added, trying to give her the credit she deserved, which he had not done that first day on the dock.

She swept her flashlight's beam along the tree line at the edge of the property.

"Thank you, but sometimes I feel like when I hit my professional peak, my personal life fell apart," she said. "I put my parents through a lot when I canceled my wedding. I don't want them to have to worry about me anymore, but I also don't want to make a mistake. Dad suggested an MBA, and he made it sound so sensible."

That first day on the dock she'd been so sure of herself, but maybe she'd been afraid to be vulnerable. It was funny how Avery could be so attuned to what others needed, but out of sync with herself. Miles desperately wanted her to recognize her own value and feel good about her accomplishments.

"Tell me what to do." She pressed her hands together, begging him. "I was living on nothing and putting all my money back into the Peppered Page. Before I sold it, I only had two hundred dollars in my checking account. These big checks arrived, and everyone suggested, 'invest in yourself,' which sounded like code for 'do something more impressive.' You sold CashCache and started your camp. You keep outdoing yourself. Tell me what to do next."

Miles pressed his lips into a thin line and spun to face her. It hadn't been easy, but he could see how it appeared seamless. He hated seeing her lose trust in herself, but he wouldn't tell her what to do. Listening to other people had brought her to this point.

"I can't do that," he said. "You're the one who has to live your life. Whatever you do next, don't let someone else pick it for you. Deep down, you know what makes you happy and energizes you. That's where you'll find your answer. Envision the life you want and make that happen."

Avery stood silently, lit by the automatic flood lights that illuminated the back of the house, her gaze elsewhere, as if something were clicking inside that gorgeous head. She studied him and parted her lips. He wanted to kiss her to make it all better. But she hadn't asked for that. He headed to the unlit side yard, shining his flashlight from side to side.

"I didn't mean to unload on you," she said, trailing behind. "But

Casper taking off like this... Everything feels so out of control. I need a friend."

"I'm here." Miles nodded, the word *friend* sinking like a rock from his heart to his stomach. He flashed his light in the crawl space under the side stoop. "Tell me what got you thinking like this."

"I was watching *13 Going on 30*, and it made me assess every choice I've ever made." She lifted a hand to her heart. "The end made me sad."

He made a mental note to thank Anna Catherine later.

"The dollhouse?" he asked, furrowing his brow.

"Yeah." He could make out her shoulder shrug in the dim light. "That's my favorite part."

He wished he could think of something like that dollhouse. Something that would magically answer all of her questions from the last decade. Something he could hand her so she'd know they still belonged together. Despite what Anna Catherine and Hayes said, life was nothing like the movies.

"Nate constantly says he has always loved Lily. Which is amazing." Avery followed him to the water-facing side of the house. "No one says that about me."

"Nate hasn't loved Lily all his life." Miles flashed the light into Casper's doghouse. "He's loved her since he met her. That's possible for anyone, at any age. Trust me. You haven't met everyone who is going to love you."

"Yeah, I guess." Her voice cracked. "But I'm a jilted bride, and it's coming."

"What's coming?" The light next to the door cast a multitude of shadows on the Cooper's long porch. Miles shined the flashlight under the rattan furniture.

"Thirty and then thirty-five," she said. "All my friends are in serious, long-term relationships, and I can't seem to find one that lasts. I don't want to be cast off more times than your favorite fishing rod."

He stared at the long, dark lawn in front of him and thought about bringing up Trent to deflect blame from himself, but Avery was at glass half empty. The goal was to fill her cup. She waited for an answer, lit by the glow of the porch.

"You'll be thirty next September. That's over a year away." He ducked his gaze into her line of sight, waiting for her to connect. "And I'm already in my thirties. It's not so bad. Look, we all feel lost sometimes. But you don't peak once. Life is a mountain range, full of peaks. Peaks have valleys. You're in one. You'll get out."

She smiled hopefully and her teeth chattered. They'd been so distracted, he hadn't noticed her wet hair and thin T-shirt. A bra strap peeked out below the shirt's loose collar.

"I want what they have," she said. "Somebody. Someday. What am I doing wrong?"

Miles wanted nothing more than to be that somebody, but he knew not to jump too far ahead. So he removed his jacket and draped it over her shoulders. She shivered into its warmth as her arms ran through the sleeves. He zipped it up and rubbed her shoulders.

"Avery, I'm no expert, but I think you try to rush things. Relationships aren't something you check off a list. They're something you grow. Isn't that the advice you gave me? Go on one date, then two, and then one day you've gone on so many with the same person, you've lost count."

Miles took a small step toward her and opened his arms. "Come here," he smiled. "I don't know the dance routine they do in the movie, but you're freezing and I give warm hugs."

She stepped into his chest and Miles wrapped his arms around her and, without thinking, planted a soft kiss on her cool forehead.

"Maybe you'll find someone at Paulson's hotel bar. What was it? Bemelmans."

She lay her ear against his chest and looked toward the dark lake.

"Yeah, Bemelmans," she said. "With the murals."

"I'd have picked Bar Chrystie at the Public Hotel for you," he said. "Everything's emerald-green. They have lighted chandeliers lying sideways on pedestals. The whole time we're there, I'll be trying to figure out if the room is making you sparkle or if you're making it sparkle. Even though I know it's the latter."

She picked her head up off his chest and in the dim light, he saw a smile. He wondered what color her eyes were. It didn't matter. She was beautiful.

"Can you follow me around and whisper all of that to me every day?" She patted his chest.

That was the dream, and Miles felt the thrill of entering a scary carnival ride. He wanted her to know how special she was.

"Sure." He smiled.

He reached up and ever so lightly ran the pad of his thumb over her cheekbone. He went liquid on the inside when she closed her eyes and leaned into his hand. As his gaze drifted over her, the idea of the dollhouse came to him. He needed to tell her what she didn't know.

"I think I see you places." He kept his voice soft and steady, so she'd know his words came from deep within him. "Crowds, lines, running ahead of me along the Hudson. I spy a reddish-blond ponytail, one that could've been rinsed in the Tabasco sauce they named you after. I catch my breath and think, *it's Avery.*"

He said her name with a hitch, as if he had seen a fish jump. When her breath hitched too, he knew his words had hit their mark. He slowly tucked a lock of hair behind her ear, softly brushing his thumb over the spot he used to kiss. Her lips parted.

Getting closer was a gamble. She might run.

All that existed in this moment was Avery and the softness of her skin under his hand. For years, he'd envisioned what he wanted. She was standing right in front of him and the prospect of getting himself where he wanted to be seemed possible.

"Obviously, she's never you." He lowered his hand. "But damn, Avery, for the last ten years, I haven't stopped looking, no matter what else is going on in my life."

Maybe he'd revealed too much, but Avery didn't run. She stayed in his embrace and wrapped her arms around his neck. It was a risk to open himself a little more, but one nudge forward and she might understand what he really wanted.

"I used to worry that at some point, I wouldn't remember you anymore." His voice fell to almost a whisper, and he grasped a handful of her jacket ... which was his jacket ... right at the small of her back. "The crinkle in your nose when you giggle, or that you smell like a flower I can't quite name. I never ever want you to fade."

Avery's lips parted ever so slightly, as if inhaling his words. In the dim light, he could have sworn she wanted a kiss, and the anticipation made him quiver. She licked her lower lip and studied him, and he wished he could read the thoughts spinning through her beautiful mind. Avery rose on her tiptoes and came closer, reducing the distance between them to mere millimeters.

Time ground to a halt. Stars collided. Planets aligned. Miles closed his eyes.

He wasn't sure their lips were touching until her mouth gave way and her tongue skirted his lower lip. She ran her hand ran up the back of his neck and into his hair, pulling him to her. Her torso pressed into his, her hips writhing against his jeans.

Avery Easton was kissing him. Like she meant it, like she wanted him.

Miles opened his eyes in shock and quickly closed them, hurrying to catch up.

The taste of mint lip balm tempted him with all the things he could do, right here, right now. And good God, he wanted to do them all. He pulled her in, wondering if she felt the rock-solid length of him through the layers of fabric between them. He was about to cup the back of her head when Avery pulled away.

His mind filled with questions. It had all happened so fast, and he'd been unprepared. That kiss meant *something*, but what? He stared as Avery rubbed her lips. A pulse jolted through him at the thought of those lips exploring every inch of him. Her kiss had turned him into a lovesick puppy. He'd follow her anywhere and everywhere if she let him.

Avery forced a smile.

"I'm sorry." She shook her head and fixed his collar. "We are supposed to be friends. I shouldn't have, um..."

Miles had waited so long for this moment. He froze, knowing whatever he said next could make or break his chances.

"The thing is," she said with a sigh, "we've changed. You have your famous friends, your red-carpet events, and your amazing apartment with the same sofa as Kendall Jenner. It's beautiful. It also costs a small fortune."

He reached a new level of regret for that one frivolous purchase.

"Avery," he started. "It's not..."

She placed her finger over his lips.

"Let me finish," she said. "I love that you have a beautiful life. You work hard, give back, and escape here to the best house on the lake. You deserve all of that. Thing is ... I'd be expecting the boy I fell in love with ten summers ago. And it's for the best that he's gone because him not loving me shattered me. I can't take that kind of heartbreak again. So thank you for being my friend and making me feel better."

Her words crashed through him like a freight train filled with cement. He didn't know where to start. With her perception of his lifestyle, or the couch he hadn't chosen, or that his goal hadn't changed in a decade, or that *she* kissed *him*.

"We need to give our best friends the conflict-free wedding they deserve," she said. "So they can take a cruise or whatever for their honeymoon, with happy memories."

Miles had been so quiet, parsing each word and figuring out how to refute every single weak argument when something dawned on him. Something more important than the defeat he felt now.

Take a cruise. Shit. He knew one more place to look for Casper.

"Avery," he said, pulling her elbow toward the waterfront. "Come on, there's one more place."

Miles took off across the lawn to Sam's private beach. There on the sand was Sam's dark-green Old Town canoe. The one he paddled around the lake with his best friend in the bow.

Come on, Casper, wanna take a cruise? The thought of Sam saying it made Miles miss Sam.

And there in the canoe lay a ghostly white lump, waiting for his best friend. Casper raised his eyes but not his head when Miles shined the light on him. Avery pulled up a second later.

"Casper, are you okay?" She clamored into the boat.

"I think he misses Sam. They go out on the lake together. Sam calls them cruises. When you said that word, I knew."

"Poor guy." She ran her hand over the dog's head. "I'll take you out on the lake."

A few minutes and a hotdog later, Casper followed them up the hill and jumped in the back of the Mail Jeep. When Miles shifted into reverse, he started to loop his hand behind Avery's headrest to look out the rear window as he backed up. It had taken so long to get her back into his passenger seat. But Casper's giant head panted between them, dripping drool onto the floorboard. She nuzzled her nose into the dog's neck.

"Casper, you scared me." She kissed the top of his head and held his muzzle in her hands. "Don't you ever leave me again."

Miles wanted her nuzzling *his* neck, her kissing *his* face, her telling *him* not to leave. So badly his stomach hurt at the realization someone who made you so happy could make you so sad. He'd done that to her once.

Miles let his eyes linger on her profile, all the time wondering at what point a man should give up on his dream. Casper gave her his paw and dropped his eyes as if to say no one had ever loved him. Completely false, but Avery lapped it up.

That dog was a player. Miles admired his skills.

Dammit, Casper, he thought as he backed up. One day he was going to print that on a T-shirt.

CHAPTER THIRTEEN

Avery

WEDNESDAY, JUNE 14 - TWO DAYS UNTIL OPENING DAY

Avery paddled along Bramble Beach, thankful for a break from a frazzled week. After witnessing Casper's hollow, sad eyes Friday night, she'd taken him out on the water every day. He ran in circles whenever she pulled out his doggy flotation vest and once in the canoe, stood in the bow the whole ride, ears cocked and tail wagging as he scanned the water. Today, they'd paddled past Red House, which commanded a view of the entire lake. On the other side of the point, sandy, unspoiled Bramble Beach was the definition of *away from it all*. Every time she came here, Avery searched the shoreline for a moose. They gravitated to quiet places with access to water.

The stillness was a welcome break. With only a week until opening day, Nate had the nervous energy of someone who'd had too many espressos—remarkable for a man who never touched caffeine. Whatever random thought entered his mind came right out, and he hadn't stopped thanking Avery and Miles for all the progress they'd made. He always said their names together, "Avery and Miles" merged into a single breath. As if they were one word.

As if they had kissed.

And gah! Did Nate know they had kissed? Avery hadn't told anyone. Miles might've told Nate, and if he had, she wanted to know what he'd said. She'd been sure Miles wanted that kiss, but his delayed response had left her wondering if he hadn't felt a spark. Maybe he'd frozen in shock.

Avery sighed and watched as bubbles floated to the surface from somewhere deep in the lake. She'd always wondered what made random bubbles finally decide it was time to float free.

The night of the kiss, it was as if her body had floated up and said *I'll take it from here.* In retrospect, *her* kissing *him* made sense. Miles had calmed her insecurities. When he'd said he'd searched for her in crowds, she'd melted. Then he'd flattered her, comparing her sparkle to a luscious hotel bar that didn't sound real. The intimate admission that he'd be taking her there as much for himself as for her, so *he* could watch her sparkle, buzzed in all the right places. No wonder she'd kissed him.

The more she tried to convince herself they'd changed, the more she realized some things remained the same. The easy way his lips fit hers. Those familiar fireflies tingling through her. The closer they got to melding seamlessly into one another, the later thoughts of him touching her kept her up at night. Avery made her bed every morning. Lately, she'd twisted the neat sheets into a wrangled mess by midnight.

There were countless similarities between that summer and this one: the attraction, the smells and tastes, those eyes, that hair. But if Miles remained the same, his breakup might still fall like an axe splitting a log. Instant division, no going back. And while a fling sounded intriguing, the aftermath meant waking with the dread that every day was another day without him. She didn't want to grieve him again.

A loon skimmed across the surface ahead. Loons were so mysterious. Despite their eerie call, they could be quiet and stealthy. Their flat bodies and pointy heads sat low to the waterline, making them easy to miss. This loon saw something beneath the water and dove under. She watched and waited for it to resurface.

Miles would resurface at Montressa soon. He'd gone back to the City the day after they'd kissed. Monday evening, @lovetrainnyc had tagged Montressa in a photo of Miles riding the 6 Train, reading *War and Peace*. A forest-green T-shirt tugged across his chest, emblazoned with Avery's drawing of five silhouetted pines—the one she'd sketched at the staff meeting a few weeks earlier. Below the pines, it read *Wood is Good - Montressa Lodge and Camps* in log-shaped letters. The post's caption summed up the way Avery was starting to feel: *Still pining for the guy who takes his commutes with a little Tolstoy #throwback.*

An hour later, Portland Graphics delivered a full run of the shirt. A Post-it note atop the box in Miles's handwriting alluded to the firefly tattoo.

Took liberties with your artwork again. Hope you don't mind. Sell these.

Avery had giggled at the note and shared the post to Montressa's stories. It was hard not to crush on a guy who'd do anything for the people who mattered to him.

She'd texted him a selfie of her wearing the shirt, and he'd immediately replied.

○ **Miles:** Ah! I picked that color to see if your eyes could turn spruce green ;)

○ **Avery:** And…

○ **Miles:** success :-{)

Miles still used punctuation emojis, and he gave them mustaches.

That was kind of swoony. So much so, she'd envisioned Miles with a mustache. By late afternoon, the shirts had sold out on the Montressa website and they'd had a few reservation inquiries.

A family of ducks swam past the canoe, the tiny ducklings following their mama. Avery stopped paddling and floated, listening to the ducklings, the songbirds, and the lapping of the water against the boat. She could sit all day in this tranquility. She reminded herself that rather than spend her morning analyzing all things Miles, she should savor the break from the front desk and Nate's exuberance.

Up ahead, a man walked along the shoreline of the corporate retreat. He was fit, but shorter and bulkier than Miles. Avery shielded the brim of her Vanderbilt baseball cap with her hand to get a better look, but she was too far away to see clearly.

As she paddled toward him, his head lifted.

"Avery?" he called.

She recognized that voice.

"Paulson?"

Avery hoped the corporate retreat wasn't the reason he'd been *in the area* so often these last few weeks.

"Well, look at you on a puppy cruise," Paulson said, as she paddled to shore. "Love the doggy life jacket."

As he helped her out of the canoe, Avery noticed dark circles under Paulson's eyes. His rumpled hair didn't know what to do without its daily dose of hair gel. A blond lock fell across his forehead.

Casper plodded up the beach and sniffed the rocks between the beach and the lawn.

"Hey." She gave Paulson a hug. "Didn't expect to see you here."

"Honestly, I'm not sure I want to be here." Paulson kicked a rock with one of his dirty Air Jordans. "Dad sent me to assess this property for our newest resort. He thinks Linden Lake needs a hotel with year-round recreation. Snowshoeing and cross-country skiing in winter, jet skis and parasailing in the summer. He wants to put in a glass-front hotel."

Oh no. Her heart stopped and then pounded faster. Miles was right. Paulson was up to something. A mega resort would crowd the lake and ruin Camp Luciole. Montressa might not survive despite its national television debut in two weeks.

On Monday morning, she had watched all three hours of *Bright and Early*, paying extra attention when Miles explained why something called "spaving," or spending to save, wasn't saving. Adding things to your cart to get perks like bonus gifts or free shipping was spending. She hadn't paid attention to his advice because she enjoyed spaving and damn, television suited him. His navy suit and the studio lights had turned his eyes the color of maple syrup. The post-segment banter had centered on the show's upcoming trip to Maine.

After the show, Victoria Evans called the lodge. The last Friday in June, she and her crew would film four live segments for her series, "Where America Vacations." She expected a vegan menu and a comped room stocked with three kinds of bottled water: Evian for washing her hair, Fiji for drinking, and Voss for brushing her teeth. Several locations needed to be "on-set ready." Everything was an order. She assumed Avery knew what she was demanding and didn't elaborate. She hadn't said thank you. Victoria hadn't changed.

That night, Avery posted a sweet photo of the birch bed in the Boathouse to the lodge's social accounts. Symona Beauvais had immediately shared it on her stories, saying she needed a getaway. Then Hazel Matheson shared Symona's story with the caption *not if I get there first*, which was also the title of one of her biggest hits. Avery had entered the lodge the next morning to find every phone ringing, and thus began a trial by fire for the new front-desk staff. By noon, the Boathouse had been booked for the entire summer and the staff had taken a few reservation requests for the following year. A behemoth resort and its jet skis could undo all of that momentum.

Paulson led her to the flat lawn.

"As usual, Dad changed my entire plan," he said. "When I pitched the idea of a small resort focused on fishing, I wanted something closer to a river. More in the pines."

Like Montressa, Avery thought, which wasn't for sale.

They stood there scanning the property. Smaller classroom-type buildings surrounded a main building, possibly a dining hall. Sweet log cabins dotted the shoreline, with enough space between each one for privacy. The place was perfect for Miles's camp. So perfect, she'd volunteer to decorate those cute cabins.

Carter Hotels would win a bidding war and knock all of it down. They'd change Linden Lake forever, destroying animal habitats and tarnishing what brought people to natural areas year after year: tranquility.

Casper picked up a stick and ran in circles with it.

"Dad asked me to assess the property so we can outbid the other group that wants it," Paulson said.

Avery hesitated. It felt like a breach of Miles's trust to leak details about Camp Luciole, but this was urgent. And Paulson seemed to be searching for a reason to pass on the property.

Casper dropped the stick at Paulson's feet. Paulson picked it up and hurled it across the lawn, and Casper set out on a chase.

"Paulson," she said. "I'm telling you this in confidence. It goes no farther than you and me. Miles is the other person trying to buy this property."

Paulson studied her, as if deciding what to do with that information. His choice would reveal whether he was the sweet guy Avery had faith in, or the devious, self-serving person Miles made him out to be.

"He wants to open a bereavement camp here. For people who've lost loved ones. With therapists and support staff and"—she felt a tinge of guilt ripple through her chest for spilling secrets—"quiet."

Paulson faced the sun, closed his eyes, and pressed his lips into a thin line.

"Miles has always been such a good guy." His voice wavered, and he cleared his throat. His Adam's apple bobbed as he swallowed. "He's a lot like maple syrup. Every drop is pure and good."

He paused and Avery tensed, anticipating a huge "but" filled with bravado and vitriol.

"But he bottles up so much. When he came back to school after his mom died, I tried to reach him, but he didn't want to talk about his pain."

"That sounds like Miles." Avery smiled as Casper dropped the stick at Paulson's feet.

"Well, I wasn't mature at twenty-one." He threw the stick again. "So maybe I came off like a know-it-all. I thought we had something in common. In a way, I lost my mom too. She's alive, but she's gone. Miles didn't see that as the same. I guess we never truly understand someone else's pain. And maybe I was being selfish. I wanted someone to help me through my grief, and I thought he might do that. Or we could do it together."

Paulson had hinted at his mother last time they talked. Avery wondered what had happened, but didn't ask. He should decide what he was comfortable revealing.

"I was ten when she left." He cleared his throat. "She moved to a compound in the desert, convinced my father belonged to *the corporation*, which in her mind was evil. Dad traveled out there and tried to get her to come home. She refused. My last semester of college, I found her. I got my diploma, ditched my graduation trip to Base Camp Everest, and drove cross-country instead. She met me at the gate and told me Dad had tainted me and nothing could be done. She sent me away without so much as a single tear. And it messed me up. I don't know if I can trust another person enough to have a relationship. It affects friendships too."

Avery didn't know what to say. She had no frame of reference for

Paulson's experience. But it was a loss. Avery wondered if Miles knew Paulson sought out his mother only to have her reject him. He must not. Miles would treat Paulson differently if he did.

"Paulson, I'm so sorry." She reached out and rubbed his arm. "Can I give you a hug?"

"Yeah, no one ever offers that."

As she pulled him in, Avery noticed Paulson smelled like leather and rain. Luxurious sadness. He let go and mustered up a too-bright smile. She put on a similar face when she needed to find something positive.

"I'm going to tell Dad there is too much granite here and we will have a fight on our hands with the environmentalists," he said. "I'll call Miles to say I heard he was the other interested party and let him know we're backing out. I won't mention I saw you. This property's sat abandoned for a few years; Miles should lowball them."

"I think he'd like getting that call." She whistled for Casper, who came running back with his stick.

Paulson picked up a piece of trash off the ground and stuffed it in his pocket. Something about the insignificant gesture reminded Avery of Miles. She hoped he came around. Paulson needed a friend.

"Okay, I have to go." Paulson pointed back and forth at Avery and Casper. "You two never saw me."

Avery nodded. "Bye, Paulson."

"Hey," he said. "Text me when you're in New York. I owe you a drink at Bemelman's."

She stuck out her hand and he shook it.

"Deal."

"Miles is lucky to have you. You're a good friend." A warm smile passed between them.

"You are too." She patted his arm. It might have sounded hollow, but she hoped he knew she meant it.

Paulson chucked the stick into the bow of the canoe and winked at Avery as Casper jumped in. Five minutes later, as she paddled past the Red House, Avery stopped and floated, lost in thought. Finding and keeping friends was so much harder once you got older. She wondered what it would be like if she, Paulson, Miles, Nate, and Lily stayed friends as adults. Maybe Hayes and Anna Catherine too, although she had never met them, and they probably didn't need more friends. They were welcome to join this fictional friend group that gathered at the lake every so often to jump off docks, paddle to islands, and toast one another.

She didn't notice the sliding door of the Red House open, but she heard it close. Out walked Miles in a pair of Ray-Bans, a bottle of chocolate milk in one hand. He swept the sunglasses off his face fighter-pilot style, furrowed his brow, and craned his neck, as if checking to see if she was real.

Avery gulped, partially because she had just told someone about his camp and partially because Miles was wearing shorts that showed off the long, toned legs of a runner. Not just any runner, a former sub-four miler.

"Welcome to the Red House." Miles held his arms out wide like he couldn't believe his luck. Confidence burst out of him. "Someone special once proclaimed it the best house on the lake, so I bought it. Bramble Beach and Loon Cove came with it."

Avery felt heat rise in her cheeks. This was what she got for choosing this spot to daydream about adult friendships.

He finished his milk and set the empty bottle on a table next to a lounge chair.

She studied Miles and his Red House, the triangular roof of the A-frame sloping down the ground behind him. He'd made every change she'd suggested. Sliding doors, a new deck that spanned the width of the front of house, and below it, a new two-level dock with navy chaise lounges. She'd suggested lobster pillows, but he'd argued lobsters didn't live in lakes. A silly argument between two young people, neither of whom expected to ever own the house, had finally been resolved. He'd chosen white pillows, each with a pine tree and star, mimicking the Maine state flag. Perfect.

Miles crouched and grabbed the canoe to avoid a dock bump, then reached in and rubbed behind Casper's ears.

"You always loved this house." His maple-syrup eyes met hers. "I'm trying to do right by it. You had such good ideas for it a decade ago."

Avery glanced at the house. He'd made her vision real, and something about that felt both sad and sweet. She didn't know what to say, so she opted for graciously accepting the truth.

"It'll never be mine, so I'm glad it's yours."

"You don't believe in never. That's how you made a fortune in stationery." He smiled. "How about if I give you the right of first refusal if I sell?"

"Okay." She giggled. He lived near his best friend on the lake he'd once said held his favorite memories. She was genuinely happy for him. "You finally get to live across the cove from Nate."

"Yeah, and check this out." He walked over to a large, round light with flaps on it and turned a knob, flipping the flaps up and down. "Nate and I got Morse code lanterns."

"That's super nerdy." She laughed.

"Not to mention horribly inefficient," he said. "Most times we flash them and then text one another." He closed the flaps and walked back to the canoe. "How 'bout I give you a tour of the inside and you help me pick a backsplash? I'll pay you in chocolate milk."

"I haven't had chocolate milk in ten years." She smirked. It was just one item on a long list of reminders of Miles she'd avoided.

"You swore off chocolate milk?" He clutched at his chest as if pierced by an arrow, and stumbled backwards. "Oof! That hits hard."

"Drama king." Avery lifted her paddle and splashed him. "I can't stay long. Thanks to you, the phones have been ringing off the hook."

"Paddle around back." He pointed a thumb behind him. "I'll meet you."

A minute later, he pulled her green canoe next to his blue one. Casper jumped out first and ran ahead. Miles waded into the water and held the boat steady as she got out. As they climbed the uneven rock steps, he held out his hand. His corded forearm muscles greeted her as he pulled her up to the top.

He kept hold of her hand, leading her to the back door. Those same hands used to gently untie her bikini strings and explore her goose-bumped skin. Avery reminded herself to be cautious. Whatever future she'd imagined for the two of them and this house at nineteen was no longer possible.

"It won't take long." He smiled. "A-frames don't have many rooms. The real estate listing described it as cozy."

A piece of her wanted to relax into a snug, simple life, fueled by his warmth, and never leave. But he dropped her hand, and a cloud moved in front of the warm sun. Her palm cooled in the breeze. A reminder that summers end, dreams die, and hearts break.

And at the first sign of frost, everyone leaves the lake.

CHAPTER FOURTEEN

Miles

JUNE 14 – THE DAY BEFORE THE DAY BEFORE OPENING DAY

Miles dropped Avery's hand because the last time he'd touched her, she'd let him down softly, as if he were an egg. The gentle *thank you for being my friend* hadn't stopped his shell from cracking. If staying friends mattered so much, he wanted to know why she'd kissed him. The only certainty was this house had once held their dreams. Those dreams depended on them being together. Currently, they drifted in an undefined space between ghosted silence and reconciliation. Every time they took a step forward, she put up the friend wall, deepening his frustration.

Once inside, Casper plodded behind and sniffed everything until he found the ideal napping spot in a patch of sun. Given Miles owned only a couple pieces of furniture, there were plenty of choices. No Boa sofa, just his full-size childhood bed in an upstairs bedroom and a small card table in the kitchen nook.

From the second Avery removed her Vanderbilt baseball hat and placed it on the counter, her eyes never stopped sparkling. She gushed over the massive stone fireplace and mentioned the house had "good bones." The short tour ended back in his kitchen, and Miles wanted her to stay. Picking a backsplash while a dog slept under a sunny window, making blueberry pancakes on Saturday mornings, doing the *Sunday Times* crossword. He'd give her anything she wanted.

He selected two small glass bottles of chocolate milk from the refrigerator and handed her one.

She removed the cap and raised her bottle in a toast.

"To your new memories in this old house. May they be happy."

"Thank you. That means a lot." He clinked bottles with hers, drank, and let out his signature "Ahh" after his first sip.

She ran her hand over the white granite and traced a gold vein with her fingernail. "The counters came out beautifully."

"I love them. Thanks for the help." He rinsed their bottle caps and set them on a towel beside the sink.

Avery crossed to his side and carefully laid out the backsplash samples, holding each one up to see how it matched other things in the kitchen. Miles watched as she discarded two, one of which he'd previously deemed a frontrunner.

"Mimi always said decorating a room is like learning to play the piano," she said as she propped the remaining tiles along the back of the counter. "It gets more complicated as you go. But you'll know when you've got it right."

He'd only met Mimi for a weekend, when she'd visited Montressa ten years ago, but Miles loved how Mimi's charm enabled her to get away with telling the truth. Mimi had sensed Miles and Avery's connection immediately.

"Mimi is the only grandmother I know who passed out condoms to her grandchildren." Miles chuckled and watched Avery's face flush.

"Only once." Avery concentrated on the samples. "We were an anomaly."

"I feel special," he said into the bottle's edge before taking a sip. "Every time I tell that story, it brings down the house."

"Miles, I swear." She shook her head and covered her eyes. Ah, her southern accent. He had flustered her enough to stretch out the long "I" in his name.

He gave her a second to let the blush fade from her cheeks.

When she regained her composure, Avery returned to the serious work of picking the backsplash. He recognized the same pensive face she made when she couldn't decide what color to use next in a painting. She narrowed her eyes and shifted side to side, assessing the samples from different angles. Miles scanned her profile. Pretty eyelashes, simple stud earrings, and full lips, twisted in thought.

Those lips had fueled his fantasies the past few nights. He wanted to kiss her again, linger there, and let it lead to exploring her everywhere. Evidently unaware of his desire, Avery started talking about ceramic versus glass tile.

He sighed and came back to the present moment.

She discarded another sample, propped the remaining choices against the wall on the opposite side of the kitchen, and settled next to him. They both stared at the samples. It made him feel better to see her struggling with a task Wes described as *easy peasy*.

"Why is this hard? I just want to eat my Cocoa Puffs and like my kitchen." He picked up one of the milk bottle caps and idly fiddled with it.

"They're all bland and impersonal." She tilted her head in thought. "Your house should give people a glimpse of you. That's why these don't work."

He twirled the bottle cap through his fingers. He wasn't sure how a grouping of tiles could say anything about him, and he didn't care about the backsplash. He'd told her how he'd sought her out in crowds, but there was more. For ten years, he had regretted those five minutes in the parking lot. Finally admitting that might change how she felt. Or it might rip the bandage off old wounds. Avery picking his backsplash kept her here in the Red House. It was too perfect a moment to tarnish.

Miles cringed when Avery's attention shifted to the tie he'd worn on *Bright and Early* last week, discarded on the counter. She picked it up and examined the tag. Chanel. That was how she saw him. Tom Ford suits. Red carpets. The Boa couch. Proof of a glamorous life he wasn't sure he belonged in.

"It was free," he said, as if that made it any better. "My date wore one of their dresses, and I was told I needed to match."

"It's lovely," she said, folding it neatly and putting it back.

Not as lovely as that kiss. Not as lovely as this house he might never have thought twice about if it hadn't been for her. He needed to convince her the life he wanted was here, in this cozy A-frame, with her in it. If he nudged her back to that, maybe she'd discover the small-town guy she once loved.

"Thank you." Avery cleared her throat. "For your much-needed perspective the night Casper bolted. I have moments where I feel so, I don't know. Lost? Misunderstood? Typically, I'm a firm believer in fixing my own problems. You inspired me to envision what I want."

"That's my girl," he blurted out. A split second later, he realized he hadn't intended to sound possessive, or imply he expected her to please him.

"I, um, that came out wrong." He leaned against the counter. "I meant you should, um, do it. One question: Do you know what you want?"

"Um, no?" She giggled and her nose crinkled. "I mean, it's hard to pick one of my brilliant ideas. Give me some time, Magrum."

The flirty swat of the back of her hand on his biceps coupled with the playful use of his last name, which she had never done, and no one ever did, felt like a victory.

"You and I were stars that night." He lightly poked her arm with the bottlecap's edge. "We found a dog no one knew was missing."

He nodded at Casper, who contentedly snored away in a sun-washed slumber.

Avery picked up her milk bottle, her eyes almost melancholy. She traced a drip of sweat down her bottle with her thumb. He let her sit with her thoughts for a moment, but as the pause grew, he wondered if he should fill the void.

With a snap of his hand, Miles flicked the milk bottle top he'd been fiddling with across the kitchen and into a red basket on top of the fridge that came from the house he grew up in. Time had frayed the edges and faded the red to pink. It reminded him of simpler times with his mom and dad. The milk top plunked off the top edge and fell inside.

"You still collect those?" She nodded at the basket.

"Ayuh, out of habit." He couldn't help but smile. "They switched from metal caps to plastic a couple of years ago. Over the years, I collected thousands of metal ones. I kept those, but I recycle the plastic ones because they aren't as cool."

"Where are they?"

Miles disappeared into the mudroom and came back with a plastic bin filled with metal milk bottle caps. Maybe seeing them would erase her impressions of the tie and sofa.

"Dad dropped them off when he and Lily's mom moved to a single-floor house a year ago. I should recycle them, but it feels like throwing out my past. It's silly."

Avery dug through the box and carefully laid caps on the counter in neat lines. Linden Dairy's milk bottle caps had a large gold star on top. Each point reached the edge rimmed in tiny stars.

"There it is." She swept a hand above the caps like a game show host showing off a prize package.

"What?" All she had done was place them in neat, offset rows.

"Your backsplash."

Miles lifted an eyebrow. She wanted him to display what others would have thrown away.

"Don't look at me like that." She laughed and pointed at the caps. "You love stars. They're from your milk, your past. These are the story of you. And the gold stars match the veining in the countertops. I am not leaving until you tell me I'm right."

She dug through the box and pulled out one with a red star.

"Why is this one red?"

"Oh, they used to do special caps at Christmas. I have more."

At that, she danced in place.

"Excellent. The red ones can form a star pattern over the stove to pull out the red in your cabinets. Damn, Miles, your kitchen will be amazing."

If he had hired Avery to decorate his penthouse, he wouldn't have bought that ridiculous sofa, and he would have had more fun.

"Perfection!" Avery snapped him back to the present. "Remember, you gave me right of first refusal when you sell."

"Well, I haven't said yes to this zany bottle-cap backsplash idea." He winked.

"But you will." She put a hand on her hip. "Right?"

He smiled at her and said nothing. She held on to both his wrists and shook them. He resisted for the fun of the flirt.

"Okay, okay. I will." He watched her face bloom with excitement. "And I think you learned how to play Chopin on the piano today. Mimi would be so proud."

The next thing he knew, she was in his arms, his hands resting at the small of her back. He wanted to kiss her again, confess he bought this house because that summer, her dream became his. The two of them in this kitchen, flirting and laughing, was the future he envisioned. Letting her pick whatever she wanted, because his favorite thing was making her happy.

He licked his lips. She moved closer. His arm tightened around her, their shared heat at odds with the need to honor her cautiousness.

"Miles," she breathed.

"Avery." He didn't let go. He kept his gaze steady. "The other night... You took me by surprise, and I think I gave you reason to doubt my interest. I want to kiss you again. This time, I'll get it right."

Her lips quivered, signaling she wanted it too. Miles held his breath, waiting for her consent. Just as it seemed she was about to say yes, Avery lurched in his arms and studied his face. Her mouth pressed into a tight line.

"It's a bad idea."

"Sometimes our worst ideas are our best." He said it firmly, so she knew he meant it. "Like me quitting my job to develop an app that helped people get out of debt. Or you opening a stationery company in a world reliant on email. We're learning to play piano, and we need another chance to get it right. Every time we touch, I feel ... I don't know. Something. Something so wonderful I want to keep feeling it."

"Something? Miles, be practical. Opening day is this weekend and before we know it, we'll be in different cities. You have your camp and an incredible life. But that's not our biggest hurdle."

That hint of her southern accent coupled with the trill in her voice told him Avery was on the verge of saying something hard to verbalize. He loosened his arms around her to give her space. She took a step back.

"Miles, all that time." Her voice cracked with the hint of a tear. "Why didn't you call me? I hurt for so long."

Out the window, a breeze had picked up. Whitecaps rippled across the lake. They had to get past this, which called for honesty on both their parts.

"You know, I suffered a trauma that day. Only a year after witnessing my mother lose her life, I saw a child almost lose his. And afterward, I treated you terribly. No argument there. But no matter how I behaved, I assumed deep down, you knew I never meant to hurt you, and you'd check on me. Instead, you left all my clothes in a bag in my car while I was at work. By the time I found it, you'd left Maine. A day early." His mouth went dry. "That seemed pretty final."

Shock filled her eyes. He didn't want to upset her, but to move past that bad day, they needed to own their regrets and their pain.

"That's unfair." She dropped her head and picked at a cuticle. "The burden shouldn't have been on me. I cried the whole way home and for months after."

"I know. But you know what else isn't fair? You spent a whole magical summer with me and decided after a few terrible minutes that I'm a demon you can't trust. You defined me by my worst moment and didn't give me the chance to apologize or defend myself."

She sighed, took another step back, and leaned against the opposite counter.

"And in those ten years, I wanted so badly to call you, Avery." He heard the desperation in his own voice. "But you'd cut me off too. I waited for a sign you wanted me to reach out. I asked Nate and Lily if you ever mentioned me. They said you never did. Not once. Nate said you barely reacted when they brought me up. It was like you didn't know me. Like you never had."

Sadness, or maybe regret, filled her eyes. "So all that time, you missed me?"

"Of course I missed you. Why do you think I never date someone more than once?"

"Come on, Miles." She rolled her eyes. "You expect me to believe I ruined commitment for you?"

Miles flexed his fist at his side and let it go.

"No, I expect you to believe there isn't another *you* for *me*."

He caught her small smile before she shook her head in disbelief.

"You think we're still the same," she said. "We aren't. You need to let us go."

"I don't want to let us go. You're back in my life and I'm feeling things I haven't felt in a long time for *this* you." He stepped across the alley kitchen and leaned close to her again. "Can you honestly tell me you're not feeling them too?"

"Miles," she said in a resigned voice. "We've lived this story. We know the ending, and it's too painful. Save us from repeating the same mistake. Let us go."

The only thing that mattered to him was her heart, and he didn't want to break it again. No amount of preparation could guarantee their happiness. Maybe her fierce protection of herself doomed her other relationships. As the man who'd done that to her, he was the last person on earth who deserved her. Keeping her heart safe from harm would splinter his into a million tiny fragments.

"Understood." He sighed.

Avery started for the door.

"I need to get back to the front desk. Thanks for the tour. This house is really, um, lovely." It all came out in one hasty burst, as if she needed to get it out as quickly as possible. "Come on, Casper."

Casper rose slowly and side-eyed Miles for ruining his sun nap.

After she shut the door, he watched her through the back window. Everything happened in real time, but he saw it in slow motion. She walked toward her canoe, turned, and took two steps toward the house. Almost instantly, she reversed course and headed back to the boat. She stood there, her gaze alternating between the canoe and his back door. Finally, she pivoted away from the house. Within seconds, she and Casper floated away.

Miles swiped his hand over the counter, bottlecaps skimming in every direction. Some bounced off her Vanderbilt baseball cap, onto the floor. As he picked up the mess, he wondered if he'd pushed her too far. At least she knew how he felt. His assumption that she had moved on easily without him was wrong. Avery had more to say. And if she needed closure, he wanted her to have it, regardless of its impact on him.

CHAPTER FIFTEEN

Avery

JUNE 15 – ONE DAY UNTIL OPENING DAY

Montressa shone bright, ready for another summer. White linens adorned the dining room tables, lounge chairs sat in a neat row along the beach, and every garden bloomed. The lake showed off with little whitecaps rippling across the cove. Avery had worked late last night, creating fresh flower arrangements for each cabin. This afternoon, she and Nate had delivered the flowers and inspected every cabin except one.

"Can you take the last flower arrangement to the Boathouse?" Nate asked. "It's already four, and I need to get over to Karaoke Bowl."

Every year, the night before the resort opened, the Coopers threw a pre-season staff meeting followed by dinner and a fun activity. This year, Nate chose the bowling alley/karaoke bar in a neighboring town. A good plan, since the forecast called for rainstorms.

"Oh, and put this bottle of Prosecco in the fridge while you're there." He placed a chilled bottle in her free hand. "A welcome gift for Maine's biggest social media star, our first guest in the new Boathouse."

"Sure." Avery took the bottle and glanced at the label. The best Prosecco Montressa carried.

"Thank you, Avery. We wouldn't be ready to open without you," Nate said. "If you don't feel like coming tonight, you'll have this whole place to yourself. Last quiet night until October."

"I can't think of any reason I'd miss singing while bowling." Avery smiled. "Is Lily coming?"

Lily had been busy with end-of-the-year school picnics and award assemblies, and Avery hoped to drag her to a corner of the bowling alley and catch her up on everything, from the kiss to Miles's kitchen.

"Ayuh." Nate winked. "She needs a night out."

Avery headed down the path to the Boathouse, thinking about the pre-season kickoff party ten years earlier, when she and Miles had shared glances across the Maine-themed mini-golf course in another nearby town. There was no bigger thrill than realizing your crush might also have a crush on you.

A day ago, as she contemplated getting back in her canoe outside Miles's house, she'd come close to running back inside. Her heart wanted him, but her head couldn't get past their fractured past and a future living apart. For a relationship to work, they needed to be more mature this time. Miles's self-awareness had grown in the last decade, but dating women only once hardly proved he was ready for commitment.

A gust of wind fractured the gentle breeze, blowing her hair back. Across the water, a swath of heavy rain darkened the horizon. Every so often, a bolt of lightning lit the billowing clouds above the storm. Beautiful from a distance, but that angry sky was headed her way. She shivered. Best to check this last thing off her list and get to the party.

It took two tries to open the Boathouse door. She made a mental note to make sure Wes fixed that doorknob first thing in the morning.

As she walked inside, Avery let out a sigh and admired her work. What was dusty and drab was now woodsy and dreamy—a room Maine's top influencer would immediately post, bringing more attention to Montressa.

Avery placed the Prosecco in the fridge and double-checked the cabin. She pulled the duvet taut on the bed, fluffed the pillows, and opened each dresser drawer to ensure they were clean and empty. She walked to the desk by the door and straightened a lampshade.

Despite the room's metamorphosis, it still brought back thoughts of Miles. Even though she'd stopped a second kiss from happening in his kitchen twenty-four hours ago, she wanted to feel his firm lips on hers again. Like that summer, his arms wrapped around her transformed her into a spinning top, kept in motion by the delicious thrum of his touch. Hearing Miles admit he felt a spark only made her own feelings burn brighter. But these days they led opposite lives; his exciting and bold, hers boring and uncertain. Miles resumed classes at NYU in the fall. And her MBA started in two months. Both programs were huge time commitments. The distance alone would be challenging.

Avery fluffed a couch pillow and shook it more vigorously than necessary. Never asking about Miles or reacting to news of him had manifested her worst fear. He'd spent the last decade longing for breadcrumbs she never dropped, which had convinced him to stay away. What could have been if she had texted him or casually brought him up to their friends?

She might have reached out if she'd been in a better place the year after they broke up. Instead, she had labeled him the villain. All over five bad minutes. Thinking of it now embarrassed her, but none of it convinced her to apologize. After all, she had been the one trying to help him after he'd resuscitated Max Perry. She might have gone about it in a misguided way, but Miles had ended things.

It had required so much willpower to keep her feelings hidden from everyone, which hadn't stopped the hurt. But maybe Avery needed to free herself from this limbo between anger and love. Once the resort was up and running smoothly, she'd sit down with him and let it all out.

The inside of the Boathouse grew dimmer by the second. The dark cloud must be closing in. She crossed to the closet and arranged the bathrobes, lost in the memory of sliding her arms into the sleeves of Miles's warm jacket the night Casper had run away. The scent of a forest after an August rain had escaped in a cloud of hot air as he wrapped it around her.

The rattling of the Boathouse doorknob startled her. Miles stood in the doorway with windswept hair, a tan face, and a navy Henley. Working on the lakefront gave him a glow-up no studio could. A heat rose in her neck and cheeks.

"Nate asked me to bring these down for the influencer, who's a charcuterie expert," he said, maneuvering a large cutting board and two brown bags inside. "There's a storm coming. What are you doing here?"

He handed Avery the cutting board, shaped like the state of Maine and perfect for social media content. Miles opened the fridge and loaded the shelves with cheese and cured meats.

"Same thing as you," she said. "Getting the room ready for Maine's biggest social media star. Are charcuteries still a thing?"

"They were all over New York couple years back, but everything takes its time reaching Maine." He laughed and closed the refrigerator.

Thunder clapped above, and a gust of wind sucked the door shut with a loud *bang*. Her thoughts went straight to the broken doorknob.

"Oh no! Are we locked in?" She walked to the door.

Miles strode to the door in what seemed like three steps and rattled the knob.

"Yep," he said, picking up his phone and typing. *He better be texting for help*.

She rattled the knob, but it wouldn't budge.

"I'm afraid we've been set up. Maine's biggest influencer"—Miles let out a laugh and held out his phone—"is a comedian who posts videos of his dog dressed as a woman. There's not a charcuterie board in sight on his feed."

It took Avery a second to piece it all together. Nate had sent her here with Prosecco, and then he'd sent Miles here with…

"Miles." She slapped a hand over her mouth. "Nate Parent-Trapped us!"

"He meant well, Pepper." Miles swept a hair off her face and let out a laugh. "I think he and Lily really want us together."

She gulped. No one would return to Montressa until well past midnight. And this room had only one perfectly made bed.

"We can climb out a window." Miles took his phone and placed it on the desk next to hers. "But as I see it, there's no one on property for a few hours, a storm's coming, and we need to talk."

A chain reaction of nerves tensed up her spine. The Boathouse was the last place she wanted to have this conversation with him. In theory, she could say what she needed to say. In reality, she wasn't so sure.

She leaned back against the locked door as Miles stepped forward, the aroma of summer rain and pine trees floating ahead of him. He placed a hand flat on the door, beside her head. Without him so much as touching her, she felt him everywhere. His heavenly scent, coupled with his unrelenting stare sent the familiar thrum of arousal pulsing through her. Avery froze.

"Here's the thing, Avery Astor Easton."

The tiny hairs at the back of her neck prickled at the sound of her middle name rolling off his lips.

He shook his head and locked his gaze with hers. "You're a fool if you think I'm going to let us go after that kiss."

Amber flecks twinkled in his chestnut eyes. She remembered Paulson comparing Miles to maple syrup, pure and good, and Avery nearly melted.

Miles closed in, his breath brushing her neck, his voice low and gravely. "I tried to walk away and forget you once. It didn't work. And I'm done dancing around this fire with you."

Avery licked her lips. This time, she wouldn't stop his kiss.

Miles cocked the slightest smile and whispered, "I can't forget you, Pepper. There's a case of your lip balm at the CVS checkout. I shop there because reminders of you? They're a welcome, daily occurrence."

Miles moved a fraction closer, the dimple in his chin shadowed like a crater in the dim light.

"There's a better ending to what we had," he said. "We both know that."

Avery couldn't tell if it was resolve or seduction in his voice. Her eyes fell to the bottom button of his Henley. Confident Miles and his exposed collarbone were taking her words away. It was all she could do to keep from imagining him pressing into her. Avery let out a tiny gasp. He studied her for a second, pushed away from the wall, and cleared his throat.

"We need to talk." Miles extended a hand, nodding toward the couch.

The first drop of rain hit the roof, clearing a path for other raindrops to follow until the cloud released them all and the sun returned. Her feelings had billowed inside long enough. If there was no blue sky after she released her truth, so be it. She could weather what came next.

The time had come to unveil her hurt.

"Okay." She took his hand. "Let's talk."

She hoped he couldn't feel her shaking as he led her to the sofa. Miles sat on the coffee table and faced her, their legs so close she felt the hairs on his calves standing on end. He furrowed his brow, rested his elbows on his knees, and steepled his fingers together.

"That last day," he said. "I didn't give you the opportunity to talk. It may be ten years too late, but I want you to have the closure you never got. Say whatever you need to say to me. I promise to listen."

Avery's stomach tightened into a ball, but she resolved to speak through her nerves. She took a deep breath.

Start at the beginning of the end.

"That day. In the parking lot," she began. "You were shaken up, and processing several traumas, so I understood why you pushed me away. But you made it clear multiple times that we weren't ... well ... what I thought we were. I loved you. I thought you felt that too."

Time had never dulled the pain radiating through her chest now. Miles waited while she breathed away the growing knot below her breastbone.

"You said you never loved me." She gulped, reliving the pain of hearing him say it. "What was I supposed to do? I haven't found the thing I want most in life, a stable relationship. And it might not be fair or true, but I blame you. I deserved better."

He stood and crossed to the fireplace, his knuckles turning white as he gripped the mantle. She tried not to jump at the next bolt of thunder. He must have noticed the chill in the room, because he took a match off the mantle and lit the fire that had already been set up. Her first thought was someone would have to clean the fireplace tomorrow. Her second was firelight transformed the birch tree bed into a lush, romantic sanctuary.

Miles watched the flame grow.

"I treated you terribly and I am so sorry. You have no idea." His voice came out soft and measured, as if he had carefully prepared for this moment. "I didn't contact you because there was no erasing what I'd done, and I didn't think I deserved forgiveness. But now? Avery. You're back, and there's this feeling I only get with you. I live for the little everyday moments we share. Doesn't it feel like we've waited long enough?"

At the word *waited*, her teeth clenched. For months afterward, she'd cried herself to sleep and cried herself awake. She'd tried so hard not to wait for someone who didn't want her. Avery stood and met him at the fire.

"Waiting wasn't an option." She pressed a finger into his chest. "You shut me out."

He fell quiet, but when she glared at him, he spoke.

"Honestly, Avery, what was supposed to happen to us?" His eyes pleaded with her. "Summer was over. We had no money. Nashville and New Haven were more than a day's travel apart. After my graduation, you still had another two years of school. Paying off my insurmountable pile of student debt meant I had to take the best job I could get, even if I was miserable. I had no connections in Tennessee and no money to visit you. How were we supposed to work all of that out? I'm not saying it's an excuse, but the odds weren't in our favor."

Avery bristled. If Miles had loved her, he would've found a way.

"I don't know!" she cried as the rain pounded the roof. "But people figure things out. They make love work. You weren't willing to try. You left me crumpled in a parking lot and ghosted me."

He sighed and thumped his fist on the mantle.

"I regret everything that happened after I pulled that little boy out of the water. You were there for me, and I was so mean." He rubbed his palm on his forehead. "You find silver linings and bright sides to everything, so I figured you'd move on. This summer, I realized the pain didn't end for you when you left Maine. I admit I should have called, but regret and grief overwhelmed me. You gave me the one thing you can never get back and never give to anyone else. I tainted a moment you should have cherished. There was no scenario under which I deserved your love."

He paused and rested his head in his palm. "You gave me your heart, and I didn't, um, I don't deserve you," he mumbled.

Outside the window, a pine tree thrashed around in the wind. She had always been thankful he'd made her feel special and safe her first time.

"Miles, I don't regret that night. Or us." Avery rested her hand on top of his. "But, grieving you swallowed me whole. Everyone kept telling me to let you go, but I couldn't. I stopped going to class. I stayed in bed and slept or cried. I hated waking up because that's when it hurt the most. You were my first so many things, including my first heartbreak."

"I didn't know." His voice shook. "I wish you had called. I would've—"

"I wasn't sure how you'd react. Rational thinking is hard when you're suffering from depression. With each passing sleepless night, it grew easier to believe the worst in you."

Tears welled in her eyes. Maybe now he understood. Miles's hand quivered under hers.

The rain poured down and neither one of them moved. What felt like minutes later, Avery looked up to find his beautiful brown eyes filled with sorrow, love, and pain. They'd each carried their own grief for what they'd lost. The last thing she ever wanted for Miles was more grief.

"It's like Tolstoy said"—she stepped closer—"'we lost because we told ourselves we lost.'"

Avery lifted her hands to his chest, her right hand over his heart. She pressed her face into his soft shirt and let his now smoky scent, the crackle of the fire, and the sound of rain falling on the roof calm her. His thumb rubbed tiny circles in the small of her back, slowly releasing her tension.

"Pepper." His tone was playful, like he'd said her name halfway through a grin. "Did you read *War and Peace*?"

He kissed the top of her head and pulled her closer.

"I read it after my engagement ended, because the person I missed most was you," she said. "I see why you like it so much. It's like a nineteenth-century scripted reality series with love, schemes, duels, soirees, religious conversions, trysts, love, and massacres."

Miles lifted a loose tendril of hair and tucked it behind her ear, letting his thumb caress the spot that made her buzz. "You said love twice."

"I like to think love can happen twice." Avery laced her fingers behind his neck.

"I hope so," he said.

"Miles." She wanted to exhale his name over and over, in the evening, in the morning, and every time in between. For so many days she lost count. "You know how you told me to envision what I want? I want this."

He lifted her hand off his chest and kissed it, never taking his eyes off hers. Avery tingled all over. They were on verge of something wonderful, and she wasn't going to stop herself this time.

As if reading her mind, he pulled her closer. Miles slowly kissed her. His hands cupped her face, each tiny movement demanding more of her until his tongue begged at her lower lip. It was nothing like the kiss the night they'd searched for Casper. This one held want. It held heat. It held promise and the smoky aroma of a glowing fire.

Somewhere outside a tree branch fell, followed by a vicious clap of thunder. Avery jolted in his arms, her lips buzzing. He quietly contemplated her, not a trace of regret in his soft eyes. She ran her thumb along his stubbled jaw, stopping at the dent in his chin. The thrum inside her went liquid.

"Avery." His brow furrowed. The care and concern in his sultry eyes echoed his voice. "I want this too, but if you need us to take our time, we can."

Consent suited Miles.

"We've already taken our time," she whispered. "I'm ready. What about you?"

"I'm a selfish man," he said between kisses. "I've wanted to explore every inch of you since I saw you on the dock in May."

His warm hand skimmed under her shirt. He brushed the soft skin above her hip as he pressed his forehead against hers. Their eyes locked, and a second wave of his deep woods scent pushed her over the edge. She had to have him. Avery rocked her hips into his. He was hard. Miles was ready for this too.

"I'll go at whatever pace you set," he said. "But first, we need to talk safety."

She pulled him to the desk and retrieved their phones. After they exchanged test results, his brow furrowed. He ran a hand down his face.

"Um, I don't have a condom with me." He placed his phone back on the desk, rocked back on his heels, and put his hands in his pockets. His eyes traveled to the ceiling and his cheeks flushed. Miles was a little embarrassed, which somehow made him more irresistible.

So he didn't carry a condom with him—a built-in pause button to consider whether sex was something he wanted. She liked that, along with his current state of dishevelment. Avery placed a hand on the middle of his chest and pushed him until he leaned against the desk, his long legs cutting a diagonal to the floor.

Miles combed his hair with his fingers, messing it up in frustration. He was a brewing storm of tumultuous angst.

He dropped his hands. "What I wouldn't give for just one..."

"Just one?" Avery smirked. She opened the desk drawer and pulled out the giant box of Golden Tiger condoms. The ones he had shoved in the drawer that day with Wes. "How long will it take us to get through two hundred fifty? Was it eight a day for a month?"

"Ha." Miles took the box and shook it. "Not to sound full of myself, but past me was a genius."

"I'm the genius." Avery wrapped her hands around his neck. "You only wished for one."

"Only because I have other tricks to make you moan and fist the bedsheets we're about to dishevel." He kissed along her clavicle. His strong, stealthy hands grazed over her curves and flirted with her waistband.

"It's only fun if we feel safe. If one of us gets overwhelmed and wants to stop, we stop. Agreed?"

"Mm-hmm." She could abide by Miles's acknowledgment of her agency and wouldn't deny herself the elation of fisting those sheets.

He pulled the paintbrush out of her topknot, gathered her hair into a loose ponytail, and gently tugged it back, blazing a path of deliberate open-mouth kisses up her neck, each one igniting a spark that rippled through her. Miles worked his way to the spot below her ear, his breath hot on her goose bumped skin. She groaned when he skimmed her earlobe with his teeth and pushed her body closer to his.

"Beautiful," he murmured. "I'll need more than one night for the things I want to do with you."

This was happening, and it was better than Avery had imagined. Her mouth went dry. Words jumbled.

He moved slowly, too slowly, pulling off her tee like he was opening a fragile gift and pushing aside her bra strap like it was tissue. He admired what he'd unwrapped and shook his head in disbelief, leaning down to kiss that freckle beside her breast.

"I missed this freckle." Kiss.

"I missed your soft skin." Kiss.

"I missed my Pepper." Nibble.

His whisper, his hands smoothing over her sides, and the tickle of his hot breath made Avery writhe in desperation. She hooked her fingers through his belt loops and pulled him to the bed. He eased her onto the mattress, hoisting himself above her so he could gaze down on her.

"You sure?" he asked.

For a split second, she realized her concept for the bed had worked. It felt like being in a tree with Miles. Hidden from the world, wrapped in a safe, warm, comfortable dream. Avery tugged his hips toward hers.

"I'm sure."

CHAPTER SIXTEEN

Miles

JUNE 21 - FIRST DAY OF SUMMER
Miles paddled onto Montressa's beach and savored the crunchy whoosh of sand parting into the shape of the blue canoe's bow. Sam had come home over the weekend. He'd sat out on Montressa's front porch and chatted with guests, but kept asking to get out on his beloved lake. After Nate finished his late morning meeting, he and Miles were taking Sam fishing.

Arriving early to make sure they had enough bait was an excuse to see Avery. They'd spent the last week savoring quiet moments together. She'd slept all but one night at the Red House. They'd made breakfast every morning in his kitchen and planned their day. In the evenings, he read on his dock while she painted, this time seated on Adirondack chairs. One day, he sat on the double lounge chair answering emails and gently playing with her hair while she dozed off with her head in his lap.

A day ago, she'd examined the firefly tattoo in depth.

"You had them keep our initials in the wings." She touched her heart. "I love it."

"Ayuh, makes it so you never leave my side."

He liked to think he'd understood the single tear in her eye. Sometimes, their years of mutual longing crashed into him too. The tear dropped onto the tattoo and she'd kissed it away.

Miles had forgotten how Avery always slept with some part of her touching him. Sometimes he'd wake to an arm across his torso, other times the tip of her little toe brushed his shin. He loved how she fell asleep with her head in the crook of his shoulder. Their bodies were making up for lost time.

Miles raised his arms, stretched his tired muscles, and climbed out of the canoe. Ever since the night in the Boathouse five days earlier, he'd been tired in the best way possible. He craved more of this exhaustion and couldn't get enough of her sweet moans as he kissed his way up her soft inner thigh. As soon as they climaxed, he wanted to make love to her all over again.

He'd had a lot of great sex in the last decade, but things had never gone past casual. This eclipsed that. He wanted Avery to know where she stood—that this relationship meant something. He never felt lonely with Avery, even when she wasn't beside him. And he didn't want to be apart from her for long.

But when he thought too much about his life melding with hers, fear crept in. If he loved her, it would hurt more to lose her. He knew what a loss like that meant. He and his father had suffered so much pain when his mother passed away. It left Miles convinced that loving someone led to losing them with no chance of getting them back.

After Maisie Magrum had passed away, Miles and his father handled the loneliness differently. His father quickly started dating Lily's mom, which seemed to fill the void. That same void consumed Miles and he convinced himself the only way to avoid losing his whole world a second time was to never to love someone so deeply again. He'd confronted some of that in therapy. And while Avery was everything he wanted, the same fear simmered below the surface. Tumbling head over heels scared him.

Miles got out of his boat and tucked his paddle inside, thinking of the easy evening routine he and Avery had settled into. They cooked dinner together and spent the night in his full-size bed. He liked being close to her, but they could use a little more room. He'd asked Wes to make him a larger bed, one with spindles. He didn't mention this to Wes, but Miles liked having something either one of them could grab onto when they made love.

In some ways, it felt like they'd settled into couple life too quickly. He'd skipped past the light-hearted thrill of asking her out and hearing her say yes. They'd missed out on the end of the first-date roller-coaster dip of *I don't want this night to end* followed by *It doesn't have to be over yet* and the emotional high of *Want to come up?*

With so much experience, Miles should know how to make a woman feel special. But most of his dates were events that he didn't plan. He'd been an arm to hold, a tall smile, a stand-in. Avery deserved to be charmed, dazzled, revered. Miles wanted to plan something that left her dancing across water.

He'd considered taking her to the City for a weekend or recreating their first date and hiking up Linden Mountain. There was always kayaking to an island for a picnic. But all of those choices seemed too easy. She deserved something unique, romantic, and intimate. Something picked just for her.

He climbed the granite ledge to the lodge, hoping to catch her for a pre-fishing kiss or two. Nate's meeting ended in about a half hour. Miles didn't know the meeting's purpose, but lately Nate had been talking about fixing the potholes in the driveway before the Fourth of

July. It made sense, given they might sell out for the summer once *Bright and Early* broadcasted live from Montressa.

When Miles didn't find Avery at the front desk, he wandered out to the front circle. At the bottom of the steps to the loft, his FaceTime rang. He slid his phone out of his pocket.

Hayes.

He should take the call. The realtor had emailed both of them the night before. The other potential buyer of the corporate retreat had backed out. He and Hayes should submit an offer. Miles sat on a bench hidden under the sweeping boughs of a pine tree. He could see out, but no one could see in. Children called it "the spy bench."

He answered, and Hayes and Anna Catherine lit up his screen. Baby Lennox sat on Hayes's lap, facing the camera.

"Hey, baby girl, I've missed you," Miles cooed. Lennox screamed in surprise at the sight of him and tried to grab the phone, but she lacked the necessary dexterity.

Miles moved his face off-camera and then back into view. "Peek-a-boo!"

He did it again and again, delighting Lennox, who cooed and giggled. A tree bough swung aside, and Avery stepped under the magnificent pine. A blush warmed his face.

"I thought you were playing peek-a-boo with me." She giggled.

He felt his entire face and chest light up at the sight of her. She'd showered, and her damp hair had started to curl; Miles's favorite look.

"Come here. I want you to meet my friends," he said.

Avery nestled beside him. He wrapped his arm around her and her heavenly floral vapor greeted him.

"Hayes, Anna Catherine, and Lennox." He pulled Avery into the frame. "Meet Avery."

Anna Catherine's jaw dropped as if she were the one meeting a celebrity.

"Avery, you exist." Hayes's big-screen voice hummed. "We're so happy to meet you."

"OMG." Avery gaped at Miles with wide eyes and pointed at the phone. "He sounds like he does in the movies."

"We can't wait to meet you in person next weekend." Anna Catherine wriggled on screen, overly giddy with excitement.

"And you too. I mean me. I mean, I can't wait to meet y'all." Her Southern accent signaled she was starstruck. Miles ran his thumb in a circle on her shoulder blade, hoping she wasn't feeling put on the spot.

"Oh my goodness." Avery palmed her face. "Let me start over. It's a pleasure to meet you."

It sounded smoother. She'd be fine. Anna and Hayes were used to bringing conversations with fans down to a normal energy level. He'd witnessed it a thousand times.

Miles kissed her temple and Anna Catherine squealed. From there, he lost control of the conversation. Anna had so many questions for Avery. Hayes and Miles smiled as the two women prattled on about Lennox, fashion, why babies loved cell phones, and how much Anna loved the Peppered Page.

Miles envisioned Avery and Anna Catherine becoming friends and sharing secrets; ones that didn't involve him and some that did. The two couples could do things together, like go to farmers markets and concerts. Nothing would make him happier.

But that little voice inside him kept telling him he'd lose her.

He cringed, hoping no one saw his rising anxiety. Having her beside him would be less overwhelming if he could get past the fear that losing her would be unbearable. Rationally, it was an unrealistic thought—one that shouldn't prevent him from moving forward with the relationship.

He wasn't sure he could ever love without this paralyzing fear. In hindsight, it had surfaced their first summer, after Avery said she loved him. He hadn't said it back, but not because he didn't love her. He'd feared what loving her could mean.

He hadn't said "I love you" to anyone since his mother's death because he and his mother had said it so many times in her last days, the words took on a new meaning. *I love you* came to mean *Goodbye. Forever.*

Seeing Hayes on FaceTime made Miles wish he could confess his fears to someone who understood heartbreaking, permanent loss. Nate tried to understand, but couldn't relate. Miles's father was inaccessible on the Appalachian Trail. After years of his father dropping subtle and not-so-subtle hints, Lily's mom had finally agreed to hike the trail this spring. Miles didn't want his problems to ruin their good time. That left Hayes, the one person who had lived almost the same story. But asking Hayes to reopen his wounds felt unfair.

This anxiety made no sense when something he had always wanted was going so well, but he worried Avery might rethink her decision to take him back if he admitted the dark thoughts roiling through him. He needed to keep things light and happy this early in their rekindling. Maintain the just-got-back-together bliss. Take her on that incredible date he had yet to plan.

Anna Catherine and Avery wrapped up and everyone said goodbye, with Hayes asking to visit the corporate retreat when he came in a couple of weeks and maybe make an offer.

"Your friends are so nice," Avery said after they hung up, nuzzling a kiss into his neck.

"You're easy to like." He leaned into her kiss and let the spark pulsing through him remind him of what made Avery so special. He could face his fears later. First, he needed to take her out. So many times they lost count.

Crunching gravel interrupted their kiss. A familiar black Rivian SUV pulled into the circle. Avery's elbow nudged Miles in the ribs as a pair of black and red Air Jordans hit the ground. Paulson.

He better not be coming on the fishing trip with Sam, Miles thought. Avery gripped Miles's leg. Whenever she touched his thigh, it made him feel simultaneously strong and needed. And hard. Thankfully, the boughs of the tree hid them well.

Paulson entered the lodge and greeted Nate as the door swung shut.

"What's he doing here?" Miles asked.

Avery ran her teeth over her lower lip as if she knew something. "Didn't he call you? He promised to call you."

"Why would he call me?"

"Carter Hotels was the other party interested in the corporate retreat, but they decided to pass," she said. "He said he'd call and let you know, so you could lower your offer."

Miles wondered if Paulson's change of heart was a trap. Maybe Paulson still wanted the retreat and had counted on Avery telling Miles in hopes he'd lower his offer, allowing Carter Hotels to buy the property without competition. That would be pretty slimy, even for Paulson. Carter Hotels could outbid anyone. Miles needed to be careful. He rarely called in favors, but maybe he should ask some local friends to dig around and find out. Jeanette heard a lot of gossip at the diner.

"Paulson wants to open a small fishing lodge near a river." Avery's green eyes widened. "What if he tries to buy Montressa? We should go in."

"Sweetheart, Nate can handle it and it's not our decision to make," Miles said, trying to sound reassuring. "He knows about Paulson. And he'd never sell Montressa."

Avery leaned her head onto his shoulder, sending an ease through him. An ease she didn't seem to feel. She picked at a hangnail and jiggled a leg.

"He promised to call you," she said.

There was nothing they could do about whatever motivated Paulson not to call, and Miles didn't want to get into it. She needed a distraction. He said the first thing that came to his mind.

"They're putting in the backsplash today. All the guys on the crew love the milk bottle caps."

The leg kept jiggling.

"I can't wait to see it," she said. "Which reminds me. Will you show me how to make your mom's macaroni and cheese?"

"Ayuh." He brushed a thumb along her hairline. His mother would have loved hearing her ask how to make her prized recipe.

They waited silently for a minute, half hidden under the giant pine, drinking in the balsam breeze.

"Speaking of dinner," she said. "You need something other than a kitchen table made of sawhorses and plywood. You also need a couch, a rug, and bedroom furniture."

"Maybe I should make a list." He winked.

"Well, I'm never gonna tell someone not to make a list." She giggled and the bouncing leg slowed to a stop.

Shopping for furniture wasn't a special outing, but Portland had furniture stores and romantic date potential. They could shop and have lunch at the same lobster shack where the spark had ignited that summer. Afterward, they'd drive up the coast and stay in the nicest suite at a waterfront boutique hotel. It felt like a natural progression and not too much, too fast.

"Decorating is overwhelming. But you're so good at it." He cleared his throat. "Will you help me find furniture? We could—"

The front door to the lodge opened, and Paulson and Nate stood under the portico with Sam. Everyone shook hands.

"That didn't take long," Avery whispered as she gripped Miles's thigh again.

"Thank you both," Paulson said. "I'm excited to help with your new bar. I have some other ideas too, for later."

"We'll gladly pay you for your time," Nate said.

"Unnecessary." Paulson studied the lodge. "This is a special place.

I admire what you and your father have here."

Miles was certain Paulson wanted something. He'd catch up with Nate on the boat.

"Wait," said Nate. "I'm having a bachelor party canoe trip on the Kennebec River the last week of July. It's me, Miles, Hayes Preston, and some of my friends from high school and college. Join us."

Miles's chest sank. While it was Nate's party, Miles wished he'd had some input. People in large groups jockeyed for position. Paulson made everything about himself. He'd be loud and insufferable.

Avery must have sensed his frustration because she swatted his knee and whispered, "Be kind."

"That's awfully nice, Nate," Paulson said. "Text me the dates and I'll see if I can make it. That reminds me, I need to call Miles."

"Mm-hmm." Avery nodded.

"But right now, I've gotta get back to the City." Paulson sighed. "I'll call him next week."

As the driveway dust from Paulson's Rivian SUV settled, Miles took Avery's hand and led her to the lobby. Sam patted his son on the back.

"Dad," said Nate. "Paulson's bar idea enables us to be a wedding destination. Guests will love it. With Avery's marketing and Miles's website, Montressa's future gets brighter every day."

"You've got good friends." Sam smiled. "Each Cooper makes our mark on Montressa. Now it's your turn. I'm glad to see you breathing new life into it."

Sam wiped away a tear.

"We owe you both so much." Nate nodded at Miles and Avery. "What's next in your plan?"

Miles felt a rush of pride. The Coopers trusted his and Avery's instincts.

"My friends from CashCache are beta testing the new reservation system," Miles said. "But the more immediate need is filling this summer's vacancies."

"I know it's early in the season, but we're just over half capacity today," Avery said. "The only cabin booked all summer is the Boathouse."

"Victoria and I broadcast live from here next week," Miles said. "That should help."

"I hope so." Sam put his hands in his pockets. "It's so nice of Victoria to come back."

Avery let out an irritated sigh only Miles seemed to notice. He couldn't figure out the tension there, especially with half a summer's worth of reservations at stake. But Avery didn't understand his distrust of Paulson. They each had people in their lives who didn't work with their personalities.

"It's national television." He squeezed Avery's hand. "And free advertising worth hundreds of thousands of dollars."

"The thing is," said Avery, "everything with Victoria comes at a price."

"You're both right," Nate said. "But we can put up with a day of diva behavior for that level of exposure."

Sam fanned his hand at the three of them and chuckled.

"Enough shop talk," he said. "Let's go fishing."

As Nate and Sam headed outside, Miles hung back with Avery. He wanted to let her know how much she mattered to him. He couldn't sort out his own feelings yet, but she checked off every box he had for the perfect partner.

"I leave for a few days in Minnesota tomorrow, and the camp I'm observing doesn't allow cell phones." He picked up a strand of her hair and tugged it. "Dinner tonight?"

She lifted a hand to his stubble and her eyes sparkled like sunlight on water.

"Yep, it's a date."

"Dinner at my house isn't a date. It's too ... every day." Miles frowned.

Nothing he came up with felt special enough. "I want to take you somewhere amazing."

She wrapped her pinkie around his.

"You already do. I love your every day. Being out on the lake with you. Stargazing on the dock. Eating dinner at your house. Those are the moments I feel most content."

Relief swept through him. She didn't want a big show. Avery shook his pinkie and gazed up at him. Her eyes were almost emerald today.

"If we're going to make this work, we'll need to share our 'real worlds' eventually," she said. "I want to see your other every day. The one in New York. Meet your friends, see your apartment, maybe go out to dinner or to one of your parties. And I want to take you to my family's house in Virginia."

Miles tried to swallow the lump in his chest. It didn't move. Those were steps to something more permanent, which sounded wonderful and frightening at the same time.

Nate stuck his head in the door. "Miles, let's go."

Avery dropped his pinky and kissed him with lips that felt warmer than the sun. He'd wished for that kiss on every birthday candle, found penny, and errant eyelash for the last ten years. Fears aside, he knew he wanted to be with her forever. He needed to figure out how to get himself there.

As he walked to the dock, the only thought running through his mind was not to mess anything up. Not this time. Not ever.

CHAPTER SEVENTEEN

Avery

JUNE 26

The last four days had felt like eight and despite the relatively quiet evening at the front desk, Avery was slightly jittery. Miles had been without a cell phone somewhere in the woods of Minnesota, and she hadn't been able to stop her mind from analyzing the time they'd spent together. In some ways, they had picked up where they left off that summer. He'd been leaving her donuts again, sometimes with quotations or poems attached. They'd shared kisses when he put the Mail Jeep in reverse and looped his arm behind her headrest. Miles had started teasing her about hoarding half his clothes.

But there were differences too. This was not the hasty, inexperienced Miles Magrum from ten years ago. The new Miles Magrum knew where to go and what to do with her body. He paid attention to her cues, responded to her moans, and took his time coaxing the euphoria out of her, sometimes twice, sometimes in sync with his own. When it was over, he'd stay in her embrace or hold her as she rested with her head in the nook below his shoulder. Lying in bed with Miles reminded Avery of lazing on a screened porch during a summer rain.

A little bit like earth, a little bit like water, a lot like heaven.

But summers came and went on the lake. When she'd joined his FaceTime with Hayes and Anna Catherine the previous week, Avery detected a glimmer of fear or regret in Miles's expression. She couldn't put her finger on it, but something seemed off.

She checked her text messages. Nothing.

Montressa had been open for ten days. Enough time for issues to surface with the front desk staff, who were all college students. The double-booked cabin was easily fixed since they had vacancies. Two staff members hadn't shown up for shifts one morning, one spent too much time chatting with other staff, and one always let the phone go to voicemail. Every minor issue had resulted in finger-pointing.

Guests hadn't noticed the discord, but the staff needed to work together once the busiest weeks of summer kicked off on the Fourth of July. Backing each other up mattered when the resort turned busy. In an effort to help the team bond, Avery had sent them on a sunset seaplane ride. She'd stayed behind and taken desk duty so everyone could go, and the quiet night left plenty of time to think about Miles.

He'd be back from Minnesota tomorrow, and she knew what he'd want to do. He'd picked up a new ski boat the day before he left and hadn't had time to take it out on the water. It sat moored at his dock. Tomorrow was her day off and she was excited to water-ski, cruise the lake, and have a picnic. Maybe he'd let her drive it. It didn't matter what they did, as long as they did it together.

Avery scrolled through her text messages. Still nothing. The week of no contact was eating at her. The camp wrapped up this afternoon, and she'd assumed he'd text her the second he got his phone back. That's what boyfriends did. Him further prolonging of a week of no contact made her question his devotion.

This wasn't a summer fling. Or was it? She wanted commitment, but she didn't know what he wanted. He'd mentioned wanting a relationship in the Boathouse. But he'd frowned when she suggested taking him to see the house she grew up in or visiting him in the City, both of which seemed like a natural progression.

When wild blueberry season drifted into pumpkin-spice-latte season, their lives would change. Canoe commutes would be replaced by long drives. Miles would go back to his glitzy parties, finishing his master's degree, and working on his bereavement camp. He might want something more casual to go along with his busy lifestyle.

Avery would start her MBA at Dartmouth—another thing she was unsure about. Given how little her first semester classes interested her, she'd begun doubting whether pursuing an MBA made sense. It felt redundant to get the degree when she'd already successfully run a business. But withdrawing meant casting herself adrift, which ran counter to her need to get things done. She didn't want confusion; she wanted a plan.

Instead of connecting with her future classmates online, she'd started exploring other career options. Maybe the Peppered Page's new owners could help her find a job in a creative field. Late one night, on a whim, she'd researched interior decorator certification and textile classes at the Fashion Institute of Technology in Manhattan. It had been fun reimagining the Boathouse and helping Miles with his house, and she seemed to have an eye for it. Textile design was a natural progression for watercolorists.

While the MBA felt more and more unsuitable with each passing day, she didn't want to move to Manhattan just for him. Part of his rationale for breaking up with her that summer had been that commitment made no sense if they lived apart. Living in the same city would test whether Miles wanted her in his every day, but she wasn't willing to go that far for something casual. She'd kept all of these thoughts to herself to avoid pressuring him into a serious relationship he wasn't expecting—or didn't want.

The closer it got to the late shift's arrival, the more time slowed. The last three taps to her phone had read 11:27. She noticed her reflection in the dark window. Mimi used to say at night, windows showed where you were, not where you could go. And maybe she needed to focus on the present and stop thinking about a future she couldn't predict. If they clarified where they stood now, they'd have a path forward, one that would avoid a repeat of what happened that summer. Three more minutes and she could get a good night's sleep, so she'd be ready to talk when Miles came back tomorrow.

Finally, the clock on her phone moved to 11:30 and the late-night shift arrived. Ten minutes later, she entered the loft and tossed her phone on the bed. A text message chimed as it hit the quilt.

💬 **Miles:** Surprise :) I'm home early. Meet me at the ski dock. 15 minutes

Avery smiled. They could talk about their relationship tomorrow. For now, she missed his hands, his mouth, his warm weight blanketing her. She'd fall asleep with her head nestled in the nook of his bare shoulder, listening to his heartbeat. She answered with a thumbs-up, threw together a small bag with her overnight necessities, and headed to the dock.

Miles's new ski boat crossed the water so quietly, she wondered if he was paddling it. She expected the loud whirr of the motor, not a gentle purr.

"Hey," he said in the soft, sultry voice she could have sworn he used only for her.

"Hey, how are you?" Avery bounced on her feet, eager to climb aboard.

He tossed a rope around a pylon and pulled the boat closer and helped her down. Once she stepped inside the boat, he held the rope in one hand, wrapped the other arm around her, and they shared a long, lingering I-missed-you kiss.

"Mmm. Much better now." he mumbled between chocolate-laced kisses. "How are you?"

"I missed you too," she whispered. "Did you just have chocolate milk?"

"Count Chocula. It turns regular milk into chocolate milk. Like magic."

"You eat like a ten-year-old."

"Scientific fact. Chocolate aids muscle recovery after long runs. Google it. You're good at that." He laughed and motioned to the passenger's seat. "Have a seat, be my first mate."

She wanted to be his only mate, but they'd discuss that tomorrow.

He put the engine in gear and maneuvered the boat away from the dock and out into the cove.

"I love this boat. It's so quiet." She ran her hand over the edge of her seat. Everything felt plush, and it smelled a little like a new car. In the captain's chair, Miles grinned like a kid with a new toy, his face aglow in the dashboard lights.

"I love it too," he said. "It's electric. Zero emissions. Maybe tomorrow you and I can take it out for its inaugural ski."

In the middle of the lake, he cut the engine and dropped anchor. He stood, took her hand, and led her to the seating area in the bow, which had been set up for sunbathing, almost like a bed. She reminded herself to live in the moment and not dull the excitement of his new boat. If Avery was being honest, she was a little afraid to hear his thoughts on commitment.

Miles sat and pulled her into his lap. As her back settled against his chest, his overwhelming warmth permeated her. He produced a blanket and covered them both. Gentle waves sloshed against the boat.

"You warm enough?" he asked.

"I'm cozy." She sank farther back into him. Floating with Miles brought its own kind of peace. She turned her head, and they kissed quickly. On the lips, nothing deeper. When they broke apart, she studied him.

"Sorry. I'm nervous," he said. "Being away made me realize we haven't discussed where we stand."

Avery felt a tinge of relief that he wasn't waiting another second to figure out the question they'd both worried about all week. If she wanted to be present for him, she needed to be honest.

He shifted underneath her.

"I feel like we should check back in with one another," he said. "Do you want a commitment? Are we doing a summer fling, or is this friends with benefits?"

Avery jolted upright and faced him.

"I don't want friends with benefits," she blurted out. Miles had a history of dating for a short time. She wanted more than casual hookups. But given their past, if she pushed too far, he'd close the door, so she backtracked. "We already had a summer fling and honestly, we were terrible at it. What about you?"

He rubbed the back of his neck.

"I don't want friends with benefits. I don't know why I brought that up. And you're right." He let out a nervous laugh. "Turning that summer from something real into a fling is my biggest failure. You're all I want. I'm never lonely when I'm with you."

A tear formed in her eye at how she often forgot how much time Miles spent alone. She touched his cheek.

"Whether or not we're together, I never want you to be lonely."

"I know." His voice cracked. "I don't want to screw this up. Last week, I tried to come up with ways to make you feel special, and

I couldn't find the perfect way to do that."

"While you were stressing about that, I plowed ahead in time. You've probably noticed when I get anxious, I plan." She motioned across the lake. "Way into the future."

"Really? I hadn't noticed." He laughed. "Truth is, I love our everyday lives. Or what they are becoming. There's no place I'd rather be than right here, with you."

"Same." She pecked his cheek. "Thank you for talking about us so openly. My mind has been working overtime trying to convince me you didn't want a relationship beyond, well, you know."

He cupped her cheek and made sure their gazes met in the dim light.

"What part of 'I spent the last decade hoping I'd see you' didn't sink in? I was full on pining for ten years. For you. Of course I want a relationship. But I want you to want it too." The corner of his mouth lifted and a second later, he gently kissed her. "No end of summer goodbyes in parking lots. No ghosting. I have no desire to find a bag of my clothing in my passenger's seat. This new us, I want it to last way beyond summer. We'll figure out the fall when we get there. Together."

Avery's stomach filled with fireflies in anticipation of them becoming the truest, most honest relationship she'd known. Her head relaxed into the nook below his shoulder, and she gazed up at the sky with renewed hope. She wasn't sure she'd ever seen so many stars.

"So, tomorrow we're water-skiing," he said. "Any chance I could get your help with a home upgrade? Maybe we could go furniture shopping in Portland one day."

Avery grabbed Miles's thighs and shook them. "Let's do it. I love furniture shopping. How about the day after tomorrow? We can squeeze it in before *Bright and Early* comes."

"I like your enthusiasm." He kissed her ear and whispered, "I'll buy you a lobster lunch."

"It's a date and this time, I'll wear the bib." She giggled and shimmied her shoulders. Lying in his arms felt like floating on a star.

As if reading her mind, Miles picked up a flashlight off the seat beside him. Avery smiled to herself. He must've planned this night for them.

"I brought you out here to see stars," he said. "Tell me what you see."

In her college astronomy class, it had been hard to locate the constellations during the rooftop nighttime exam. The teaching assistant grading her took pity and passed her.

Her finger rose into the air. "Orion's belt, the Big Dipper, and the Milky Way. I only remember the basics."

"So follow my light up the Milky Way"—he switched on the flashlight and swept it up the galaxy—"to right there."

The light stopped near a very bright star.

"That's Vega, the second brightest star in the sky after Polaris."

Miles made it so easy to find the stars, he almost plucked them out of the sky for her.

"So Vega is part of the Summer Triangle with Deneb, down there, and Altair, across the Milky Way."

Avery followed as he aimed the flashlight's beam at Vega and then Altair.

"Vega was a goddess and Altair a mortal. They fell in love, and Vega promised he'd join her in the heavens one day. But the gods forbade love between a mortal and a goddess." He turned off the flashlight and put it down, wrapping his arm around her. "When Vega's father found out, he granted Vega's wish and hoisted Altair into the heavens, but he placed them on opposite shores of the great Celestial River, the Milky Way as punishment. They're stuck on either side, with no way to cross."

Avery stared at the sky. "Wait, that's so sad."

"Ayuh." His hand slid under her shirt and rested on her hip. "Every year on the seventh day of the seventh moon, July seventh, magpies fly into the heavens and form a bridge over the Milky Way so Vega and Altair can cross and reunite for one day."

Safe in his arms, Avery compared the fate of Vega and Altair to the decade she and Miles had spent apart.

"I couldn't bear an eternity of seeing you one day a year," she said. "Waiting ten years to have you every day was worth it."

He quietly circled his thumb over her hipbone. "I'm not doing that again. That'd be torture."

She felt a rush at his description of not seeing her as torture.

Miles's breathing steadied as they stared at the vast sky. The boat swayed a little.

"Does your boat have a name?" she asked.

"Pole Position. It's already painted on the back."

Avery sat up and pivoted to face him. "That is not its name."

"What? It's the best position to start from in the mile. Or any race." Due to the crescent moon, she couldn't get a good look at his face to figure out if he was joking.

"So you don't like the name?" He sounded serious, but as an avid reader and all-around brainiac, Miles had to understand double entendre.

"I hate to break it to you but"—she giggled—"that name has more than one meaning. Or was that intentional?"

"Oh, you're cute." He pulled her face to his and kissed her forehead.

"I think you knew what you were doing," she murmured, kissing the dip in his clavicle. "Tell everyone whatever you want, but I know the truth."

Avery shifted off to his side and rolled onto her back, staring up at the sky. Miles pushed himself up and straddled her, hovering over her on all fours.

"You're the one who thought of it. What's on your mind, Pepper? Is there something you want tonight?" His hand trailed the length of her inner thigh, each pass moving inward, upward. He licked his lips. Avery's lips buzzed in anticipation of tasting him again.

"We're here to stargaze." She rested a hand on his hip and tugged his waistband. "Except you aren't looking at the sky."

In the dim light, she could make out a faint smile. Moonlight suited Miles.

"I don't need to. You're the only star in my sky."

Avery wrapped one hand around his back and cupped his cheek with the other.

"Miles," she said in a delighted haze. "I'm so happy right now."

He kissed her softly, and she nibbled at his lower lip. At some point his mouth worked its way to the spot below her ear.

"Help me solve the mystery of your undefinable, unmistakable floral scent," he murmured, goosebumps blooming on her skin under his breath.

"It's some kind of flower," he said into her clavicle. "But I don't know which one."

"Magnolia," she said. "Their flowers can be almost the size of a dinner plate. Their massive blooms sweeten the hot, humid air on summer evenings back home. There was a tree full of them by Mimi's pool. I used to float in the water at night, ponder the stars, and lose myself in the scent."

"It's intoxicating." He stopped kissing her and ran his thumb up to the band of her bralette.

She shivered into the buzz humming through her. Out on the lake, a loon called.

"We didn't have loons, but it was a lot like this."

"Lucky me. I'm getting the best of both worlds." His thumb slipped under her bralette and slowly traced the curve of her breast. "I've waited a long few days and all I want to do is make you see more stars."

"How about we both see stars? At the same time."

Out on the lake, Avery savored every inch of Miles's heavenly body, taking her time, giving him little bits of pleasure until he begged for all of her.

Afterward, she lay in that nook below his shoulder, the heady scent warm pine after an August rain filling her head. His long fingers stroked the length of her spine over and over. The boat swayed, as if still in their rhythm.

"The boat's not done" She laughed.

"Give her a break." He kissed the top of her head. " She just got christened, and I'd say she lived up to her name."

"So you do understand double entendre," she said.

"In more ways than one." He chuckled. "By the way, I didn't name my boat Pole Position."

"What?" She covered her face with her hands. "Ugh. I can't believe I fell for that."

"Hook, line and sinker." He arced his hand in the air and plunked it down as if it were a cast fishing line sinking into the water. Miles's shoulders shook as his laughter grew. "But the way it inspired you? I'm here for it."

Avery smacked his chest and grinned. "What did you name it?"

"Another Summer," he said, wiping a happy tear before kissing her forehead. "Because that's always been the dream."

"Perfect." Avery pulled the blanket over them. Their breathing mingled, combined, and became steady. He kissed her forehead and left his lips there as they drifted off to sleep.

CHAPTER EIGHTEEN

Miles

JUNE 27 - PORTLAND, MAINE

Miles lowered himself onto the picnic table bench. Ah, soothing sunshine, salt air, and warm wood. Like getting into a car on a hot day, his entire body melted into a relaxed state. He and Avery had been shopping for furniture in Portland for the last few hours and it felt good to finally sit down and not have to evaluate what he was sitting on. Ever since they'd arrived, he'd tested countless couches and chairs to determine if he liked any of them enough to live with them for the foreseeable future.

"Miles," she had said on the hour-long drive down that morning. "The goal today is to put you in your comfort zone, not take you out of it. I want you to love coming home. Snap your fingers if you don't like something."

A few nights ago, Miles had suggested finger snapping as their safe sign. He'd found it funny when she appropriated it for his interior decorating anxiety. Picking a piece of furniture only to have to pick another piece in a complimentary color, while keeping the mood of the room consistent, required talent beyond his faculties. Had he been alone, he'd have left the store overwhelmed and empty-handed.

What would've taken him years took Avery three hours. She'd zig-zagged all over the showroom, equipped with a clipboard containing measured layouts of each room. Every time she discovered something perfect, she called him over, asked his opinion, and made him sit or lie down on it.

"You're going to nap on this couch. Make sure you like it," she had said. "Lie there while I see what else they have."

Avery's concern with his comfort made him trust he'd like the end results. Miles needed her genius. And there were a lot of other people like him. What felt onerous to him was a breeze for her. She took charge, but in a relaxed, comfortable way. When she found the right thing, her eyes lit up. It clearly made her happy.

His decorator in New York had never asked if he liked an item, much less made him test it out. She'd repeatedly mentioned "creating a curated aesthetic" and he'd never wanted to admit he didn't know what she meant. Today was the polar opposite. Avery was carefully crafting a home. His home. All that mattered was his comfort and that he liked it.

Avery returned from freshening up and sat across the table.

The patio was almost empty, given the late lunch hour. The warm sun felt so good he wanted to take a nap. A couple of seagulls landed on the roof next door. He wondered if she recognized this restaurant, this sunny patio, this table. She'd said nothing when they'd placed their orders. Ten years ago, they'd had lunch here the day Sam sent them to pick up boats in Portland. He considered that day their very first date, even though he didn't officially ask her out until a week later.

"We got a lot done today." She pulled her lip balm from her pocket, slathered it on, and smacked her lips with satisfaction. "I want to be sure we didn't forget anything."

She flipped through her room plans, double checking her lists.

"We didn't get bedside tables," she said. "But I think you should wait until Wes installs your bed, so we have exact dimensions."

Miles nodded. He was fine with boxes, old milk crates, or stacks of books for a while.

"Pepper, I love all of it." He reached across the table and took the clipboard. "If we forgot something, we'll come back. Thank you."

He placed the clipboard on the bench beside him. They'd done enough for one day and he wanted to enjoy one another.

"Do you recognize this place?" he asked, as the other table of late lunch diners stood to leave.

"Of course I do." Avery blushed and arranged her napkins and utensils. "You taught me how to eat a lobster here. I just reunited with the hand dryer I used when I tried to dry off my shirt in the bathroom after I refused to wear the plastic bib and got soaked with lobster juice."

The other diners passed by and walked off the deck.

Avery ran a hand down her pink cheek. "Ugh, I was an embarrassed, southern girl, eating lunch with a cute New England boy. I didn't want to come across like I had no idea what I was doing."

"It was a good thing I'd already fallen for you." He laughed. Back then, she'd been everything he hadn't known he needed. Flirty, fun, kind. And new. He'd become enchanted with her on the drive to Portland when she noticed a digital clock bank sign and asked him his favorite time of day—as in actual time. Hers was 10:01 because she liked symmetry and 11:11 was too popular an answer.

"I got cold. You gave me your sweatshirt." She smiled.

Avery still seemed to enjoy collecting his clothes. She hadn't returned his jacket or his flannel yet. He'd hung onto her Vanderbilt baseball hat as collateral.

"What happened to that sweatshirt? You gave everything back at the end of the summer. Except that." He winked.

"It's back home under my bed, in a bin of college stuff. It doesn't smell like you anymore."

Miles's chest expanded. The idea that she knew its exact location and that it no longer held his scent meant she'd wanted to hold onto the memory of their day in Portland. That day had marked a turning point for him. With a simple hug on the beach, and a piece of sea glass, Avery had opened his eyes to the potential for happiness in his future.

He rested a hand on top of hers.

"That day," he said, brushing his fingers over her knuckles. "You changed my life. You took my crippling sadness and despair and gave me hope. Without you and your hug, I'd have just kept sinking."

Her blush returned and she swatted her hand away. "You give me too much credit."

He shook his head. She never gave herself enough credit. He said nothing because their server arrived with a tray of food.

"One salad and two watahs." The server placed the items between them. "Lobstahs'll be right up."

Avery let go of his hand and drizzled her side of the salad with balsamic vinaigrette. She stuck her fork in a tomato, then a carrot, and finally lettuce. It occurred to Miles that Avery ate like she did everything else: precisely.

"Victoria's coming and she's requested a specific French-milled bath soap and the matching hand and body creams." Avery rolled her eyes. "There's a store on Commercial Street that carries them. They might carry the sea-salt-scented candle she wants. Can we stop in after lunch?"

"Of course."

"Her poor assistant."

"Oh, she's not bad. Vic has eczema, so she's careful with skincare." Miles tested the waters. "Admit it, you're irritated because you've never liked her."

Avery grimaced and concentrated on adding more dressing to her side of the salad.

"Wanna tell me why?" he asked.

"I imagine it's a lot like the reason you don't like Paulson," she said. "Hard to explain, but something doesn't sit right."

Touché. Paulson grated on him, even though everyone else loved the guy. Come to think of it, he had never called Miles about the retreat. Miles gritted his teeth and held back a growl.

"It's okay," she said. "Once I survive Queen Victoria's visit, and I will, I get to meet Hayes and Anna Catherine, and we can all have fun on the Fourth of July. After that, it's smooth sailing for the rest of the summer."

"I'll be in Wyoming the third week in July to observe another bereavement camp. I get back the day before the Camp Luciole fundraiser in the City."

"Do you have a lot to do? Fundraisers are a lot of work."

"Nope. Anna Catherine and Hayes put together a party committee, and all I have to do is show up and give a speech."

He'd been thinking about whether he should take her. She'd have to find a dress, fly to the City, and get all done up. If Victoria's requests were too much, who knew how she'd feel about an over-the-top Manhattan charity gala. He didn't want the stresses of his life to become an inconvenience to her.

Avery stabbed her fork into a cucumber, then a tomato, and scooped a crouton on top.

"After that, I have Lily's bachelorette, and you have the bachelor party."

"Are you sure you don't mind overseeing the furniture delivery while I'm on the river?" he asked. The earliest possible delivery date had been the Friday he returned from Nate's canoe trip.

"Not a problem. The next available day they had was in late August, and I want to see the new furniture in your house before I leave for Hanover."

"Wait," he said. "When do your classes begin?"

"Assuming I get around to signing a lease, I'll move in the tenth for orientation. The landlord is taking forever to email it to me. Classes start on the fifteenth."

Miles gulped a bite of salad. He'd assumed she started around Labor Day.

"That's so early," he groaned. "You'll miss the Perseid meteor shower."

She seemed so laid back for someone who had so many events coming up. Hearing it all laid out made his head spin. Adult summers were nothing like carefree college summers. Their obligations were stacked like dominoes. Ready to topple. Calendars that didn't mesh would grow more complicated in the fall when she was five hours away.

Avery let out a long sigh and put down her fork.

"I know," she said.

Miles mixed the remaining salad around in the bowl. He'd been so hungry a minute ago, and now he'd lost his appetite. His chest felt tight, and the warm wood table prickled under his forearms.

Avery took his hand back in hers.

"Miles, tell me what you're thinking?"

He focused on the salad. That night on the boat, she'd been so honest about what she wanted. A relationship. And he wanted one too. In the Boathouse, she'd mentioned that people who made a commitment to one another tackled their obstacles together to make the relationship work. He now stood at one of his emotional roadblocks and he owed it to her to try.

He squeezed her hand and met her gaze.

"When did summer become so busy? I just want to spend time on the lake with my girlfriend."

Girlfriend. It had slipped out naturally and somehow, he felt a shift. Miles and Avery. They were a couple now. Avery's gorgeous smile almost knocked him over.

"We will make the most of this summer, I promise." She threaded her fingers through his and rocked their hands side to side. "Most of our commitments for the next month are two or three days each. That leaves four or five days in the week to be together."

When she put it that way, it sounded better. Except she'd leave halfway through August. He couldn't bring that up because he refused to insert his opinion into her MBA. She'd never had a boyfriend who supported her choices and celebrated her accomplishments. And Miles wanted to be the partner she deserved.

But he also wished they could stay suspended in some kind of perpetual summer, free of obligations. The only time he could visit other camps was in the coming weeks. Regardless of how busy they might be, this summer was already one of the best he could remember. Ever since they committed to this relationship, they'd been discussing their challenges and figuring out solutions.

"So what do we do?" he asked. "Let's make this work."

As the warmth of her smile washed over him, Miles grew confident Avery's plans would set everything right.

"We sit down with our calendars and treat the days we're both available as sacred," she said. "More sacred than Hazel Matheson tickets or Super Bowl tickets."

"More sacred than Hazel Matheson playing the Super Bowl halftime show." He nodded.

"Exactly. Nothing interrupts our time together unless we discuss it first. It's what modern, professional couples do."

Leave it to the girl who made lists and mapped out rooms before buying furniture to suggest merging calendars. Miles liked the idea. And he could take it a step farther.

"So we share a calendar," he said, excited by the idea of taking such a big step.

Avery's eyes fell as she smoothed her napkin over her lap. Miles felt a knot in his stomach. He'd hit a nerve. Maybe sharing calendars was too personal.

"I won't make you do that." She huffed, as if trying to make something big feel smaller.

"I thought it made sense. To keep us from booking something else during our time."

"Yeah, but—" She shook her head. "I asked Trent to do that once, and he called me a nuisance. He said his calendar was his business, and no men he knew did that."

The hairs on Miles's neck rippled in protective response. He had never punched another person. If he ever met Trent, that might change. He couldn't tolerate anyone who made his sweet, kind Avery feel bothersome and insignificant. Miles's Yale Track sweatshirt wasn't the only thing Avery had hidden away. She'd kept her hurts and dreams to herself. Little bits came out when she felt safe, like now, or as a last-ditch effort, like when she'd told him she loved him that summer.

That day on the beach ten summers ago, she'd acknowledged and respected his pain, like she'd done with his furniture aversion earlier in the day. He wanted to be there for her. Where Trent made her feel little, Miles wanted her to never question how much he valued her. He didn't need a sky full of stars. He only needed one.

"I don't see what's a nuisance about sharing a calendar with my girlfriend." Miles lifted his chin to demonstrate he'd take on the challenge. "It's the easiest way to keep track of the only thing more important than Hazel's Super Bowl Halftime show tickets."

He took a bite of their salad. As he chewed, he thought about how things would go down if he met Trent. More specifically, how Trent would go down. Hard. Miles filled his fork again. If her ex showed up, Miles would show him a different kind of stars.

Her wide grin beamed across the table and his MMA ass-kicking fantasy faded to black, replaced by a vision of the sectional sofa he'd just bought. He'd lay her down on that couch the day it arrived and kiss his way up her inner thighs, her gasps and moans filling the quiet house.

Their server arrived with a full tray. "Two lobstah plattahs, one with steamahs."

"The one with steamahs belongs to my boyfriend." Avery's eyes darted toward the tray and back to him.

Steamahs. Avery had nailed the northern accent.

He winked at her because he wanted her to feel appreciated. Every day. She could fill his house, his calendar, and all other blank spaces in his life, including the one in his heart. His girlfriend. She checked every item off his list. The one she didn't know existed because he, Miles Magrum, had been too afraid to admit that what he wanted, more than anything in this world, was her. The woman who took away his loneliness.

CHAPTER NINETEEN

Avery

JUNE 30 - BRIGHT AND EARLY

Avery unzipped her wet suit and toweled off as she stood on the beach next to the dock. *Bright and Early's* opening, featuring her water-skiing, had gone well. Despite the stress of jumping the wake one-handed while wearing a microphone, she managed to smile while saying the show's famous tagline, "Wake up! It's *Bright and Early* in Maine." Usually they said "America," but this was a special episode.

She slipped into the sauna, changed into warm sweats and Birkenstocks, and took the path to the lodge, hoping to catch Sam's live segment during the show's second half hour. She checked her phone to find it ablaze with notifications. The Easton family chat was busy this morning. They'd all watched her open the show and loved it.

In some ways, she'd begun a new chapter with Miles three days earlier in Portland. That night, at the boutique seaside inn he'd taken her to, they'd spent an hour coordinating calendars and setting aside time to be together. Their shared calendar looked tidy all laid out on her iPad. It felt like a big step from ten years ago when distance alone made him not want to try.

Despite everything going well, Avery couldn't help but put their relationship under her own microscope. He'd taken a big step and called her his girlfriend. She should be content, but every time he mentioned the fundraiser in New York, he didn't invite her. She knew he wouldn't take someone else, but the lack of an invitation without an explanation felt like he was holding back. She'd let her mind get carried away, picking out dresses on her phone when bored, only to remind herself she wasn't going.

Sam's interview began as she arrived at the lodge. Avery tiptoed across the porch and stood next to Lily, behind the crew. They exchanged a quiet smile and watched the monitors.

Sam sat near the railing, fidgeting under all the lights with the lake sparkling behind him. Victoria knew how to make her guests comfortable, especially those with no prior TV experience. She asked about the lake, and his face lit up as he described Montressa as the most peaceful place he knew of to rest a weary soul. Peace was the last thing Avery had felt with *Bright and Early*'s crew on site.

Ever since Victoria had checked in, she'd treated Avery as her personal concierge. Despite her low-key on-air personality, Victoria issued diva-level requests every twenty minutes. The extra cases of three different bottled waters hadn't placated her. Neither had the French-milled soap or the sea salt candle.

Victoria only drank one kind of champagne. Montressa served Moet, but Avery had to fetch a bottle of Veuve Clicquot and a bottle of Veuve Clicquot Brut Rosé because visiting Montressa put Victoria in the mood for summer, and summer called for pink bubbles.

Thankfully, one of the housekeeping staff was in Portland and picked up a skincare fridge, which Avery learned was a tiny bathroom refrigerator made especially for beauty products.

"I'm doing Montressa a favor." Victoria had lifted a hand to her heart. "Once you try it, you'll understand why every cabin needs one. I'll leave mine so you can have it when I leave."

"So magnanimous of you," Avery muttered to herself when she'd finally trudged back down the stairs of Victoria's cabin for the umpteenth time. The skincare fridge wasn't Victoria's to give away anyway. Montressa had purchased it.

When Avery's phone pinged well after dinner last night, she'd immediately regretted ever having given Victoria her number. The Queen, as Avery and Lily called her, requested a higher-thread-count bathrobe and a security guard, despite there being no danger to her safety. Luke, a bellhop who played football and lacrosse at Winslow College, was thrilled to take the job because, *it's Victoria Evans!* The robe request had felt aggressive. Montressa's new robes were made from a plush, sustainable bamboo fiber. So Avery had firmly said they didn't have an alternative, which ended the texts.

When she'd promised Nate she'd ski the show open, it hadn't occurred to Avery that if she wanted to watch the taping, she'd be standing in the lodge with wet hair, among the made-up and camera-ready. She looked around at the crew. Everyone else was dry and not in sweats. This experience rivaled the time in middle school when she'd arrived at Mary Kaitlyn Smyth's Halloween party to find she was the only one wearing a costume.

She felt a tap on her shoulder the second Sam's segment finished.

"Avery." Nate pulled her out of her thoughts. "I'm up next, and Lily is biased. She calls me a hottie no matter what I wear. How do I look?"

He had on a Montressa polo and a wide grin, his golden hair combed into place. That rugged, handsome, friendly outdoorsman vibe so many men tried to emulate came naturally to Nate.

"Great. Like Thor, if he managed a lodge and went fishing in his spare time." She patted his arm. "You've got this."

"You look hot, babe." Lily kissed Nate.

"See," Nate shrugged at Avery. Their wedding was going to be so much fun.

"All right, everyone," one of the producers shouted. "Next segment is in the lobby, with Nate Cooper."

The crew moved equipment while the show paused for the local news and weather. Avery left Nate and Lily in the lobby near the hearth and headed to the bathroom to neaten her wet hair just as Miles strode through the back door. His navy fisherman's sweater perfectly alluded to the sculpture underneath, but his jeans still hung from his hips as if he hadn't tried very hard.

"Hey you," he said.

"Hey," Avery said. "Isn't your segment on the dock?"

"Ayuh, but I wanted to tell you that everyone says that was our best show open ever." Miles ripped off his Velcro watchband and wrapped his digital watch around her wrist. "I'm entrusting this to you. The producers insist I wear a smartwatch so viewers can see I'm a techie."

It was a tiny thing, but his warm watch on her wrist made her feel chosen. She recognized it as the same watch he'd worn in college. Most girlfriends would replace a beat-up watch with a new one, but Avery knew he used this watch to time his runs. It was sacred to him.

"You're the prettiest one here. Lucky me," Miles whispered as he kissed her forehead. "I'm off to get made up."

Avery didn't think Miles needed enhancing, but she nodded anyway.

He pointed at her and clicked his tongue as he walked through the conference room door, now embellished with a Sharpie-scribbled sign that read *Hair and Makeup*. Avery had posted a photo of it on Montressa's Social media profiles earlier in the day with the caption, *Ready for our close-up. Are you watching Bright and Early?*

A cheer erupted as Miles entered the room.

"The hair and makeup crew never greet me like that." Victoria pouted as she walked out of the hair and makeup room with a cell phone attached to her ear. The haggard production assistant in her wake held two additional phones, both showing hold screens.

"Nate, your father was perfect. I'm doing you next. By the fireplace." Victoria pointed and continued her conversation. "This is non-negotiable, Charles. Call me back when they've agreed."

She hung up and grabbed the other phone out of her assistant's hand. "Hello? Yes. Yes. No."

By the time she finished, the next caller had given up.

"I told you to keep them on the phone," Victoria chided her quivering assistant.

"Avery, get me a Montressa polo." Victoria's command was more of a bark. "I want to be on brand for my nostalgia piece with Nate. They'll be running a photo of me wearing mine from that summer. I am still an extra small, unless you have extra-extra small. That robe you brought me last night was way too big."

Avery left to find a shirt, and Lily accompanied her.

"She's driving me insane," Avery said through gritted teeth. "I've brought her French milled soap, a special candle, three types of bottled water, champagne we don't carry, and a special refrigerator for her skin creams. Nothing satisfies her."

"That's a whole spa." Lily giggled. "No wonder she texted me asking for a robe last night. Nate had a cabin steward take one over."

Avery's jaw dropped open. "I wonder if that was before or after she asked me for one and I told her to use the one in her cabin. Please help me through this day!"

"As soon as those trucks pull out, you and I are hitting the water," Lily said. "Wes used the air compressor to inflate our floats. Yours is definitely a loon, but I'm not sure about mine. Is it a deer? Is it a moose? Is it a *doose*? We can debate this and other hot topics on our way out to Lone Pine Island."

Avery laughed. Lily always brightened the mood.

Back in the lobby, Miles returned from makeup, tissue stuck in his neckline for touchups before he went live on the dock. Victoria stopped him and ran her hands over his pecs.

"Just getting some lint off," she said, and smiled at him. "So, who's your date for the fundraiser?"

"No comment." He scowled at Victoria.

"Off the record?" She picked another piece of invisible lint off his shoulder.

"Victoria, private life, private. You know this." Miles's face transformed into a bed of chiseled rock.

"Look at you, so cute when you're mad. I'm going solo." She smoothed a hand down his arm. "Now get to the dock for your segment."

Miles didn't budge. As Victoria interviewed Nate, Avery wondered if Paulson was going to the fundraiser. If he showed up, someone should introduce him to Victoria. Miles wouldn't do that for Paulson. If Avery were there, she would finagle a meeting so Paulson could get her out of his system.

When Nate's interview cut to commercial, Miles winked at Avery and sped down to the dock, possibly to avoid Victoria.

But Victoria had her eyes on another companion.

"Avery, my friend. I feel bad we haven't had time to catch up." She used her sweetest voice, as if ten years ago, Victoria hadn't called Avery a prude and predicted Miles's end-of-summer breakup. "Come with me."

Another command. As Avery walked slowly to the dock with Victoria, she braced for another ridiculous request. Those trucks pulling out couldn't come soon enough.

"So, you and Miles have reunited," Victoria said.

"We're both here to help the Coopers. That's all." Avery centered her gaze straight ahead to where Miles joked with the crew in the middle of the ski dock.

Victoria clicked her tongue. "His watch around your wrist and your stolen glances don't fool me."

Avery knew to be cautious. Miles had given Victoria nothing.

"Thank you so much for taking time out of your busy schedule to come here." She attempted to change course. "I know the Coopers appreciate the—"

"He doesn't fall in love." Victoria eyed Avery up and down, as if assessing her and finding her lacking. "But you already know that."

"What?" Avery stopped short. How dare she try this again?

"Miles doesn't do love. He's Mr. One and Done."

Avery grabbed a loose towel hanging off the back of a chair and squeezed it to hide her shaking fists, reminding herself a shared calendar said otherwise.

"Woman to woman," Victoria said in a sickeningly sweet, I'm-your-best-friend voice. "In the City, his life is different. Actors. Models. Rock stars. It's no place for a girl who ogles at loons and paints pretty pictures."

Avery bit her cheek to keep from exploding. It took every ounce of energy not to tell Victoria to pack her chilled face cream and leave.

"Think about it, Aves. You and Miles have different love languages. Like most Southern women, you crave attention and words of affirmation. Miles is all about physical touch. A guy that hot can have his needs met anywhere, anytime, with anyone. That's why he never stays with the same woman. I'm just trying to prepare you for the inevitable. When you leave this lake, he'll find someone else."

Avery swallowed. Somehow Victoria had not lost the ability to make her simultaneously implode and explode. How dare she pick them apart? That was Avery's job. Except Miles did love touch. Whenever they were alone, his hands were all over her. Trent had loved touch too ... and look where that had landed her.

The time she and Miles carved out together on their shared calendar was all at the lake, and they hadn't discussed their lives off the lake yet. She wanted to take him home to Virginia the next time she visited her family, but it would be a while before she went again. However, he frequently returned to New York and always by himself. Blending their lives shouldn't fall on him, but she worried absence would make his heart lose interest. What if they couldn't coordinate their separate lives come fall? What if weekends here and there weren't enough?

Avery's stomach sank as a small voice inside of her said, *You're fooling yourself, Avery Easton. This will never work.*

She didn't watch Miles's segment. Avery curled up in the loft and cried. Half an hour later, someone knocked on her door. When she opened it, her best friend pulled her in for a hug.

"Oh sweetie, the Queen emotionally guillotined you." Lily gave her a sad pout.

Avery sat on her bed and filled Lily in. Lily quietly contemplated the conversation.

"Everything she said could have applied to Trent," Avery said. "And I know Miles is not Trent, but in some convoluted way, it makes sense. Maybe I have a type."

"Don't you think Miles's love language is acts of service though?" Lily asked. "It's why he's opening the camp and why he pays every table's check whenever he eats at the Lakeside Diner."

"He does that? Every time?" Avery asked. This explained why Wes had prodded Miles to come by the diner.

"He thinks it's a secret, but this is a small town. Nate and I noticed Jeanette asks him if he wants 'the usual' at the end of the meal. Wouldn't you ask that *before* the person ordered?"

"Yeah." Avery also assumed "the usual" was chocolate milk. Avery put a hand to her mouth. Lily might as well have discovered the answer to getting the *Friends* couch up the stairwell wasn't to yell "pivot."

Lily proudly tapped her temple. "The 'usual' is him paying for everyone's breakfast. It's his way of giving back. The camp is too."

Avery had never been more thankful for Lily. Yes, Miles loved through acts of service. It explained why he insisted on giving Avery pleasure before seeking his own. Miles thought so much about other people, he sometimes forgot about himself. Between helping the Coopers, planning a camp, and reuniting with her, he might've forgotten his other life existed. This summer was already different. He'd proven he wanted to make things work. Maybe it hadn't occurred to him that she might be interested in going to his events. Hayes and Anna Catherine's visit the following weekend could be the gateway to taking her to New York.

"Wow, the usual. He's sly." Avery wiped away a sniffle and smiled at how Paulson had been right. Miles was like maple syrup. Good to the last drop.

"Yep." Lily popped her lips in satisfaction.

"I love him," Avery blurted out. In an instant, a pang of panic rose in her throat at admitting her feelings so freely to the woman who might tell Miles's best friend.

"I know." Lily nodded with a comforting smile. "And I'm guessing you haven't told him, so I won't say a word. Now go put on a swimsuit so I can try out my half moose, half deer float."

Avery chose a string bikini. He wasn't going with them, but if she saw Miles, she wanted to look like all his dreams. As luck would have it, Nate and Miles were waiting on the dock, ready to send them off. Lily jumped right in but Avery let Miles's gaze linger. His devilish grin said his mind had gone elsewhere at the sight of those strings tied at her hips.

"She's gone," he whispered to Avery as he took back his watch. "And Anna Catherine and Hayes arrive tonight. I promise they're more fun. For starters, they won't need a skincare fridge. After that, it's you, me, and a bunch of sunsets."

"I love the sound of that."

"I love that in four pulls, I could have you naked right now." His breath tickled her neck.

"Let's go," Lily yelled. "The doose is on the loose."

Avery swatted Miles's bicep, kissed him, and jumped into the cool water. Halfway to Lone Pine Island, it occurred to her that if Lily could tell how she felt, Miles might have sensed it too. He hadn't been ready for her to say she loved him that summer. But surely he had changed since then. After all, he was talking about a sunset-filled future. Given that he didn't go on second dates, he might never have been close enough to someone to say he loved them.

Avery wanted to be the one to break the mold.

CHAPTER TWENTY

Miles

JULY 3

Like rocks at the bottom of a river, everything had fallen into place. Miles could tell Hayes and Anna Catherine adored Avery. The previous night, the two couples had shared cocktails on his dock. A mother loon had swum by with two fluffy gray chicks on her back, prompting Avery and Anna Catherine to take at least a thousand photos. Avery posted one on Montressa's socials and within an hour, ninety-two people had shared it. After dinner at the lodge, Lily and Nate joined them for a spirited round of Anna Catherine's favorite game, couples charades. Miles and Avery won, which meant something given that Hayes and Anna routinely read each other's minds.

This morning, Miles and Avery were taking Lennox for a walk. It had been his idea, so Hayes and Anna could have a quiet breakfast before he and Hayes visited the corporate retreat. Miles wanted to make an offer, but he needed Hayes's approval, and they needed to raise some capital.

Bright and Early's live broadcast had worked. Montressa was officially fully booked for the summer, but Miles felt certain Victoria had said something mean to Avery. When she and Lily had left for their float, Avery's eyes were puffy, as if she'd been crying. She'd smiled, but something felt off. Miles wasn't afraid to confront Victoria if she'd convinced Avery to doubt his intentions. He hoped getting to know his friends helped Avery feel welcome in his life.

Casper had tagged along on their walk. Sam walked him farther and farther each day, but Casper still needed to chase a ball. Sam's stitches had healed, but he hadn't reached ball-throwing shape yet.

Avery threw terribly, but Miles enjoyed pushing the stroller. Despite his lack of experience with babies, Lennox had a special attachment to Miles. Anna Catherine called him "the baby whisperer" because he could calm Lennox in seconds. At first, he assumed she had liked something about his face. But Hayes had mentioned babies liked the sound of a heartbeat. Thanks to all his running, Miles's heart rate rested at a nice, slow forty-eight beats per minute. It probably lulled her into contentment, and often, when no one else could soothe her, Lennox fell asleep on Miles's chest.

"My arm is getting tired." Avery handed him the ball. "Switch?"

He ceded control of the stroller and threw the ball. Lennox cooed in her seat and pointed at Casper as he retrieved it. Miles launched the next throw high into a tree. Casper jumped in a circle when he lost sight of it and Lennox screamed in delight as it came crashing through the branch canopy ahead, landing with a *thunk* on the compressed gravel. Casper took off, jumped, and caught it on the second bounce.

"You should have been throwing the whole time." Avery smiled.

Lennox wiggled in her seat and pointed at Casper. "Da, da, da."

"Are you saying dog?" He stood in front of the stroller, blocking Avery's progress to point at Casper. "Dog?"

Lennox lifted both her hands, waving at him.

"Oh, you want me to pick you up." Within seconds, he had Lennox in his arms and Casper chasing a throw.

"Ba," Lennox cooed.

"Did you hear that? She said ball. I've taught her two words."

Avery rolled her eyes.

They were almost back to the parking lot, where he'd arranged to meet Hayes. "Now I am going to teach her to throw."

Avery sighed. "Miles, she is too young to throw. She's only ten months old."

He put the wet ball in Lennox's hand. She dropped it.

"You threw it!" Miles exaggerated his excitement.

"She dropped it."

"I say she threw it." He rubbed noses with Lennox, who laughed.

"Miles, Anna's right." Avery's eyes turned gooey. "You're a natural."

He thought luck explained why Lennox liked him, especially given his lack of parenting experience.

"You haven't seen me change a diaper," he laughed. "I babysat for them once when Hayes cut himself cooking and needed to go to the ER for stitches. I put the diaper on backwards. Anytime it comes up, Anna laughs so hard she pees."

"That's karma, if you think about it." Avery dropped her head to the side in thought. "But really, you're great with her."

"Thanks. This is fun for a while, but I don't know. I never had siblings or cousins. And my family kind of dissolved during my formative years, so I'm not sure I know how to parent."

A child needed guidance and understanding. Avery could probably do that without thinking. He wasn't convinced he could. Miles wasn't entirely sure he was a good enough boyfriend, and Avery deserved the best of everything.

His heartbeat quickened. He didn't want to ruin the starry-eyed, fireflies-in-the-stomach feeling that had recently resurfaced, even though it felt like they had been together for a long time. Life with a stroller, a dog, and Avery seemed like it could be so fluid, so easy. This wasn't just a walk. They were trying on a future and silently asking themselves if it fit. Avery might be imagining them as a family. What else was she supposed to think?

The next logical step for Avery would be marriage. With Lily's wedding looming, she had to be thinking about it. He didn't know if Avery wanted to get married, especially after what happened with Trent. Victoria had given Miles the nickname *Mr. One and Done*. And in some way, the moniker fit. Being a boyfriend was new to him. If Avery expected him to leapfrog right into a proposal, he wasn't there yet.

He handed Lennox the ball again, and she dropped it. This time, his praise was less enthusiastic. His mouth went dry. He heard his own heart pounding rapidly and placed his free hand on his chest to check. This was not forty-eight beats per minute. It was double that. His forehead broke out in a cold sweat.

Avery put a hand on his shoulder and the other on Lennox's back.

"Miles." Her calm voice carried a hint of alarm as she tried to lock eyes.

He focused on the Mail Jeep and walked toward it. If only he could climb inside and hide until whatever this feeling was passed.

"Do you need me to take her?"

Avery moved her hand to his forearm, walking beside him, still trying to catch his eye. He gazed at Lennox instead, aware of the concern in Avery's voice and touch. After marriage came kids—and yes, he wanted to be a parent, but something could happen to one of his children, or him, or his wife. Loss was a lonely path. Robert Frost lied. Sometimes, the road less traveled was riddled with brambles and thorns.

Anna Catherine's laugh cackled from over near the lodge, coming their way. It was not the time to discuss their future. He needed to pull himself together so Avery didn't think she'd done something wrong.

"Mama's coming and we need to clean your hands. Uncle Miles gave you gross dog-slobber-ball hands." Avery fished out a wipe from the diaper bag.

She automatically knew what to do. And although Hayes and Anna Catherine called him "the baby whisperer," Mr. One and Done had a lot to learn. Right now, he needed to stop thinking about the future and lighten the present mood. As much for himself as for everyone else.

"Hey, hypocrite." His raspy voice hinted at his anxiety. He forced a smile, determined to smooth out his tone. "You told me dog saliva was equivalent to hand sanitizer."

Avery let out a laugh and shook her head.

Lennox dropped the ball again. Casper caught it and she squealed.

"Teaching her to throw, I like it." Hayes strode across the parking lot, Anna Catherine holding his hand.

"Miles, the two of you are so cute with a baby." Anna Catherine sighed, putting a hand to her heart. "Your kids will be so adorable."

For a second, everything stood still. Hayes shot Anna a questioning look, Avery busied herself cleaning Lennox with the wipe, Casper pooped in the corner of the parking lot, and Miles wondered if everyone could tell he wasn't himself. A teardrop of cool sweat trickled down his spine.

Anna shrugged. "All the girls love Miles."

"He hypnotizes her with all that charm." Avery put the wipe away and pulled a poop bag out of her pocket.

"That's our baby whisperer." Anna grinned proudly.

Avery's brow furrowed. Miles felt for Avery. This conversation had to be hard for her. He wondered if she assumed she'd have a baby by now. She probably did. Her sister was about to have her third.

He handed Lennox back to Anna, who placed her in the stroller. He wiped the cool sweat off his lip as his mouth went dry. His chest pounded in his ears again. His lungs tightened. He unlocked the Mail Jeep as a distraction, hoping no one else noticed his shaking hand.

"Hayes, we should go." They'd be early if they left now, but Miles had an overwhelming urge to be anywhere but in this parking lot, keeping a cyclone of anxiety at bay.

Miles locked eyes with Avery, who had a poop bag over her hand, ready for the pickup. Her expression spun through a pain-stricken kaleidoscope of sympathy, fear, worry, melancholy. Emotions blended together, spread apart, and fell back together. She had to be questioning if they could weather all storms.

"I'll see you after lunch. We'll swim." He quickly pecked her warm cheek.

Her arms wrapped around him, and her mouth came to his ear.

"You're pale," she whispered. "Are you okay?"

He nodded quickly, so she wouldn't have time to decipher the truth in his eyes. He'd be fine. All he needed was space.

"I'm fine." He placed another kiss on her forehead and left her with something normal to reassure her. "Have fun with Lily and Anna Catherine. We'll swim later."

Hayes kissed Anna and got into the Mail Jeep. Within seconds, Miles started the car, backed out of his spot, and raced from the parking lot. Only later did it occur to him he'd left a shocked Avery in the same parking lot twice. At least this time, she wasn't crying. If she was, he wouldn't know. Either way, he'd left her with a mess to clean up.

As they drove to the retreat, Miles tapped the steering wheel. Whenever he envisioned himself with kids, it was with Avery. He should've told her that. But there were a lot of steps beforehand—first comes love, then comes marriage, maybe. A lot needed to happen before a baby arrived, and they hadn't discussed any of it because they'd only been back together a short time.

None of it was possible until he let go of this fear he was destined to lose anyone he loved.

Hayes sat quietly to his left, giving Miles a moment to think.

A couple of minutes later, Hayes spoke first. "Dude, I can feel your mind churning. What happened back there?"

"I'm trying to figure that out." Miles drummed his thumb on the steering wheel.

"I've never seen you so shaken," Hayes said. "I think Anna got ahead of herself and put you on the spot. We always assumed you wanted children."

"It started before you got there. Avery and I are still in the fun phase. We've touched on what happens in the fall, when we're living in two different cities, but nothing beyond that. And definitely no mention of kids." Miles stopped at a four-way stop and stared at the road ahead. "All those women I dated were just dates. I want more with Avery. When I think of the future, she's in the dream, you know?"

He put the car in gear and drove ahead.

"That's great."

"Ayuh, but it's also terrifying." Miles sighed. He slowed as they approached the covered bridge across the river, looked through to make sure no cars were coming, and drove through at a a snail's pace. "Avery used to love this bridge. The inside reminded her of a cathedral, and she thought it would look magical if someone lit the trusses under the roof. I want to light it for her." Miles pressed his mouth into a fine line and nodded. "That summer, I imagined proposing to her here one day, but things are different for her now. She's been hurt before and she'll need a place where she's comfortable enough to answer honestly. And I don't know why I'm telling you all of this since I don't know if we'll ever get there."

"It's a pretty cool bridge." Hayes leaned forward and peered up through the windshield at the trusses. "Sounds like you're ready for the fun to turn serious. What's the holdup?"

"I'm terrified of getting what I want. Half the time it's a dream, the other half it's a nightmare. I'm afraid of losing her."

"Losing her because she won't want what you want?" Hayes asked.

"No, because I won't be able to get her back. That she'll ... you know, be gone." Miles spun his finger in the air and saw Hayes' confusion. "Like my mom."

Hayes's mouth rounded into an "O," and he let out a whistle. "You're afraid to love her because you worry she'll..."

Hayes didn't need to finish the sentence. Both men knew what Miles meant. A tear formed in Miles's eye as he pulled into the retreat's driveway. He stopped the car.

"Were you ever afraid of that?" He swallowed. "With Anna?"

Hayes gently rested a hand on Miles's shoulder.

"Yeah," he said. "It happens to a lot of us who've suffered a loss. They call it philophobia. The fear of falling in love. You can date casually and have sex but never make a long-term commitment. Women I dated got so frustrated with me because I couldn't get past the casual stage. Unlike you, I'd string them along until they gave up and left. Such a jerk move and so immature. Anna wouldn't give up. She got me to open up, found me the help I needed, and stayed by me. Every time our marriage gets challenging, I think about how she stuck it out when others would've understandably left." Hayes shook his head and stared out his window. "So much about you makes sense now. I can't believe I never saw it."

"Ayuh." Miles felt a sad smile come to him. "I'm panicking like I did that summer. I understand myself a little better now, but I feel myself falling into a spiral that ends with me hurting her and that's the last thing I want to do."

"You can get to the other side of this. And it'll be worth it. Promise," Hayes said. "But you need to tell her all this, because there is no perfect in love. Every relationship has challenges."

"I want our relationship to be easy for her. I already put her through so much." Miles rubbed his forehead. "Unloading my issues feels unfair."

"Let her decide that. I think Avery will do anything for you. You'd help her if she felt this way, right?"

Miles nodded. When she hit rock bottom after that summer, he hadn't been there for her. If she ever needed him again, he'd get there as fast as he could. He shouldn't try to predict whether his life or his issues would overwhelm her. She could make up her own mind. Maybe his panic would fade if he invited her into his whole life. This weekend was a start. Next, he'd ask her to the fundraiser. They could build from there.

"Tell her what you're feeling. Right now, she's analyzing what she witnessed this morning and possibly blaming herself." Hayes sighed. "And talk to a professional. Don't be the guy who runs a bereavement camp but hasn't dealt with his own grief."

Miles nodded again. "I have a good one back in the City. I'll call her when I get back in the fall."

"Hey, Mr. Tech Start-up, ever heard of Zoom? That's how I do therapy on set. Don't wait. Do it now." Hayes rolled his eyes. "Letting love into your life is better for your health, your anxiety, and your outlook. But you'll never know true love until you allow yourself to be vulnerable. Make the call. Put in the work. Trust me, the only way you'll win the love lottery is if you confront what's holding you back. Anna says you need a sprinkle of kismet too, but I think you got that when Avery came back to the lake."

"Thank you." Miles shifted the Jeep into gear, grateful they could talk things out with one another. "I know we share a similar pain, and I appreciate your willingness to revisit your own trauma to help me. I hope our camp helps others find the same support."

"I'm always here for you, like you've been for me," Hayes said as they pulled past the sign welcoming guests to the corporate retreat. "And I can't wait to replace that sign and start helping grieving families find what they need."

They passed an overgrown archery course and two dilapidated tennis courts. Miles imagined them filled with families redefining themselves.

"Dang, Miles, I think you found the perfect spot." Hayes leaned forward and stared out the windshield with an open mouth as they passed the small outdoor amphitheater. The log cabins were straight ahead.

"Here comes the crown jewel." Miles steered the Jeep toward the long lawn overlooking the shimmering water and blue sky. "The lake is the best part. Always."

CHAPTER TWENTY-ONE

Avery

JULY 4

Avery climbed the ladder, toweled dry, and plopped down on the chaise lounge next to Lily. They'd spent the morning relaxing on Miles's dock with Anna Catherine while Miles and Hayes visited the corporate retreat. When Lennox went down for a late morning nap, Anna stayed inside and napped too. To cool off, Avery and Lily swam all the way out to the large rock everyone called King of the Rocks and back.

"I know this sounds weird, but this lake reminds me of the sweet tea we drink down south." Avery reapplied sunscreen to her forehead. "They're both so refreshing."

"Like when you pour a sugar packet into iced tea?" Lily asked.

"Bless you heart." Avery placed a hand to her chest in feigned shock and conjured up her most delicate southern accent. "Sweet tea is not iced tea with sugar, darling. It's carefully crafted."

Mimi had always added a pinch of baking soda and slowly dissolved the sugar in the water before adding the tea. Avery made the Easton's sweet tea now because her family agreed hers tasted exactly like Mimi's recipe. She needed to make some for Miles and their friends. Miles would love southern food. Grits, country ham biscuits, pimento cheese, cucumber sandwiches, lemon bars. She couldn't wait for him to taste it all.

She and Lily sat quietly surveying the bustle of waterfront activity over at Montressa. Children played Marco Polo and parents stood along the beach shore, supervising their toddlers. People came and went in kayaks and stand-up paddleboards. The ski captains were giving lessons. Casper slept on the main dock under the Montressa flag, flapping and snapping in the breeze. The lodge looked happier with people around.

"Surveying your work?" asked Lily.

"Our work." Avery nodded. "You, me, Miles, Nate, Wes, and then some."

All of them contributed to the success of Montressa, and none of it would've happened if she and Miles hadn't moved past their rocky start in May. Now her relationship with Miles reminded Avery of holding hands while running down a steep hill. Exhilarating at first. But they'd reached the point where their bodies were moving faster than their feet, and the hurtling pace felt unstoppable. It remained to be seen whether they fell or miraculously reached the bottom together.

Earlier in the day, Miles seemed ready to topple over the second Anna mentioned their hypothetically cute children. He couldn't leave fast enough. Yes, he and Hayes had an appointment with their realtor to see the retreat, but he'd peeled out of the parking lot and left her standing in a cloud of driveway dust.

Avery's focus drifted to Lily, who lay on her back, eyes closed, soaking in the warmth of the midday sun. Ever since Lily and Nate started dating, they'd worked toward a shared future. The wedding planning seemed easy. Within twenty-four hours of their engagement, Lily and

Nate had set a date and booked Montressa. Avery and Miles were the only attendants. Lily and her mother bought the dress before her mother left to hike the Appalachian Trail with Miles's father. Once she and Nate married, Lily planned to keep teaching, Nate would run the resort and every summer, they'd run Montressa together, just like Sam and Laurie had done. An entire shared future fell into place with little effort.

Avery didn't know what she and Miles were doing six weeks from now when she left to start her MBA. At some point, the shared calendar conversation would become whether they wanted similar things out of life.

A dragonfly landed on Lily's thigh. She shaded her eyes with her hand and studied Avery. "You're thinking about something."

Avery let out an exasperated sigh and rubbed a droplet of water off her freckled thigh.

"Lily, do you and Nate have your whole lives planned? Not just that you'll live here. Things like how many kids you'll have?"

"Kinda." Lily took a sip from her mammoth water bottle. "Not that we agree. He says four children. I say two and then decide. We'll run Montressa, but I don't know how long I'll keep teaching. I may burn out or maybe I'll want more time with Nate. So, I guess the answer is yes and no."

So maybe they hadn't etched every detail in stone, but at least they agreed that they'd be together. Avery watched another dragonfly hover over the surface of the water as she smoothed out her towel.

"Miles and I have no plan past mid-August." She picked a loose towel thread. "When we're together at the lake, we're on the same page. It's all little things, like whether to make blueberry muffins or blueberry pancakes. I'm afraid to ask the bigger questions because I'm catching glimpses of his answers, and I think I assumed things that aren't correct."

"Like what?" Lily asked.

"I'm not sure he wants a long-term commitment." A tear stung the corner of Avery's eye. "And I don't care if we get married. I'm okay with that. But I want a partner who's in it for the long haul."

The door to the Red House slid open and Anna Catherine emerged carrying Lennox who looked adorable in her tiny swimsuit and a floppy hat.

"Hey." Anna Catherine grinned from under a matching floppy sun hat as she bounced Lennox on her hip. Her other hand held a small pink inflatable swim float. "I thought I'd take her for a swim."

Anna Catherine passed the lounge chairs and walked to the edge of the dock.

"I want to get in, but I don't know how to do it with the baby. Can one of you help me put her in this little floatie?"

"Sure." Avery held Lennox as Anna Catherine slid into the water and kept the tiny inner tube still. Lennox's eyes grew large at the sensation of the cool water as Avery lowered her into the tube.

"I can't tell if she's petrified or happy." Anna Catherine snickered as she guided Lennox's tiny feet through the leg holes. She pulled up the collapsible sunshade and spun Lennox around so she could see Avery. "Say thank you to Avery, Lennox."

Lennox cooed and splashed her hand in the water. Anna Catherine steered Lennox back and forth in front of the dock.

"That floatie is the cutest thing I've ever seen," said Lily.

"Miles bought it," Anna said. "He had everything ready for us. Diapers, Boudreaux's Butt Paste, this, and a portable crib so she could nap inside it while we hang out. It has a mobile with little moose and fish, which is so Miles. He's the sweetest."

Lily smacked Avery's arm. "See! That's not something a man who wants to stay solo does."

"Wait, what did I miss?" Anna Catherine asked.

"Avery thinks Miles doesn't want a long-term commitment." Lily offered.

"Oh Avery, I'm so sorry. I'm partially to blame," Anna said. "When I said you and Miles would be great parents, I overstepped. We talk about personal stuff with Miles all the time. But I went too far. I hope I didn't upset things. I forgot you're new to our group. It feels like I've known you forever."

Miles always said Anna Catherine and Hayes were regular people, but Avery savored someone famous bonding with her.

"It's okay." Avery glanced back at the Red House. "But his reaction worries me."

"I think I made him sweat." Anna let out an uneasy laugh. "I have a habit of pushing too hard."

Except Miles seemed anxious on the walk, way before Anna had entered the conversation. Walking a baby with a dog made Avery imagine the two of them in a few years. He could've envisioned the same thing. Maybe Victoria was right, and Miles didn't want a family, despite being a natural with children.

"No, Anna, it wasn't you. It was already weird." Avery bent over and dragged a finger through the water. "I got the sense he doesn't want children."

Anna spun around, mouth wide open in shock. "What?"

"He doesn't have siblings. I get the impression he didn't feel parented as a teen, because of his mother's illness. He told me he isn't sure he's equipped to be a parent."

"No one is sure until they do it," Anna Catherine said.

"The part about his teenage years is true." Lily put on her sunglasses. "Miles was such a good kid. Never missed an assignment, overachieved at everything, never misbehaved. Never drank or smoked. His mother was in and out of the hospital all through high school. The guy parented himself, and he did a damn good job."

Whenever Miles talked about the things he'd missed out on, Avery turned to mush and felt compelled not to challenge him. Doing so could take him farther into his pain. Besides, a lifetime together was a touchy subject for two people who just reunited.

"He had panic in his eyes and couldn't get out of there fast enough." Avery noticed a group of kids swimming out to the King of the Rocks. "The only other time he left that parking lot that quickly was the day we broke up. Maybe he doesn't see himself with me after this summer. Victoria said we'd never last. She called him Mr. One and Done."

"What? He never talks about the women he's dated, except you." Anna Catherine swam closer, pushing Lennox ahead of her. "He used to tell us he thought he'd seen you in random places, like in crowds or waiting for the subway. He wanted to know our opinion on whether he could be forgiven. Occasionally, he contemplated texting or calling you."

"He did that with us too," Lily said. "He always asked about you. And he wanted to know if you asked about him."

Avery had never once asked about him, afraid of reopening the hole he'd left in her heart. When he asked about Avery, it must've been hard for Lily. If she'd been in Lily's shoes, she'd have lied to make him feel better.

"One time, I asked if he had a photo of you," Anna Catherine said. "He didn't have one on him, so we googled you and when your photo came up... Avery, the warmth in his eyes could have melted an iceberg. Everything stopped. The house fell quiet. The kind of stillness where you can tell something is about to happen. He decided to find you that night. In the end, he didn't contact you because Nate told him you were engaged. He said all he wanted was for you to be happy. But he said it with regret, like he wished he'd been the one who'd made you happy."

"He might need more time," Lily added. "He's relied on himself for so long. Maybe his dreams are coming true, and it's overwhelming."

They'd also entered the relationship with their own trepidations. Avery couldn't let go of the worry that whomever she fell for might not love her the way she loved them. That fear stayed glued to her like an invisible tattoo. In the Boathouse, Miles had admitted he'd spent a long time telling himself all the reasons he didn't deserve her. Maybe a piece of that still lurked in him.

"This morning was stressful." Anna Catherine shook her head. "But I promise he's different with you. Hayes and I were just saying last night how this is the first time we've seen him so relaxed and content."

It helped to hear Miles's best friends had noticed a change.

"Thank you," Avery said. "He called me his girlfriend. That's great, but it also feels like whatever I say becomes clouded with motive. I don't want to push him into something he isn't ready for, and this morning wasn't the best time to take a deep dive into our future."

"Hang in there," Anna said. "Let him get used to the idea of the two of you. It may take him longer than the average guy to open up about the big stuff."

All three of them stared out at the lake where the group of kids had made it to the King of the Rocks.

"I used to be petrified of swimming out to that rock. It's so far out and so deep all around it." Lily took another sip of water. "The cool thing about people is we learn how to do all kinds of things we were once afraid of. Miles'll get there."

"Yeah." Avery stood. She needed a moment to herself and a glass of water. "I'm going inside to get something to drink. Y'all need anything?"

As Avery walked into the A-frame, she decided this weekend was for having fun. Miles took a big step introducing her to his friends. They could discuss their futures over time, which they'd already set aside. After a quick trip to the bathroom, she opened the refrigerator. The entire top shelf was filled with pint-sized bottles of chocolate milk. For one man. She let out a chuckle and chose sparkling water.

The back door creaked.

"Avery."

His voice prickled every hair on her neck. She closed the refrigerator door and met his gaze. The color had returned to his face. Miles opened his arms wide. He wanted the same thing she did. She put down her can.

As soon as he wrapped her in his embrace, her entire body relaxed. His did the same. He squeezed her tighter, taking a long inhale, as if he were smelling something he loved.

Miles was a conundrum. Sometimes he pushed her away. Other times, like now, it felt like he'd never let her go.

He kissed her neck and murmured into her hair. "I'm so sorry I bolted this morning."

They needed this right now. The two of them, holding each other. Nothing else mattered.

"This morning was a jump I didn't see coming." She pulled back to gauge his reaction and chuckled. "We haven't even seen each other's apartments."

Miles laughed and a spark lit his eyes. He pushed her back to the counter and settled his hips into hers. Avery massaged the knots in his shoulders.

"Let's change that," he said. "Come see my apartment next weekend. We'll go to the camp fundraiser together. Sunday morning, you can fly back to Maine with Anna for Lily's bachelorette. What do you think?"

A step forward. He was ready to let her into his life, ready for her to meet more of his friends.

"I'd like that." She kissed him.

"It's a date." He leaned over and scooped an arm behind her knees, lifting her and carrying her to the stairs.

"Miles, we should be friendly hosts and go swim with your guests," she said, putting up no fight. After the morning they'd had, she needed to feel him.

"I need to change into my swim trunks," he said, his voice rough and ragged. "You know what your coconut sunscreen does to me, and if I don't untie your bikini before I go out there"—he growled into her neck—"our guests are going to be acutely aware of how much I want you. And that's rude."

"So considerate." She kissed his neck.

"Nah, I'm about to get wicked selfish."

CHAPTER TWENTY-TWO

Miles

JULY 22 - NEW YORK, NEW YORK

Before the elevator reached the floor labeled *PH*, Miles stuffed his speech notes into his pocket, pulled out his keys, and glanced at his watch. Thanks to a weather delay, he'd been a day late getting home, and now had less than an hour to get ready for the gala. He let out a tired sigh. At least he'd made it back to New York in time for the fundraiser.

The doorman had let Avery into his apartment the previous night and she'd texted him a picture of herself grinning on the Boa sofa. Miles's heart soared at the anticipation of seeing of her smile after five long days in Wyoming. Waiting the extra day to hold her again had felt longer than the entire week he'd been away.

He'd wanted to be there when she entered his apartment for the first time. He'd always imagined sharing champagne on his terrace and pointing out landmarks like he pointed out stars. *There's Central Park, the Empire State Building. That's lower Manhattan. The planes fly up the East River and down the Hudson.*

After that, a tour of the interior. *This is the statement couch the interior decorator insisted I buy to match the modern style of my apartment. I spend all my time over in that navy Eames lounge chair instead. I can't wait to make love on the couch we picked for the Red House and nap on it, holding you. Maybe we should buy a second one for here and get rid of this one.*

He wasn't sure when his "I" had become a "we," but he couldn't wait for the Saturdays when they'd wake up next to one another, make love, and amble to the kitchen to throw together some blueberry pancakes. New York might be big and bold compared to small, quaint Maine but no matter where you were, you needed breakfast. He wished they could start that life tomorrow, but Avery and Anna Catherine were flying out for Lily's bachelorette in Boothbay first thing in the morning.

He walked off the elevator and headed to the door on the left. One day, Avery wouldn't be a guest in Penthouse A. He'd overcome his anxiety and ask her to live here. But it'd be two years until any of that happened. Her MBA came first. She'd have an internship the following summer, possibly with a consulting firm, who knew where, but it wouldn't be at the lake.

They needed to savor their little bits of time together over the next month. They might cross paths for a brief second between her return to the lake from Lily's bachelorette and his departure for Nate's canoe trip. After that, they'd have two weeks until her classes began. She'd be busier than ever in the fall—and he planned to finish his masters, recruit new board members, write grants, and if they raised enough money, purchase and renovate the corporate retreat.

Miles needed August to do what August did best: slow everything down. He unlocked the door and glanced at his watch again. This would be a quick hello.

As the door swung open, the sweet scent of magnolia permeated his senses in the best way possible. Within seconds of the door closing, she ran out of the guest bedroom wearing his plaid flannel bathrobe. She'd wrapped her hair in a lovely chignon and wore a wide grin on her face. He only caught a glimpse before Avery flew into his open arms. Miles imagined coming home every day and wrapping himself in this happy energy.

"I'm so excited to be here," she said. "I slept in the guest room last night because it felt weird to sleep in your bed for the first time without you."

If only they could stay in for the night. But he needed to shower, shave, and memorize his speech. His dream of opening a camp for grieving families depended on raising enough money for a down payment and securing financing on the corporate retreat. He and Hayes couldn't make an offer without proving they could afford it. He'd happily add more to whatever they raised, but a large donor base gave grant-making foundations a reason to believe the project could succeed.

"Get going." Avery smacked his backside. "The car will be here soon."

He recited his speech from memory while he shaved. In the shower, he went over it again and forgot half of it. The time crunch sabotaged his confidence, and schmoozing people for money wasn't his forte.

While he believed in the mission and knew his fundraising target, Miles doubted his ability to sway people to donate to a camp that hadn't affected a single person yet. And he rarely spoke to crowds. On *Bright and Early,* he talked to a camera. There was no audience inside the studio, only out on the plaza. CashCache's success had happened in a room, at a computer, after work hours and on weekends. Later, it had grown in rented conference rooms and when CashCache took off, in a real office.

This gala called for convincing a large public audience. He needed the stage presence of Hayes and the persuasiveness of Paulson, who could fearlessly convince anyone of anything. Miles hated to admit it, but he admired Paulson's ability to sell Avery on her hotel bar in seconds flat.

Thankfully, Hayes and Anna Catherine were a huge draw for the event. *Counterblow*, Hayes's latest film, was smashing box office records this summer. People vacated Manhattan in summer, spending their days in the Hamptons or on Nantucket. But they'd returned to the City for this event and the chance to be in the same room with Hayes Preston and Anna Catherine Page.

Hayes had mentioned the Camp Luciole project during a recent appearance on *The Tonight Show*. He'd teared up talking about his own loss. The clip had gone viral, a sign others cared about the camp. Miles would rely on that to buoy him through the night.

Thirty minutes later, Miles leaned against his kitchen counter, wearing navy pants and a dress shirt, his jacket hanging on a nearby dining-room chair. His tie looped over his shoulders and his cufflinks sat beside him as he gave his speech one last pass.

"How do I look?" Avery walked out of the guest bedroom, a vision in midnight blue. An embellished crop top showed a hint of her midriff above a long skirt with sparkling beads fading down its length. On her feet were matching heels. The added height brought her eyes closer to his.

"Oh, Pepper." His throat tightened. "You're prettier than the night sky."

She twirled around and finished with a curtsey.

"The invitation said the theme is summer camp." She skimmed her hand down the skirt. "This ensemble reminds me of stargazing with you."

He put down his notes and stepped to her, tracing his thumb along the exposed skin above her waistband, his eyes holding hers.

"I don't want to dishevel perfection." His voice cracked. "How about if I touch you right here all night?"

She folded his tie under his collar, her fingers brushing the back of his neck, and began tying a knot. No woman had ever dressed Miles, only undressed him. It felt caring and incredibly intimate. Avery focused on the task, her forehead close to his lips, as they breathed the same air. In the silence, his breathing became ragged. Avery patted the tie and kissed him, melting his nerves. She wiped her lipstick from the edge of his mouth, and he felt the urge to kiss her so she'd have to rub off another smudge.

"You can dishevel me later." She tugged his belt loops and winked.

As they stepped away from one another, a chill washed over him. They never used air conditioning at the lake and Miles didn't like it. Cold air billowing out of a rectangle in the ceiling was not the same as a cool breeze blowing off the water. He missed the heat she generated in him.

Avery glided over to the enormous windows facing his terrace.

"This apartment is something," she said in a way that didn't sound like she loved it. "It's like a decorator's show house."

True. He lived inside a glossy magazine photo. Staged and sterile, with nothing personal anywhere. It could easily have been a rental because it said nothing about him. He didn't collect things like airplane propellers or flags; things that hinted at his interests. His hobbies were running and reading, but his bookshelves were filled with modern sculptures and massive black and white photography books he'd never cracked open.

Avery crossed to the Eames chair and ran her finger along the back, swiveling it.

"I think this is your favorite spot." She smiled. "It's the only thing in here with your imprint."

"You know me and decorating." Miles fiddled with his shirt cuff. "I figured the designer knew her stuff. The couch looks cool, but it's meant for a media room. It makes you recline, even if you don't want to."

"You're leaning back to where it's hard to get up," she said. "It's like being stuck in a comfy dentist chair."

"Maybe I should pull out my drill." He winked.

"Slow down, doctor. I need Mr. Thirsty first." Avery made the slurping sound of the dentist's suction tube. "On second thought, he sucks."

Miles loved when they relaxed and joked like this, even if she wasn't wild about this apartment. Purchasing the Penthouse A had been like buying a new pair of pants only to discover they chafed. He'd moved to this brand-new building from a small prewar studio on a vibrant, sometimes noisy street in the East Village. What his old apartment had lacked in size, it made up for in charm and warmth.

"I'll redo the whole place if you don't like it," he said.

She straightened and walked over to him.

"Oh, I didn't mean for you to change it. It's beautiful; the polar opposite of the Red House. Maybe because your life in the City is different from your life at the lake. They're worlds apart."

He winced. Miles felt like the same person, no matter where he was, but she had a point. This apartment was extravagant but uncomfortable, which summed up how he felt about his city life.

He pulled her closer and rested his hand on that bare spot again, letting her warmth permeate his fingers and run straight to his heart.

"I want you to feel at home here," he said.

"At the end of summer, I'll still be a visitor. I know you hate talking about the future and now is not the best time, but at some point, we need to discuss what happens when we leave the lake."

What came next after leaving the lake loomed large. Denying it wasn't fair to Avery. He'd never asked her where she wanted to land. Surely, she had dreams and plans that were important to her. Supporting each other required love and commitment, which sounded amazing and overwhelming at the same time. Miles's chest tightened, and his heartbeat sped up. He'd noticed a pattern to this gripping fear. Next came the sweat.

"I want us to try," he said. "But I don't know how to figure this out, and maybe we can't until we are living in it."

Avery placed a hand around his wrist, circling his veins with her thumb. Her touch was meant to soothe but it did the opposite. Their eyes met and her brow furrowed. He hooked a finger into his shirt collar and pulled. Miles wanted to know for sure he loved her. But love should feel easy, not frightening. He didn't know how they'd make it work with his rising anxiety.

She picked up a cufflink from the counter.

"You've stepped away from your life this summer." She matched up the holes on his shirt cuff. "I know you need to get back to it. I need to figure out my next steps. I'm having second thoughts about the MBA, but I don't know what else to do."

She'd mentioned her doubts since the night Casper went missing, and once again, he didn't want to weigh in on a big decision that shouldn't involve him. He would celebrate and support whatever she chose.

"The thing is," she said, smiling at him, "I don't see myself as a consultant or investment banker. I know we have the party right now and this isn't the time for a deep discussion. But there's a fork in my road, and I don't know how to navigate all of it. Maybe we could talk about it later."

She finished putting on the right cufflink and lifted her hand to his cheek, running the back of her knuckles along the edge of his jaw. For a second, he thought about telling her that her deep blue eyes matched her dress, but she spoke first.

"All I know is I love you," she said as her eyes melted into a lovely starlit haze. "That's all that matters. And this time, we'll figure it out."

It caught him by surprise, how easily she said those words. Ten years ago, she could have interpreted saying *I love you* as the beginning of their end.

He wasn't sure how his face reacted to a moment he hadn't seen coming. He should have treated her words as what they were: the best news. Whatever shape his face took, it clearly wasn't the joyful expression Avery must've hoped for. She lowered her gaze and picked up the left cufflink, intent on her work.

She'd taken a major step in their relationship and once again, he couldn't keep pace. Sweat burst out on his brow, across his sternum, and under his arms. His silence had to hurt, but he couldn't move. Part of him screamed to lift her chin, kiss her, and repeat the same words back to her. Not loving her would break her heart again. But expressing his love could lead them down a path of profound and painful loss. Losing her would decimate him.

Miles rubbed his right hand over his heart and inhaled deeply to calm the internal cyclone swirling inside his chest. It was no use. His heart raced faster than it had when he had run a sub-four-minute mile in college. His collar squeezed his neck.

"Avery, I can't..."

Breathe.

The doorman buzzed just as she finished with his left sleeve.

Breathe. He inhaled, held it, and exhaled. One more time. She didn't seem to notice. His internal storm began to quiet.

"There." Avery adjusted his tie. "You're hot to go and ready for your speech."

She stepped back and excused herself to get her lipstick and handbag. He rested both hands on the edge of the counter and took a few more deep breaths to calm himself. When she came out of his guest bedroom, his heart had stopped racing. Miles focused on her crystal purse, shaped like a tiny camp tent, looped over her arm. Avery loved a theme, and she'd nailed this one. For him.

For the first half of the ride, they stared out their respective windows, the tent handbag between them. Neither one said a word. About halfway to the Carter Park Avenue Hotel, he'd rested a hand on her leg.

"I need more time." He heard the melancholy in his own voice. This night should be fun for her. He'd made it tense, maybe unbearable.

"I know." Avery smoothed her skirt and picked up her purse, fishing through it for something. If he had to guess, she wanted her lip balm.

Miles wished for a way to tell her his fears and not cause her to worry the two of them would never get things right, or worse, think she was to blame. But the next thing he knew, the car had turned onto Park Avenue. The Carter's awning was straight ahead. There wasn't time to discuss this now.

Her phone buzzed in her lap. His buzzed a second later. She opened her texts, and her hand rose to her mouth.

"Oh."

"Everything okay?" he asked.

"It's Wes. He and Jeanette from the diner just got engaged." She turned the screen to Miles, but he barely glanced at the photo because the smile on Avery's face didn't match the hurt in her eyes.

A rush of guilt came over him. If he'd handled the *I love you* better, those eyes would be bright and happy. Saying it back now seemed like trying to even the score. His silence had delivered a blow, and it occurred to Miles that Avery knew unanswered love all too well. He reached across the seat and took her shaky hand as her other hand scrolled through photo after photo of Jeanette and Wes.

"I don't get it." She put the phone in her lap, and Miles braced himself for her realization that at almost the same time she'd professed her love to him, their friend had professed his love to someone too, each event leading to wildly different outcomes.

"He proposed at the Wildlife Park, but not in the pretty center part with the otters. Or by the baby moose. He dropped to one knee in the bat house." She let out a snort. "Who proposes at the bats? It's dark and bats are gross."

She had to be thinking about something else, but Miles needed her to arrive at this party in a better place. So he kept it light.

"It's Wes. He probably said something silly." Miles shifted into his smoothest, lowest voice. "Something like, 'Jeanette, these bats have me wondering, would you like to hang out for the rest of our lives?'"

Avery pressed her lips together in amusement, but he wanted her full smile.

"The only way this story works for me is if Jeanette's first reaction was, 'I didn't see this coming.'" Miles held back a laugh. "And Wes replied, 'bats what she said.'"

Avery's eyes lit up, and the balloon of tension between them burst into a sweet swell of laughter. Ten seconds later, she was laughing tears. He offered her his clean, white handkerchief.

"I'm going to get it messy." She held up a hand to refuse it. "I've made enough messes tonight."

"It'll be like us," he said. "A little messy, but worth having with you all the time."

"I shouldn't have said ... you know. But I missed you last week." She took the cloth and gently dabbed an eye. "I put pressure on you when you already had too much going on, which wasn't very thoughtful."

As the car door opened to let them out, he kissed her forehead. "Let's go out there and have fun. We'll talk later. Promise."

She nodded and took his hand as he helped her out of the car.

CHAPTER TWENTY-THREE

Avery

JUNE 22 - NEW YORK, NEW YORK

The elevator's beep at each passing floor sounded louder than Avery remembered. She'd grown used to silence on the sullen ride home. Miles hadn't said a word, despite the fundraiser's success. After he and Hayes raised hundreds of thousands of dollars for a camp that hadn't opened its doors yet, he should be jovial, celebratory, or at least proud of himself. He wasn't even smiling.

Avery had barely seen Miles the entire night. They'd drifted from talking to a few people together to having separate conversations while standing next to each other. She hadn't noticed the sea of people filling in between them and before she knew it, they were on opposite sides of the room. Every time she caught a glimpse and headed in his direction, he'd vanished by the time she arrived. There was no indication he'd looked for her in the swollen crowd. As the night wore on, Avery wondered if Miles remembered he'd brought a date.

After an hour of cat and mouse, Avery gave up on looking for him, vowed to stop worrying about everything that happened before the party, and walked toward the band. Miles hated to dance, but the almost empty dance floor seemed like the easiest place for him to find her, if he wanted to. She felt a tap on her shoulder and spun around to find Paulson. He motioned to the floor, and they danced an entire set.

The evening had worked out for Paulson. When the band started a slow song, he and Avery headed to the bar. Victoria waved to Avery and came over to say hello. A spark ignited the second Avery introduced the two of them. Avery declined an invitation to join Paulson and Victoria out on the rooftop terrace, allowing them space to get acquainted. Again she'd gone in search of Miles.

"This elevator is taking forever," she said into the silence.

"Ayuh." He leaned his head back, sighed, and closed his eyes.

Maybe he was exhausted. Due to bad weather, it had taken more than a day for him to get home from Wyoming. In the car on the way to the Carter Park Avenue, he'd promised to discuss the fall once they got home. Perhaps he dreaded that conversation now that she'd made everything so serious between them.

It was possible the *I love you* explained everything that had happened at the event. He might have used the crowd as a buffer to gather his thoughts. Once they exited this semi-private elevator and entered his apartment, they could talk freely.

She needed to apologize. The last week without him at the lake had been hard. She'd felt adrift, uncertain of what to do with her career and her life. Avery was never one for throwing cards into the wind and seeing where they landed. She craved the predictability of a solid outline. Her need to plan everything had driven her to say something intimate at the worst time and she'd been unfair to Miles, though truthful.

He stared straight ahead, his jaw tight. A vein at his temple pulsed.

Maybe they should go to bed and deal with it in the morning. A shiver snaked down her spine. The tension was eerily similar to the moments right before their breakup that summer. He'd been sopping wet after pulling Max Perry from the lake and resuscitating him. Water droplets falling off Miles's shorts left small dots in the dust on the surface of the staff parking lot. Something about walking out of the water carrying a limp child had taken Miles somewhere else. After he'd breathed life back into the little boy and the ambulance arrived, Sam had asked Avery to take Miles home. At the parking lot he'd insisted on going home alone, staring straight ahead, jaw tensing and letting go. She'd called him a hero, and he'd denied it. She'd told him she loved him and wanted to help. He'd clutched his chest and called their relationship spoiled milk, well past its expiration date, before he got in the Mail Jeep and peeled out of the parking lot.

A pressure built behind Avery's eyes. He'd clutched his chest that same way before they left for the gala too, a grip so tight it seemed like he was devoting all his energy to stopping something. The elevator pinged and the doors slid open. She stepped out into the hallway and waited as he unlocked his door.

As soon as they were inside the apartment, she started to apologize but stopped short when Miles's face hardened into a chiseled bedrock of ridges and crevices like it had when Victoria asked about his private life. Avery removed her strappy sandals instead. When she finished, his face was no softer.

"You must have dazzled Paulson," he said through gritted teeth, holding his phone so she could see the six-figure donation Paulson had made to the camp.

This couldn't be the root of his anger. The point of a fundraiser was to make money.

"Wow, that's so nice." She tried to sound upbeat. "The second you mentioned people could give through the camp's app, everyone around me pulled out their phones. Your story inspired so many people to donate."

"Oh, he didn't do it for me." Miles put his phone down and crossed his arms, leaning back on the kitchen counter.

Avery's mouth fell open. Neither anger nor jealousy suited anyone, even him.

"Wait, are you mad because he gave a huge donation? That had nothing to do with me. Your camp motivated him." Avery leaned a hip against the counter beside him. "You know Paulson has a personal history of loss, right? His mom left him and his father when he was ten. She's alive, but she's in something that sounds like a cult. He's tried, but they've never reconnected."

"That's not the same thing." Miles glared at her, his darkened chestnut eyes narrowing.

"It's a loss, Miles. His mom chose not to love him. That's painful."

"You spent most of the night dancing with him." He shook his head.

"Because you left me all alone. I tried to locate you so many times, I gave up. It felt like you didn't care where I was. I couldn't find anyone I knew except for him. All Paulson and I did was dance. We made the best of a room where we knew almost no one. He never so much as touched me. He's wanted to meet Victoria for a while and once I introduced them, I left them to chat and looked for you. Again!"

Miles massaged his jaw. "You know how I feel about him. And you danced for the entire set. You left me."

Avery removed the bracelets from her wrist and stacked them on the counter. She knew he wasn't jealous of Paulson. His behavior was about something bigger. Maybe she'd told him she loved him at the wrong time, but she would not let him talk to her this way.

"The dance floor wasn't full. Why didn't *you* come over and ask me to dance? Or ask me to go get a drink? Or any of the million other things you could have asked me? All I wanted was to be with you. I would have done whatever you suggested. I actively looked for you. Forgive me if I didn't want to stand at the edge of the party like a jilted wallflower."

For a long minute, Miles said nothing. A hurt rose within her. Trent had iced her out at parties too. Avery had initially assumed his habit of flirting his way through a room was part of his charm. Later, she learned it was part of his game. Miles wasn't the type to enchant women for the sake of his own ego, but he'd left her out in the cold.

"I don't like feeling jilted, Miles," she said. "I was alone in a sea of beautiful people who didn't seem to know I existed. The last thing I wanted to do was bother you with my insecurities. You had enough going on."

Miles opened the fridge and poured himself a glass of chocolate milk without asking if she wanted anything. She let him gather his thoughts in hopes he might gain some perspective.

"I had a full plate," he said, screwing the cap back on the milk bottle. "It was a lot of pressure, raising money while making sure everyone had fun. I'm not used to that."

"You go to parties, premieres, and galas all the time." Avery placed a hand on her hip, right where he had touched her earlier in the night, back when he couldn't wait to dishevel her. His wish had been granted. Things between them were rapidly disheveling now.

"Those are different. I'm not an interesting person, I just know interesting people," he said. "It's never *my* party. I'm always a guest."

"Then you should know how I felt," she said, trying to keep herself calm despite the growing storm inside her. He had to understand the humiliation of not belonging somewhere.

He stood quietly and drank half his milk.

"I wanted you next to me," he said, peering into the glass. "Even though we were in the same room, it hurt that you were somewhere else. Did you hear my speech?"

"Of course I heard it. Your speech was brilliant and moving. So many people around me teared up," Avery said. "And I kept moving to where I saw you and when I got there, you were gone. At some point, I felt iced out."

Miles began to pace. "What is happening? When did we start moving so fast? We were fine this morning, and now we're..."

He ran his hand down his face, shook his head, and stared at the floor.

Avery needed him to finish the sentence, but he didn't. So she filled in the blank for herself.

Now, we're ... having our first fight. Okay, maybe our second.

She gripped the edge of the counter as a giant bubble of hurt expanded through her chest. One fight shouldn't be enough to establish a pattern, but both their fights had started with her saying she loved him.

And him saying nothing.

She knew the pattern. Miles was, after all, a runner.

Avery didn't like city Miles. She loved the boy in the Boathouse who pointed out constellations to her. Saying *I love you* hadn't protected them from the cold, hard truth. Once again, Victoria was correct. Avery and Miles would *never* work outside the lake.

That summer, she had said nothing as they stood in the parking lot. He hadn't given her any choice other than to accept his decree and watch as he drove off. This time, Avery was going to say her piece.

"Maybe things started moving fast when we were locked in the Boathouse that night, and you said it had always been me." She swallowed the growing lump in her throat. "Or maybe it was when you told me you didn't need to look at the heavens because I was the only star in your sky. I'm beginning to think you only mean those things at the lake. All I know is tonight, I wasn't in your sky. I was in your way."

"I never said that," he said.

"You didn't have to. I can't be yours only at the lake, Miles. I've been in a relationship with someone who had another life, and I'm not doing it again."

"Dammit, Avery." Miles slammed a fist on the counter. "I'm not Trent. Don't compare me to him."

"Then don't give me a reason to!"

It was the first time in the history of Miles and Avery that she had yelled at him. Maybe he wasn't Trent, but he wasn't being kind or caring either.

They both stood there, quietly contemplating the night, the summer, their past. A few minutes later, he pushed off the counter and walked away.

"I'm tired," he said. "I'm going to bed."

Miles walked into his room and shut the door, making it clear she wasn't invited. She didn't like how he fled when things got sticky. Working something out with him was impossible, especially since he didn't seem to have worked it out for himself.

Her doubts were coming true. They'd left the lake and fallen apart. Maybe the lake was their haven from the pains of life, or maybe it put them into a continuous loop of reliving that summer. Ten years ago, it would've been tremendous a challenge to stay together after the summer ended, given the eight states between them.

Now they could overcome the physical distance, but it wouldn't resolve the emotional and social gaps. It wouldn't quell his instinct to run. Miles bolted when faced with too big of an emotional jump. Not being able to tell him she loved him was no way to have a relationship.

She didn't need to be the only star in his entire universe, but she wanted to be the brightest one. The North Star, guiding him home. When he scanned the crowded sky, she wanted *him* to find *her*. He could do it at the lake, but he couldn't do it in the real world. Summer only lasted ten weeks. The other forty-two weeks, life got real. Avery wanted love, commitment, and trust. The things that made Miles flee.

After taking off her makeup and going to bed in the guest bedroom, Avery tossed and turned, chasing sleep for what felt like hours. Her heart was breaking all over again. At three in the morning, Miles came into the guest room and climbed into bed with her.

At least he hadn't waited ten years to return.

"Avery," he whispered. "I'm screwing us up."

He snuggled into the nook of her shoulder, as if he couldn't get close enough.

"We'll figure it out," she murmured. "Mimi used to say our problems look different in the light of day."

She spent an hour listening to him breathe, thinking about that summer, this summer, Maine, New York City, all of it. Avery wanted to believe Mimi was right, but the light of day wouldn't resolve whatever had happened after the gala. Some of their problems remained the same. Miles couldn't commit to Avery the way she committed to him. Once again, she'd given away too much of herself. The pain of that raw vulnerability was simply too much to bear.

Consciously or not, he'd made her fears come true. She loved him, but she wasn't sure he knew how to let himself love or be loved. Some part of Miles was always closed off and she couldn't open it. Being together all the time, like they were in Maine, wasn't sustainable.

Years ago, she and Miles had bonded together fast and fallen apart faster. A few hours ago, they'd gone from *I love you* to broken in the blink of an eye. If history repeated itself, he'd say goodbye soon.

Unless she said it first.

CHAPTER TWENTY-FOUR

Miles

JULY 23 - THE NEXT DAY

Miles woke the next morning clouded in brain fog, aware of the daylight but unsure of the time. His hands skimmed the mattress. Alone again. Not a trace of Avery's warmth remained on the cool percale sheets. For a second, he thought she'd gone to the airport until he heard the shower shut off. He exhaled his relief and massaged his forehead.

They needed to talk about last night.

Mimi was right. Last night looked different today. He didn't know why the second Avery said she loved him, everything inside him shut down, but he knew she'd meant it and he'd hurt her. There had to be a way through this. Other people entered long-distance relationships every day. With the pressure of the fundraiser gone, he felt calmer and a little more level-headed.

When Miles thought about it from Avery's perspective, she had every reason to be upset. She was right; he hadn't looked for her in the crowd last night. He'd needed space to process the way he'd felt when she'd admitted she loved him. He should have told her about his anxiety instead of shutting her out. Given his inattentiveness, it was a wonder she'd stayed at the party. Of course she danced with Paulson.

Hayes had managed the party so easily while doting on Anna Catherine. Anna knew people there, yet Hayes had included her in every conversation. Miles should have done the same for Avery. Instead, he had ignored her so he could stay in control of his emotions. Seeing her doe-eyed gaze would've reminded him of his silence, or worse, brought back the heart palpitations. No one wanted to donate to a cause led by a man covered in a sheen of anxious sweat. They wanted confidence, not distress. He'd accomplished a calm demeanor, but Avery had paid the price.

He rolled over to her side of the mattress and sunk his head into her pillow, surrounding himself in her divine floral aroma. He wanted to be the guy who knew what love was and gave it away easily. He thought about the couples he knew. Anna Catherine and Hayes. Lily and Nate. His parents. They opened their hearts easily, sure they had found *the one*. If they could do it, he must be able to get there somehow.

If he was honest, it had been a relief not to have to introduce her to every single person he talked to last night. He wasn't ready for the panic of being asked if he'd finally found his person. His person. He hated that term. She was more than his person. She was everything, but somehow acknowledging her love felt like taking an exit labeled *Road to Ruin*. The one where Miles freezes. And runs.

He needed to make last night's fumble up to her, but she was flying to Portland later that morning for Lily's bachelorette in Boothbay Harbor. *Bright and Early* had him hosting three live segments on "Building Your Nest Egg at Any Age" this week, so he had to stay in the City. As soon as Wednesday's show wrapped, he'd fly to Maine for Nate's bachelor canoe trip. What a mess.

Last night he'd given her no reason to believe he loved her. He needed time to fix that. Time he didn't have.

He sat on the edge of the bed and ran his hand down his face. It made no sense for Avery's love to paralyze him. She was everything he wanted: smart, kind, loving, honest, invested. Whenever he imagined his future, it was Avery sitting across from him at the end of the dock and standing beside him on the subway so he wouldn't have to read alone to keep the world away. It was Avery leaning in for a kiss in his Mail Jeep as he turned around from looking out the back window and shifted out of reverse.

Miles wanted to be what she needed. Support her through her highs and lows. He'd get a dog, and that dog would be so much better than Casper because it was theirs. He'd train it. That sounded like love, and maybe it was, but he needed more time to figure out how to lean into his dreams without panic.

He had to apologize. Tell her about the tightness in his chest, the racing heartbeat, and the irrational, but real to him, parallel he'd drawn between love and loss. How he wasn't sure he could say the one thing she needed to hear.

Winning her back needed more than flowers and *I'm sorry*. Maybe he should drop everything and fly to Maine with her today. Or show up tomorrow, at the bachelorette party, *Jerry Maguire* style. Except that wouldn't be fair to Lily.

Through the bathroom door, he heard Avery's hair dryer. He went to the kitchen, brewed tea for her, and left it on the bedside table next to her earrings and lip balm. Miles waited in the living room, semi-reclined on his nest couch, drumming his fingers on the velvet armrest. His mind scrolled through various ways to start a discussion. When Avery finally came out, dressed for her flight, he took it as a good sign when she sat next to him and not as far away as possible.

"Thank you for the tea." She glanced at her phone, where the bright-pink Lyft app showed a map of his neighborhood. "Not sure I'll finish it. My car will be here in four minutes."

He reached for her hand and she let him hold it, but didn't clasp his in return. She was a little shaky.

"Avery, about last night." The couch squeaked as he shifted to face her. "I do know what it's like to feel alone at a party. I didn't handle the evening well, especially after we got home. And I'm sorry."

His long legs didn't know where to go on this low a couch, so he kept adjusting them. She drank a sip of tea and took a deep breath, slowly, as if preparing to say something she was afraid to say.

"Miles." She smiled with a huff. "This summer is a giant déjà vu. All the way down to me telling you I love you, you not saying it back, and you putting physical distance between us. It doesn't matter if it's across ten states or across a ballroom. We are heading for the same end. And I can't live through that a second time. I guess our love has muscle memory and is destined make the same mistake over and over again."

His heart skipped a beat. They weren't a mistake. She was everything.

"Wait. We're so great together." He squeezed her hand. "I walked into this damaged and afraid of truly enjoying the good things. Big feelings scare me, because so much can go wrong. And that's on me, not us, not you."

Avery again took her hand away and smoothed a wrinkle out of her jeans.

"We've been down this path." Her voice cracked. "We spend every second together at the lake, and it's great. But summer ends. Isolation and heartbreak follow. If last night proved anything, it's that I don't fit in your life here. It's best if we end this amicably. Our best friends are getting married. We need to get along for them."

Avery sat back on the couch and jiggled her leg. She checked the Lyft app. He could see the car was two blocks away and silently wished for a red light at the next intersection. Miles's chest was splitting in half.

They had the power to make this summer different, better than that summer. It didn't have to end.

"Avery." He reached over and caressed her cheek. "This summer is only like that one if we make it that way. Back then, I was a poor college athlete with a full schedule. You had three years left at Vanderbilt. That's all changed. I can travel to see you, and I can make it easy for you to come here. I'll do whatever it takes. I can lease time in a jet, so you never have to wait in an airport."

She stared at her lap, and then her phone buzzed.

"My car is here." She stood and he followed her to her bag, wrapping his hand around her wrist.

"If you think about it, we went into last night wanting the same thing. To be together. And a whole slew of people got in our way. I'm sorry I ignored you. Leaving you alone at a party should be easy to fix. Give me another chance at another party. And what you said to me before we left, I reacted poorly. And I want to say it back to you, but I'm slower at this than you. I have, um, issues I need to work through."

She lifted the handle on her suitcase and faced him, tears brimming in her eyes. He stepped closer and wrapped his arms around her, wishing she didn't have to leave now. When she buried her face in his chest, he took it as a sign she didn't believe they were over. Telling him she loved him only to attempt to break up with him less than twenty-four hours later might be an act of protection. Avery was trying to break her own heart before he could. Miles knew the signs. He'd done it once to himself.

He reached over to the counter, grabbed his handkerchief from last night, and handed it to her. She took it, let out a small laugh, and wiped her tears.

"The thing is, Miles, Victoria's right. You and I only work at the lake."

Rage billowed in his chest. Victoria had no business putting that in her head.

"She said that to you?"

"Twice." Avery wiped her nose. "That summer and this one."

No wonder Avery didn't like Victoria. Those were next-level head games. It had to sting when Victoria's prediction came true. He needed to tell her about his anxiety, but not now, not when it sounded like an excuse, or worse, a plea.

Her phone rang. The driver. She asked him to wait and promised to be right down.

"I have to go," she said as she hung up.

He followed her into the elevator and hugged her again.

"I don't want to be the guy who makes you sad." He kissed the top of her head. "I think we can fix this. I need to go back to therapy again. Last night I discovered I have some things I need to work on, but right now you have Lily's bachelorette, and I have three live segments this week. As soon as I am done, I'm off to Nate's canoe trip. After that, we have the first two weeks of August with no other commitments. Can you give me time to get my bearings? There's so much I need to tell you, but it's too big a conversation for an elevator ride. Please don't end us yet. Hit the pause button. And after we get through our obligations, give me an afternoon or maybe a day so we can discuss a different ending to our story."

"Like when Ross and Rachel took a break?"

"Nothing like that. Do you remember the week before we started dating a decade ago?"

"No." Avery shook her head and let out a tearful snort.

"I ran into you in the woods and quoted Robert Frost." Miles eyed the elevator's floor counter. They were only halfway down, moving more slowly than last night. "I quoted the first two lines of 'The Road Not Taken,'" he said. "You answered with the ending of 'Stopping by the Woods on a Snowy Evening.'"

She nodded and let out a trace of a giggle. "You corrected me and said that wasn't the same poem."

"You told me you didn't care because 'Stopping by the Woods' was better."

He had loved that Avery hadn't been afraid to be herself. He still did.

"I remember you said when you were little, your mom used to read you that poem and you thought the 'miles to go' part was about you." She refolded the handkerchief she'd been clutching all this time. "So cute."

He chuckled. She remembered.

"Both those poems are about taking pauses and the difference it made." Miles was so sure this was one of his genius moments, if she bought into what he was saying. "This is us taking a Robert Frost moment. One that will make a difference. Think of it as a pause to consider our path. And after the pause, if you still think we won't work, I'll respect your decision."

Not great, but it was the best elevator speech he could come up with on such short notice. And the twist in her lips told him she was considering it.

"No sleeping with other people," she said, going back to *Friends* and probably Trent.

"Of course not," he said. "I'll go tantric. A sexual version of when Aaron Rodgers took that darkness retreat."

Avery giggled, and he told himself to savor it. He wouldn't hear her laugh for a week. Besides, her right eye twinkled, a sign she didn't want to end it.

"Text me all you want," he said. "If we want to talk, we call or FaceTime. But let's wait until we can be together to discuss the big stuff."

She concentrated on the display above the elevator buttons, watching the floors slowly tick down.

"Avery." He cupped her chin and ran his thumb along her cheek. "Whatever happens, I do not want to walk through the world as ghosts ever again."

She nodded, and he wasn't sure if she agreed not to be ghosts or to his plan.

"In the grand scope of our lives, this pause will be a tiny blip," he said. "But it has the potential to be the most important, most meaningful, and most mature moment you and I have ever experienced."

"I'd like us to have that," she said. "Especially the mature and meaningful parts."

The elevator chimed. They'd reached the lobby. As they hugged goodbye, he took a breath of magnolia, imprinting the moment for himself. She let go and gazed up at him. He took her wistful smile as her being okay with their pause.

The doors still hadn't opened. Maybe they were stuck. It wouldn't be the worst thing.

"Miles, I have to go," she said. But she didn't wriggle out of his arms. She stayed put.

He leaned in and whisked his lips over hers.

"Pepper," he said. "Next time we're together, I promise to be a better man than the one who wants to kiss you right now. Can I kiss you anyway?"

She nodded and he slowly kissed her, building the intensity until the elevator doors whooshed open. No one kissed him like she did. It had to be love, but he didn't say it.

When he let go, Symona Beauvais and Hazel Matheson stepped into the elevator. Hazel raised an eyebrow at Miles. Avery scurried out and waved goodbye. Miles stood in his pajamas and bare feet next to a model and a rock star but kept his eyes on Avery's beautiful face as the doors closed. His last thought, as he blew her a kiss, was that he'd turned her eyes gray and dull, and he'd do everything in his power to make them shine again.

CHAPTER TWENTY-FIVE

Avery

JULY 23 - BRUNSWICK, MAINE

Ah, salt air. Avery stepped out into the sunny street, tasted her gelato, and walked toward their parked car. She'd departed LaGuardia with Anna Catherine at nine. After the flight up and a little over an hour on the road, they'd stopped for food in Brunswick, thankful for a break from the rental car, which reminded Avery of a roller coaster cart that had no Bluetooth. Lily and her high school friends planned to drive from Montressa to Boothbay this afternoon.

Over lunch, Avery spotted the gelato store across the street and after reading the rave reviews online, announced she couldn't leave town without trying some. Cold, creamy desserts were the perfect way to pass a fraction of the three hours of free time they had until they could check into their charming rental cottage and start the bachelorette festivities.

This trip marked the first time Avery had been alone in public with

Anna Catherine Page, television star. On the flight, Avery gave Anna Catherine her window seat, partly to stop the gawkers. Most of them were nice, but nearly everyone stole a glance as they boarded. The whole flight, it felt like anyone could be eavesdropping. Avery had been careful not to have a conversation that might be juicy enough to resurface on Deuxmoi an hour later. They discussed the weather, growled at the day's *New York Times* Connections, and ranked their favorite Nancy Meyers movies.

Avery stopped to window shop, savoring a spoonful of gelato. In her peripheral vision, a group of women raised their phones. Anna Catherine, oblivious to someone snapping a photo of them, looked up from her maps app.

"It looks like there's a pretty college a few blocks up this street. Let's check it out." Anna Catherine popped her spoon in her mouth and her face melted in delight. "Oh. My. Gelato. Blueberry crumble is divine. What flavor did you get?"

"Blueberry cheesecake."

"Miles would be so proud of us." Anna pointed her tiny spoon at Avery. "He told me not to come back unless I ordered blueberry everything. I read the reviews for tonight's restaurant. We all need to order a blueberry Lemon Drop martini. I hope Lily's ready for a blueberrypalooza."

A nostalgic ripple pierced Avery's heart. During that summer and this one, Miles's blueberry enthusiasm was contagious. She couldn't wait to try them in her favorite cocktail.

"Miles loves his blueberries almost as much as he loves chocolate milk," Avery said. "Maine should make him their blueberry ambassador."

"Mr. Blueberry." Anna giggled. "That's our Miles."

Avery frowned. *Our Miles* turned ashen and grabbed his chest when she said she loved him. She wanted her dream version of Miles, the one who didn't exist. He would have said he loved her back. Knowing what she knew now, before the party had been the absolute worst time to proclaim her love for him for the second time. She should have waited. It had been selfish to expect an overwhelmed Miles to attend to her throughout the night. Healthy couples took turns holding one another up. Last night was her chance to support him.

Avery stirred her gelato as they walked along the tree-lined street. It had been less than three hours since she'd exited his elevator and waved goodbye, and she already missed him. After getting some distance, she appreciated him suggesting a pause would help them figure out what they needed to say. Mimi used to say everyone loved with their heart first and their head second. Avery wanted to know what was going through both every time he lifted his hand and rubbed his chest. If this pause helped him verbalize it, the wait would be worth it.

No day moved slower than a summer Sunday, and the college campus was almost empty. Avery and Anna Catherine were free to talk normally again. It must have been challenging for Anna Catherine, being under so much scrutiny. Once they joined Lily and the rest of the party, they'd be in a private cottage, where they'd be able to let loose and be themselves.

"I didn't realize how intense it is for you when you're in public," Avery said.

"Comes with the job, but I'm not sure I'll ever get used to it." Anna smiled. "Not as many people recognize me if I wear a baseball cap and sunglasses. But on an airplane, sunglasses single me out. Most of my fans are nice. Miles is always giving me disguise ideas like Princess Leia or Hermione Granger. He tries to make me stand out when I need to blend in."

Avery finished her gelato and thought about how Miles loved to tease people. Ahead on the path, two squirrels jumped out of a trash can, darted across the green grass, and chased one another in a spiral up a tree.

"Did you and Miles have fun last night?"

Avery finished her last spoonful of gelato.

"Eh." Avery wiped her mouth with her napkin. "We got separated by the crowd and ended up mad at each other. I didn't know many people there so I felt iced out, and he felt unsupported."

"Ugh, I hate when that happens," Anna Catherine said. "It's easy to lose each other in a huge crowd. I couldn't believe how many people came back for that party. Usually people stay in their homes in the Hamptons or wherever until September."

"I tried to get to him, but when I couldn't, I danced with Paulson. Miles considers Paulson his nemesis, and Paulson thinks Miles is his friend. It's a weird dynamic." Avery pitched her napkin and empty gelato cup in the trash can, half expecting another squirrel to pop out.

"What beef could Miles possibly have with Paulson Carter?" Anna asked. "He donated the rooftop rental for that party, which is so generous and kind."

"They went to college together, and I guess old habits die hard." Avery shook her head. "I don't think Miles ever tried to get to know Paulson. He assumed Paulson was a nepo baby, which he is. But he's not mean. He's actually sweet."

"He left with Victoria Evans." Anna Catherine wiped her mouth with her napkin and threw it into the can. "They were in front of us outside the hotel. Both of them were so gooey-eyed, I don't think they noticed us."

"No way!" Avery pumped a fist in victory. "I introduced them. He's had a crush on her."

"For real?" Anna waited for Avery's nod. "We could all hang out together when you're visiting Miles in the City. And maybe Miles'll warm up to him."

Avery didn't respond and kept walking. She'd said enough, maybe too much, about the disagreement and didn't want to tell Anna Catherine about her feelings toward Victoria. This was supposed to be a fun weekend. Lily's weekend.

Anna stopped at a Gothic-style granite building, complete with a pointed archway, and glanced at the sign in front.

"Ooh, it's their theater," she said. "Can we go in?"

Avery checked the clock on her phone. Dessert had taken fifteen minutes, and Boothbay Harbor was less than an hour away.

"We've got loads of time."

Anna Catherine pulled open one of the creaky double doors. Once their eyes adjusted to the dim lobby, Anna and Avery perused the schedule of summer stock plays and still photos of past stage productions. Anna peeked inside the theater and squealed. The stage lights were on. After calling out a hello and getting no answer, she sauntered down the aisle, climbed the left side stairs, and flittered to center stage. Avery followed, walking normally, hoping if someone caught them, they'd recognize Anna Catherine.

"I never went to college." Anna spun around and her face found the lights. "I got discovered in middle school and bam!"—she clapped loudly—"I moved to New York to star on Broadway in *The Secret Garden*. I rejoined my class for the first half of ninth grade but left when the Disney Channel cast me in *So High School*. After that, it was tutoring on set. College always looked fun, at least in the movies. Well, except *Scream 2*. What was it like?"

It had never occurred to Avery that Anna might have regrets.

"College was all the things your twenties probably were," she said. "Disorienting, confusing, exciting. You make new friends, maybe become someone new. Your mind expands, your world too. You fall in love and get your heart broken. It's an unpredictable mash-up of miserable and fun, and I'd do it over again in a heartbeat."

"Is that why you're going back to school?"

Avery ran her teeth over her lower lip.

"I didn't know what else to do. An MBA seems practical and will help me get a great job." The words fell out robotically, absent of feeling.

Lately, the MBA made less and less sense. College had been about discovering new things. Graduate school focused on one thing, to prepare for a career. She should have a clear goal before she invested so much time and money.

"Can I be honest?" Anna pivoted on one foot and faced Avery.

Avery wasn't sure she wanted to hear what Anna had to say, especially if she said Avery would make a great girl boss. Sure, the girl inside her was still a dreamer. But in the corporate world, Avery viewed herself as a woman. Starting her own business hadn't been easy. Managing inventory, cash flows, and employees had nothing to do with why she'd founded the Peppered Page, but those skills allowed her to do what she loved, design stationery.

"You're like me." Anna waved her hand out over the invisible audience. "We're creators. Imagination fills our cups. Will an MBA do that for you?"

Avery swished the pendant on her necklace back and forth along the chain. Anna Catherine had joined the list of people who saw straight to Avery's core. Miles and Lily had hinted at the same thing. Anna Catherine saying it felt like a revelation.

Avery had picked an academic discipline anyone could benefit from. But would it satisfy her?

"I don't know," Avery said as the truth rose in her throat. *Probably not.*

Anna reached out and touched Avery's arm, as if in solidarity.

"I know I'm standing here talking about how I wish I'd gone to college," she said in a stage whisper. "But I wouldn't change a thing about my life. When I lay my head on my pillow every night, I'm thankful I get to do something I love. What do you love, Avery?"

Avery traced the "X" of stage-marking tape with her foot. Someone knew to stand right here and deliver a line. They probably felt a rush when they got the line right. The way she felt seeing the joy on someone's face when they loved their wedding invitations or milk-bottle-cap backsplash. Crafting something from nothing, be it a watercolor painting or a new look for an old room, nourished her soul like nothing else.

She'd felt a pull to be more like her siblings. Her sister became a lawyer, just like their father. Her brother had an MBA and worked at a hedge fund. He never worried about health insurance or retirement, things Avery had found intimidating setting up for her employees at the Peppered Page. But no matter how many times he described what he did, Avery still didn't know what a hedge fund was.

Anna's hand worried at her mouth.

"I don't mean to judge you. I'm sorry if I crossed a line," Anna blurted out. "But I hate to see people throw away talent. The baby announcements I bought for Lennox from the Peppered Page were spectacular. The watercolor bassinet made of flowers." She lifted her hand to her heart. "*Vie de Luxe* magazine featured me in a cover story on working mothers. They asked to put the announcement in their issue, but I refused for privacy reasons. *Vie de Luxe*. That's high praise."

Pride bloomed in Avery's chest. She'd had a lot of celebrity clients, some of whom had posted her work. But a magazine's approval came from a discerning editorial board. Validation in any form always helped ease the self-doubt all artists experienced. The night she had signed the paperwork for the sale of the Peppered Page, Avery dreamed the buyer backed out of the offer. She'd woken in a cold sweat, afraid the new company would realize they'd made a terrible mistake. The underlying worry that she might be a fraud had inspired her to apply to business school, which provided measurable markers to protect her from feeling like an imposter. But bypassing that pain meant missing out on incredible joy.

She'd miss the high of Wes bringing her birch tree bed to life or watching Lily tear up when she saw her wedding invitations. There'd be no more working through the first sketches of a project and tossing out the inevitable failures before finally getting it right.

Avery thought back to the night they'd lost Casper when Miles told her to envision what she wanted and go for it. At the time, she hadn't seen the answer right in front of her. Redecorating the Boathouse and helping Miles pick finishes and furniture for the Red House had come so easily. Not everyone knew how to make their space into something they loved.

Perhaps selling the Peppered Page hadn't been the end of something, but the beginning of something else. She'd loved designing stationery, but the non-compete clause in her contract meant she had to move on from paper. It didn't mean she had to abandon all creativity.

"You okay?" Anna rubbed her elbow. "I hope I didn't make you doubt yourself."

Avery stepped on the stage marker, her feet covering the "X." She wasn't sure why she could finally hear her own inner voice. Or why it had taken so long for it to show up. Yes, her future with Miles and her career were uncertain. But for the first time in a long time, Avery could see she'd known the answer all along and hadn't admitted it to herself until now.

"I'm okay. Thank you, Anna, for saying the hard stuff I needed to hear," Avery said. "I'm not sure where I'm going or where I'll land. This summer, I've discovered some things I'd never considered. I can feel an idea coming together and for this first time in a long time, I'm excited."

"Oh sweetie, you've got this." Anna gave her a hug. "Can we do one thing before we leave? I want to sing."

Avery smiled. "I'd be honored to hear you sing."

Avery sat in the audience as Anna sang her favorite song from *The Secret Garden*. Anna's a cappella rendition prickled every hair on Avery's arm, so she gave Anna a standing ovation, whistles, and a few shouts of "bravo!" It might have been the stage lights, but Anna glowed, as if she'd just worked out.

"Take a bow," Avery yelled.

"Thank you for indulging me." Anna tilted her head back toward the building after they walked outside. "Ever since Lennox arrived, I've been a little lost myself. Being on stage just now, something clicked. I want to go back to my roots. I'm going to start auditioning for plays."

"Do. Please share what I just witnessed with the world." Avery smiled. "But first, blueberry everything and puffins."

CHAPTER TWENTY-SIX

Miles

TUESDAY, JULY 25 - NEW YORK, NEW YORK

Miles walked off set and down the back hallway to his dressing room. Day two of "Building Your Nest Egg at Any Age" had just wrapped. Today's guests were empty nesters, Sara Beth and Jeff, an overly friendly couple from Atlanta who wore matching shirts and wide grins. They'd managed to send two children to college but were behind on saving for retirement. The segment had gone well, although the overly flirty Sara Beth had grabbed Miles's biceps several times.

Every time Sara Beth said "y'all," Miles felt a pang in his gut as he thought of Avery. The past two nights, he'd replayed the moments before and after the fundraiser more times than a HazMat with the newly dropped Hazel Matheson album. He'd examined every nuance, and it all came down to his silence. As much as he hated to admit it,

Miles hadn't gone to find her at the party. He'd found it easier talk to people alone, which saved him the stress of working her into the conversation. Avery deserved a pass for not sticking by his side that night.

He wanted to explain what roiled through him every time he grabbed his chest, but that needed to be said face-to-face. Avery had texted him a photo of her blueberry Lemon Drop martini last night. Her focus today was Lily and the puffins, as it should be.

He'd join the hosts out on the plaza in a few minutes for the last segment. After that, he had a Zoom with tomorrow's guest, a woman his age who'd almost paid off her debts using the CashCache app and needed advice on how to start saving. This was his favorite financial challenge, because nothing compared to the feeling of conquering your debt.

Miles nimbly maneuvered around the dog crates crowding the *Bright and Early* hallway. This week was National Pet Adoption Week, and Victoria had partnered with FLOP—For the Love of Pups—a local rescue, for a special series. All week, the on-air personalities played with pets awaiting adoption during the show's closing minutes. At the end of the previous day's show, Miles brought out an older dog who loved to play fetch. Someone in the crowd had adopted him while the segment aired. Victoria had closed the show while wiping away happy tears.

Miles wanted to duck into his dressing room for a minute of downtime. The banter leading into commercial sometimes wore down his social battery, and a few minutes alone helped him recharge so he could be vibrant and engaging on air. Ahead in the hallway, Paulson leaned against the wall outside Victoria's dressing room, holding a tiny white puppy. Miles was still sore over Paulson occupying so much of Avery's time at the party, but he smiled because Paulson's donation meant they could buy the retreat.

"Hey, Miles," Paulson called.

"Paulson." Miles walked over and gave Paulson a fist bump.

"Vic wants me to adopt this pup." He held the puppy to his nose. "What do you think?"

Seeing Paulson here could only mean one thing. Avery's introduction had worked. Miles could've done it a year ago, and he felt bad for denying Paulson the beaming grin on his face. Paulson was already calling her "Vic," visiting her at work, and considering adopting a dog for her. After three days. *Bright and Early* had done a segment on insta-love once. This scenario checked all the boxes.

"He's awfully cute." Miles smiled as the puppy licked Paulson's nose. "And I think he likes you."

"I bet he likes to fish," Paulson said.

Any situation involving an endless supply of food sounded like a dog's dream, but Miles kept that to himself. A sanitation worker had found the dog when dumping out a trash can. Paulson had already vastly improved this puppy's life.

"Thank you so much for your support on Saturday." Miles scratched the puppy's head. "It meant a lot."

A blush rose in Paulson's cheeks. "You don't need to thank me." He settled the puppy on his arm and rubbed its ears. "As someone who's essentially lost a parent, I appreciate the difference Camp Luciole will make in people's lives. Which reminds me, I've been meaning to call you."

Ah, the famous phone call. Miles pressed his lips into a line, wondering what was so important that Avery had mentioned it, yet so trivial Paulson had let it wait for almost a month.

"Avery said you were going to call me a while back," Miles said.

"Sorry." Paulson glanced at the puppy. "I could lie and blame my reluctance on being busy, but honestly, Miles, you intimidate the hell out of me."

If Miles had been drinking water, he'd have done a spit take. Paulson had never seemed intimidated by anyone. In college, Paulson told extravagant stories and took his friends on ridiculous spring break trips, like sailing the Carter yacht in the Seychelles. Miles had assumed Paulson never included him because Paulson found Miles beneath him. But Miles ran track and couldn't have gone on spring break anyway.

"I intimidate you?" He paused between each word. The puppy gave Miles a sleepy side-eye reminiscent of Casper, and Miles wondered why some dogs seemed to read him the wrong way.

"Yeah." Paulson smiled. "Don't you get that a lot? You never open up, at least not with me. No matter what I do, I seem to irritate you."

He had a point. Miles often gave one-word responses to Paulson's questions. The semester after Miles's mother died, Paulson had gone beyond the usual condolences and attempted to talk to Miles about his grief. And maybe there had been good intentions, but it felt intrusive when all Miles wanted was to dissociate. He couldn't carry Paulson's pain too, which made him feel inadequate as a friend. Miles had gone to great lengths to avoid Paulson ever since, which was intimidating, rude, and unfriendly.

Miles rubbed his clean-shaven face, aware he'd learned a lot about himself in the last couple days.

"Paulson, how about you tell me what the phone call was supposed to be about, and I'll listen." *For once.* Everyone had to start somewhere.

"The corporate retreat on Linden Lake," Paulson said. "Carter Hotels was the other interested party. My father wanted to open a lake resort, so he sent me to check the place out."

So when Paulson had shown up at Montressa, he *had* been up to something.

"Okay." Miles clenched his jaw. If he'd needed to, he'd have fought Carter Hotels to preserve his camp, the Red House, and Montressa. But none of that made sense anymore, given Paulson's donation. He needed to hear whatever Paulson had to say.

"I got to know Nate at a hotel conference and when I stopped by

Montressa, Avery really sold me on what a special place it was. One day I was on a site visit at the retreat, and she paddled by in a canoe with Casper."

The only day Miles knew Avery took Casper out in a canoe was the day she had visited the Red House and picked his backsplash. The day she first mentioned Paulson would call him. Miles reminded himself to listen and tried to relax his intimidating rock-hard expression.

"When I told her we wanted to buy it, she spilled the tea about your camp." Paulson wiped his brow. "That convinced me to pass the retreat. I asked her to let me call you, but I never did. I'm sorry."

Sweet Avery, she valued people and honored promises. When she could've walked away or said nothing, she'd protected Camp Luciole because she knew how much it mattered to Miles.

"So, I told Dad it wasn't the right spot," Paulson said. "But we thoroughly studied that land. I hate to see you pay what they're asking, which is too much. Especially since it needs a new septic field. It seems wasteful for you to repeat what we already did. I can email the report over and I'd be willing to help you draft an offer, if you want help."

Miles had only bought property twice, and both the Red House and his apartment were residences. Commercial real estate transactions were more complicated, and he could use some help from a seasoned expert like Paulson. There was only one thing to say.

"Um, yes to all of that." Miles couldn't control his smile. "This is ... wow. Paulson, this is so generous."

Paulson's phone rang.

"Hang on a second, Miles. This'll be quick." He pressed accept, put the phone to his ear, and stepped into Victoria's open dressing room. "Hello..."

A production assistant and the FLOP rescue coordinator appeared with a shaggy red puppy.

"Mr. Magrum." The production assistant checked her clipboard and handed him a blue card. "Your dog for the show closing is Tabasco. Here's her information."

Miles picked up the puppy and stared into its almond-shaped eyes. Tabasco whimpered and Miles settled her in his arm, determined to protect her. She needed a safe, loving home. Avery would love this puppy. He wanted to give it to her, but when the rescue agency had been on the show during the holidays, they'd said gifting someone a puppy was giving them a fifteen-year obligation.

The Coopers never seemed to mind their finite commitment to Casper. He ate her lip balm and ran away sometimes, and Avery loved Casper as if he were her own. Miles imagined himself with a dog, throwing a stick off his dock and watching the dog leap in after it. Or riding on his boat. He could get one of those rope leashes, throw on his sunglasses, and walk her around the City.

While he'd been petting Tabasco, his mind stilled, his body relaxed, and his jaw unwound. This must be why dog owners didn't mind picking up poop or getting sneezed on. Miles watched as Tabasco nuzzled the crook of his elbow. He could've sworn he saw the dog smile as she drifted off to sleep.

Pet owners were signing up for his biggest fear. People adopted dogs knowing they would outlive them. Again and again, they signed up for love, despite the inevitable loss. They chose to walk into a situation they knew ended with sadness and grief. Hayes must be right. Winning the love lottery must be worth whatever pain lay ahead.

Miles bounced on his toes, adjusting to the hope filling his heart. He'd discuss this people and dogs revelation and what it meant for his future with his therapist later this afternoon.

Paulson stepped back into the hallway, still holding his puppy. "My office is sending over the documents now."

"Thank you, Paulson," Miles said. "I can pay you, or we can work out a donation."

"Pfft, you don't need to pay me." Paulson waved off the offer. "Take me out for a drink at the Marlton. And if a spot opens up on your board, consider me. I know our losses are different, but I believe in what you're doing. Camp Luciole will have a tremendous impact to the families you serve. Thank you for taking that on."

Miles had never fully appreciated Paulson's suffering. And he never would, because grief differed for everyone. Grief didn't discriminate. So why was he? It was unfair to compare losses. A loss was a loss. A familiar ache rose in Miles's chest at the thought of Paulson losing his mother.

"I need to give this snowball to Vic." Paulson shuffled toward the plaza door. "She's taking him on camera. Will you tell her I want him back as soon as she's done?"

"Ayuh," Miles said. "That means yes. It's a Maine thing."

"I know." Paulson laughed. "You say it all the time. It took me a while to figure it out, but I got there."

As Paulson walked down the hall, Miles realized most of what he'd learned about how people dealt with loss hadn't come from observing grief camps. Like him, Hayes had feared love after loss. There were other kinds of grief too. Paulson still felt pain over his mother's abandonment. Sam grieved the loss of his physical fitness. Avery arrived at Montressa still processing the sale of the Peppered Page and her failed engagement. Perhaps he and Avery had grieved one another after that summer.

"Mr. Magrum?" The production assistant tapped her clipboard with her pen. "Um, they want you on the plaza."

Tabasco let out a dream whimper and snuggled closer. The only thing more perfect than this would be having Avery here. He'd found a goal to work toward. For now, the sleeping puppy would be cute on camera.

"You can call me Miles." He smiled, hoping to make himself less intimidating. He pulled out his phone. "Hey, can you do me a favor and take my picture?"

She snapped a few. He quickly sent one to Avery and stepped out into the sunlit plaza to a loud, collective "Aw," which did not awaken Tabasco.

CHAPTER TWENTY-SEVEN

Avery

TUESDAY, JULY 25 - BOOTHBAY HARBOR, MAINE

"Look at this one." Lily spun her laptop around and took a sip of her frosé. They'd discovered a slushie maker in the cottage, perfect for the bottle of rosé Avery had bought at the cute wine shop, next to the cozy bookshop and across the street from the quaint bakery. If social media influencers built a town, it would be Boothbay Harbor.

"Amazing," Avery said for the millionth time, wondering how many puffin pictures Lily had taken on the cruise. Avery had ogled over at least five hundred already. Each photo refreshed Lily's cruise euphoria. The adorable puffins flitted back and forth from the rock island to the sea. Some floated on the water, which made for the best views of their colorful beaks. Lily loved it so much, she'd immediately plopped down at the dining table next to the window with views of the busy harbor, downloaded her photos, and started editing them while Anna Catherine FaceTimed with Hayes and Lennox on the porch. The rest of the group smartly avoided rehashing the entire morning frame-by-frame and were resting upstairs.

Lily rotated the laptop, cropping and filtering, then scrolling to the next photo. Avery spun her straw in her frosé and took a long sip. Miles would've loved the puffin cruise. He and Nate loved any excuse to be on the water. Most guys, Trent included, flew to Vegas for a bachelor party. Nate chose three days on a river.

Avery dreaded going back to the lake and waiting for Miles's return from the bachelor trip, four days from now. They'd texted and Miles sent her an adorable photo of himself with a sleeping puppy in his arms. She half-hoped he'd bring the puppy back with him. Avery let out a long exhale. A few days paled in comparison to ten years. And unlike that summer, this time she'd say what she needed to say, once she figured it out.

"You okay?" Lily arched an eyebrow.

"Great." Avery took another sip of her frosé to hide her frustration.

Except Lily saw through everything, thanks to her teacher radar.

"Ayuh, there's a lot of heavy sighing coming from you." Lily let down the eyebrow and narrowed her eyes. "You don't need to keep things in, just because this is my bachelorette. Spill the tea, Aves."

"It's Miles."

"Of course it is. What did he do this time?" Lily returned to her photos, as if Miles causing discontent was a common occurrence requiring little brainpower.

"Well, I tried to break up with him, and—"

"Wait. What?" Lily raised a hand to her gaping mouth.

Avery puffed her cheeks and blew out a long breath. As much as she hated to bother Lily, she needed the comfort only a best friend could provide.

"Things went south at the gala. We got into a fight, and ugh, Lily, it wasn't about the party. I told him I loved him while we were getting ready. And he didn't say it back."

Lily closed her computer. "He didn't?"

"Not even close. He froze, like I'd delivered devastating news. To be fair, I should've picked a better time to say it. We were about to leave, and he was stressed about his speech."

Avery traced the icy sweat forming on her glass. She'd wanted him to repeat it back, so she'd feel secure. Declaring your love should be about the person you're saying it to. She'd denied Miles the chance to feel cared for, cherished, and understood by seeking her own validation and saying it on a frenzied night.

"The party was so crowded, we couldn't find each other. I kept looking for him, but it didn't seem like he was looking for me. I felt like everything Victoria said came true. Like he iced me out because I don't fit in his life. And he"—Avery choked back tears—"I'm not sure he wants a long-term commitment. I mean, it's not just that he can't say he loves me. He was great at communicating when we first got back together, and I thought he had changed. But when it's time for big feelings, he's like a clam that won't open. You pry and pry and eventually, you give up. Either that, or he runs. I tried to break up with him to save myself the heartbreak of hearing him say he doesn't love me."

"Hey." Lily rested a reassuring hand on top of Avery's. "We know love is complicated for Miles and he bottles up his feelings. But so many of his actions say he loves you. You know he outbid the Coopers to get the Red House? They wanted to expand Montressa. It blew up into a huge thing and one night, he and Nate went at it. When Nate asked him why he needed *that* house, Miles said, 'because she loves that red A-frame. There's no other house like it and if she ever comes back here, she'll paddle by and I want to be there.' He didn't need to say who 'she' was because Nate knew. Everyone knows."

Avery twirled her glass. While buying the house she loved sounded romantic, it also put the burden on her. Miles relied on his actions to make up for what he couldn't or wouldn't say, but his inactions communicated things as well.

"That is the stupidest way to get someone back." Avery threw her hands in the air. "This isn't *The Notebook*. Instead of waiting for me to show up, he could've called or come found me. Either way, we'd have to talk. To be fair, this summer he's better about working through things. Except when talk turns to love, he runs."

Avery picked up her glass and aggressively slurped the last drop of frosé at the bottom of her glass. Lily rubbed her hand down her face. A second later, the porch door swung open and Anna Catherine walked in.

"Did someone mention *The Notebook*? I love that movie. Their love story had so much chemistry even though Ryan and Rachel did not get along during filming and... Oh no." Her enthusiasm disappeared. "What'd I miss?"

She plunked into the open chair across the table.

"Miles is being Miles." Lily rolled her eyes, reached across the table for Avery's empty glass, stood, and walked back to the kitchen. "I think we all need a refresh."

"Lily," Avery called after her. "I should get your frosé."

"You'll have plenty of opportunities"—Lily paused for a beat and sang out—"at my wedding."

Avery filled in Anna Catherine until Lily returned with a tray of drinks and tissues.

"Just in case," she said as she put the tissue box between them.

Once they were all seated, Avery shrugged. "So, what do y'all think?"

"When Hayes and I reached this point, we had a bump in the road too," Anna Catherine said. "He thought loving me somehow diluted his love for his mom. Like love was finite."

Avery felt her heart flutter. Poor Hayes and Miles shared a sadness, but she wasn't sure Miles had the same misconceptions about love. She'd seen fear in his eyes when he rubbed his chest. Still, Anna Catherine might have an idea how to coax the issue out of him.

"So what did you do?" Avery asked.

"I told him he didn't have to love me, but I loved him and planned to stick by him. It was slow going for a while, but worth it. He lined up a therapist who could do telehealth while he was on location. I think being apart for work helped us. He had the space to work through his issues away on set, and so did I. By the time we came back, we knew what we wanted and thankfully, it was the same thing."

Avery hoped she and Miles regarded their pause the same way.

"These guys." Anna swirled her straw in her frosé. "They lost their moms, and their hearts got jumbled. Give him time. He'll talk."

"It seems natural for Hayes and Miles to have issues with intimacy," Lily said. "Moms love unconditionally. Losing that so young must alter your sense of what forever means."

Uncertainty about whether love could last a lifetime might explain why Miles had avoided a relationship ten years earlier. She wished their second chance hadn't come with the risk of suffering heartbreak again. But that was how relationships worked.

"Maybe." Avery mixed the melted and frozen frosé in her glass into a slushier slush. "I can tell he keeps things from me. Whenever our future comes up, he turns white as a ghost, grabs his chest, and freezes. Then he flees. Like he did that day in the parking lot when having children came up. He couldn't get out of there fast enough."

Anna Catherine covered her eyes with her hand. "I feel so bad about that."

"Don't. It was a natural thing to say. Most people would've let it slide, but he got so worked up, I worried about his well-being. And when I said I loved him this weekend, it happened again."

Avery carefully placed her glass back in the water ring it had left on the coaster. If Miles needed space, she could wait a little while, but not another ten years.

"Hang on." Lily leaned her elbows on the table. "Describe what he does again."

"Goes pale, grabs at his chest," Avery said. "His breathing gets uneven."

"He broke out in a sweat too," Anna Catherine added.

"That sounds like a panic attack." Lily snapped her fingers. "Some of my students have them. One told me she grabs her chest so she can count her heartbeats. I have another who takes his pulse."

Avery closed her eyes and asked herself how she hadn't seen it before. Her chest sank like a rock in water. She'd made the moments about her. Miles was hurting, and regardless of whether he loved her, she loved him. It made sense for him to be wary of love. Love had made him suffer the unimaginable. Whatever he needed, she'd do.

She glanced out the window, hoping to stop the expanding lump in her throat.

"How do I help him?" she asked, tears stinging her eyes.

"Accept you can't fix it. He can't make it go away either," Anna Catherine said. "Maybe gently ask if he knows what a panic attack is. From there, see if he's willing to get professional help."

When middle school friendships got hard, Avery's mother used to take her for long drives. She'd always felt safer pouring her heart out in the car, when she could focus on the road instead of her mother. Perhaps if Miles didn't have to look her in the eye, he'd feel safe enough to open up. Nighttime might work. They were good at having deep conversations in the dark, like when they'd stargazed or searched for Casper.

"Develop some sort of code so he can alert you he's having one, without other people catching on," Lily said. "I have a deal with my students. There's a quiet corner in my classroom, with curtains you can pull shut. It was the best I could come up with. If they ask me if they can study quietly, I let them. One said they do deep breathing exercises there."

"My brother uses repetition to get through them," Anna Catherine said. "Like counting or playing an app on his phone called Bubble Wrap. It's designed to mimic popping bubble wrap. He finds it soothing."

Avery imagined Miles popping bubble wrap on his phone. "I can't wait to suggest to the founder of the CashCache that he download an app called Bubble Wrap."

"My amateur diagnosis only goes so far," Lily smiled. "But if they are panic attacks, Miles can get through this. Therapy and finding what else works for him may take time, but he'll get there."

Avery wasn't ready to give up on Miles. In their best moments, he felt like combination of kismet and a soulmate, what Mimi had termed a *kis-mate*. He'd come back to her bed the other night, a sign he might still let her in. If that happened again, she'd ask Miles how to help and suggest some of the ideas Lily and Anna Catherine had shared.

"Thanks, y'all."

"I love when from-aways say y'all" Lily giggled.

Avery remembered everyone that summer calling her a *from-away*. It meant you weren't from Maine. Who cared? You didn't have to be from Maine to love a Mainer.

Lily reopened her computer and scrolled to the next picture. Her eyes widened and she spun the screen to Avery. The perfect puffin photo existed. Mid-flight, its head turned to the camera. Tiny orange feet trailed straight behind its body. The wispy clouds in the blue sky looked airbrushed.

"Lily," Avery gasped. "This one is next level."

"I agree." Anna held her hand to her mouth. "They're all cute, but this one has such life and movement."

"I think it's the best photo I've ever taken." Lily grinned at her work and closed her laptop. "Puffins are too cute."

Mimi used to say some things were better left unsaid, so Avery didn't tell Lily Miles's puppy photo was cuter. She picked up her phone instead and sent Miles a text.

○ **Avery:** Hey. Just want to say I'm thinking of you. Hope all is well

○ **Miles:** Hey. Walking home from therapy. Tired but feeling hopeful. How were the puffins?

Her chest lifted at the mention of therapy. Miles was trying. Maybe they both could find out how to communicate better. She hearted his message.

○ **Avery:** I always need a nap after therapy. The puffins were so much fun. So cute. Have you ever seen them?

○ **Miles:** No. I'll put it on my list

○ **Avery:** List?

○ **Miles:** Someone taught me the virtues of having one … or several … going at the same time :)

○ **Avery:** She sounds like a keeper

○ **Miles:** Yeah, I miss her

Avery put down her phone and reminded herself that giving him the time and space he needed could turn that last text to *I love her.*

CHAPTER TWENTY-EIGHT

Miles

THURSDAY, JULY 27
THE KENNEBEC RIVER

The river was in charge. Bubbles shot up Miles's nose and whooshed past his ears. Once he surfaced, Miles lay flat, pointed his feet downstream, and protected his head as he coursed through the rapid. He hadn't seen whether Paulson had also fallen out of the canoe, but he hoped not. Given that they were in the last boat, the other boats could be far downstream and might not have seen him go in. Thankfully, Miles had insisted everyone wear flotation vests and helmets.

Body-surfing a rapid was wildly invigorating and frightening at the same time, but he wasn't having what his therapist had diagnosed as a panic attack. He only seemed to get those when he considered a future filled with love.

It made no sense that loving Avery, who understood him in ways no one else ever had, could elicit more fear than he felt right now. The only difference he could come up with between facing his feelings for her and being carried by a raging rapid was preparation. He'd had little training in the ways of love, but he'd studied and rehearsed water safety. As a child, he and his father practiced falling out of a canoe hundreds of times. When the moment came, Miles knew how to stay present and remain calm.

You couldn't prepare for an out of the blue *I love you*. If anything, he'd conditioned himself to avoid love and flee from commitment. But choosing to be alone wasn't fulfilling anymore. Avery made him want to be a better man, one who could figure out how to love and support her. Getting to the best version of himself required going through rough waters.

"*Rope!*" a voice yelled.

A thick rope landed with a thud on Miles's chest. He grabbed onto a knotted end, lifted his hand, and gave a thumbs-up.

"Got it!" he yelled.

A few seconds later, Nate pulled him to shore at the bottom of the rapids. Miles waded out of the water and sat on a big rock, his breath ragged. A dry Paulson handed him a towel and patted him hard twice on the shoulder.

"Dude, you good?" Nate removed Miles's helmet and held his cheeks as he examined Miles's face.

Miles nodded between breaths.

"What day is it?" Nate studied the spot Miles felt throbbing on his cheek.

"July twenty-seventh," Miles said.

"Where are you?"

"The Kennebec River, below Katahdin."

"What's the state bird of Maine?"

"The black-capped chickadee."

"Who is your best friend?"

Miles smiled at the trick question. "I'm good, Nate. Promise. I assume the other boats went on their way?"

"Yeah, they were pretty far ahead," Hayes said. "They'll be sorry they missed the show."

"Since we're already pulled over, I'll patch you up and we'll have lunch," Nate said.

Miles leaned over and shook the water out of his left ear.

"I'm so sorry," Paulson said.

"Nah, it was my fault. I wasn't paying attention and dropped my paddle when it collided with a rock. I should've let it float behind me, but I reached for it just as we hit the first swell. When the boat popped up, I popped out." Miles took off his shirt and wrung it out. "First rule of canoeing is keep your mind on the water. I let my thoughts wander."

"A rare misstep by the best paddler I know." Nate dug through his dry bag and pulled out a first-aid kit. "Must've been some big thoughts."

So big, Miles needed advice. Nate and Hayes both were in long-term relationships. He wasn't sure Paulson had anything useful to add, but they had reached a point in their friendship where Miles could trust him.

"I've been having panic attacks. I had them in college, but I didn't know what they were, and at some point, they dissipated." He wiped his face with his wet shirt and blotted his cheek. Blood, but not a lot. He must've scraped against something on his way down the rapid.

"Panic attacks suck." Hayes handed Miles his water bottle. "You ever get that help I suggested?"

"Ayuh. I saw my therapist every day this week and we have a plan." Miles loosened his boots, kicked them off, and set them in the sun to dry. He hated having wet feet. He'd grab his Crocs once the group relaunched and floated down the calm stretch of the river to their campsite.

"Daily appointments?" Hayes grimaced. "What brought that on?"

"Before the party Saturday night, Avery said she loved me, and I … I didn't say it back." Miles touched his tender cheek, feeling for a bump. "We got separated at the fundraiser and when we got home, things came to a head. I blamed her, she blamed me."

He took a sip of water. Nate dug through the first-aid kit.

"She looked for you the whole time I was with her." Paulson rubbed his forehead. "I tried to help. We spotted you three or four times, but every time we got ready to head your way, you'd moved. She figured you'd find her on the dance floor."

"I know," Miles said, wincing as Nate cleaned his cheek with antiseptic foam. "I was self-absorbed and anxious about my speech. Not the best time to drop that she loved me. Maybe she said it because she was anxious too. I knew almost everyone at the party. She knew three people. In the heat of the argument, I bolted into my bedroom. The next morning, she tried to break up with me."

Nate handed him clean gauze and Miles held it over the wound, applying pressure to his cheek while Nate inspected the various bandages.

"Sounds like she tried to protect herself," Nate said, selecting a pack of butterfly bandages. "Can't say I blame her after everything that happened the first time you two dated. You're a runner, Miles, but you can't outrun love."

When they met up after this trip, Miles hoped Avery didn't see breaking up as their only option.

"I talked her out of it," he said. "She had to go to Lily's bachelorette, and we're planning to talk after I get back."

Miles studied the gauze. There was a moderate amount of blood. Enough for a regular adhesive bandage.

"Nate, I think this cut is small. I don't need all that."

Nate moved Miles's cheek into the light and studied the cut. "I'm sticking with butterflies."

Miles decided not to argue. Nate had already peeled the backing off one, and the glint in his eye said he couldn't wait to apply it. He'd always been heavy-handed when it came to first aid. After they'd pricked their thumbs with a sewing needle and become blood brothers at age ten, Nate wound an entire roll of gauze around their thumbs. He'd also put Miles's arm in a sling.

"So what do you want to say to Avery?" Hayes asked.

Miles sat still as Nate applied the first bandage. He wanted to say he loved her, but that felt too big to admit now.

"I'm never lonely when I'm with her. I know that's selfish, but it's true. I want a future with her where we bring joy to each other's lives."

"So you want to say you love her too?" Paulson said.

It sounded so simple, yet the thought of saying it made Miles's pulse quicken and his chest tighten. He'd learned a couple methods for managing panic attacks in therapy. They were also tackling his instinct to push Avery away when she often made his most intense feelings seem bearable.

As Nate opened the second bandage, Miles touched his cheek again, wondering if he should admit the real reason he couldn't say it. His therapist had asked a question that kept replaying in his head.

If you knew it would end in hurt, would you do it anyway?

They'd been discussing his revelation that people loved their pets knowing they'd outlive them. His therapist suggested a dog might help Miles accept unconditional love and lessen his fear of loving anyone, including Avery. Could he love Avery if it ended the way his parents' relationship had?

"I want to fully commit, but if I think about it too much, a rush of fear comes over me." He turned his cheek to Nate. "I have a history of losing the people I love, and I don't know if I can put myself in that position again."

"Do you know how mad I get when you say that?" Nate pressed the second bandage onto Miles's cheek and stood back. "I know your mom's passing left an enormous hole in your heart. But sometimes I wonder if you woke up one day and decided to be lonely. Look around you, Miles." He waved at Paulson and Hayes. "You haven't lost me or any of these guys here. You've got your whole hometown rooting for you. Heck, my parents think you're their second son. You're rich with people who love you. And I know you love us."

"You didn't lose me, Anna Catherine, and Lennox," Hayes said.

"Or me." Paulson smirked. "But good God, did you try."

Miles laughed. He didn't deserve Paulson's friendship, but he welcomed it. But Avery's love felt bigger and riskier than friendship.

"I want to say I love her," he said. "But every time I get close, I panic. And I can see how much I'm hurting her. It's all over her face."

Hayes sighed and rubbed the back of his neck. Paulson tilted his head to the side and grimaced, as if he knew a little about Miles's predicament.

"Saying you love someone is like jumping off a dock," Nate said, packing up the first-aid supplies. "The first time is the hardest. You get so worked up about saying it, it becomes its own life force. But I promise, it gets easier each time. One day, you'll find yourself saying it all the time."

He wondered if Nate chose the dock analogy on purpose. When Miles was about six, all he'd wanted was to jump off Montressa's dock. Nate and his other friends were already doing it, and they were having fun. He'd watched them jump in enough times to know you sank when you hit the water. Everyone always floated back up, but what if he kept sinking?

He'd stood at the end of the dock, thought about it, and tried a running start but each time, he'd stopped himself and backed away. The anxiety of sinking grew into a roadblock. Finally, his parents intervened. His father stood in the water and offered to catch him. His mother offered to hold his hand and jump in with him. It had taken one jump with her before he'd done it by himself time after time. The safety they had given him set him up for a lifetime of fun on the water.

"I know you love her, Miles." Hayes passed him a sandwich. "People don't hope for another chance with someone they feel lukewarm about."

True, but their chance would be short-lived. She'd leave for school in a couple weeks.

"Is all of this worth it if we won't be in the same town in two weeks?" he asked.

"Hell yeah. Lily and I had an entire ocean between us when she lived in France," Nate said. "You can make it work."

"If she can't come to you, could you go to her?" Paulson asked. "You tech guys are always bragging about how you can work from anywhere. Do it."

"I'm a retired tech guy, and I have other commitments," Miles said. "I'd have to put my classes on hold at NYU."

"Or do what I did in college," Paulson said. "No Friday classes and no Monday classes equals a four-day weekend."

"Paulson, you might be the smartest guy I know." Miles unwrapped the sandwich. "Now I regret not listening to you sooner."

"Hey, I'm a nepo baby." Paulson winked. "We live for shortcuts. Training begins early, in our Gucci strollers."

As the four of them ate lunch, Miles did something else his therapist had suggested. He practiced a little gratitude.

Ever since his mother passed away, Miles had envisioned himself as an island. Alone and lonely. All that time, his friends had been there for him, ready to pull him up. Perhaps he should stop pushing away the love that embraced him every day. If his friends accepted his panic attacks, Avery might too. If her understanding resulted in a deeper connection, it would be worth the effort.

He wanted things. Avery. Tabasco. Waking up on Saturday morning and figuring out the weekend together. That sounded like contentment. Trying to protect himself from pain had become bigger than it should've.

So big, it kept him from leaping off the proverbial dock.

"Thanks, guys." Miles wrapped up the last of his lunch. "I'm lucky to have you."

"We all find our own families," Hayes said. "And you'll always be a part of ours. That's why people have Friendsgiving."

"Okay, family." Nate clapped his hands together. "If we want to celebrate Friendsgiving this year, we should get back on the river so we can make it to camp, meet up with our party, and catch some fish for dinner."

Miles stood and extended a hand to Paulson. "Willing to give me another chance? I promise to hold onto my paddle."

"Of course." Paulson reached out and let Miles pull him up. "The great thing about second chances is our mistakes become part of our story as opposed to the entire story."

Miles took out his phone and typed Paulson's words into his notes app. "Who said that?"

"I did. It's a Paulson original." Paulson climbed into the stern of the canoe. "But you can use it."

"I don't want to use it. I want to live by it." Miles shoved the canoe off the riverbank and jumped into the bow.

CHAPTER TWENTY-NINE

Avery

JULY 29

Avery walked through Miles's living room and admired her work. The new furniture had transformed the Red House from a construction zone into a warm and inviting home. Miles asked for comfort, and that's exactly what she'd delivered. She'd fluffed every cushion, draped a throw blanket neatly across the base of the sectional, and built a ready-to-light fire in the fireplace. The room beckoned for someone to lie down and take a nap.

Miles should be home any minute and after a couple days on the river, he'd be tired.

Nate returned home mid-afternoon, while Miles dropped off Hayes and Paulson at the Portland Jetport. Part of her worried he'd volunteered to drive so he could put off their inevitable conversation. If he was stalling, she would wait.

She paced to the sliding glass door. The lake's glassy surface reflected the purply-pink sunset. She needed content for Montressa's Instagram. Maybe she'd paint it later, now that she had time.

Avery slid open the glass door and walked to the end of the dock, snapping a photo every few feet. Regardless of what happened with Miles, she wouldn't wait ten years to come back to Linden Lake. She loved it too much, and at the very least, she and Miles could be friends now.

The loon family broke the placid surface as they glided home to their cove, a V-shaped ripple fanning out in their wake. The babies trailed behind, too big to ride on their mama's back anymore. One of the adults let out a long, lonely cry, echoed moments later by another cry far out on the lake. Avery closed her eyes. Crunching gravel behind her broke the stillness. As the car turned in the driveway, the headlights behind her lengthened her shadow in front of her.

Miles parked, unloaded his gear, and walked up the path from the garage. It took everything in her not to run to him, jump into his arms, and wrap her legs around his middle like a love-starved contestant on *The Bachelor*. Instead, she stood frozen, the hem of her white sundress tickling her knees. Avery slid her phone into her pocket and wiped her hands down her hips. Anxiety twirled in her stomach.

As much as she'd tried to shake it off, their breakup ten years ago still left her cautious. She needed him to come to her.

He saw her, threw his gear bag to the ground at the side door, and jogged down the dock, slowing a few steps from her. He stopped and pushed back his hair.

"Pepper." For a split second, she interpreted the quiver in his voice as the beginning of the end. Until Miles threw open his arms. Bathed in the pink of the setting sun, his smile glowed like the crescent moon.

Miles Magrum wanted a hug.

She leapt into his embrace, steadied by the warmth of his body. She'd missed his back muscles under her palms. His tight hold around her middle felt like proof he wouldn't run.

"I'm so glad you're back." She breathed deeply, inhaling a combination of mud, sweat, and dirty laundry. Miles smelled like a minivan full of her brother's lacrosse friends. Her mother had called it DTS for "damn, that stinks." Cologne could not save this man right now, but he felt so warm, so full, and so strong, she ignored the odor. If all went well, she'd wash it off him later and he'd return to smelling like a pine forest after an August rain.

"I missed you." He let go enough to gaze at her, his Adam's apple bobbing as he swallowed. "That few days felt like another ten years."

Miles clearly hadn't shaved on the trip. Avery grew goosebumps thinking about that thick, bristly stubble brushing her skin. Her eyes stopped on the cut on his cheek, held together with muddy butterfly bandages. She gasped and ran her finger over the sticky canvas.

"What happened? Are you okay?" she asked, not leaving his gaze long enough to give the injury thorough inspection.

"I'm fine. I fell out of the canoe, and Nate went a little overboard with the bandages. Come here," he said and led her to a lounge chair. "Can we talk before I forget everything I need to say and lose my courage?"

Avery nodded and sat at the end of a chaise lounge. Miles sat opposite her, on the neighboring chaise, their legs tangled together. He picked up both her hands, and her breath hitched.

"Miles," she said, unable to help herself. "I told you how I felt at the worst possible time, and I've been kicking myself ever since. It's okay if you don't feel the same way."

"Stop." He ran his thumb over her knuckles and shook his head. "Please don't apologize. I spent ten long years yearning to hear you say that again. Yearning should be a circle of Hell, by the way."

He let out a ragged laugh and shook his head.

"I'm sorry I didn't handle that night better." His gaze lifted to her, his warm eyes reinforcing his sincerity. "It's kind of hard to admit, but the deep feelings I have for you frighten me. After I lost mom, I convinced myself I'm destined to lose the people I love most. It's irrational, but it feels so real."

He broke their stare and glanced at the sunset. His brow furrowed in the golden glow. She rubbed his knuckles and reminded herself vulnerability didn't come naturally to him. She needed to listen.

"That summer when I broke us apart, that day in the parking lot, I had a panic attack." He sighed and dropped one of her hands to rub his stubble. "I'd had a couple before then but back then, I didn't know what they were. They went away for a while, then resurfaced when I sold CashCache, and I'm beginning to see a pattern. I think they happen when my dreams seem possible, or maybe it's when the future seems uncertain. I had one before the gala."

"And the day we walked Lennox?"

He nodded and closed his eyes.

Avery gulped back a tear and shook her head, focusing on a knothole on a dock plank. When Anna Catherine and Lily had talked about Miles's panic attacks, Avery hadn't considered that her *I love you* sent him spiraling.

"Miles." She let out a tiny gasp. "I'm so sorry."

"Pepper." He lifted her chin and brushed his thumb across her jaw. "You have nothing to be sorry about. This isn't anyone's fault. I had them before I left for college too. I haven't told you because I thought I'd get a handle on it. And asking you to put up with all that felt like too big of an ask."

"It's not." Avery never wanted him to isolate himself, alone with his darkest fears. The best she could do was hold his hand as he walked through it. "Let me be there beside you. We'll lean on each other."

She reached up, cupped the back of his neck, and waited for his gorgeous black eyelashes to lift so his eyes could meet hers.

"Miles, your openness makes me love you even more." Avery dropped her hand to the spot he often rubbed on his chest. His heart beat steadily below her palm.

"Tell me when you have one," she said. "I'll help you through it. But you need to communicate. Let me know what helps, okay?"

He nodded.

"You're so brave." She squeezed his hand.

"I don't feel very brave." Miles winced.

"But you are." Avery squeezed his shaking hand. "You've carried an enormous burden by yourself for a long time. But you aren't alone. Rely on your village. Me, Nate, Lily, Hayes and Anna Catherine, your dad. We love you and would do anything for you. I'll walk beside you and hold your hand in the darkness. And if you need someone to protect your need for time and space, I'll step between you and the world and ask the world to wait, if that helps."

"Thank you for all of that. I already told the guys. And I've had a couple therapy appointments this week. That's why I'm late getting back today. I did a session by Zoom in the parking lot of the Portland Jetport. My therapist has some ideas she thinks might help," he said with a tinge of hope. "I'm going to take a mindfulness class. And maybe adopt a dog."

"A dog?" Avery wondered if she'd misheard him. "But you hate Casper."

Miles rolled his eyes.

"I don't hate Casper, and my dog will be different," he said. "Studies show pets ease anxiety. She thinks a dog might teach me about unconditional love. The responsibility of owning a dog means you can't run away from a problem. I do that, you know?"

"Do I know?" They both laughed.

"I'm glad we can use humor to help us through this," he said. "Anyway, I put in an application for Tabasco. I might train her to be a therapy dog for the camp."

"I love that idea."

Miles kissed her forehead and everything felt lighter. She and Miles were getting somewhere. Facing their difficulties required time, but she didn't want to miss a second of it.

I love this man, she thought to herself, but didn't say it aloud. She needed to be honest with him but grant him the time and space to get there.

"Miles, I want a relationship with you. And I'm willing to wade through the muck with you," she said. "If it means I get to kiss you every morning and every night, it'll be worth it."

Their knees knocked together as Miles pulled her toward him. He ran a hand down her back and kissed the spot below her ear. His hair smelled like river dirt, which didn't smell as sweet as lake dirt.

"I couldn't bear to lose you forever." he whispered. "You make me want to learn to love again."

Avery had never felt so honored. She climbed across the space between them and straddled his lap. He tugged one of her dress's shoulder straps down and greeted the top of her shoulder with stubbled kisses. She cupped the back of his head and pulled his face to hers. His hands splayed across her back and his lips buzzed over hers, sending a ripple of warmth down her middle. Miles's hands slid down her sides, worked under her skirt, and skimmed her thigh. She wanted his stubble there. If not now, soon. The rhythm of his kiss broke when his hand drifted higher. Miles lurched back in surprise, his hand rapidly exploring her goose bumped skin. His eyes grew wide.

"You're naked under here. A man needs a warning."

Avery pulled the dress over her head, feeling him grow hard beneath her.

"It's the middle of summer," she murmured into his parted lips. "We haven't been skinny dipping yet."

She yanked at the hem of his shirt. "And you need to clean off before you sit on your new furniture."

She stood and pulled the shirt over his head.

In the dim light, she saw his cocked eyebrow too late. He stood and picked her up and before she knew what was happening, Miles ran off the end of the dock, holding her tight. Cool water rushed around them as they sank in a whirl of bubbles. When they surfaced, he pulled off the rest of his clothing and tossed it on the dock. She wrapped her legs around his middle and shivered at the sensation of her skin gliding over his warm hips. He rested his arms at her lower back, holding her in place.

She caressed his cheek with her thumb. "I'm not going to business school."

Miles's brow furrowed. He pivoted her into the waning light, presumably so he could see her reaction. "Why not?"

"I love designing things." Avery felt a burst of adrenaline hearing her own confidence. "This summer I enjoyed decorating, and each day I found myself less excited about studying finance and economics. I'm considering taking my art into the home, maybe with fabric or wallpaper. I'm a little lost, a bit confused. There's a lot to figure out. But I'm at peace. This feels right."

"All that matters is you feel fulfilled." Miles kissed her nose. "I'm so proud of you. I can't wait to see what you do. I guess I can stop looking for a house to buy in Hanover."

"You were going to buy a house there?"

"Paulson said if you couldn't come to me, I should come to you," he said. "I scoured Zillow in my tent last night."

"Wait." She shook her head. "You took advice from Paulson?"

"I did. He's going to help with the grief camp. Paulson and I have a lot in common." Miles winked. "If only someone had pointed that out."

He playfully splashed water at her. Enough to wash over her shoulders but not hit her face. She splashed him back.

The warm tickle of fireflies lit up her middle. She wasn't used to this level of support. Miles was willing to pivot so she could shine. Actions that conveyed his love. Avery lifted her hand to the bandages on his cheek, lightly touching them.

"Pull them off," he said. "And beware of Nate with a first-aid kit."

The first bandage came right off. The second needed some coaxing from her fingernail.

Miles's mouth lifted into a bemused, teasing smile.

"That cut," he said as the second one peeled away, "was your fault."

"It's a tiny cut, and I wasn't there." She took her wet thumb and rubbed the adhesive off his cheek, examining the small abrasion. He had not needed butterfly bandages. "How is it my fault?"

"I fell out of the boat because I was thinking about how much I love you."

Avery's thumb stopped midway across his cheek. For a second she wondered if he'd meant to say it. But his gaze and his gorgeous moonbeam grin signaled his intent. Those three words stopped the sun from setting and lifted it enough to pool a ray of warmth around them.

"You heard that, right?" His whisper roared between them, and he shivered beneath her hands.

She placed a hand on his heart, aware of what it had taken for him to get there.

"I love you, Pepper. I've made so many mistakes. Never saying I love you is the biggest one."

"And I love you too. So very much." The water droplets on her face might've blended with the tear in her eyes. Or maybe not. Avery pulled him into another embrace and rested her head on his shoulder, looking out at the ever-darkening lake.

"I see Venus," she said. "The sky will fill with stars soon."

"I'm already holding the only star in my sky, Pepper. You know that."

They didn't go to bed until they'd taken a long shower together and made love on the new sectional sofa. *Twice.*

"I'm so happy we got another summer," he whispered as they fell asleep. "Now, *that summer* is part of our story and not all of it."

"Mm-hmm." Avery nestled into the nook below his shoulder and smiled herself to sleep.

CHAPTER THIRTY

Miles

SATURDAY, OCTOBER 7TH

Miles stepped to the edge of the party and scanned Lily and Nate's wedding reception. It was a little weird, wearing a designer suit in a place reserved for flip-flops and bathing suits, but Montressa had risen to the occasion. Edison bulbs lit the lodge's porch and fanned out over the lakeside ledge, casting everyone in a sepia-toned glow. He hoped the photographer took a photo from this spot, just outside of the party, looking in at the celebration. He wanted the dreamy image on his bookshelf, where he could pick it up years later and instantly remember this night, when everything was perfect.

Lily and Nate stood on the porch, in the center near the stairs leading into the lodge. Sam and Laurie sat under the eaves, listening to Miles's father tell Dorothea his favorite story about Nate and Miles. At age ten, they'd built their own pirate raft during an extended playdate and decided to take it out for a spin. They forgot flotation vests, and when the raft sank in the middle of the lake, Miles's father had taken a canoe out and made them swim back to Montressa's dock. He'd paddled along beside them to keep the boys safe.

"It totally backfired." Sam's bellowing laugh echoed through the party. "The boys became obsessed with swimming across the lake and spent the rest of the summer trying to get there. Mark grew biceps paddling after them."

Miles chuckled at the memory of his father's toned arms. That winter, his father had done a hundred push-ups a day to keep those biceps.

At another table near the porch, Hayes and Anna Catherine were finally eating dinner after indulging every guest's request for a selfie. Paulson sat next to them, flying a spoon around as if it were an airplane. Lennox's bright eyes tracked the spoon right into her mouth and she clapped. Across the table, Victoria cooed and snapped their picture with one of the thirty vintage cameras she and Paulson had bought, loaded with film. They'd set one at every table and were planning to make a photo album for Lily and Nate.

At Victoria's feet, Casper happily chewed on the large bone Miles had given him. Without the bone, Casper would've stolen a plate of hors d'oeuvres by now and started a *Sandlot* style chase through the reception, demolishing the wedding cake and anything else in his path.

That save alone made Miles congratulate himself for being the ultimate best man.

He kept it to himself that at only a few months old, Tabasco already behaved better than Casper. Of course, she hadn't come to the reception. He'd checked his nanny cam app a few minutes ago to find her snuggled in her crate in the Red House, curled in a ball. At first it seemed ridiculous to buy a nanny cam for his dog, but after experiencing anxiety the first couple of times they'd left her alone, Avery declared it worth it if it reassured him and he didn't spend the whole time checking it.

Avery should've been easy to spot in the crowd in her slinky dress. She looked almost as gorgeous as she'd looked naked in his bed that morning. He'd hovered over her, placing kisses along her jaw, murmuring, "I already let the dog out," as he continued down her body.

If he stood in one place long enough, he'd find her.

In September, she'd rented her own apartment in New York, only to spend most nights at his place. Two mornings a week, they walked to the Fashion Institute of Technology for her textile class. He left her there and continued on to NYU. Their sidewalk commute conversations were his favorite part of his day.

Saturday mornings were exactly what he'd always wanted. Waking up beside his girlfriend, making blueberry pancakes, and planning their day together. One Saturday, they'd explored Central Park with Tabasco and wound up at Anna Catherine and Hayes's brownstone where, over midnight grilled cheese sandwiches, Avery had confessed she'd had a poster of Hayes on her wall in middle school. Another, they'd shopped in Brooklyn and met Hazel and Symona for dinner. Last Saturday, they'd bought Miles a new sofa. Avery insisted he put the nest sofa in storage because she had "ideas" for it. He couldn't wait to see what that meant. Every night, he felt grateful for Avery's head nestled into his shoulder.

Miles was happy, and no longer lonely. Out of gratitude, he touched his heart.

A few seconds later, Avery appeared beside him, her brow furrowed.

"I took a few photos from back there so I can paint this scene for Lily and Nate." She covered the hand on his chest with her own. "Is everything okay?"

She must've noticed his hand on his heart and worried he was having a panic attack. But the wave rushing over him now was love.

"I'm fine." He tucked a loose strand of hair behind her ear. "I'm just standing here wondering why I feared feeling this complete."

Avery held up three fingers, his cue to employ the 3-3-3 rule. *Identify three objects. Identify three sounds. Move three body parts.* The distraction of the exercise helped calm his anxiety.

"Pepper, I'm going to do it, but I want you to know I'm okay. I came over here to watch the party and had a realization. My hand is on my heart because my life feels right. I'm happy. Promise."

Avery teared up, and her smile lit up the night.

"Cake, your green eyes." He brushed his thumb across her temple and closed the space between them. "This dress shows off that freckle I like to kiss. The one beside your breast. I've been staring at it all night."

Someone at the party clinked the side of a glass with a knife, prompting Nate and Lily to kiss.

"Laughter, glasses clinking, the jingle of your charm bracelet." He tugged a charm and shook it.

With his free arm, Miles pulled her closer. He kissed her softly, the way people kissed in a public place: mindfully and demurely. He rested his forehead on hers and looked into her gorgeous green eyes.

"When we get home," he whispered, "I'm planning on moving more than three body parts. For starters, I'm going to lift your hands above your head and hold them against the wall the way you like. At some point, this dress is coming off. Correct me if I'm wrong, but you bought this for me to take off, right?"

She gave him a coy smirk and ran her hands down the silky fabric. The dress shifted enough for him to see beyond the freckle.

Miles licked his lips.

"I bought it in April," she said, "with the sole purpose of making you jealous."

She wrapped her hands around his neck and her low, raspy purr tickled his ear.

"Is it working, Magrum? Are you jealous?"

Miles subtly ran a thumb under a strap and swallowed. Avery raised an eyebrow and waited for an answer.

"Completely jealous. I've always wanted a dress like this." He winked.

"On my floor."

"The best man needs to behave." She lightly smacked his chest and fixed his tie. "Later, you can misbehave all you want."

He'd always assumed playful flirting waned once you fell into a life with someone. Avery showed him the freedom of being more playful within the safety of a relationship. Miles gently brushed her smile with his lips. A sweet gentle kiss passed between them.

"I love you, Pepper."

"And I love you too." Avery leaned her head against his shoulder and they stared out at the party.

Lily and Nate stood alone on the porch, sharing a conversation and every so often, a kiss. Wes quietly took a photo of them. Miles imagined himself there one day with Avery and squeezed her closer.

For a second he thought about asking her if she wanted a wedding like this one. But this was Lily and Nate's big day. And he had a speech to give in a few minutes. They had plenty of time to figure out their future, which felt less scary and more natural every minute.

Avery squeezed his hip. "What a magical moment in a magical place."

A server carrying a tray of champagne stopped in front of them. Paulson, Victoria, Hayes, and Anna Catherine stepped on either side of Miles and Avery, each grabbing a glass.

"Looks like it's time to cut the cake," Paulson said.

Miles glanced at Avery and pulled out his notes. "I've got a speech to give."

Her warm, loving smile said *I'm right here if you need me.*

"You got this." Paulson patted his shoulder.

"Now go break a leg," Anna said. "Make everyone cry."

Miles threaded his fingers through Avery's, and they walked toward Montressa's front steps while Lily and Nate tasted their wedding cake.

Glasses clinked back where his friends all stood.

"Speech!" yelled Hayes.

Miles climbed the porch steps, smiled at Lily and Nate, winked at Avery, and took a deep breath.

"Hello everyone, I'm Miles, the best man, and I grew up with Lily and Nate. I don't need to tell you how special they are. Thank you for coming today. I think we can all agree Lily looks stunning, as we all knew she would. She's the only one of us who could ever convince Nate to trade his L.L. Bean tuxedo for the real thing. For those of you who don't know, an L.L. Bean tuxedo is a multi-pocketed khaki fishing vest and matching cargo shorts. Or if you're classy or it's cold out, cargo pants. It's a Cooper Family staple. Even Casper has one."

Everyone laughed. Casper stood and carried his bone over to the steps and sat at Miles's feet. He lifted his nose to Miles and wagged his tail, and for the first time in as long as Miles could remember, Casper didn't seem annoyed with him.

"I'm sorry, Casper, I know you think you're the star, but we're here for Lily and Nate." More laughter. He waited for everyone to settle.

"When you grow up in a small town where everyone knows each other, everyone's lives weave together until the town becomes one giant family. We work together, grieve together, and celebrate together. So we rejoice when two of our own fall in love. Some of you showed up early to fix flowers or construct wedding arches. Some of you closed your businesses because the only place you wanted to be today was here at Montressa, celebrating the love between our Nate and our Lily.

"Falling in love is a mysterious process. Like many things we don't fully understand, people often try to make sense of it. There's love at first sight, fate, kismet, stars aligning. Call it whatever you want. In the end, it's pretty simple. Our soul realizes there is something about this person that feels different. And that inspires us to make a choice.

"A couple of months ago, something Nate said resonated with me. He said sometimes he thought I woke up one day and decided to be alone. At first, I denied it, but as I thought about it, I understood the truth. It wasn't the alone part. I know a lot about being alone and being lonely. It was the 'decided' part that got me. To truly fall in love requires a choice."

Miles scanned the crowd. The guests were hanging on his every word. Hayes winked at him; a subtle sign Miles was on the right track.

"One Christmas Eve a couple years ago, Lily and Nate ran into one another at the Portland Jetport, Lily on her way home from France for the holidays and Nate returning from our annual fishing trip in Virgin Gorda. This is the part of my toast where I take credit for their entire relationship because, thanks to me, Nate had unlocked 'golden-boy mode'. His bleach-blond hair and bronzed skin stood out in Maine in December. That sun-kissed glow gave Nate confidence and Lily goose bumps. His rippled forearms from playing all that hockey didn't hurt either.

"Lily accepted his offer of a ride home and asked to stop at her favorite donut place. She'd missed a good old-fashioned Maine donut after a year abroad. And there in the Holy Donut, Nate made his move. When Lily couldn't decide which flavor she had missed most, Nate bought one of every flavor and insisted they do a taste test. According to Lily, they grabbed neighboring donuts and their pinkies brushed. The donuts weren't the only thing that was glazed. They stared into one another's glazy eyes and made the same choice.

"Sometimes, love tells us it's time. We choose to open our hearts and be vulnerable. We choose to say what we mean, even if it's hard."

Miles felt a tickle that might lead to fully choking up, so he paused and scanned the reception. Dorothea wiped away a tear. Miles's father wrapped an arm around her, pulled her close, and planted a kiss on her forehead. Miles cleared his throat to stave off his emotion at seeing his father happy again.

"And if we're Nate, we decide to take the chance Lily will pledge her heart to the guy with the sun-kissed glow, the one who tries all the donuts and gives his love freely. Thankfully, she did.

"Lily and Nate, thank you for including us in your big day. I think I speak for all of us. It is an honor to share your love. May you have a long, healthy, and happy life in love together. Cheers!"

After everyone lowered their glasses, they clapped, whistled and whooped. During Lily and Nate's first dance, Miles leaned into Avery's ear.

"Ready to dance with me?"

She shook her head. "Oh Miles, I won't make you do that. I know you don't dance."

"What if I told you I learned?" he asked. "For you?"

"You did?" Avery's jaw dropped to the floor as her hand rose to her heart.

"Hayes and Anna Catherine made me watch *Hitch*." He smirked. "They were a little disappointed when I identified with the Kevin James character. I do a mean Sprinkler. They intervened and gave me lessons. And I kinda like dancing now."

He threaded his fingers in hers. "Come on, Pepper. Let's go have some fun."

EPILOGUE

AUGUST, A YEAR LATER

Avery plodded out of the lakefront door of the Red House to join Miles, who sat at the end of the dock, reading in an Adirondack chair. Unlike most nights, she'd brought nothing with her. All she wanted to do was watch the sunset. Miles could keep reading. They didn't need to talk. After a great but busy week, being next to him was the balm she needed.

The underbelly of each cloud in the sky glowed pale pink, highlighting Miles in a warm glow. Tabasco lay beside him, head up, scanning the lake for anything she might need to bark at. Her tail thumped the dock as Avery approach. Miles reached down, patted Tabasco's head, and smiled at Avery before turning to the next page of the latest bestseller.

The final week-long session of Camp Luciole's first summer had ended a day before and the experience had been exhausting and rewarding. Miles and Hayes oversaw everything and while they had a legal pad full of suggestions for next year, their inaugural year had been a resounding success. Every departing family commented on how grateful they were for the opportunity to be away from their daily lives, in a calming place, finding the healing they needed. They'd made friends and found support in the group sessions and lake activities. Avery caught Miles and Hayes tearing up more than once during the goodbyes. She wasn't sure she'd ever seen him hug so many people and felt a swelling of pride in her throat.

At the end of the dock, Avery kicked off her Birkenstocks, pulled her lip balm out of the pocket of her sundress, slathered the minty freshness on her lips, and looked out at the clouds reflection in the rose-colored water. This might be the prettiest night she'd ever seen on Linden Lake.

In addition to the amazing therapy team Hayes had assembled, their friends and families pitched in too. Miles's father and Dorothea led daily hikes and kayaking excursions. Avery's parents had flown up from Virginia for a couple of weeks. Her mother taught yoga and her father, a trusts and estates lawyer, helped grieving widows and widowers with probate questions and referrals for attorneys who could draft new wills given their changed family situations. Ned and Lily popped over from Montressa, sometimes with a couple off-duty staff who wanted to volunteer, and led the evening activities, including Bingo night and s'mores around the campfire. Sam told campfire stories. Anna led a theater class while Avery worked in arts and crafts with the art therapists. And Paulson ran the immensely popular catch-and-release fishing program.

Casper, Tabasco, and Paulson and Victoria's dog, Snowball, visited everyone who wanted to pet or play with a dog. Somehow the three pups never discovered the two emotional support cats one of the therapists kept in the office building where they held sessions with families.

Avery plopped down in the empty chair next to Miles. This chair had become her chair in the past year, and this was her favorite part of their day, sitting on the dock, sometimes way past when the stars came out. Skinny dipping once it got dark enough, sometimes swimming out to the floating dock, and on nights where a light breeze kept the bugs away, laying naked under the stars. There was no place she would rather be than here, with him.

She relaxed back into her chair and checked out her freshly painted nails. She never got manicures, but she and Lily had gone to get pedicures after the camp wrapped up yesterday and Lily insisted they get "the works". Watercolor paint often dyed Avery's cuticles and got under her nailbeds. She hoped she could keep her hands looking this nice, at least for a day or two.

"Hey." Miles looked up from his book. "Did you come down here empty handed?"

"Yeah." She tilted her head to the sky, closed her eyes, and took a deep inhale. After painting murals in each cabin at Camp Luciole this spring and then working in arts and crafts, Avery had far surpassed her normal artistic output for the summer. Her daily sixteen hour shifts behind her, she looked forward to the next two weeks of sleeping late, nestled in the Red House's birch tree bed. Waking up, with nothing to do but gaze up at the pitched ceiling and plan her day however she pleased.

Miles reached across the armrests and rubbed her forearm.

"You okay?"

"I'm great." She turned her head and cracked open her eyes, further relaxing into the chair. "I'm appreciating this moment of quiet. It's been a full throttle summer, and I'm ready to cruise for a while."

Miles had worked harder than she had. Where he got the energy, she didn't know. He should be dog tired by now.

"Oh, you don't fool me." He turned a page in his book. "I know you have the whole next year planned."

Avery smiled to herself. Over the last year, she'd learned to let go of her need to always have a plan. When she'd moved to Manhattan, she told herself she was going exploring. She'd taken classes in pottery, wood working, interior design, even a rom-com seminar so she could keep up with Hayes and Anna Catherine's references. By Thanksgiving, she'd designed a line of wallpaper and fabric. She found a manufacturer in South Carolina and convinced an elite Manhattan design studio to carry her line. Since she couldn't call it the Peppered Page and she didn't want her name in her brand, Miles had come up with the name: Paprika Home. Her camp-themed line was doing quite well and after being around toddling Lennox, she had a plethora of ideas for children's rooms.

Miles traced the webs where her fingers met her hand. "What's on the schedule for next year?"

"I've been thinking about something for a while. I want to spend more time here."

Miles closed his book. "Here?"

"In Maine," she said.

A week before camp started, Hayes and Anna Catherine announced they were moving to London for a few months while Anna headlined a play in the West End. Lily and Ned were here all year. With the camp, Miles commuted to and from Portland frequently. Now that they had a successful summer in the books and hoped to offer more sessions next year, he'd mentioned needing to hire year round office staff. Avery loved Maine in summer and wanted a taste of winter.

"Remember when we came up here for Valentine's Day?" she asked. "You took me ice skating on the lake. I keep thinking about that. It was so cool."

"I liked what we did next better." He raised an eyebrow. They'd made love in front of the fire. "I'm always up for more of that."

He winked.

Avery asked herself how once upon a time, she'd not only resisted that sultry wink, but managed to find it utterly vexing. These days, when

Miles winked, she melted. He knew this and used it to his advantage. And she loved him for it. Avery knew what drove him wild too.

"Yes, I want more of that too." She ran her finger along her lower lip and watched him lick his own lips. "After you give me lessons."

"Lessons." The word hung in midair while he absorbed it. Miles swallowed, a dark flicker in his chestnut eyes. He shifted his lips like he was assessing her suggestion and adjusted his pants.

"Not those kind of lessons," she giggled. "Teach me to cross-country ski and snowshoe. Maybe we'll even see a moose."

She laughed as his face fell flat. Yes, she loved sleeping with him. But Avery also wanted to get outside.

"Just so you know," he said, "I have never seen a moose while skiing."

"And you won't if you don't get out there. It's not like a moose will magically appear while you're banging me either."

"If I can make you see stars, I can make you see a moose."

"Now, there's some big dock energy." She laughed.

Tabasco barked at the sight of Sam and Casper, out on the lake in their canoe, taking a cruise. Everybody waved to one another and Casper barked in return. They paddled away under a purple sky. It was heartwarming to see Sam happy and healthy.

Miles stood, took out his phone, and snapped a photo of the man and his dog. He picked up the base of his chair, turned it to face hers, sat down, and rested his elbows on his knees. His brow furrowed as he steepled his fingers. A sign he was considering her seriously.

"Back to this Maine thing. I'm confused. Are you asking to move here? Or visit more often?"

Avery bit her lip and met his gaze. He was so intently focused on her, she couldn't read his emotion. And she didn't know what she wanted. She'd never lived in Maine and the winters seemed long.

"I don't know," she said. "I'm trying this out. You have experience with winter here. Is this some pipe dream that ends with us snowed in and driving one another crazy? I don't know if I would like it."

"We don't have to move here. One option is to spend more time here this coming fall and winter." His eyes were brightening. "You can get your feet wet. Well, hopefully not. It'll be cold and you'll want dry feet. That's what Bean boots are for. We can test it out. See how we like it. And if we don't, call it quits with little investment."

"I like that idea. I don't want to make you leave the city. I like it there and I need to be there for my work."

"You could travel up here with me when I come for camp business and we could tack on a couple days. And maybe we try a couple extended work-from-home visits."

Avery nodded and looked out at the lake. She couldn't wait to find out if she, a "from away" as Mainers called out-of-staters, could handle the winter here. It could be harsh or a winter wonderland. She envisioned drinking hot cocoa in the little red A-frame and finding out if people really ventured into the woods and chopped down their Christmas trees like they did in the movies.

"Pepper, I see wheels turning in your pretty head." He took both her hands. "Tell me your worries."

"I'm imagining it all." She let out a laugh. "Would we chop down our own Christmas tree?"

He smoothed his hands over her knuckles and laughed. "We don't have to figure everything out tonight. There's plenty of time to make a final decision. And, yes, we can chop down a tree or buy one in a lot. Whatever makes you happy. My only request is you wear one of those knitted caps with a pompom on top."

"Ooh, I want to see you wearing a flannel and wielding an axe. Maybe don't shave for a day or two before?" She wiggled in her seat.

"I like this plan." He rolled his lower lip through his teeth and smiled.

Miles ran his hand through his hair and messed it up. This time, a piece stuck out to the side. She reached up and put it back in place.

Miles was so gorgeous, with his dark eyes and tan face. Some days she couldn't believe he was her boyfriend. Over the last year, he'd continued his thearpy. He still had panic attacks but a few weeks ago, he'd told her that he'd come to the realization they were temporary and he knew how to utilize his various tools to manage them until they'd passed.

They'd worked together on his flight instinct. He now asked for time and space to think instead of running away. Avery had learned to let him process their issues on his own before they addressed them together. She now trusted he'd return to the discussion when he was ready. Giving a problem space to breathe helped them resolve disagreements rationally. Seeing him struggle and try so hard made loving him easy.

"So the next year is figured out." He laced his fingers through hers and rocked their hands back and forth. "What about the rest of your life?"

"The rest of my life?"

"Yeah, what are you doing for the rest of your life?" Miles smirked.

Out on the lake, a fish jumped and flipped midair. Avery's stomach did the same.

"Miles, we just figured out the next year, how far do you expect us to go?"

"The thing is, I've lost count of how many dates we've been on. And that feels monumental," he said. "I love you, Avery. You sit with me in my rain and share your sunshine. I never want to hear your laugh or giggle and know you aren't mine. From the day I met you, from that hug on the beach, I knew you possessed the truest heart of anyone I had ever met and would ever meet again. I can't imagine a day without you and your lost lip balms and your lists. I wanted to know if you'd like to maintain this love, this kismet, for the rest of our lives."

Avery swallowed and tried to keep her tears at bay. Was this really happening right now? She'd imagined this moment a million ways but never expected it tonight.

"I'd love to spend the rest of my life with you." She let the joy burst out of her. A wide smile, followed by a tear or two, wiped away by her perfectly manicured hands. "You know that, right? I used to think I would never find someone who loved me the way I loved them. It turns out I found him. At nineteen. And again a decade later. I never want to let that go."

Everything fell very still. Avery caught her breath and sunk into the feeling that this, being with Miles, felt right.

"You're my kis-mate," he said with a half-smile. Miles had come so far. He used to think he couldn't love someone at all. And look at him now, lit in a pinkish haze and getting all gushy.

"And you'll always be mine."

Miles cleared his throat. He cupped her jaw with both hands and ran his thumbs along her cheekbones before clasping both of her hands again. His gaze was so intense, he might not have noticed the sunset. Avery sure hadn't.

"Avery, will you marry me?"

Time, the lake, Miles, Tabasco. They all stood still.

"Miles," she croaked as another, even wider smile burst out of her. "Yes. Of course I'll marry you."

Miles's shoulders relaxed. She ran her hand along his smooth jaw. Miles had shaved sometime this afternoon. He'd planned this. She leaned forward and kissed him. One of those deep ethereal kisses where she could've sworn she and Miles stood still while the sky and lake spun around them.

"Do you want me to get on one knee?" he asked sheepishly. "I will, but I wasn't sure you'd want that."

It dawned on Avery why he'd asked her while they were doing something they did all the time, in a place she felt comfortable. He'd ensured she'd have the freedom to say no if that was what she wanted. Sweet Miles. He was trying to keep this as unlike her first engagement as he could. Truth was, she would've said yes if he'd asked her on a jumbotron.

"I don't need a knee," she said.

"How about a ring?"

"I'll take one of those." She giggled.

"It's a good thing I convinced Lily get you a manicure." Miles smiled.

"What?" Avery palmed her forehead. "Lily knew? Oh my stars. She was so stealthy. I didn't have any clue. And I never get manicures."

He fished inside the zippered side pocket of his pants and pulled something out. He kept his fingers over the top as he slid it onto her finger.

"I can honestly say that this is the best day of my life," he said. "And I'm looking forward to saying that a lot in the future."

Avery's breath hitched. The ring was perfect. Not so big as to get in her way but large enough to look significant. Minimalist in style, to let the emerald cut stone take center stage.

"Oh Miles, it's gorgeous. I love it." She tilted her hand back and forth and admired the stone in the light. "But not as much as I love you."

Tabasco knew something was up. She stood and wiggled her way between their knees, wanting to be part of whatever was happening. Avery climbed over the dog, over to Miles's lap and cupped his face in her hands. Tabasco worked her way bedside Miles, perched her front paws on his armrest and rose to join them. She gave them both kisses.

"Somebody needs to train that dog." Avery smiled into the space between them and kissed Miles.

His laugh broke the kiss. "Lighten up, dog kisses are basically hand sanitizer."

Avery snuggled across his lap, her legs hanging over one armrest and her back leaning against the other armrest. Miles placed a hand on her thigh, his thumb playing hide-and-seek with the hem of her sundress. Neither one of them could stop smiling. Tabasco settled at Miles's feet. Somewhere out on the lake, a loon called.

"I think we're missing the sunset."

"There'll be another sunset," she said. "But not like this one. This is the best sunset ever."

For the next half hour, they talked about their wedding. It was easy. They'd get married on the lake, ask Sam to officiate, and get Hayes to do a reading. Miles admitted that Hazel helped him pick the ring and had already agreed to drop whatever she was doing and come sing at their wedding. But Anna Catherine also wanted to sing, and they giggled about a potential competing divas situation, especially once Victoria joined the mix. They'd rent out all of Montressa and have the reception on the granite ledge. The only question was which dock to get married on. After some deliberation, they decided to tie the knot on the Red House's dock. The A-frame would make a lovely backdrop, and it was their dock now.

Avery patted his chest and let out a happy sigh. She looked at her ring and smiled. What a great day. What a great summer. Their best summer yet.

"Hey Miles."

"Mm-hmm."

"I'm so happy. Thank you for making our proposal so perfect."

"I'm not done yet. Tonight we'll celebrate by ourselves. There's champagne in the fridge and a fire ready to be lit." He shifted under her and sat up straighter. "Tomorrow, I invited everyone to the Lakeside Diner before your parents fly out. It'll be our parents, our friends, and a whole mess of blueberries and maple syrup."

"And will you be having the usual?" She winked.

"Of course." He winked back. "That chocolate milk costs a fortune."

Avery rested her head on his shoulder as they watched the last sliver of sun sink in the western sky and waited for the stars to come out. Except one star was already out. And he was the only star in her sky.

DEAR READER,

Thank you so much for reading *Another Summer*. I hope you enjoyed Miles and Avery's story as much as I enjoyed writing it.

Reviews are extremely important for independently published authors because we lack the marketing department and distribution channels of a traditional publisher. Our readers have to work to find us. Reviews are the main way they choose their next book. If you have a moment to leave a review on Amazon, Goodreads, Barnes and Noble, and/or any other platform, I would be grateful.

If you would like to receive bonus content related to Miles and Avery's story or hear about upcoming releases, please subscribe to my newsletter. And I'll always appreciate a follow on social media. All the links for newsletter and social media can be found at karakentley.com

Happy reading,

Kara

ACKNOWLEDGEMENTS

I never thought I would say this but thank you, insomnia. Ever since I was a child, I've passed my sleepless nights making up stories until sleep finally came. The stories are my own personal soap opera, often continuing night after night for months at a time. They comfort me and keep my worries at bay. I always wondered what would happen if I wrote one down. And here we are!

I'm so grateful to the people who made writing a novel less of a solitary process. My developmental editor, Savannah Gilbo, let me wander off on tangents before reigning me back into the heart of my story. Sometimes, we spent an entire Zoom call discussing our dogs and I'm good with that. I took her Notes to Novel course and joined her Story Lab, both of which helped me craft this book.

I'm in an indie author self-publishing group with Emily Klein, Jennifer Lauer, and Stefanie Medrek. We write in different genres but speak the same language. I asked a million questions, and they answered them all. They deserve an award.

Caroline and Jim read this book first and encouraged me to keep going.

My beta readers told me what was and wasn't working and that was no small feat. Thank you to the fabulous Coffin Screw Crew: Steph Alta, Kelly Beck, Kevin Peoples, Haley Phelan, and Emma Vail. I cannot wait to see your books out in the world.

Two Birds Author Services line edited and proofread for me. I'm a terrible typist, so they had a big job on their hands.

Thank you to my pre-release readers, Jim, Stefanie and Stephanie.

Nicolette S. Ruggiero designed my stunning cover. Zoe Norvell created the gorgeous interior. It was an honor to work with both of them.

Established authors who help new authors are what makes the romance community so special. I had the best time discussing my meet-cute with #thewritinglush, Melonie Johnson. I had an equally enjoyable back-and-forth on banter with Sara Whitney while getting her feedback on my opening pages. I really appreciate both of you taking time to help a new author and hope I can pay it forward one day.

Stephanie, thank you for calling me several times a week and asking, "what are you doing?" as soon as I pick up the phone. Your almost thirty years of friendship have kept me sane.

No one knows you like the people you met at age four in ballet class, at nine during Girl Scout camp, at sixteen at field hockey practice, at eighteen while working at a resort for the summer, at nineteen at the sorority house, at twenty-two in the running store, at twenty-eight in the NICU and the Little Gym, or at twenty-nine and beyond through workplaces, gyms, book clubs, and fundraisers. Friends make the world go round. I cherish every one of you.

Vacations create lifetime memories. My parents, siblings, and cousins gave me a love the lakes of Maine. It's where we spent our summers swimming between islands, hiking, camping, canoeing, picnicking, water skiing, stargazing and listening to the loons call to one another across the water.

Two sweet dogs kept me company while I wrote this book. Macy, may you rest in peace. I miss your warm body draped over my feet as I write. And Linden, thank you for laying your head in my lap when I've been typing too long and looking up at me with your sweet, soulful eyes. I'm grateful for your quiet reminders that it's time to take a break.

To my children, what a gift you have been. I've loved watching you grow and bloom. Thank you for doing the same for me. You are awesome cheerleaders and all around great human beings.

Jim, I love you with all my heart. My life changed the day I met you. You've walked through my anxiety with me, let me fall asleep with my head nestled in the nook of your shoulder, and learned how to make my tea just the way I like it. You are what the romance world calls *swoonworthy*. One of my favorite lines in this book is something you've said to me countless times. I'm not sure I've ever said it back to you, but I hope you know that *I am never lonely when I'm with you.*

Books are for readers and so I am grateful for those who pick this up and read it start to finish.

xo

Kara Kentley was born in New England and raised in Virginia, but spent her summer vacations reading, swimming, camping, and visiting family on Lake Mooselookmeguntic in Oquossoc, Maine. An avid contemporary romance reader, she grew up in a house without a television and passed her time creating stories with meet-cutes and happily-ever-after endings.

Kara is afraid of getting stuck in an elevator, so her real-life meet-cute happened on the ground floor. They were never enemies, never fake dated, and he wasn't her older brother's best friend. She is eagerly awaiting the moment she discovers he is either a secret billionaire or a prince. Until then, they're content sharing a rescue sheepadoodle, a love of movies and television, and a room with only one bed.

When she is not writing, Kara works with community non-profits and searches for heart shaped objects in everyday places.

Another Summer is her debut novel.

Made in the USA
Middletown, DE
16 July 2025

10362237R00209